Waltzing Matilda

Jon Gray Lang

WALTZING MATILDA

Cover Image by Tithi Luadthong

ISBN 978-17323305-4-2

Library of Congress Control Number: 20293901312

Jon Gray Lang

To Desha, you'll always be my Captain.

Jon Gray Lang

THE MATILDA SERIES
The Matilda
Twistin' Matilda
Black Matilda
Secret Matilda
Waltzing Matilda

Also, by Jon Gray Lang
Nun With a Gun: Town with No Name

one

End of Time

The Cluster, home of the nomadic D'ziageno, slowed as it neared the end of its journey toward the last port it would see in a year. Suspended by cables beneath the amalgamation of ships and living containers hung a beat-up freighter with the name Matilda emblazoned across its flank.

Luli yawned as she stretched in the pilot's seat of the old scow. It had been a long night, but her last evening on the Cluster had been fun and exactly what she needed. She glanced over as Captain Delahaye wandered over to the Nav console. She waited while Jacquie flipped through the star maps until the one they occupied blossomed into being.

The comm blinked briefly as Luli slipped the jack snuggly into the back of her skull. As her eyes opened within the Matilda's interface, the star map expanded around her. The ship's computer assembled a mock-up of the Cluster and the Matilda's position amongst the other connected vessels. She refocused on an oblong shape far ahead that slowly resolved itself into a huge asteroid. Bits of ship wreckage dotted the surface of the rock and with its higher power output it glowed brighter than the Cluster.

"That must be the Scrapheap we've all been hearing about," she muttered to no one in particular.

The comm blinked again within her immersed view. Her eyes activated the icon, "This is Luli Qing of the Matilda, receiving."

Joy rang out through the wide beam comm as Lucia, the All-Mother spoke, "Deep spacer, I had to give you a last farewell. Thank you for spending time with this old woman. Though I will miss your songs of old Sol, I will miss our conversations more."

"Lucia! I will cherish our time together," replied Luli. "But I thought we said our goodbyes last night!"

"It is not every day that one gets to say goodbye to a true legend, never mind twice! More than that, I wanted to give you my heartfelt blessings for finding your friend."

"The universe is a huge place," murmured Luli. "By Tom, I pray that the Cluster's inhabitants find everything they need and you live a long life."

"Don't pray to that old demon on my account," huffed Lucia. "We will do as we always have. Fortunes be with you, Luli Qing."

Jon Gray Lang

"And with you, All-Mother. This is the Matilda signing off."

The comm light stuttered into darkness and the star map filled her vision. The Scrapheap hovered ahead of her as the Cluster receded behind. Luli crossed her fingers, "Come on Tom, favor our mission and get us underway."

Luli heard Jacquie's voice in the background, "Cables have been disconnected. You are free to ferry us. Matilda out."

***

"Message received, Matilda," answered Derain. "You hear that Anton?"

"Sure did. Separating now."

The Cyclops and the Waratah pulled the Matilda free of the Cluster and towed it toward the asteroid called the Scrapheap, a place known as a colony of pirates, smugglers, and others avoiding the eye and arm of the Consortium.

"I haven't been here since I was a child," Anton remarked over the comm.

"You've been here?" replied Derain. "Didn't think anyone but pirates and the like came way out here."

"Oh, I used to live here with my father. He used to say it was the best place to give the slip to all the hatchet men out there. I haven't seen her contours in a long, long time. Man, she's just as ugly as I remember."

"I didn't know you were from here, Anton," Luli commented into the comm.

Anton wryly remarked, "I'm not from the 'Heap! Well, I don't think so anyway. We hid out here for years. It's a good place to disappear when you need to. And we always needed to disappear." The comm chattered with static as Anton said, "I wonder if the Old Nag is still kicking. I'm switching comms, Rabbit out."

"Any thoughts on where we can park the Matilda," asked Jacquie. "Anton? Hello? Gah! I swear that man is trying to make me crazy."

***

"Cyclops to Scrapheap, come in Scrapheap. Cyclops to Scrapheap, come in Scrapheap."

A bored technician's voice replied, "Scrapheap to Cyclops. What do you want?"

"Holy shit, is this Sanford? This is Rabbit."

"Rabbit? Rabbit of the Roane's? I figured you'd be dead by now!"

"Ha, ha! Not yet, but it isn't from people's lack of trying," joked Anton. "Hey, I've got a broken boat on my hook and I'm looking for a dock to drop her. Is the Old Nag still kicking?"

"Kicking it live. You know the Major can't take her without a fight that he don't want any part of," replied Sanford. "Her son handles most of the business up front, but she keeps him in line."

"Can you patch me through?"

Jon Gray Lang

There was a long pause, "... sure Rabbit. Hold on a moment."

Rabbit kept pace with the Waratah as they slowed the drag on the Matilda. He glanced out the port window and gazed over the surface of the Scrapheap. The place had grown since he'd been gone. Newer ship carcasses dotted the surface of the huge asteroid. Sky bridges connected some of the shinier wrecks to the domes that beckoned with humanity and all its pleasures and problems.

A couple of large sloops shot past and curved their trajectory around the Matilda. They disappeared behind the far edge of the asteroid.

"Well, that's a bit curious," remarked Anton.

An old woman's codgy voice crackled through the comm, "... that you Rabbit? I figured you'd be dead by now."

"Hello, Orla!" Anton replied. "I hope I didn't wake you. I know you think you need that beauty sleep, gorgeous as you are."

"Yep, that's the Rabbit I remember. Always the charmer. What do you want, you scoundrel?"

"Now I don't expect charity, but I've got a busted-up ship that needs repairs."

"Did you steal it?" she asked.

"What? No! I don't do that anymore." Anton exclaimed in consternation. "And before you ask, I am not looking for a handout."

"Ahh, that doesn't sound like the Rabbit I know..." she replied.

"I'll give you the jump on a prospect, if you'll

help me out. I've got a line on a beaut of a shipwreck," he mouthed into the comm. "Only a couple weeks out."

"There," Orla giggled. "Now that sounds like the Rabbit I know. And you got my attention."

"It has an FTL drive though I can't promise it's intact," he said. "I'll give you dibs on it, if you get my boat up and running."

"Never could keep your mouth shut," she growled. "Let's discuss this behind closed doors, boy. Bring your boat around back... you know where. Orla out."

Anton switched the comm channel, "Derain, follow me in. I got us a dock for repairs."

"About time," replied Derain. "Following you in."

The Cyclops and the Waratah tugged the Matilda behind them and rounded the asteroid. Following Anton's commands, the two ships were able to bring the Matilda around and settle it onto a platform. Once they unhooked their lines, the two ships flew back into the Matilda's hangar. Space suited figures strapped the Matilda down to the platform and the whole assembly slid inside the asteroid. A gigantic blast door closed behind them and shut out the night sky.

***

Derain was the last one to join the others waiting in the lift on the top deck. As the door shut, he asked, "What did you do to get us a dock so fast?"

"Relax," Anton answered. "I used to live here. I know these people. You can trust me."

"Oh boy," intoned Barney. "Last time you said that we had to jump port and we couldn't go back for a year."

"Calgorlie was a one-time fluke..."

Luli piped in, "Or what about that time at Gichi where we had to leave without getting new cargo? Jacq was pissed!"

Jacquie interrupted them, "You sure about this, Anton? We don't have the mazuma to cover the fees."

"You couldn't be more wrong about that, Jacq. We have a line on exactly what this place wants," answered Anton.

"And what is that, pray tell?" asked Derain.

Anton stared expectantly at each one of them in turn, but received only honest blank looks in reply. The doors to the lift parted and he stepped into the cargo bay. He looked back at everyone trailing behind him, but no one offered an answer.

"It's pretty simple, folks," Anton replied. "Physically, this asteroid is as big as it can get. Adding ship wreckage is the only way the place can grow. And we just left a ton of wreckage out there."

"I don't like where this is going," Derain said with an uneasy look. The rest of the crew's expression mirrored his.

Anton quipped, "Come on folks, we're

dripping in mazuma!"

***

The crew followed Anton as he led the way out onto the open landing pad. Jacquie's nose tickled in the dry air. The slipway had that musty smell of old metals, rust, and burnt oil. Another freighter lay in pieces on the next pad over and darkness swallowed up the rest of the place. The huge docking facility may be old but it was kept very tidy. Whoever Anton's friend was, she kept the place organized.

Leaning against the far wall was a spry old woman, surprisingly short and plump. Standing in front of her was a younger man. In contrast to her stockiness, he was tall and willowy, but in appearance his face eerily matched her, feature by feature.

Anton nudged Jacquie in the ribs and whispered, "That's her son, Emy. He was born on this rock and the light gravity affected his health. Orla would've left this dump years ago, but he can't live anywhere else." He shrugged, "He used to be a bit angry about it."

"That you, Rabbit?" exclaimed Emy. "You're bigger, but you still look like that bouncy piece of garbage that was always underfoot."

"Good to see you too, Emy," Anton replied. "It's always nice to remember that I'm younger than you, because I'd hate to have been your pa."

Orla laughed heartily as she latched onto

Emy's arm, "Calm down, boy. The two of you constantly tease each other." Stepping ahead of her son, she gestured to the group, Who are your friends, Rabbit?"

Anton approached and kissed the knuckle on her right hand. "They're my crew, Orla. Or technically, I'm hers," he said as he pointed out Jacquie. He swept the old woman into a deep embrace, "It is good to see you, Auntie." He grabbed Emy and dragged him into the hug, "You too, Emy. I've missed you both."

"Don't forget how you left us high and dry, you bastard," complained Emy.

Anton just pulled the pair of them in tighter.

Emy relented, "We got through it alright, though. Damn, it's hard to stay mad at you."

"I love you too," Anton said as he patted him on the back. "So are we continuing this business out here on the pad or should we head in?"

Jacquie's expression was dubious, but she motioned for the crew to join her as she followed Orla and Rabbit to the stairs.

As they walked, Luli whispered, "Did you know that Rabbit was from here?"

Jacquie whispered back, "I didn't think he'd stayed anywhere long enough to be from anywhere, to be honest."

***

Orla settled herself behind a desk while Emy

filled a bunch of flimsy cups with a thick, dark liquid. He kept one for himself, then handed out the others. Orla waved him to a seat but he moved behind her and leaned into the wall. Orla just shook her head at his contrary posturing.

"Before we go any farther, let me see what you've brought," she said.

Anton chuckled and pulled a data pad free of his coat, "Of course, Auntie. A jump on salvage only helps if you've got it." He pulled up a list of files and shunted it over to her ancient desk holo. The light flickered briefly, then grew strong as a visual copy of the M33 appeared.

Emy switched off the overhead lamps and the office was bathed in the greenish-blue glow of the holo. He whistled in appreciation at the image of the ship. "You have the coordinates for that?" Emy asked.

"We do," answered Jacquie. She ignored Anton as he tried to shush her, "Like Anton said, it's about two weeks out on a slow drift. With a full burn, you could get there within one."

Anton jumped in, "Now as this image shows, she's not in the best shape." He shunted over another image showing the M33 split into two jagged pieces with flotsam orbiting the main hull.

Orla moved the new image around, "What happened?"

Luli peeped, "To be honest, we don't really know. One minute we're being transported to the brig and the next, the ship is on fire."

Orla laughed, "To the brig, eh? Yeah, that's the Rabbit I know and love."

Derain laughed as Anton struggled to defend himself, "It wasn't me this time, Auntie. I swear!"

"Consortium military, eh? What about survivors?" asked Emy. "Or didn't you leave any?"

Barney grimaced, "We checked, but couldn't find a soul. There might be some sections deep inside that still have an atmosphere, but I wouldn't bet on there being any survivors."

"You said it had an FTL drive?" asked Orla.

"It sure does!" Anton affirmed. "The tunnel collapsed and we got thrown out into this system."

"Yeah, the tunnel mysteriously collapsed," added Jacquie as she stared daggers into the back of Derain's head.

Barney hopped onto the desktop so he could reach the holo image. His fingers spun it upside down and expanded it, "If I remember correctly, this is where the drive is. And the emitter should be here," the nose of the destroyer grew larger until the boxlike structure right underneath was easy to see.

"We can't promise it'll work, but most of the heavy equipment is intact," added Anton. "Here's her draft and potential mass. So, what do you say?"

"The local mercs aren't looking for her?" asked Emy.

Derain smiled bitterly, "The ship wasn't set to come out in this system. The locals shouldn't be aware of it. And Consortium military wouldn't know where to begin to look for her if she's even been classified as missing."

Orla laughed deeply, "Knowing them, they wouldn't broadcast the loss of one of their own unless they had something to gain."

"No doubt," chimed in Anton. "So, do we have a deal?"

"We have a deal. Emy, wake Idam and get the tug prepped. Tell her she needs to get her team together yesterday and to keep it on the quiet side."

"On it, Ma." Emy pushed off the wall and bounded through the door. His haranguing echoed back into the office as another voice joined his in the outer hallway.

Orla winked at Anton, "So, we fix your busted boat and we get primary salvage rights on that one."

"You've got it to a T, Auntie."

Orla placed her scarred palm over his hand and clamped down hard. "If the lead is worthless, I'm keeping your boat and I'll take the rest of what you owe me out of your hide. Deal?"

"Deal." Anton winced as his fingers were crushed. Flexing the pain out of his hand, he said, "We've had a long day and I for one am famished. So, if you'll excuse us, we'll be on our way."

Orla watched the ragtag crew walk out of her office. As soon as they reached the bottom of the stairs, she stepped out into the hall and motioned Emy to return to the office.

"What is it, Ma?"

She opened her desk drawer and pulled out a beat-up data card. "I don't know how the boss knew, but these folks? They're the ones we were told to look for."

Emy glanced toward the door, "Them?"

Orla nodded as she slipped the card into Emy's hand. "The boss wants whatever is on this card input into their ship's computer. You got that?"

"I'll have one of the boys take care of it," Emy said as he closed his hand over the data card.

***

Orla's warning burned in Anton's mind as he led the crew out onto the streets of the Scrapheap. "You and your people need to stay close and you all better keep your people's mouths shut on this. Do you hear me, boy?"

He had laughed when he walked out the door, but Anton knew the "Old Nag" meant business. Friends were one thing, but business with friends was still business.

"Thanks for letting me take the lead, Jacq," said Anton. "You know, since I speak the local lingo and all."

He glanced over his shoulder at the Captain. No change. She was still staring daggers into his back.

"Uhh, let's head over to the Royale Pho 303 and grab some lunch," Anton said as he headed off toward a blinking neon sign.

***

Jon Gray Lang

"Royale Pho 303?" asked Luli.

She looked up at the word Royale, emblazoned along a metal panel that appeared once to have been part of the hull of a ship. In glow paint beneath it was written the word, PHO. The remaining 303 of the ship's Ident stood out in stark contrast underneath. It took her a moment to realize she was standing alone in the lobby and some of the people were giving her appraising looks. She moved quickly through the entrance.

The interior of the cafe was dim, lit only by strips of neon in blue and purple. Scattered across the ceiling were pinpricks of light that resembled the night sky outside of the planetoid. She found her people seated around a small table and slid in between Barney and Jacquie.

"Five bowls of the house pho," Anton ordered. "Add a little extra of your special seasoning, too, will you? Thanks, Binh." A secretive expression lit up Anton's face, "You guys are in for a treat!"

Jacquie drummed her fingers against the table, "Can we trust Orla?"

Anton barked in amusement, "As far as the deal goes, yes. So everybody keeps their mouths shut. Any leaks about this business will cost us our hides."

"Noted." Jacquie continued to angrily stare at him.

Anton deflated a little under her glare and he

lowered his voice, "We're operating on promises in the land of lies, Captain. It's a good chance that our conversation is being recorded by somebody. We can get through this, but we have to play it close to the chest."

"Our choices are limited," interrupted Derain. "This is his home territory and he knows it best." He scratched at the stubble growing on his cheek, "We'll need somewhere to crash in the meantime. Got a place in mind?"

A squat older man in a filthy apron balancing a large tray stacked with gigantic bowls approached the little round table. He gingerly placed a bowl in front of each person. But as he set a steaming serving in front of Anton, he paused and blurted, "By the Gods! It is you, my boy! When Binh said with special seasoning, I had to double-check."

"Quoc! It is good to see you!" Anton beamed as he stood up and wrapped his arms around the cook.

The old man laughed, "Only two people ever ordered extra seasoning. You and your papa." He shrugged derisively, "All these Scrappers have weak tongues."

"Weak as babes," agreed Anton. "Everyone, this is Quoc. This is the man who taught me everything there is to know in the galley."

Luli made an 'oh' face and bowed deeply, "I thank you from the bottom of my stomach. His cooking skills have kept the love between us more than once."

Jon Gray Lang

"The boy was willing and I needed the help. It didn't hurt that he would work for food. Another hand, no matter how small, is always appreciated. Well Rabbit, I will leave you and your friends to it." Quoc winked at Anton, turned slowly and tottled back to the kitchen.

Jacquie waited until Quoc was out of sight before she spoke, "So we're here for at least a couple weeks before the Matilda can fly."

"If we're lucky," muttered Derain.

"If we're lucky," Jacquie commiserated. "We need to figure out our next step."

"Get off this rock," stated Anton. "Then we start looking for Galena."

"Do we even know where to look?" asked Luli. "Last we saw of her, she was in a med tube being carted off by a woman in a lab coat.

"That woman was Dr. Wyeth," grated Derain. "We should be able to find something on her, but it won't be easy. And before you ask, yes I was hired to track her."

"Track her or kill her?" asked Barney. "By the way, this pho is absolutely amazing! Where did they find the mushrooms?"

"Don't ask questions you really don't want the answers to," warned Derain.

"Which question?"

"Probably both," answered Jacquie.

Anton lit up, "Well the mushrooms are grown in the waste bin on deck three..."

"I don't want to know," gritted Barney.

Jon Gray Lang

Anton slurped in some of the broth and wiped his face, "Is that why you wanted to blow the ship?"

Derain ground out, "Listening devices..."

"So we need to find information on this Doctor," interrupted Jacquie. "Anything else?"

"A place to crash would be nice. I am exhausted," answered Luli.

"I know a place," asserted Anton. "It's a bit of a shit-hole, though."

"Fewer listeners," Derain rejoined.

Jacquie slapped the table, "It's a start. Let's finish this meal and find some crash space. Then on to the next step."

***

Quoc watched from the kitchen as his guests wholeheartedly dug into the pho. It was good to see Rabbit again. He was leaner, and more rugged, but still had that quirky look about him. "I'll miss the boy."

Binh walked up and whispered into Quoc's ear, "I let the boss know that they're here. He said to leave it at that."

Quoc sighed, "Always in trouble, that one. Well, the less we're involved, the better."

"The less we're involved, the better," agreed Binh.

Jon Gray Lang

two

The Streets of Forbes

The rock walls of the Scrapheap passed by as the crew followed Anton deeper into the core. As they made their way through, some sections of the Scrapheap were brightly lit with neon and noisy with the chatter of people and music. Other areas were dark and the only sound was the drip of water carving pools into the stone floor.

"From all the rumors I've heard about this place, I've got a serious question." Barney peered into the shadows, "Are we inviting trouble walking back here?"

"Shouldn't be a concern," answered Anton. "There are too many of us."

Derain almost laughed, "Too many of us? We're a party of five."

"No one wants a hard mark," scoffed Anton. A rattling sound receded into the distance, "But keep

Jon Gray Lang

an eye out, just the same."

They all rounded a corner and saw a lodge of sorts at the end of the corridor. A Vacancy sign blinked intermittently below an image that some artist had rendered as their vision of the Taj Mahal. A double door was propped open and a dim light filtered through the blinds of the single nearby porthole.

With a dramatic sweep of his outstretched hand, Anton declared, "And this will be our palace."

"You weren't lying about it being a shit-hole," smirked Luli. "Did they pull this section out of an old personnel carrier?"

"The Taj may not look great on the outside, but inside it's even worse," chuckled Anton. "On the plus side, no one will look for us here."

"I wouldn't look for us here, either," remarked Derain.

Jacquie swiped through her data pad, "Can we afford it? Those Consortium brutes stripped our funds."

Anton bowed, "Leave it to me, my Captain. I... know people. Now just stand out here and wait."

"If I didn't know better, I would think he was enjoying this," grumbled Jacquie.

"Of course, he is," added Barney. "How many times has it been us pulling his ass out of the fire and not the other way around?"

Derain glanced back down the long hallway and a slight movement caught his eye. The rocky walls created shadows amongst the bits of twisted metal that poked through. A pair of eyes glinted as they caught the light from the remaining tube light that dangled loosely from the ceiling. "Hey Jacq, I'll be back. Just let me know what room."

"I got you," answered Luli. She breathed in deeply, "It's nice to be off the ship, nice to be out and about again. Makes me want to sing."

Jacquie rubbed her back, "We can make that happen, girl."

Anton popped out of the office, "Follow me. I got us a suite."

***

The poly-wood door swung open and part of the lock spilled out onto the stained taupe carpet. Sections of the flooring were bowed inward and the spiral pattern within the weave was matted into place.

"You weren't lying," Jacquie asserted through gritted teeth. "We better be vaccinated against whatever is growing in those threads."

"I'll put the lock back together," said Barney as he picked up the pieces. "Good luck with finding the cure."

"Hey now, it's not that bad," Anton insisted. He looked at the floor a little harder, "Though I don't think the carpet's been replaced since the last time I stayed here. Yeah, don't touch it, if possible."

Luli shot past and called out from the back room, "There are only a couple of beds. Been a long time since we bunked up like this. I'm off to take a nap."

Barney scoffed, "A very long time. Jacq? If you don't mind, I'd like to check in on the Matilda. I'll have my comm with me."

"Please do. I'll figure out a place to meet up for dinner. Anton, join me." Jacquie wandered over to the small table and slipped into one of the three chairs.

"Sure, Jacq." Anton slid into one of the other chairs. "I got a city map from the front desk, everyone should get a copy shortly."

Jacquie drummed her fingers as she waited for him to finish. When he finally put down his data pad, she blurted "Galena's trail is getting too damn cold! We can't stay cooped up in this place for two weeks."

Anton reached out and gripped her hands, "We'll find her. I'm sure of it."

"But where?" she demanded as she pulled her hands free. "I finally had all six of us together and then we lost Galena when you and Derain murdered everyone on a Consortium vessel! There's no way we can escape karma for that kind of justice."

"Was it justice when they shot the Matilda to pieces? Was it justice when they yanked us off our boat and stuck us in the brig?" His mouth quirked in a grimace, "Is it justice that they treat the genorgs as less than human? Fuck them, they deserve what they got."

Jacquie leaned back, "Be careful, Rabbit. Your

revolutionary tendencies are making an appearance. Remember how that went?"

"I can't ever forget. Memories like those never go away. They just sit in the back of your mind and come out when you can least handle them. But you know what I mean, don't you?"

"We all have our own." She couldn't meet his eyes as she slid back into the chair, "Okay. We've only got one lead to Galena and that's the woman from the M33. Any ideas on where we might find this Dr. Wyeth?"

He replied distractedly, "... I've got a few ideas. Let me check around first. The bonus here is this place never sleeps and it is seething with info-gatherers. Someone will have a lead on her. While I'm at it, I'll check on a place for Luli to do her musical magic, too." His fingertip traced a surge stain on the table, "I better get started. I think it's best if the rest of you stay inside tonight. I'll pick up some grab-n-go on my way back."

Jacquie watched as Rabbit opened the door and slipped out past the poorly lit signage. The door swung back and clicked closed with a sharp finality. She grumbled to herself in the quiet, "Hard being the Captain when you're stuck on a rock with a dead ship and missing crew. Damn hard."

***

The snoop ahead of him was elusive, but Derain kept him in sight. He almost lost the

Jon Gray Lang

slippery fellow when he shot down a staircase and around a corner, but the man didn't seem to be aware that Derain was tracking him. Which was good, because it was much darker down on this level.

Derain kept a surreptitious eye on the snoop who sauntered over to a small table staged out front of a drinking establishment. The man nonchalantly glanced around at his surroundings as he settled into a seat.

Derain also surveyed the scene. "Now, if I only knew where on this bloody rock I am." His data pad lit up, and an old map of the Scrapheap appeared like an answer to his prayer.

Derain smiled at Anton's digital signature attached to the map, "Don't know how he does it, but somehow Rabbit always comes through when it's really needed," he murmured.

He looked up. The snoop still sat at the little table out in front of the tiny bar. The dark coat that encircled the squirrely-looking fellow looked like what was left of an optical camo poncho that had shorted out. His mark kept glancing inside the bar. *'Was he waiting for someone?'*

Derain studied the map. It appeared he was on the deepest level of the asteroid. The little bar and sandwich shop wasn't listed on the map, so Derain tagged the name to it, Bröt 790. A moment later, someone came out of the establishment and waved the mark in. Derain lost sight of him.

The comm chirped, "Derain here."

Jon Gray Lang

"Come on back to the room," said Jacquie. "We're planning on an early start tomorrow."

Derain watched the front of the bar, but he couldn't see past the entrance. "Good enough. On my way Captain."

***

Getting back to the docking facility had been easier than Barney had expected. The map Anton sent was good backup, but Barney had remembered most of the route. He wrinkled his nose, "Spend enough time on different worlds and stations, and eventually you can find your way around by smell alone."

Barney waved at Orla as he walked back to her office. His eyes settled on the Matilda as he rested his hands on his hips. The freighter sat on the deck while work lights played over the new engine cores and exposed the empty brackets on the hull. The engines they had stolen from the Consortium destroyer were larger than the ones they would be replacing.

His eyes traveled along the scars on the hull. Some sucked in the light like a deep ravine across a flat expanse. On the starboard side, two of the armored plates near the articulated short engine wing were buckled inward. A batch of the hydraulics hung freely exposed to the elements.

"We might get her flight-ready, but her days as a beauty are far behind her," Orla remarked.

"She's still a beauty on the inside."

Orla laughed, "You sure about that? I've been in her hold."

"Eye of the beholder. And to mine, she is the most beautiful thing in the universe."

"You mind telling me what that ball thing is in the engine room?"

He glanced sideways at her, "Not my ship, not mine to tell. Besides, it wouldn't make any sense."

"Try me."

He shook his head, "Still not mine to tell."

Barney's data pad chimed and a marker hovered over a section of the map, "Looks like I've been called back. Direct any correspondence our way. We're staying at the Taj."

"That shit-hole?" she replied. "I don't know what Rabbit sees in the place."

"Maybe he thinks it's beautiful."

She chortled, "I doubt that. You and your people did good work with the heavy lifting. After we retrofit the sublight engine cores, there'll just be the electrics left to re-run. We'll keep working on her."

As he made his way out of the bay he heard her say, "I hope Rabbit comes through this time. I'd almost feel bad for selling this ship out from under him."

***

Anton stumbled in through the motel room

door with his arms overloaded with bags. Unappealing grease spots had formed on the bottom of some, but the aroma that wafted into the room set many a stomach to a growl.

He set the bags down on the scratched and chipped table and pulled the staples free of the fold. The stomachs in the small apartment only growled louder as the aroma grew stronger.

"You guys are in for another treat! I can't believe Guilo Guiseppe's is still open. I was sure he'd have been chased off by the pirates' press-gangs by now," Anton grinned as he pulled out various small boxes and bowls from the bags. He placed them around the table until there wasn't room for more, "Those press-gangs are rough. I never thought they'd catch me but they did and off this rock I went."

There was a pregnant pause, "What?" Jacquie asked stonily.

"Uh," replied Anton as he blinked at her. "Oh... Oh look, Barney is here!"

"It smells heavenly in here," Barney stated as he walked in through the doorway and stepped over to the table. "Alright if I dig in?"

"Yeah, of course," answered Anton. "Grab a bowl and go, go, go! I'm going to go out and check on Derain."

"No, you're not," Jacquie insisted as she blocked the doorway.

"Derain!" Barney hailed the crew member who suddenly appeared over Jacquie's shoulder.

"Where have you been?"

Anton seized the moment to slip past Jacquie and wrap an arm around the bounty hunter. He hauled him over to the table, "What have you been up to?"

Derain slid out of Anton's grip and checked out the food, "We had a tail on us after we left the repair bay. I figured I'd see what they were up to. What is the yellowy-orange stuff?"

"Oh, that's a curry noodle dish," answered Anton.

"It is bloody fantastic!" added Luli. "Somewhere between a golden curry and a ragu."

Derain glanced at the contented expression on Luli's face as he spooned some into his own bowl, "Our trace stopped at a rinky-dink bar on the bottom level. A tiny place with a couple tables out front."

"Bröt 790?" At Derain's nod, Anton continued, "The Entro-Pita there is to die for, but not surprised. The place is a big info trading hub on the 'heap. One of Orla's folks would've sold the news of our arrival eventually. She might have partnered with your tail, truth be told."

"And you trust this woman?" asked Jacquie.

Anton smiled slightly, "Trust is a strong word. More like I know what I'm in for than actual trust. Besides, I won't stop her from making a bit of mazuma on the side. Life is hard enough out here and she has plenty of mouths to feed. Including us at the moment."

Luli's voice piped up in the background, "These bean-paste ravioli are to die for!"

Anton's grinned, "I could never get those to come out the right way." He touched Jacquie on the shoulder and led her to a corner, "I know some places we can ask around about this Dr. Wyeth character. Some of them are going to be your kind of place."

"Down and dirty, huh? Great."

Anton shrugged, "It could be worse. Could be like that creepy place on Abos IV. Just thinking about it and I have that taste in my mouth again. Ugh."

Jacquie grimaced, "Thanks for that memory. I could've lived the rest of my days without remembering that hellhole. We'll make an early start of it. And don't think we've finished that conversation about you in a pirate press gang."

Anton replied, "I wasn't in the press gang. They pressed me into service on one of their ships. It's not like I had a choice."

Jacquie backed him up against the wall, "We will finish that conversation and we will talk about the cost."

"Have I died? Ginger, tomato, and garlic lo mein with fried tofu balls? We have got to come back to this place, Jacq!" mumbled Luli through another mouthful. "You guys better get some of this, or I am going to eat it!"

Anton laughed nervously, "After you, Captain?"

three

By the Light of the Silvery Moon

The front room was a flurry of activity. Anton bustled around the single burner hob, scooped out some protein pudding and shoveled it onto plates. Barney took the plates and dropped them on the table where Luli circled and grazed to her heart's content.

Jacquie stretched as she came out of the back room with her hair still wet. She smiled at the domestic scene, "I still can't believe this dump has an actual water 'fresher'. This place is better than I gave it credit."

"Better than being in vacuum," quipped Derain from the couch.

Jacquie rubbed the towel through her hair once more, then tossed it onto the bed. She heard Anton's admonishment, "You couldn't hang it back up?"

Jon Gray Lang

She wickedly grinned as she flopped next to Derain, and flicked her wet hair around. But he was all business. Jacquie grumbled and leaned into Derain's ear, "Looks like someone has a plan. So what is it?"

Derain wiped the water droplets from his face and scowled at her, but the comments he might have made were cut short when a breakfast plate was set on his lap along with a napkin.

"I'll have your plate ready in a mo," Barney told Jacquie as he returned to the table.

Derain picked up a strip of something unrecognizable and bit down hard on it. A look of surprise appeared on his face, "That's pretty good." He cleared his throat, "Well, we've only got a couple weeks on this rock and we don't know how long ago Galena arrived at her final destination."

"Or if she even has," groused Anton.

Derain nodded in agreement, "Or if she has. Either way, we need to gather as much info as we can. I suggest we split up to cover more ground."

A plate dropped into Jacquie's lap as a cup of something hot was pressed into her hand. She took a sip, "Mmm... thanks, Barney. Two weeks in the same room is going to send me over the edge. I need to blow off some steam."

"We all know what you mean, Jacq," Luli sighed.

Derain choked for a moment, "You're used to ferreting out smuggling jobs. See what you can find."

Jon Gray Lang

"Mm, hmm," she conceded over a spoonful of the protein pudding. "You paired me up with Rabbit, right? We need to work some things out."

"We don't have time for your grudge right now," grumbled Derain. "I told you he was a pirate before we pulled him off the Vogelgesang and you didn't want to hear it then."

Jacquie settled the plate on the arm of the couch and jumped to her feet, "I'll do this my way, thank you very much. She roughly slapped Anton on the back and gripped his shoulder, "It's you and me, Rabbit. Everyone else know where they're heading?"

Barney held up his data pad and pointed to the glowing markers on the screen. "Rabbit gave us the locations and a line on some mazuma from who knows where." He saw the look of fear on Anton's face and said, "You sure you don't want to partner up with me?"

"I'm good."

Luli pulled Jacquie back, "We can't have you stuffing Rabbit in a dumpster because of something that happened a long time ago. You'd best pair up with Barney, Captain. Maybe he can hammer some sense into you." She saluted as she stood between Jacquie and Anton. "I, on the other hand, have our local boy lined up to give me the grand tour. And I expect to be shown everything."

"I am not going to stuff him into a dumpster!"

Derain hopped off the couch and grabbed

the last piece of toast, "Works for me. I'll check the bail office and maybe wander down to that bar. Keep all avenues open, folks. Good hunting everyone."

The rest of the crew watched as he stepped out the front door and activated his optical camo. As Derain disappeared from view, the crew's banter dwindled.

"You ready, Lu? If you want me to show you everything, it's going to take a while."

"Right behind you!" declared Luli as she tossed a licked-clean spoon into the sink.

Jacquie looked down at Barney as he adjusted his work belt, "Looks like all of you are against me. Fine, let's get this rolling."

"After you, Captain."

***

Derain had worried that he might be followed from the Taj, but the invisibility jacket he wore allowed him to slip through the Scrapheap corridors completely unnoticed. "My value must've dropped," he mused.

As he neared the end of another rock and metal corridor, he switched off his optical camo and stopped at a fork in the path. From the map that Anton had given him, the bail bonds office should be off the upper deck in an old ship called the Hobart. He wasn't sure how that actually worked. He sighed as he pocketed his data pad and headed off to the right. The lift he needed should just be straight ahead.

There were more pedestrians traversing this length of corridor now than had been here last night. He passed several groups of young punks before he finally caught sight of the lift. Without even looking, he sensed that at least one of the groups was tailing him. Once he made it to the lift and keyed the button to bring it down, he felt someone tapping him on the shoulder.

"Hey old man, you got any mazuma to spare? Me and my fellow travelers could use some help."

Derain turned around to face three teenagers pressed up close to him. Beyond them was a couple more and it looked like the other bunch were moving up to join their compatriots. Derain half-lidded his eyes as he catalogued their threat value. Some were armed with blades, while others carried short blunts and at least one had metal knucklers on both hands.

"I don't have time for this," he grumbled as the gangs joined together. Behind him, the lift dinged and the door slid open. "Should we postpone this party?" he asked as he stepped inside.

One of the kids in the back seemed intent on her data pad. She kept staring at Derain and then back at the screen, "Hey guys? I think we should let this one go."

One of the older boys slapped his hand against the lift door to keep it from closing, "Naw, I think he wants to help us out. He recognizes those in need. Don't you, old man?"

Derain's hand flashed out, snapped the boy's wrist, and pushed him back into the gang, "Seriously, does that line actually work?"

The boy screamed in pain as he fell on his ass. The other kids stopped in their tracks. The only other sound was the girl with the data pad. "This guy is a killer!" she stammered. "Let's get out of here before he hunts us down and murders us!"

The look of fear on her face was emblazoned in his mind as the doors closed. He sighed as the lift began its rickety journey up, "Wonder which compilation of me that girl found?" His hands clenched into fists as he grunted, "Doesn't matter, I know what I've done and I can't change that. No excuses."

When the doors slowly split open, Derain slipped out. He pushed through the crowd waiting for the lift and kept his head down. He bee-lined straight through the mass of people until the throng thinned out.

His eyes tracked the options available and he veered off to the left. This corridor had more metal plating built into the rocky stone of the asteroid. The air seemed a bit thinner as well. Derain scanned the area looking for any sign of the Hobart, but there was only a scattering of cheap brothels and junk joints littering the way.

"Hey sailor, looking for something quick?"

"Don't listen to him, honey. Save a few mazuma bills with me. Really come and get off..."

Jon Gray Lang

The neon-colored mirages blinked in and out of existence promising all the ecstasies of the flesh and the mind, dreams and beyond. He ignored them and continued past their dusty lies and broken promises. Off to the right was a corroded staircase similar to an old lander escape way that caught his eye. A rusted signatory plate was bolted into the fuselage and the name HOBART was barely legible.

"Finally," he declared as he swung the old hatch open. Inside, the chairs bolted to the walls indicated this must be a waiting area. He strode to the desk at the far end of the room and spoke to the receptionist. "I am looking for some information."

"Is it contract related?" asked the woman behind the desk with the plas-glass shield.

Derain hesitated a moment, "Yes."

"Which contract?"

"Private. I only have a name and occupation. Dr. Wyeth, in the employ of the Consortium."

She swiped through her entries and shock radiated across her face, "... Oh. You would need to refer back to the contractee."

Derain's shoulders slumped, "Let me guess, he has an office here, too."

The woman looked up blankly, "He? I don't show a single individual listed here. The docket shows the contract was processed through a subsidiary of Unifreight Inc."

"Does Unifreight have an office here?"

"They run a part-time desk in the shipping office. Just south of the third loading dock on the main level." She looked up at him with misgiving, "You can't miss it. Now, good day to you, sir."

The woman opaqued the plas-glass shield and left Derain staring at his reflection.

***

The sign glowed in the poorly lit hallway. The name, Eclectic Electric reflected in the pools of stagnant water that puddled out front. A patron stumbled out the front door and fell to his knees in the filthy water.

"Wha' da hell? Why am I all wet?" echoed down the corridor.

Barney looked up at Jacquie, "One of these places? Preparing myself then."

Jacquie just grinned and waltzed into the establishment. Once past the fur-covered hatch, the interior emitted a bashful pink glow. Brass bolts were plugged into the wall giving the room an off-kilter lean to the hull of a ship. Heavy bass music thumped loudly in the establishment while spiraling lights slid across the open walls and highlighted chromium cages. Some of them were occupied with cavorting figures.

An official-looking woman in a fancy outfit walked up to Jacquie and asked, "You here for the dance job?" Her eyes slid over every inch of the Captain and a faint appraisal crossed her lips, "You'll do well. We have costumes in the back, if you can start within the hour."

Barney chuckled lightly behind Jacquie, "Oh... One of these places. We'll fit right in."

The woman peered around Jacquie's hip and gave Barney the once over as well, "We have a backroom that requested a dancer like your friend, too. We only have a couple costumes in your size, sweetness. How do you feel about being a bear cub?"

Jacquie rested her hand on the woman's arm and gave a slight push back, "We're not here to work, we're here to watch. Got it?"

The bored expression on the woman's face didn't change as she murmured an insincere apology and then said, "Follow me."

She brought them up to the bar and slapped her palm against the counter. A couple digi-drink tickets appeared by the robotic bartender. "Free drinks for the new customers." She edged over to Jacquie's ear and confided, "If you want the dancing job, just let me know. We have customers that are very into your look." She winked, "Including me."

"Color me flattered," Jacquie replied. "If it all goes pear-shaped, I'll keep that in mind."

Barney picked up the glowing glass that contained some form of liquid that the robotic bartender slid their way. While the glass had a heliotrope pink-purple glow the liquid inside had a faint blue tinge. The fragrance of synthetic raspberries and an alcohol that smelled raw undulated from the concoction. He shrugged, "Shaping up to be one hell of a day, bottom's up!"

Jacquie struggled to grab her glass in time as Barney's clinked against hers. The slosh left luminescent bluish streaks on her hand. "Bottom's up is right."

Barney coughed as the burn of the liquor rushed up his nose and down his throat. He leaned over and coughed harder. His glass tipped over, rebounded off the bar, and rolled into a tight circle.

Jacquie laughed and began choking too, "By Tom, that's going to need a chaser." She waved the bartender down, "Open a tab and a couple shots of your best whiskey. What can you recommend for snacks?"

The bartender duly poured out a couple shots of a whiskey that neither of them recognized. Jacquie inserted her data pad into the bar table. Her ID chit clicked over and her image blossomed on the screen before it dropped to the side with a tally next to it.

"Menu's on pad..." it buzzed as it rolled away.

Barney grabbed the shot, drank it swiftly, and slammed the glass against the counter, "Pretty simple programming on that bot. I haven't seen another automaton besides Doc in what feels like decades."

Jacquie wiped her mouth, "You know the story. The Consortium outlawed the mobile ones once genorgs were released into the workforce. All because that military android went nuts and slaughtered its handlers."

"True," he replied as he scanned the interior.

It was still early and the room only had a few other customers who were mostly clustered around a man and woman dancing on the stage performing a strange, nude, mock combat sequence. Or at least that's what Barney could make of it. Only two of the four cages were currently occupied and he wasn't sure what the aesthetic was that they were trying to achieve. 'Hospital' came to mind. Bandages strategically adorned one of the dancers while the other wore an old lab coat with holes cut out for a peek-a-boo show.

Jacquie grimaced, "Looks like we're going to be here a while. I'm ordering another round."

Barney nodded as his eyes followed the walls of the chamber. The bartender bot rolled over and served them a couple tumblers of what could only be described as a cheaper whiskey, if not the cheapest. Jacquie slid one of the glasses over to Barney and grabbed the other for herself.

She nudged the Titan, "You hear what Anton let slip?"

Barney looked up at her questioningly, "What?"

"About him getting nabbed for a pirate crew. He said it offhandedly like it was a normal thing."

Barney spread his arms wide, "Maybe it is here. This is close to no man's land, Captain. Different rules apply here than anywhere else in the Consortium."

"But still..."

Barney looked her in the eye, "I'll say this

once and only once. As bad as your life has been, it's been pretty sheltered on the Matilda. Same goes for me. She's kept us safe as best she can. But he's seen things, I don't ever want to know about. He's probably done things to survive we don't want to hear. Maybe being a pirate was one of them. To be honest, we've all done things we're not exactly proud of."

"But what if he was part of the crew that killed my parents?"

Barney sighed, "When I was thrown in that cage, he was in the one next to me, looking like a scared kid. But he broke me out and helped you carry me back to the Matilda. Far as I'm concerned, that's all that matters. And all that should matter to you."

***

Jacquie looked down at the man who had seen her through thick and thin as he angrily drank from the tumbler and a small frown etched her face. He was looking a lot worse for wear. She supposed they all probably did. But something about his appearance bothered her. He looked thinner and his skin looked more worn, more creased. His eyes didn't seem to glow as brightly as she remembered and his hair had more silver in it than she thought it should.

"You're right, it doesn't matter. You know me, just trying to keep my shit together. Might as well get a move on this. Figure I'll bug our host for information. I might be spending the night without the crew, if you get my drift."

"Drift gotten. I'll wander around and see what I can hear."

Jacquie grabbed his hand and squeezed, "Fingers crossed we get something." As she let his hand go, she shouted, "Barkeep, my companion is authorized for the tab."

***

Luli looked all around as Anton led her to the upper levels of the Scrapheap. In many ways, it reminded her of her childhood home back in the belt of Sol and that was an almost forgotten concept. The lighting and the tunnel construction bore the scars of asteroid miners. Many of the shop fronts looked like the remnants that had at one time catered to them.

In other ways, it was shockingly different. Smugglers and pirates intermingled with bounty hunters, info brokers, body sellers, and other businesses that thrived in these sorts of environments. She recognized some of the faces in the crowd, but couldn't quite place a name for any of them. Anton was the complete opposite.

He seemed to know everyone, though they all just called him by his nickname. It was interesting to watch him in action as he told jokes, anecdotes, or insults depending on who he was talking to. It was refreshing in a way to not be the center of attention for a change, able to slip her way through the crowds and just enjoy the scene.

She breathed in deeply. The stench of rust, oils, ozone, and brackish water filled her nose and it brought back memories. She remembered chasing her cousins through tunnels just like these and that memory of laughter echoed in her head. The way the music sounded when her father played the ukulele, reverberated down the rocky walls and pooled in the corners. A melancholy smile settled across her face, "So long ago and now all dust. It feels good to be in a place like home, but it holds too much woe for me right now."

She looked around and realized that Anton had wandered off. She could just make him out in the dimly lit distance, standing strangely still in front of a break in the wall. She hurried to catch up and he turned as he heard her approach. He forced a grin to hide the grief in his face, but the sorrow hid away in the corners of his eyes.

"And what is the great mystery of this place?" she asked.

He pointed to a dark alley and waited for the humorous "oohs and aahs" from Luli. "This is the alley that I hid in after my father was permanently taken from me."

Luli grimaced, "More fun, less boo, okay? I've had enough boo to last me a lifetime."

Anton struck a pose and bowed deeply, "Your wish is my command, oh princess of the galaxy. So let's see, you've been to the restaurant district, you've been to the dock. I've taken you to the nice bars... Oh! I know. How do you feel about a bit of gambling?"

"I've been known to throw down a deck or two. Why, do you have a place in mind?"

"Oh, I definitely do. Only problem is, I gave all my mazuma away. You got any on you?"

***

Derain wandered to the main level. He pulled up the map and found the shipping office location. As he put the data pad away, he noticed that a few people had their eyes on him and one looked familiar. He kept the same pace as he slowly edged toward the storefronts that littered the main corridor.

He glanced up and ducked into the first store that looked mostly empty. When the bell over the door dinged as he entered, loud squawks, yips and yowls erupted in profusion. His lips pursed in chagrin as he realized he had wandered into a critter shop.

"Good day to you, sir!" the proprietor shouted, making his way forward from the storeroom. "How might I be of service to you? Are you looking for a maritime pet or a mascot for your vessel or crew? We have many wondrous creatures on display and each one can be purchased at a minimal price."

"Not looking for one, thank you," Derain grunted as he slid between a couple of the enclosures and kept an eye on the front door. "I'd stay in the back, if I were you."

"Stay in the back of my own store? Why ever would I do such a thing?"

The shop door's bell dinged again and a large man strode in. Tattoos covered every exposed inch of his head, but the lower half of his face was hidden behind a breather. Handles on at least three different knives clearly stuck out from the bravado's armored vest. And the augment glove that completed his attire replaced at least three missing digits.

"Good day to you, sir!" proclaimed the shopkeep.

The bravado grabbed the shopkeep by the apron and pulled him close, "You seen a tall man come in here? He owes the Abandoned an apology and I mean to get it."

"He's right over there..." blubbered the shopkeep before he was unceremoniously dropped.

Derain sprung from his hiding spot and slammed his fist into the back of the goon's head, to no effect. The man's elbow flew up and Derain leaned far to the side to avoid it. The brute spun around and threw a blow to Derain's abdomen. It landed hard. Derain backpedaled while struggling to breathe and the big man laid into him.

"Disrespect the Abandoned and you pay the price!" the thug yelled as he laid in blow after blow

Jon Gray Lang

to Derain's abdomen.

Derain threw his arms up and did his best to avoid getting hit, but the man was fast. One fist clipped Derain in the cheek and he staggered to the side. Then suddenly, the bravado's eyes grew wide and he keeled over sideways. Behind him stood a woman brandishing a Billie stick.

Derain blinked as recognition struck him, "Vania? What are you doing way out here?"

Vania sneered and struck him in the temple with the Billie stick. Derain went down like a sack of grain, "Long time no see, boyo, but you got a price on yer head, see? And I mean to collect."

***

Anton held onto Luli's hand and dragged her down to the bottom deck of the asteroid. The stink of overworked air circulation systems drenched the hallway in a fine mist. These tunnels were narrower and the overall temperature was cooler than the other levels of the 'heap. The pools of stagnant water and grease were more prevalent here as well.

"Are you sure there's a good parlor down here?" asked Luli as she swerved to avoid stepping into a pile of... something.

"The best one on this rock... or used to be." He glanced over his shoulder at her, "Derain reminded me of it when he tracked that louse into the bar. If we can buy any info on that Doctor character, this is the place. All the big info sellers play in this club. It's exclusive."

"If you say so," Luli shrugged as she hopped over a puddle that stank of coolant and plant rot.

Once she cleared the puddle and was out in the corridor, proper, Anton slapped his hand flat against her chest and pushed her into a shadowed alcove. A person with a recognizable face and his entourage walked through the dark entrance.

"Was that...?" asked Luli.

Anton whispered, "What's Stanislav Tenden doing way out here?"

Both of their comms chirped and Barney's slurred voice warbled, "Hey everyone. Cap'n wants us all in the dance club, pronto! So get your skinny asses up here now!"

Anton grimaced, "Jacquie and her damn timing. Let's go or we'll never hear the end of it."

four

Green Eyes

Galena Chadov opened her eyes and found herself curled into the corner of her room. She had no memory of arriving or how long she had been there. The lighting was dim, but the cyclical calendar showed that days had passed since her arrival on the moon of Ogun.

"Has it been that long already?" She blinked as she pushed away from the wall and jumped to her feet.

A half-eaten meal festered on a tray near the large mirror on one wall and her bunk appeared untouched. She blinked at her reflection but didn't sense the presence of the creature in her mind.

"What did it call itself again," she pondered. "The Master? Wouldn't the Captain be amused at that?"

The door to her room swung open and cool

air buffeted her. A middle-aged man decked out in a Consortium military uniform stood in the frame. She looked over his shoulder, but he was alone.

He noticed her interest and fingered his stun baton, "The Captain you say? I thought you were the lucky drone to command a platoon. What Captain do you speak of?"

She pulled up the zipper on her coveralls and stood at attention, "No one of consequence, sir."

"No one of consequence," he quipped as he strolled up to her. He used the baton to lift one of the lapels left hanging open from her hastily closed coveralls. He slowly walked around her, "I thought the one and only officer of your kind would better recognize rank, Lieutenant."

Since he stood so close to her, part of her brain focused on his scent and how it seemed so familiar, but another part of her mind replied, "I stand corrected, Corporal."

The man laughed as he signaled her toward the door, "I'm glad to see you're cognizant today, but we don't have time to dally. The Commander wishes to speak with you."

"Understood," she said as she stepped into the hallway. A railing ran along the edge and she could see she was not on the ground floor. She leaned over the railing and counted four balconies between her level and the broad floor at the base. A strange armored half sphere dominated that space. "What's down there?"

"You'll find out soon enough, Lieutenant," he

assured her. "And now, you will please follow me."

***

This new stretch of hallway looked exactly the same as the previous hall had looked. *'And the one before that, and the one before that,'* Galena thought as she followed the Corporal. She'd lost count of how many turns they'd made. "Is no one else bunked here?" she asked.

"No one likes the screams... or the ghosts," he grimaced.

She stopped and stared, "Ghosts?"

The Corporal nodded, but didn't stop which forced her to walk quickly to catch up with him. Eventually, the familiar sight of lift doors came into view. The controls were locked, but responded to commands the Corporal typed into his data pad. When the lift doors parted Galena was surprised to see heavy padding on the walls. A line of genorgs were escorted out of the lift by uniformed soldiers.

"Come on, get in, Lieutenant," the Corporal grunted. He slapped at the controls until the doors shut and the lift began its upward journey. "Those genorgs?" he sighed. "Those are ghosts. Or soon to be, anyway."

Galena didn't respond as her eyes studied the walls and floor of the lift. They settled on an old rust-colored stain intermixed with deep scratches into the padding. Her fingertips brushed against the ridge of slashed cloth as she leaned into the padding on the wall. She sniffed at the air and a part of her mind glittered, "Blood. Old, but blood all the same."

She felt the soldier's eyes on her, so she turned to face her escort. "What is your moniker, Corporal?"

"Jerald Cook, Lieutenant. I've been assigned to you during your stay at the Doctor's facility. We're almost there, so let's keep the chitchat down to nonexistent."

The lift finally came to a stop and the doors parted to reveal yet another open stretch of hallway. She stepped out ahead of him and waited. He raised an eyebrow and reached for his shock stick.

"Which way?" she asked nonplussed.

A couple of women in lab coats headed toward the lift deep in conversation. Corporal Cook glanced in their direction and his hand strayed away from the shock stick. As they passed by, Galena swore she saw one of the women throw a covert smile her way, but she remained unsure. She stuck close to the Corporal and gasped in awe as the hallway opened up into a large room.

The low metal ceiling gave way to an enormous bubble of plas-glass high overhead. The floor they walked on became a floating bridge above the core of the moon base. Overhead, stars flew by in a flurry of dust and gasses disappearing into complete darkness. A pair of heavily armored doors lay ahead that opened onto a central platform under the dome. The doors, while thicker than a standard airlock, weren't as thick as the cargo bay doors on the Matilda.

Jerald Cook stepped up to the door and rapped out a quick staccato beat. A small panel slid open and the face of a guard appeared. She acknowledged the soldier with a slight nod as the doors parted open.

Corporal Cook grabbed Galena's wrist, "The Commander is expecting you so be on your best behavior," he hissed as he pulled her into the command center where officers in a gray version of the Army uniform he wore manned multiple stations.

Her mind clicked in recognition, "Consortium Navy."

In the center of the chamber stood a raised platform overseen by three people. One of them, Galena noticed, had a bit more gold emblazoned on his collar and wrists.

Her eyes traveled up to the dome that covered the command center. Beyond the double domes and far to the right hung the edge of a tiny planet that was completely dwarfed by a huge ball of fire that dominated the entire horizon.

"It's so beautiful..." she said in hushed tones as she tried to take it all in.

"It is, isn't it?" a man's voice replied.

Galena realized that the heavily decorated officer now stood in front of her. Suddenly, she slammed to attention and threw a hard salute, "Sir! Lieutenant Chadov reporting."

He smiled and saluted in return. "I am Commander Diego."

The Commander turned his attention to Galena's escort, "Thank you for delivering the Lieutenant to me, Corporal Cook. Dr. Wyeth requests that you bring her by her office once my time with her has concluded. You may wait over there."

"Sir, yes sir." Corporal Cook saluted and backed away to the far edge of the platform and stood at parade rest.

"You may stand at ease, Lieutenant. I am the officer in charge of this facility. I have wanted to meet you for a long time."

Galena shifted into a more relaxed stance and spoke freely, "Me, sir?"

"Yes, you," he replied. He extended his arm to her and gave her hand a firm grasp, "It is a pleasure to meet our most successful export, the infamous Butcher of Timmony Bay."

***

Yeoman Hamza Fitzpatrick casually wandered the hallways of the moon base. Distracted by one of the wall screens that played a feed from the surface, he paused to watch. But his memory kept replaying his recent meeting with the Doctor. Curt and scathing as always, she said she wasn't his nursemaid and would call for him when he was needed. Then she'd gone back to her data pad and pointedly ignored him.

Commander Diego hadn't been any better. He hadn't given him any orders. He had only reminded the Yeoman that he was in the personal employ of Dr. Wyeth. Hamza pounded his fist against the wall, *'Thwarted again. Every time I choose a side, I get waylaid and left in the background. If I'd stuck with Captain Kaplean, at least I'd be on a ship with those interrogation recordings I could trade to a Family with promises.'*

The sound of a couple women chattering echoed down the hall ahead of their appearance. Hamza put on one of his ingratiating smiles, "Good evening, ladies. Would either of you be so kind as to tell me the name of the moon we're on?"

"New here?" smirked one.

"Leave him be," said the other. She pointed at a display on the wall screen, "You know that's the planet Ogun out there. The Wyeth family named it after an old creator God from Earth. The God's companion was a dog, so they named this moon Ogun's Aja."

"Nobody calls it that, though," added the first woman. "We all just call it Aja. Original, right?"

"Ogun's Aja? I'm guessing Aja means dog?"

"You got it in one!" cheered the other woman.

His finger tapped at his lower lip, "Dr. Wyeth's family named this rock? I didn't realize they'd been around since the founding."

"Her family established the base you're standing in." The woman checked her data pad and groaned, "We're running a little late. Maybe we'll meet again?"

Hamza Fitzpatrick smiled broadly, "I'll be around."

He watched as the two women hustled down the hall and left him alone with his thoughts. *'Everything here belongs to the Doctor, eh? There have to be some skeletons in the closets I can use to get a leg up... or a commission out of here.'*

His smile broadened as he wandered off with purpose, "No one lives that long without making enemies. Enemies that would pay good mazuma to bring them down."

***

Galena stumbled out of the base command center as Corporal Cook shoved her through the door. She felt his hand on her shoulder pushing her further along the sky bridge. She ignored his aggressive antics as she thought back over the conversation with Commander Diego. His "their only successful export" remark had surprised her. She had met other genorg soldiers since her return to this space.

"How can I be the only success?" she had asked. "I have met many capable genorg soldiers."

The Commander had grimaced, "One of the competitor families stole early documentation from the Wyeth Family's research. They didn't find all of the contingencies and focused only on the genorgs as being used as cannon fodder."

"Cannon fodder?" Galena mouthed in confusion.

Commander Diego had continued, "Even trained as well as they were, genorgs weren't expected to survive the battles as well as natural-borns. Those fools couldn't grasp the idea that the genorgs might be able to survive 'the change' just as you did. They completely discounted that possibility."

Galena felt off-kilter at this statement, "Am I changed? I do not feel that way."

"That is what the Doctor intends to find out," replied the Commander. "We have all been monitoring your progress and looked forward to your return. But then you disappeared and we thought you were lost forever. We are happy to have you back amongst the fold, Lieutenant. The base is proud of how well you proved to the Ruling Families that you and your sisters can be so much more than menial laborers. Especially how you can make decisions that many natural-borns would find distasteful."

"Distasteful?" she wondered what he meant.

"It is an honor to have met you, Lieutenant," Commander Diego had concluded.

Galena blinked the memories away as Corporal Cook grabbed her shoulder to halt her movement at the lift doors. "And now I go back to where I began."

***

When the lift doors parted again a suspended platform lay just beyond them. The platform formed a floating pathway high above the bottom floor she had spied earlier. The peculiar armored half-sphere grew out of the flooring in the giant room. A compulsion emanated from the enclosure and pulled at Galena. It called to her and whispered secrets into the corners of her mind that she couldn't fully grasp.

She plodded her way to the railing and looked down. The heavily armored dome was situated in the dead center of the ground floor and it was easily twenty feet tall. Slivers of plas-glass windows ringed the enclosure and pulsed with a sickly light. Red-orange spikes of color fluctuated within the bruised purple-blue maelstrom that flickered from the interior of the armored sphere.

But it was the deep hum the dome emitted that drew her rapt attention. Faint bits of conversations seemed to be hidden within the matrix of sound, but she wasn't able to catch enough to understand what was said. Something underlying in the tones tantalized her. She leaned farther and farther over the railing. Then suddenly, she felt a presence in her mind awaken.

"Home!" the creature screamed in her mind. "Power! Control..."

With all her might she pulled away from the railing and stumbled to her knees. Her mind snapped back to where she was and who was with her. And the fear she saw in the Corporal's eyes brought her back to her senses.

"What are you doing, drone?" he barked. "Can't have you jumping yet. You have places to be and I won't be held accountable for your absence."

He yanked her to her feet with one hand while keeping the other close to his shock stick. Once he felt she was stable, he brushed the dust from her shoulders and smoothed the wrinkles out of her coveralls.

He gripped her shoulder and stared into her eyes, "We don't have time for your doltish behavior. The Doctor wants to question you and you need to be coherent. Are you, Lieutenant? Coherent, I mean?"

She felt her eyes blink of their own volition as she pondered his odd concern for her welfare. "Yes, Corporal Cook. I am fine." She shook her shoulder free of his grasp, "Let's not keep the Doctor waiting."

He stood back a little nonplussed. "Yes, well. Follow me, Lieutenant."

***

Dr. Wyeth glanced up when the door to her office opened. Subject 4296-E-2631-H walked in, followed by a young man in one of the darker green uniforms. She always had trouble telling them all apart and cared even less to try.

Jon Gray Lang

She stood up and beckoned Galena, "Please, come and sit here. Corporal, thank you for delivering her. You may go now."

"As you wish, Doctor," he replied as he saluted, spun on his heel, and departed.

Dr. Judith Wyeth sat back down and rested her elbows on the desk. Her hands rose to a steeple in front of her. "I find the military personnel somewhat obnoxious, don't you? Oh, but you were granted membership into their ranks, weren't you?" Her false smile faded, "My apologies."

Galena shifted uncomfortably in the chair as she studied the room. Recognizable things stood out to her. An old 2D picture of a couple that resembled the Doctor. A stack of mind puzzles that looked well handled. And a small holo of a youthful Judith playing with a boy who looked suspiciously like an adolescent version of Mr. Leon.

Dr. Wyeth watched all of this from behind her desk. Once the genorg's eyes focused on her again, she asked, "You appear to be recovering from the surgery. How do you feel?"

Galena glanced down at her hands and then looked up again, "I am sufficiently functional, but I feel strange. What is that thing out there?"

Dr. Wyeth looked surprised, "You don't remember? Hmm, that's interesting." She tapped out some notes on her data pad, "What do you remember of your time here?"

Galena nodded, "Something about this place is familiar. I feel that I have been here before, but I remember very little... like it was a lifetime ago..."

"Do you remember your time before coming here?" asked the Doctor.

"I remember most of my life, up to coming here and then the battles on Timmony Bay. There are blank spots between those memories and then other blank spots after my arrest and jailing." She peered at the Doctor, "Can you help me put the pieces back together?"

Galena's gaze searched the Doctor's eyes and Judith felt something more intense than just the genorg waiting for a reply. She struggled to pull herself away from Galena's scrutiny when suddenly the genorg's eyes dimmed and released her.

Judith tapped more notes into her data pad, "I can help you put them back together, yes. Would you like to start now?"

Galena reverted to her training and segued into the standard genorg response patterns, right down to her body language, "Yes, please."

Judith leaned back and slowly began to explain, "You have known of me for your entire life. I am the voice that walked you through the training processes for every function you have ever displayed."

Galena nodded in understanding.

"You were assembled in one of the many factories that dot the Consortium. After you were sold," continued the Doctor, "you became an anomaly when you survived multiple accidents that killed off most of the other genorgs from your generation. It was suggested that your resiliency, learned or not, would make you an ideal candidate for a new project."

"The military project," filled in Galena.

The Doctor smiled, "That was the cover plan, but you still had to succeed at the lie before we would be able to place you within the real project."

"The real project?"

The Doctor nodded, "Correct. And luckily for all of us, you did exceptionally well in your military training. So well, in fact, that the council decided to test your training on the front line during the last rebellion. Battle after battle, field after field, you survived. And you learned. You had gained a name for yourself within the Consortium council even before your exploits on Timmony Bay."

"A name?"

"You had proven that the old genorg stock, which was routinely disposed of, could still fill a purpose for the people of the Consortium. Because of the incursions by the Masters into our space, we needed soldiers who could fend them off. Then Tigron happened and funding was pushed through. But not through our facilities, damn the fools."

'The Masters?' wondered Galena. "Is that why there are genorg soldiers now?"

The Doctor nodded, "But their training was not as involved. They are only trained to be ground pounders, not officers. That is why you are so special. You had risen above the designs of the cover program and were deemed the perfect candidate for the true project."

"And what project is that? What is my true purpose, as you put it?" asked Galena.

"I'll get to that," replied Judith. "After you were prosecuted for war crimes, we had your prison transport destroyed. All aboard were listed as lost and you effectively disappeared. You were brought to this facility and once again you were under my control."

The Doctor studied the genorg, "Your times abroad have changed you. They made you tougher, more resolute in your decisions, and unfortunately, more difficult to work with. But we needed a subject with a history of finding creative ways out of tough situations. A subject that can handle the horrors she would be subjected to in the real war."

Galena's eyebrow peaked in surprise, "The real war?"

"Yes, the real war," replied the Doctor. "The war against those monstrosities that live outside our universe and want into ours. Those creatures function like white blood cells fighting off a virus... in this case, a virus of humans. But with the sample I stripped from your skull, I can now see that they are making headway."

Galena touched the scar that ran along her forehead, "A sample?"

Judith nodded and pointed to the enclosure beyond her office doors, "The things that exist within the spheres like the one we have in lock-down out there, can't survive in our space. They collapse into themselves and leave behind a fine black dust devoid of life. But the specimen that came from inside of you still lives in liquid form. And it survives because it has added your DNA to its own. Those things have figured out a way to survive here and flourish."

five

The Sky is a Poisonous Garden

Jerald Cook waited outside the Doctor's office and watched as another gang of drones was led toward the spherical enclosure. The heavy chains that hung from their wrists and feet swayed as they moved together in a line. They were called to a halt and their shackles were removed. The first one in line was singled out and unceremoniously pushed through the airlock of the armored sphere.

He looked away as he closed his eyes. The armoring made the enclosure soundproof, but he still felt the abject fear as whatever power was inside sucked the genorg within itself.

"The first one is used as the control. The next will have the new tech module they want to test. And the result will be the same. It will fail and they'll throw the next few in to see if the one with the module was an anomaly," he grumbled under his breath. "We all know the Lieutenant is special, and only the Gods know why."

The next genorg was dragged to the enclosure and pushed in. A scream rent the air, then faded away. And so it continued until Jerr's comm beeped.

He clicked it on, "Mr. Cook, please come collect the Lieutenant and return her to her quarters."

"On my way ma'am," he replied.

***

Corporal Cook stopped in front of his cabin and stared at the door. The Lieutenant had been out of sorts when he took her back to her room. It felt wrong to lock her in, but those were his orders.

He triggered the cabin's lock and while he waited for the door to slide in, Cook pulled the beret free from his head. He stepped inside, removed his belt, and tossed it onto the top of his bed. From his pocket, he tugged free a partially charred set of dog tags and dropped them into a drawer.

The sound of water running caught his ear. When the sound stopped Fitzpatrick exited the room's fresher wrapped only in a towel. Cook tried to ignore Hamza's muscular frame, but he couldn't stop staring. He took one last surreptitious glance before he spun around and fumbled with random things on his dresser.

"Afternoon," Fitzpatrick said. "At least I think it's afternoon. It's hard to tell on some rocks, isn't it?"

"I wouldn't bother trying to track the days here," Cook advised. "They only last about 18 minutes or so. At least the light does."

"That fast, huh?"

Jerald relaxed as the conversation took a more conventional route, "You'll see clocks just about everywhere you go. It may take a bit to get used to it, but knowing the time won't be a big issue."

"Glad to hear it," replied Fitzpatrick as he pulled on his trousers. "I don't want to be late for my first meeting with the Doctor in her sanctuary. You happen to know where that is?"

"Yeah, sure. Let me just drop it on your data pad." Jerald keyed through a few screens and swiped a map over to his roommate's data pad. "She'll want you to go through the indoctrination anyway." At Fitzpatrick's concern, he continued, "It's more of a formality than anything."

Fitzpatrick flashed a grateful smile, "Got it. Thanks for the directions. I'll keep you in mind as my future unfolds before me."

"Good luck to you, my friend." Jerald's jovial expression faded as he watched Fitzpatrick pull his uniform shirt over his head and shuffle out the door. When the door closed, he sighed, "Dr. Wyeth doesn't suffer those who want to use her for very long."

***

As Galena's mind cleared, she realized she was staring at herself in the large mirror. She didn't look any worse for wear than she had this morning. But tired creases etched her face and she looked a little more pallid than she remembered.

"Probably a two-way mirror," she reckoned.

"It is," whispered something from deep inside her.

Galena backed away from the mirror as her reflection morphed into something like, yet unlike her. Whatever lived within her eyes stared back at her. Anger radiated from her new reflection.

Galena stuttered, "How are you still inside me? After my surgery, you should be gone."

"No. I am with you forever."

"I'll tell the Doctor," she stammered.

The voice spoke within her mind, "Do you trust your Doctor? Do you remember what she did with you, to you?"

"It was all to help the natural-borns survive your effects."

The voice gritted, "What have these natural-borns done for you besides use you? For all that they have done to you, why are they worth saving?"

"I was made to serve," she argued.

The being replied, "Made. These natural-borns did not create you! They found you and split your life from you. You are not what you believe yourself to be."

"What do you mean?" replied Galena. A spark of pain lanced from her brain down to her core but she realized the anguish she felt was not hers. When she was able to talk again, she shouted, "What do you mean?"

There was no answer.

***

Jerald woke up when the door to his room opened and in walked Fitzpatrick. The Yeoman looked tired and angry as he yanked his shirt off and threw it across the room.

"Evening Fitzpatrick; everything alright?"

"No, everything isn't alright," he replied. "I was lured out here with promises, but so far none are being kept."

"With the Doctor?"

Fitzpatrick stared sardonically at him, "How'd you guess? Was the big clue the fact that I arrived on this rock along with her?"

Jerald sat up in his bed still rubbing the sleep from his eyes.

Fitzpatrick sighed and sat on the edge of his bed, "Sorry man. I don't mean to snap at you. I just thought things would move faster once we were in system."

"It takes a while even for communications to come and go from here. If she brought you this far, she has plans for you."

Fitzpatrick looked up and smiled, "You've been working with the Doctor for long?"

Jerald nodded, "Close to a decade before she

went after the Lieutenant. How about you?"

"Pretty much since she joined us on the M33."

Jerald quirked his head to the side, "Did you run into the Lieutenant much?"

"Just her aftermath," replied Fitzpatrick. "That genorg left a trail of bodies in every system she visited. I've never seen the like."

"Was she on her own?"

Fitzpatrick smirked, "She found others like her. We caught her traveling on a ship full of thieves and murderers, but they are no more. We left them and the M33 as dust in our wake."

The Yeoman made eye contact with the corporal, "What's your name anyway?"

"You can call me Jerald, or Jerr if you like."

"I like Jerald," he replied. "Anyway, my name is Hamza. What do you guys do for fun on this base? I could use a drink."

Jerald snickered as he pulled a bottle of gin out from under his mattress, "The base frowns on contraband, but sometimes..."

"... you gotta break the rules," agreed Hamza. "Let's save that for a rainy. I'll buy you one at the commissary."

Jerr slid the bottle back into its hiding place and watched surreptitiously as Hamza retrieved his shirt and wriggled back into it. "Um, yeah sure. That sounds great. I'll show you where it is."

***

Down at the commissary, Hamza looked into Jerald's eyes, "Salud!" He clinked his canister with Jerald's, then the big man took a swig.

"Salud," replied Jerr as he sipped from his own canister.

Fitzpatrick coughed as the cheap liquor burned down his throat. "That enclosure near the Doctor's office ain't no joke. What is she doing with all those drones?"

Jerr set his drink down, "It's all part of the project."

"What project? I'm pretty new here and that is some otherworld shit down there."

Jerr entwined his fingers and sighed. Back when he had first been stationed here, he'd been fascinated with the project. As one of the few thousand survivors after the invasion of Potune, he'd believed wholeheartedly that the Doctor would succeed.

He glanced away and studied the nearest wall. "You saw drones get pushed inside it, right?"

At Fitzpatrick's nod, he continued, "I watched the process for months, then for years and nothing changed. Every single one died. Hundreds, if not thousands, of genorgs were shuffled into the enclosure like cattle and not a one survived. When I still had hope, I looked in through the windows and saw what happened to those that fought against it. They warped into horrors before my eyes as they succumbed to whatever power lies inside."

Jon Gray Lang

Fitzpatrick stared in surprise and shock, "What?"

Jerr closed his eyes, "Then around four years ago, something changed and it took the base by storm. The last batch of genorgs didn't completely succumb. They looked changed... distorted, yet were still genorg. The scientists hypothesized the latest module must've worked to some degree, even though the control batch survived, too."

Fitzpatrick's eyes gleamed, "Really? Tell me more."

Jerald continued as if he hadn't heard, "During the excitement, some of the genorgs were released from inside the enclosure for study. They left a bloodbath in their wake. The distorted drones wreaked havoc on everything in the storage bay. By the time my squad was sent down to quell the violence, the bodies of dead scientists and guards littered the floor."

"We ended up cutting the oxygen to the storage bay and ejecting everything onto the moon's surface." Jerald's hands grasped at nothing as his voice shook, "That night haunts my nightmares. Sometimes I wake up sweating. All I can see are the drones struggling to get back into the base before being burned alive by the local star. Their eyes blacker than the night."

"That sounds insane."

Corporal Cook took a long heavy swig before he spoke again, "We heard that the attack on Ninguiz happened around the same time. Our scientists agreed that an outside force was responsible. They kept developing new modules for testing, but Dr. Wyeth had already gone after the Lieutenant. With the constant failures of the experimental modules, the whole base believes that Galena Chadov is our only hope."

"Hope against what, the aliens the Doctor keeps talking about?"

Cook nodded as he postulated under his breath, "But with all she's seen, is the Lieutenant still on our side?"

***

For Galena, the days flowed by monotonously. There would be a knock at her door and the Corporal would stand there looking dour. He would direct her to the Doctor's office where she and Judith would discuss how she was doing after the surgery. Galena never mentioned the creature's voice and the Doctor never noticed the omission.

But today seemed different. As they made their way onto the lift, she noticed that Corporal Cook pushed the bottom floor button on the control pad.

"Where are we headed?" she asked.

Corporal Cook glanced in her direction, "The Doctor has requested your presence at the dome."

Galena nodded as if that meant something to her. She went back to her inner thoughts. Eventually, the doors parted and the raised decking of the bottom level spread out before them. Galena looked down and could see the stone surface of the moon just below with pools of stagnant water in the cracks and crevasses.

Even before she stepped out of the lift, she could feel the attraction from the dome enclosure. Compulsion pulled at her core as she walked toward it. Dark red and orange light splayed from the window slivers and onto her legs. Streaks of blues and greens slithered their way through the lavenders and heliotrope purples. She barely noticed Dr. Wyeth standing next to a raised console roughly nine meters out from the airlock hatch built into the side of the enclosure.

"Lieutenant, this way," directed Corporal Cook.

Galena responded to his prodding and followed. The Doctor, with two assistants, waited patiently for her to approach. Once she was close enough, the assistants stepped forward and began applying sensors to her skin. One slid a headband across her forehead and she felt it tighten in place.

"Good day, Doctor, what is it you need me to do?" asked Galena.

Judith checked the systems to verify that the sensor feeds were working before she replied, "We will be running some tests to catalog your responses to the environment."

Galena noted that she used the word environment to denote a particular place. Her eyes traveled to the enclosure and then back to the

Doctor, "Understood."

She turned and moved toward the airlock, but Judith called her back, "You may need these."

Galena looked down at the service pistol that lay on a small table by the console. Next to it was a magazine of lethal rounds and another magazine stacked with stun rounds. Galena picked up the pistol and reached for the stun rounds, but something within her pulled back and her hand reached instead for the lethal ones. Without her control, her hand slammed the magazine in place and ratcheted the first round into the chamber.

The Doctor's eyes glinted as she purred, "Go ahead and take the other one, too."

Galena hesitantly reached for the stun rounds, but her fingers closed around them without issue. She slid the magazine into her right pocket and slipped the gun into the waistband of her fatigues.

She threw a quick, quizzical salute and turned back to the hatch. The airlock popped open and she stepped into the vacant space. The outer hatch cycled closed behind her and the inner hatch opened. Fog roiled around the area and she had trouble seeing anything clearly. Then the odor of rotting vegetation, and soured meat, with a burning undertone of an abrasive cleaner hit her hard.

But nothing startled her more than the sudden pained screaming of indistinct beings between the walls of the enclosure and the enormous sphere of light and darkness that had caught sight of her. The sound increased as each being's voice added to the cacophony. She struggled to step past the hatch as the volume only grew ever louder.

Something humanoid stepped out of the fog and something clicked in Galena's mind. "I know you," she mouthed.

"Ssssiiisssterrrr..." it spoke through a mouth no longer shaped for speech.

Behind it, other voices matched the cadence and drawl of the genorg's voice and other humanoid shapes stepped out of the mist. She watched in horror as they spread out and formed a semicircle with her in the center and called out to her.

Galena's inner voice spoke through her lips, "Sisters, I have come for you. Do you wish to be saved?"

The screaming of the other voices quieted at Galena's words and the wheezing of breath through malformed lungs sounded loud in the chamber. When the hatch clicked shut behind her, she reached out to the altered genorgs before her, "My sisters, do you know me?"

Suddenly a command came over her comm link. The Doctor's voice spoke quickly, "You are being threatened, take action. No survivors."

Galena felt her personality being overridden by the machine's intelligence. It invaded her body and seized control. She watched in horror as her left hand pulled the pistol free and began shooting. The screeching escalated with each shot, but the machine kept firing until the magazine was empty.

Jon Gray Lang

Galena's hand pulled the other magazine free and quickly slid out the three stun rounds. They dropped to the decking and glinted in the hazy light. Then the machine quickly slapped the new magazine home and fired all of its remaining rounds. At last, the trigger clicked on an empty chamber. In horror, she watched as her hand reversed its grip on the pistol and smashed the butt of the gun into the skull of the nearest squirming body.

The screaming crescendoed and at some point Galena realized her voice had joined the chorus. The machine finally terminated it's control over the Lieutenant and she blacked out.

six

Burn With Me

Amid the blackness of space, a bright whirlpool made from the reflections of stars slowly formed. The Peking Empress slipped through the newly formed wormhole gracefully. The old luxury liner entered the Coldani system on the far side of the last planet. While this was one of the prime systems of the Consortium, with only five planets it was also the smallest.

Mr. Leon stared out the bow port and said in hushed tones, "And so it beckons, burning as a beacon in the night with all its oaths and power."

"Admiral, we are one solar hour away from the Consortium Navy contingent," Ovi stated from navigation.

"Broadcast our arrival to the jump gate and let's see if we catch anything," ordered Admiral Kaur.

Jon Gray Lang

Mr. Leon looked concerned, "This tactic worked in the last two systems, Admiral. Do you think a third time is the best idea?"

She looked over at her employer, "Those two inner strikes were against outer systems and they went off without a hitch. Why fix what isn't broken?"

Mr. Leon glanced away, "Dependence breeds weakness. I will push for a different tactic after this action. We can't afford a mistake. We still need to come across as invincible in the press coverage."

"By your command," smirked the Captain.

Communications spoke up, "Wide broadcast sent. Receiving laser comm pings against the hull."

"We have their attention people," stated Admiral Kaur. "Release the sharks in the tank. Let's bloody the waters." She glanced at Mr. Leon, "Let's hope our allies arrive in time."

Mr. Leon smiled tightly as he looked on through the bow port.

***

We've got our orders, people!" Commander Keri shouted as the hold doors of the Peking Empress swung open. "Keep the Empress afloat and knock those Navy ships down a notch."

She waited on the clips to release. Once the clunk echoed through the hull, Rosa stroked the attitude jets and pushed the Independence free of the hold. She could just make out the Scorpio to starboard doing the same and knew that the Copperhead would be behind them.

As her ship broke free of the Empress, Navigation stated, "Two Consortium vessels en route to our position."

"We're being hailed, Commander," announced Comms. "They are requesting us to shut down and prepare to be boarded."

"And what do we say to that?" asked Delta.

The bridge crew shouted, "The Consortium holds no dominion over us!"

***

Gamma fired the Scorpio's attitude jets and brought the ore hauler out past the bow of the Empress. She waited on the targeting system to pinpoint the incoming ships and the old system took its time. One of the funny things about this old asteroid breaker was the tracking sensor suite. It had been built to track thousands of targets that flowed by their own gravitational forces. Once the genorgs figured this out, she had requested that the Scorpio take point.

"Let our partners know we're ready, Tau."

"Message relayed," replied Tau-SA43. She glanced up to the targeting screen above the bow window, "Looks like the two Navy ships are splitting up to try and flank us."

"Ship configs?"

"One destroyer ahead followed by a cruiser.

Standard accompaniment, Gamma."

"Do you see any fighters released?"

Nu-M12 pulled up the sensor array and ran a report. "Skies are clear."

***

The Copperhead pulled free of the hold and rolled to the starboard side of the Empress. The Scorpio could be seen out in the black like a hulking mass past the nose of the Peking Empress.

"Any status from the Scorpio?" asked Captain Kahn.

Siede replied, "Standard jump gate accompaniment, Captain. Two, no five fighters have just split from the cruiser and are headed our way."

"This is the part I hate," groused Ariel.

Mr. Leon patted her lightly on the back, "Me too."

***

"Fighters en route, Admiral," reported Thadie Dumba from comms.

Admiral Kaur looked down at Mr. Leon, "Now?" At his nod, she ordered, "Tight beam the manifesto to Hammond, the main planet."

"Tight beam message sent and shows as received."

"Nav, how far out are the attackers?" asked Harjeet.

"Umm, forty-three minutes."

"Long enough," growled the Admiral. "Where are our allies, Mr. Leon?"

"They are on the way."

***

On board the stolen ship previously known as M86, Mr. Leon tilted his head to the side and nodded. He stared out past the bow at the walls of the wormhole tunnel as it slipped past. His eyes roved over the gallery of rogues that populated the bridge of this high-tech destroyer. Pirates, merchants, and the other disenfranchised of the Consortium all beholden to him.

"Captain Zed, the enemy ships are engaged. Arrival time?"

Captain Zed's hands gripped the rail tightly as he replied, "That would be... now."

The wormhole opened up and stars showed through. The ship, now called Valkyrie, shot through and entered normal space. Off the starboard side lay the pristine view of an unguarded jump gate.

"Target sighted and locked, Captain. Permission to fire?" asked the Gunner.

Captain Zed's voice grew grim, "Permission granted."

"Firing now."

A series of rockets launched from the ship and headed toward the jump gate station locked to the ring. Heavy rounds from the coil guns sprayed out in an arc aimed to slam into the scaffolding of the ring.

"Automatic guns are working their way through the rockets, sir," said Gunnery.

Fiery blossoms popped around the jump gate station, but their defensive system couldn't stop them all. Explosions tore into the bulwarks of the station and the lights went dark. The heavy spheres from the coil guns splintered the ring into shards.

"Direct hits, sir."

The Captain grunted, "You heard the man, cycle up the wormhole engine and prep for our next destination."

Mr. Leon looked on as the jump gate exploded into pieces and spiraled further outward. "That's the third jump gate we've brought down. Let's hope our other fleets are faring as well."

***

"The Consortium ships have slowed their forward travel. Fighters still on their way," announced the Gunner.

Far off in the distance, past the cruiser and destroyer, a bright light bloomed into being and dissipated quickly in the blackness.

Captain Kahn crossed her arms, "That's our cue. Get us back to the Empress. Siede, relay that directive to the other ships, please."

"On it, Captain."

Jon Gray Lang

"Another success under our belt. Time to head back home people," murmured Captain Kahn.

seven

Shadow Dancing

The glow from the sign hanging in the front of the Eclectic Electric flooded the alley. The crowd milling out front of the establishment was lively, loud, and looped.

"The place sure is hopping tonight, isn't it?" Anton declared as he walked up to the doorway.

"Do they use a twenty-four-hour schedule here?" asked Luli.

"Well, the clock rolls over, but I don't remember which hours are meant for sleeping" said Anton. He walked up to one of the patrons who had stumbled out into the corridor, "Hey man, what's with the big crowd tonight?" He winked at Luli, "Or today?"

"They got a new dancer! Been a while since we had something new to stare at, if you catch my drift."

Jon Gray Lang

Another patron bumped into Anton, "Those new dancers are something too! They're already up in the cages and they have some crazy moves going."

Luli squinted at Anton, "New dancers, huh? Why do I feel like I should be concerned?"

"You? Concerned? I figured you'd be through the door already!" shouted Anton as the doors parted and the thumping bass track boomed out into the corridor.

Varicolored smoke billowed from the doorway and multi-colored lights flashed in all directions as holographic images floated on the mist. Luli shot past Anton and disappeared into the brightness. Anton struggled to follow her in, but the crowd trapped him. The deejay's voice cut through the cheers as the previous song ended and the next track began. But before the room could recover, a new song blasted out and sucked the air from the room. Squeals erupted in unison as Anton peeked inside.

All of the lights shone brightly on one of the cages and Anton's eyes followed the beams up to a familiar figure behind the chromium bars. "Oh!" he shouted. "How long has it been since Jacquie danced?"

Lights played over one of the cages where a diminutive form ground out some steps in a rhythmic pattern. "Barney too, huh?" Another cage was being raised and he could clearly make out Luli grinding in time with the heavy beat.

Anton chortled loudly at the sight when he

felt a hand on his shoulder. Emy pulled him into a quieter corner, "I got here too late to keep them in check. And now I see you've added your pilot to the event."

"It's not like we have anywhere to go or any way to get there anytime soon." He looked down at the mostly empty drink in the Emy's hands, "I'm heading to the bar. You want another?"

"I'll take a Chanterelle shot. Your Captain left a tab open."

"Oh, she did, did she?" Anton laughed, "I'll be right back!"

Anton disappeared into the crowd, "It's going to be an amazing night!"

***

Anton struggled to support both Luli and Barney as the trio plodded along the corridor. Barney had a huge wad of mazuma sticking out of the front of his vest. Luli had a bundle clutched in her left hand and Anton's pockets bulged with a big bunch of bills. The Captain had shoved the three of them out the door. Her last words had been that Anton better have breakfast ready for her in the morning.

A chuckle bubbled up as he remembered the blissful look on her face. It was old news, but sometimes Jacquie needed to blow off some steam and preferred to do it away from her crew. *'Even so, she still looked out for her people'*, Anton thought, as he patted his pockets.

This made him wonder through his bleary state, "Where did Derain disappear to?" Anton was sure he'd seen him at the club with a rough and tumble looking group of people. Anton didn't recognize any of their faces, though.

Nothing he could do about it now. He had to get these two back to the Taj motel and then maybe he could focus on something else.

"We almost there?" asked Luli. "I don't feel too good."

Barney stopped moving and swayed back and forth in front of him, "Me either..." He gripped his knees and vomited under a street lamp.

At the sound and smell, Luli grimaced and cursed, "Oh Tom!" She pushed Anton away and began puking loudly into the gutter.

Anton lost his balance and fell hard to the ground while his two shipmates retched onto the street. Luckily this was a quiet part of the 'heap and they seemed to be alone.

Suddenly, the voice of a young man sounded from the darkness, "Well, well, well. Nothing like easy pickings is there, Deepa?"

"No, there ain't. There's nothing like it at all."

Laughter from several others bounced around the corridor. Anton cursed as he staggered to his feet. He shook his head to clear his mind and barked, "de Lagnel, get it together! Qing, clear out your system!"

Luli whimpered from over the gutter, "That's

what I'm trying to do." She looked up at the small gang that had stepped from the shadows into the light.

Barney straightened up and slapped his face repeatedly, "I hear and I obey." He turned around with his hands curled into fists and began moving toward the first person he saw.

Deepa laughed, "Whoa, we got an active one, don't we? And he's so little."

Anton waved his finger, "It's not wise to piss off a Titan."

The young man who had spoken first stepped forward, "A Titan? I thought those were old fairy tales or something."

Anton blinked and stared at the young man, "Wait a minute. That you, Joyo?"

The young man tensed, "Where'd you hear that name?"

Anton squinted at him, "No way you can be Joyo. Man, you haven't aged at all since the last time I was here."

"I'll ask again, where'd you hear that name?"

The youth was maybe in his late teens and didn't seem as bulky as he appeared to be in the shadows. He looked scared or angry. But with that name floating around, scared was more like it. As the others came out into the light, not one of them looked very old. Still, numbers counted for a lot, especially when their targets were inebriated.

"Shit," grunted Anton. "I don't feel like fighting tonight."

"Where did you hear that name?" asked the teenager.

Anton shook his hands to loosen up his fingers, "You look just like a friend I used to run with when I was a kid." He brought his hands up in a classic boxer's stance, "Alright, let's get this over with."

The boy waved the gang back, "You used to run with Joyo?"

"Yeah," admitted Anton. "His family gave me a place to stay after my father was shot down on deck three."

The youth stopped and stared at Anton hard, "You wouldn't happen to be Rabbit?"

"Yeah, why?"

"Joyo's my older brother."

Anton stopped and dropped his arms, "Niran?"

***

Derain awoke in complete darkness. He was sitting upright with his back against a wall. The floor beneath him felt cold. But his hands, restrained at the wrists, felt warm. He reached out and discovered the walls were close on both sides. And when he reached above his head, he felt something soft like a jacket.

"Am I in a bloody closet?"

The ties around his wrist felt soft and had some give so they weren't plas-steel. The stretch in the restraints was pretty minimal and they didn't feel organic. He sighed as he checked his pockets. His pistol was missing but Vania had left him the gun belt. "That's something anyway."

Further investigation revealed that everything electronic had been lifted, too. Only an old slip of paper remained in one of the deep recesses of one pocket. They had even found the small knife that had been hidden in the lining of his gun belt.

When Derain stretched out his legs his heels hit a door. He pulled back and kicked it hard. The reverberation told him it was a cheap aluminum door, so he kicked it again and again.

"Hey! Vania!" he shouted. "Are you going to open this damn door or am I going to kick it out? Vania!"

He kept it up and eventually the door swung open to a hideously bright light that shocked his eyes, "Can you dim that down, damn it?"

"Keep quiet," was the only response.

Derain shouted again, "Vania! What the hell? I thought we were friends?"

Her voice rumbled from a far distance, "Bring him out. Be as gentle as you want."

Whoever had opened the door reached in and slapped Derain hard, then jerked him to his feet by the restraint that tethered his wrists. He was fairly dragged out into an apartment hallway. Derain staggered to his feet as a squat brute of a man pulled him into the living room.

As the restraint was removed from his wrists,

Derain cursed, "God damn it, Vania! What the bleeding hell?"

She looked up at him from her data pad, "We are friends, Tiwi, but this is business."

His shoulders slumped, "And business will always win out," he sighed.

She smirked, "Glad you remember." As she set the data pad down, she added, "I don't enjoy this, but times are tough. What with the war and all."

Derain ran through his memory as quickly as he could, "War? What war?"

Vania's brittle laughter was like a chop to the neck, "Where in Bralgu have you been hiding? A bunch of yahoos have declared war against the Consortium, if you can believe it."

"Like they'd have a chance," Derain scoffed. "Who the hell did that?"

Vania paused and stared at Derain like he was crazy, "Seriously, where have you been? Some drone with a name shouted out to the stars, that she and her kind wouldn't stand for their maltreatment anymore. Kian, what was her name again?"

"Gally something? She was a butcher. There was a rank tied to it if I remember."

Derain's disbelief was writ large across his face, "Lieutenant Galena Chadov?"

Kian's eyes brightened, "That's the one!"

Vania's eyes pierced through Derain's, "You know her? You know her whereabouts? The bounty on her head is... impressive."

Derain blinked and his face darkened, "You

know I don't give a shit about a drone. Why would I share, if I had the lead on this?"

Vania smiled, "Now that's the Tiwi I remember. He'd leave you for dead, if it would cut his losses."

Derain sneered cruelly, "I don't make the rules..."

"... I just make them work in my favor," finished Vania. "Now we understand each other."

Derain stood solemnly in the center of the room, "We do."

***

Anton frowned, "What are you doing out here, Niran? Hassling people for mazuma?"

Niran looked away, "You know mazuma is tight on the 'heap. It's the whole reason you left Joyo to suffer by himself," he lashed out bitterly.

Anton's reaction was surprising even to the youth, "What? I didn't leave! The gods-be-damned press gangs caught me out here! Three years I suffered under that bastard Captain's whip. Locked in a fucking cage at every port, all to force me to realize there was no escape from him." Anton's eyes flared angrily, "You think I wanted to leave? The only place I'd ever stayed long enough to even consider a home? Fuck you, boy. You don't know what I've seen... What I've done... to keep living in this shit bag of a universe."

"Looks like you've done alright for yourself,"

Jon Gray Lang

sneered Niran. "You've got friends and you ain't dying."

Anton's hands clenched hard until he forced his face to soften, "You're right. Times are hard for everyone these days. You can't escape the past that made you, can you?"

Suddenly, Barney passed out, toppled over and rolled face down into a puddle. Anton rushed over and pushed him to his side to keep him from drowning. Luli, still woozy from drink, kneeled in the dirt as she held her head in both hands.

Anton looked up at Niran and could see the youthful rebellion in the boy's face. He was what, fourteen now, maybe fifteen? Anton reflected, *'Had I looked any different at his age?'*

"Niran, can your friends help me get my people back to our motel? I'll give you what I can." He pulled a wad of mazuma free from his pocket and held it up, "You help me and I'll pay you."

"You know this guy?" said a voice from the crowd.

Deepa's eyes glowed at the stack of bills, "He's gonna pay us and we don't have to beat the crap out of him? Take it, Niran! This is easy mazuma no matter how you look at it!" She ran over to Barney and tried to lift him, "This tiny man is heavy! He made of rocks or sometin?"

"This one an antique spacer?" asked another, whose shoulder popped as she hoisted Luli to her feet.

Anton chuckled as the rest of the teenagers

shot past Niran and struggled to lift Barney and Luli, "Just about. And she's mostly made out of metal." His eyes shifted back to the boy, "We got a deal, Niran?"

Niran watched his friends as they worked hard to lift Anton's two companions, "We got things to do. How far?"

Anton smiled slightly, "Just to the Taj. You think you and your crew can find the time?"

Niran got the leveled meaning, "Yeah, I think so. Let's get 'em to the Taj and then we can party."

***

Derain had no idea where he was going. Vania and her team had shoved him into an enclosed litter with a sack over his head. The only thing he was aware of was the number of steps his bearers were taking. That and the sudden stops and starts.

One of his bearers must be remarkably shorter than the other as there was a noticeable dip to the back of the palanquin. He decided to stop counting the number of steps since he didn't even know where they had started from. He paid attention to how many floors they traversed, but after a while, he wasn't sure if they were just going up and down for the hell of it.

"Knowing Vania, it's all on purpose," he mumbled through his gag.

The journey had taken long enough that his backside was beginning to ache from the tight interior of the palanquin. The noises and smells outside of the litter were many and varied. Just from the mixture of aromas and accents, they must be going through a bazaar.

Muffled though it was, he heard Vania shout, "Out of the way, woman, unless you're looking for trouble! That's better. Come on me boyos. We're almost there."

"Glad this ride will be done with soon," grumbled Derain as the palanquin leaned drunkenly to the right.

After another flight of stairs downward and a sharp turn, the litter leveled out. Derain felt the box settle on the ground and heard the pounding of feet heading away from where he was. What seemed like an eternity passed before he heard a pair of boots click-clack across the ground and come to a stop near the palanquin. He wasn't able to make out the exact conversation between Vania and the other person, but it carried the tone of a completed job.

Suddenly there was a heavy rapping on the top of the box. "You still awake in there?" asked Vania.

With the gag in his mouth, Derain didn't bother answering.

Vania's voice boomed loud and strong, "Was good to see you again, Tiwi. If you get out of this, we should have a drink." She snickered sardonically, "You'd need some crazy luck to make that happen, though."

The palanquin was lifted again. The new

bearers were more of an equal size and there was less jostling. But suddenly things grew dark as the hum of a sensor vibrated overhead and down the side of the box as it moved. Eventually, the litter was placed on the ground and the creak of a door being shut was the last sound that Derain heard.

At least two hours passed before the door opened again. Faint light filtered into the litter and Derain could see a little bit. A key rattled in the lock on the palanquin and the side panel opened. Two large hands reached in, grasped Derain by the arms and pulled him out.

In complete silence, he was unceremoniously dropped to the floor. Derain took a minute to stretch out his legs and roll his shoulders. His hands remained locked in their restraints and the sack didn't leave his head.

"Well, you've got me. Now what?"

*****

Anton unlocked the motel door and ushered everyone into the room. Luli collapsed on the bed without a second thought and Barney quickly followed her. Barney's arm encircled Luli's waist as he sank into a deep slumber. Luli's breathing smoothed out once his arm was around her and she slipped into peaceful sleep.

Anton looked up into the expectant eyes of the teens as he dropped the wad of mazuma into Niran's hands. The gang divvied up the bills and disappeared out into the darkness, but the leader hung back. Anton grasped Niran lightly by the shoulder and handed him a small stack of mazuma, "This is for Joyo and your mom. I wish I had more, but times have been hard. Take care of yourself and your family." His voice choked up a bit, "Tell Joyo I love him, will you?"

He pushed Niran out past the door and it clicked shut in the boy's face. Anton stumbled to the bed and struggled to pull the sheet free from under Luli and Barney's comatose forms. He yanked at the sheet and grumbled, "Come on, guys! Help me out! The two of you are heavy!"

Luli moaned as Barney shifted and the sheet finally slipped free. Anton flipped the sheet out and flattened it over the two of them. He tucked in the corners and made sure that both of his friends looked comfortable enough. He scrubbed his fingers through his hair and yawned deeply.

Anton emptied his pockets and slumped into the big chair in the corner. Jacquie would be pissed about the mazuma he had given away. Then again, maybe she wouldn't remember this whole night. But that was a fight for later. He threw his jacket over his chest and closed his eyes. Tomorrow was probably going to suck.

eight

Orange Colored Sky

The Peking Empress plowed deep into the Geminus system. Even before the energies of the collapsed wormhole dissipated, her comms were blasting their ultimatum on all channels.

Admiral Kaur paced the bridge while Mr. Leon stood with his eyes closed, communing with his other selves. When his eyes slowly opened, he glanced out the bow port. The Admiral acknowledged his glance and nodded.

"Any response, Thadie?" she asked.

Thadie shook her head in the negative. "Nothing from the planet and no hails from the jump gate."

Harjeet stopped pacing and pressed her palms into the railing. "Any movement from the Consortium Navy?"

"Nothing at all," replied Latiff. "I'd say we're

effectively being ignored."

"Seems the Consortium is finally catching on," mused the Admiral.

"It is," said Mr. Leon, standing at her side. "We'll have to depend on the others to read the situation and figure out a way to achieve our goals."

"Prep the FTL," ordered the Admiral. "Keep the Empress ready to roll out of here, if those Navy ships make a move."

"Sir, yes, sir."

***

A contingent of the rebel ships flitted between the stars and their next target. The Peking Empress should have arrived already and made her presence known to the Consortium Navy. Captain McEevey checked his timepiece and they were still on schedule.

"Entering normal space in five, four, three, two, and one..." stated the comm officer.

The end of the wormhole opened into the Geminus system and the edge of a jump gate could be seen floating amongst the stars. The stolen destroyer, now called Sparta, slipped out of their wormhole close to the jump gate and was quickly followed by the destroyer, Bhagat.

Captain McEevey gripped the console, "Rinchlear, report."

"Consortium Naval craft about one hundred clicks out. Consortium support vessel far to port."

The Captain cursed under his breath. The ruse had failed and the Consortium two-ship detachment was waiting for them. Luckily, the cloaking on the two M class ships held.

"Looks like the Peking Empress didn't grab their attention this time. Looks like we got a fight, me lads."

***

On the Consortium destroyer Ambition, the comm blared, "Tight beam from the jump gate incoming."

The Captain nodded. "Play it on the overhead."

"Ambition, please come in. This is Geminus Station."

"We are receiving you, Geminus. Repeat, we are receiving you."

"Ambition, our instruments are picking up energy fluctuations close to the station."

The Captain glanced over at his sensor tech, "Are we getting anything?"

"No sir," replied the technician. "Running a wider scan."

"Geminus, are you able to pinpoint?" asked the Captain.

The station technician replied, "Negative, Ambition. Fluctuations are too close to the station to get a clear reading."

"Understood, Geminus. Ambition out. So,

we are next." The Captain queried the sensor tech, "Anything?"

"Nothing so far. Wait... there it is. There are two." The sensor tech flicked the findings to the holo.

The holo lit up with the Ambition at the center point. It listed the jump gate station and the cruiser Horizon within its sphere. Slowly, two amorphous clouds appeared within the bubble.

"Gunnery, track the one closest to us," ordered the Captain. "Comm, please let the Horizon know our target."

The Comm Officer nodded and contacted the Horizon. The pilot of the Ambition pulled the destroyer out of its orbit of the jump gate and headed toward the closest of the two disturbances. The burgeoning wormhole could barely be detected by the naked eye before it dissipated.

"Anything come through?" the Captain asked.

Gunnery stated, "Nothing on my screens."

"Cloaked," assumed the Captain. "Triangulate as best you can, Gunnery. You have permission to fire."

"Yes, Captain," replied Gunnery. "Missiles away."

***

"Missiles incoming, sir," said Rinchlear. "Wide of the mark."

Captain McEevey sighed, "Looks like we've

been spotted. The game is afoot, folks."

They had successfully disabled the jump gates without too much fuss using smaller ordinances. Of course, the transponder echoing the Peking Empress ident further into the system also had been able to peel the Navy ships away.

"Still, we did manage to take down seven jump gates on our own," affirmed the Captain. "Change in tactics. Comm, have the Bhagat fire on the two ships, then cycle the hell out of here. Gunnery, launch one of the big ones. Nav, get us cycled up and a way out."

"Sir, yes sir!"

All eyes were glued to the jump gate hanging in space. The flares of multiple rockets sprang out of nowhere and pelted the Consortium cruiser. The destroyer swung wide and launched a spray of rockets of its own. Small bursts exploded against the hull of the Bhagat and the cloaking fell.

The Bhagat swung wide burning its way out of there. The destroyer gave the ship chase, but couldn't catch her before their wormhole appeared.

"Missile prepped and launching... now!" exclaimed the Gunnery.

Navigation quickly followed with, "Cycling the FTL, Captain."

One of the planet killers that had been appropriated from the Consortium dropped out of the hold and blazed its way to the jump gate.

The Captain tracked the missile with his fingers crossed for luck. If everything went as planned, the detonation should destroy the station and leave the ring dysfunctional. If the Consortium cruiser took the heavy missile out, the electromagnetic pulse would disable all of the electrical systems in the jump gate station and bring it down, even if only temporarily.

"Target that destroyer and keep it busy."

"On it, Captain."

***

"Missiles went wide, sir," Gunnery inflected.

"Sir!" shouted the sensor tech. "We have a wormhole building up off the port side!"

"Gunny, knock that corsair out of our skies!" growled the Captain.

"I have a lock. Missile spread away."

The crew waited with bated breath and minutes later, Gunny cried, "We have contact! Their cloak is down."

"Are they slowing?"

"We have rockets incoming!" shouted Gunny.

The Captain commanded, "Full evasives! Full evasives!"

As the Destroyer swung wide, the sensor tech stated, "They got away, sir."

"Damn!" barked the Captain.

***

Admiral Kaur counted down the seconds as

first the Bhagat, then the Sparta jumped away. "Did they get a shot off?"

"A planet killer is on its way," Latiff confirmed.

Mr. Leon kept an eye on the missile's trajectory as he went over their continued strategy to break the Consortium. The M-class vessels they had appropriated had been destroying as many jump gates as they could all to separate the core worlds from the outer fringes. Genorg forces were bringing down factories, mines, and other large facilities from the inside.

The Servant Uprisings, as the news chans called them, kept the Consortium busy enough that the burgeoning fleet of rebel FTL ships was coming out ahead. While some of the colonies and factories were lost to the Consortium military response, the new ships had been able to slip in and retrieve many of the genorgs involved in the uprisings.

The loss of goods and materials from the fringe systems to the core worlds was already creating a shortage. The loss of the jump gates was hamstringing the flow of materials and communication even further. Not that a regular citizen would know much as the full spectrum of attacks was barely covered on any of the news brackets.

A bright flash lit up the holo and Geminus station disappeared from within the bubble. Admiral Kaur breathed a sigh of relief, "They did it. Let's get out of here."

nine

Ball and Chain

Jacquie woke up to bright light shining in her eyes. She didn't recognize the ceiling of the place, but that wasn't a big surprise; they'd only been on this rock a couple days. As her eyes acclimated, she looked around. Personal items littered the room as well as discarded clothing, but the furnishings seemed well kept.

She glanced over and realized she was not alone in the bed. The woman lying there was not someone she immediately recognized and that unnerved her.

She dropped her head into the pillow, "Crap. What the hell did I do last night?"

The woman she shared the bed with slipped to her side and propped herself on one elbow, "You and your mates put on one hell of a show, is what you did." The woman flopped to her back, "So much mazuma rolling in. We even had to regulate the number of people going in and out! It's been a long time since new blood shook up this rock." The woman snuggled into Jacquie's side and moaned, "You weren't lying about bringing a great spread, either. Dessert was entirely worth it."

Jacquie's memories of the previous evening trickled back slowly. A sly smile of satisfaction revealed her feelings as Jacquie kissed the woman on her lips, "Yes, it was. Gods I needed last night, if only to feel normal again." She repeated it to herself, *'If only to feel normal again.'*

She rolled over, "I should be going. Any idea what the local time is?"

The woman smirked and pointed above her, "Time?"

A display blinking on the ceiling showed the number 11:03 ...11:03 ...11:04.

"Thanks," answered Jacquie. "Now, if only I could remember your name."

"Basima," giggled the woman. "My name is Basima."

***

A loud, insistent beeping woke Anton from his slumber. He futilely punched at the air until his brain realized the noise was his comm alarm.

"What? Hello? Damn it, where is the button... Hello?"

"Rabbit! Glad you're awake. Your Captain is

a wild woman. I can see why you stay with her."

Anton grimaced, "Yeah. We... have a special relationship."

The voice on the comm chortled, "I bet you do."

"Gods-be-damned, who is this?"

"It's Emy. How much did you have to drink yesterday?"

Anton groaned tiredly, "To be honest, too much and not enough. How are you doing, Emy?"

"Me? I'm doing great, though sore in places I didn't know I had. Orla wanted me to ring you. Our freighter should've arrived at the wreck last night and we're expecting an update via laser comm. She wanted your people to be there in case...."

"In case we're lying."

Anton wiped the sleep from his eyes and he glanced over at the bed. Barney and Luli were a tangle of arms and legs. Suddenly, the front door banged opened and in staggered a disheveled Jacquie.

"Where's breakfast?" she grumbled. She peered into the bedroom, assessed her crew members, and headed to the kitchen.

Anton had waved to her, but continued his conversation, "What time do we need to be there?"

"Probably around one," answered Emy.

The sound of cabinet doors opening and banging shut came from the kitchen. Jacquie yelled, "How does this place not have surge of some kind? Any kind?"

"I'll get everyone there," Anton assured as clicked off the comm.

***

A familiar chuckle announced a new presence and the sack over Derain's eyes was pulled free. He winced from the burst of light and blinked wildly until he could make out a tall figure sitting in a chair across the room. The tall man held a cup of a steaming liquid. He sipped briefly then set the cup down on a side table.

Derain's eyes had fully adjusted, but he continued to stare in sheer surprise. "Stanislav? Stanislav Tenden?"

The large man nodded but said nothing in response.

Derain flexed his stiff legs and stood up slowly. He adjusted his posture, and his spine popped so loudly that it startled one of the body guards. His wrists were still restrained and the bind around his ankles allowed him to move only in short half-steps.

Derain closed his eyes, swiveled his head, and cracked his neck. He slowly opened them and watched Stanislav take another sip from the cup. "How much am I... was I worth?"

Stanislav's expression changed to mild amusement, a look that did not suit his face, "For here? Enough to live a month. Back home? A nice dinner maybe."

Jon Gray Lang

Derain snorted, "Vania must be desperate."

Stanislav set the cup down and waved at one of the bodyguards to take it away. "She has fallen on hard times of late. The fuel regulator to her ship turned up missing soon after she made port. There are no replacements available... Way. Out. Here. Strange, no?"

Derain shuffled over to a recliner, settled into it, and sighed from the effort. "Not so strange considering where we are. But how did you end up on the ass end of the universe?"

Stanislav shrugged, "Consortium jackboots showed up soon after you left. Viktor's operation was shut down and all of us were arrested. Someone leaked info about where your smuggler Captain had gone and the troops deserted us. The local ships blockaded the planet until other naval vessels arrived." Stanislav shook his head, "Viktor did not survive the expungement process. I found it difficult to run a smuggling business on a blockaded rock."

A sense of loss hit Derain at Viktor's passing. The old smuggler had been an honest man in a business built on dishonesty; one of the old guard. But something still sat funny, "I get that, but what are you doing out here of all places? You don't look much older either."

Stanislav shrugged and stood up to his impressive height. "The benefits of being put on ice to escape sensors during a blockade will do wonders for the passing of time. This is where I was sent once travel off planet was possible. I run this end of the operation now."

Derain nodded appreciatively, "Moving up in the organization. I congratulate you." He glanced inquisitively at his host, "But why put a bounty on me? Are you working for those government wowsers?"

"Oh no, Mr. Tiwi. My employment has not changed." He grinned at Derain, "I like you, bounty hunter. I did not expect to ever see you again. And yet, here we are." He indicated the door and stepped toward it, "Time is of the essence. If you would follow me?"

Derain groaned as the sack was dropped over his head again and he was helped to a standing position, "Where to?"

Mr. Tenden rendered an odd half-smile. "Mr. Leon would have words with you," he said.

***

Orla shifted as the hatch to her repair docking bay swung open and in walked Rabbit and his people. She cackled at the sight of them. Rabbit and his Captain were bickering loudly. Their pilot and engineer just tried to steer clear of them. The bounty hunter didn't seem to be with them. Orla pointed one thumb down and one thumb up at Emy and he replied with crossed fingers on both his hands. She grinned. Looked like that little bit of info had a return value.

"Rabbit! Your crew looks like shit!" Orla shouted. "But you're here on time and that's what counts. Come on up to the office."

She turned around and made her way forward without looking to see if they followed. Anton took the steps two at a time. Barney and Luli followed at a slower pace. Jacquie glared at Anton and stood her ground at first, but eventually she brought up the rear.

When Jacquie caught up, she yanked Anton back, "You better tell that 'Auntie' of yours that I'm the Captain. I'm getting pretty tired of this garbage."

Anton patted her shoulder knowingly, "Oh, she's aware, Jacq. She's pushing to see what she can get from us or what we let slip. Introductions are done. By all means, take the lead."

Jacquie folded her arms across her chest, "Great, more games. Fine."

Jacquie shouldered her way through the door and sat across from Orla. She slid back into the chair and threw her booted feet up onto the desk. "You got any surge in this tugurio?"

"Got it right here, Captain," answered Barney as he brought over a couple cups. One he set in front of Jacquie while the other he delivered to Luli.

"Thanks, Barney. Always looking out for the rest of us," quipped Luli as she swallowed the contents in one gulp.

"Uhh, I'll get you another, Lu," said Anton as he walked over to the scullery.

Jon Gray Lang

Barney filled the empty cup with another generous serving of the local surge made from fermented mushrooms and adrenal additives. Anton quickly delivered the energy drink to Luli. "Your hands are looking better, Lu," he remarked.

She nodded absently as she cupped the vessel with both scarred hands and stared wistfully out the office window at the Matilda.

"She looks worse than I remember," Luli lamented.

Orla smiled, "She may look like hell, but she's in better shape than you. We're almost done running the main electrics. Just have the thousands of end connectors left. She'll be ready to fly in a couple days."

"About a week, then?" piped in Barney.

Orla laughed and slapped the desk, "Forgot your engineer was equipped with a bullshit meter. I'll tell my people to stick to the more honest estimate."

Anton barked with laughter, "As much as you can and survive on the 'heap."

"As much as you can," added Emy from the doorway. "Ma, I've routed the incoming laser to the desk comm. Just waiting for it to initiate."

"Grab a seat, son."

Emy stepped into the now crowded office and poured himself a hot cup. As he leaned against a wall he studied the traits of the others in the room. The Captain looked hungover and angry and the pilot was definitely feeling the effects of the night before as well. The short one seemed to be masking his discomforts and Rabbit, of course, looked fine. Emy mischievously grinned, "You can take the rat out of the scrap, but you can't take the scrap out of the rat."

"What?" asked Luli.

"Nothing."

The comm crackled and a woman's voice came through sharp and clear, "Goblin calling Goa shipyard, come in Goa. Repeat, Goblin calling Goa shipyard. Come in Goa."

Orla flipped the switch on the comm, "Goa here. Repeat, Goa here. What did you find?"

"Good to hear your voice, Orla. Initial findings agree with what was offered. Will tight beam you imagery."

"Waiting for imagery, Goblin." Orla looked up and winked at Jacquie, "Sounds like your people are telling the truth."

"Or playing a good game of bait-n-hide," added Emy from the back.

Rabbit looked genuinely hurt, "I might lie to you Emy, but why would I lie to Auntie? I only love her with all my heart."

"With that little rock in your chest?" laughed Orla. "When are you going to learn, boy?"

The holo unit on the comm flickered and a three-dimensional image of the M33 hovered above it. The holo showed the giant rent in the front third of the craft and revealed bits of flotsam floating within the gravitational pull of the destroyer. Orla reached out her hands and manipulated the visual until the Goblin could be seen within the image.

"You blew that up and escaped?" Orla whistled, "Color me impressed, Rabbit."

"Well, it exploded while we were escaping... oof," Anton admitted as Jacquie's elbow jabbed into his gut.

"Either way, I am still impressed," said Orla.

She zoomed the image into the rent in the craft and the vast amount of damage that the ship had taken immediately became apparent. Holo bodies floated forlornly amongst the shredded decks and half-opened airlocks. Orla shifted the image to the tail of the craft and focused on the outer engines. Except where some of the equipment had been detached for the Matilda, everything else seemed intact. She swung the image over to the bow and other than some old wear and tear, it looked sound as well.

"She looks like she could still fly, why didn't you just take her?" asked Orla.

"She can," answered Luli. "The bridge didn't suffer any damage except for some small arms fire. Navigation and piloting controls are still intact. Sublight engines should still be working, but the wormhole drive is another question."

"The explosion that occurred was two-fold," Barney added. "The hangar had been lined with explosives that caused the ship to fall out of the wormhole. The drive couldn't handle it and overloaded the power core. The fuel went up in a blaze and here we are. We barely had enough fuel on the Matilda to even get her rudimentary systems up and running. The sublights for all intents and purposes were shut down and remain undamaged. The main parts of the wormhole drive escaped damage, but the power core for the whole ship? Boom."

Orla nodded as she added notes to the holo image. She keyed the comm, "Goblin, what's your on-site assessment?"

There was a long pause, longer than the time it took for the laser to travel back and forth, before the Captain of the Goblin replied. "As stated, initial findings match what was brought to you. Even if the wormhole drive is nonfunctional, there are more than enough parts to make us all rich for a generation or two. If we can get the drive up and running? We'll be gods-be-damned royalty."

Orla's eyes brightened and her fingers twitched with excitement, "How long to bring it back?"

The Goblin replied, "She's hooked, just trying to generate enough force to get her moving. She's one heavy bitch of a boat. Say, three days with two days deceleration?"

"We'll be expecting you Goblin. Goa out." Orla switched off the comm and made eye contact with Jacquie, "I didn't expect your fool to come through. Whatever you did to make him honest, keep it up." She reached her hand across the desk, "You've made good on your end. We'll get your boat space worthy. Deal?"

Jacquie shook the old woman's hand, "The deal is set. Since you're coming out ahead on this, how about some additions?"

"Like extra parts," interrupted Barney.

Anton added, "Some local proteins, too. As much as we can carry."

Luli threw in, "Maybe some bloody headache pills."

Jacquie laughed, "Maybe keep our presence on the quiet end of the spectrum."

"Oh, the whole 'heap knows who you are Captain," chortled Emy. "You didn't keep your presence hidden and word spreads fast."

Orla nodded to the Captain, "But, I know what you're asking. We can work something out."

***

When the door to the docking bay closed behind them, Anton whispered in Jacquie's ear, "Have you heard anything from Derain? The Scrapheap isn't the best place to go lone wolf."

Jacquie shrugged as they all headed back to the motel, "Derain does as he pleases. If we don't hear from him in a day or two, we can worry then. Right now, I want something to eat."

"Me too!" giggled Luli. "Dancing the night away always makes me hungry."

Barney laughed, "Everything makes you hungry."

"Now that's a gross generalization," pouted Luli. "While it is true that many things make me hungry, not everything does!" She turned and shouted at Anton, "Where to, Rabbit man? I need some food in my belly!"

Anton strutted his way to the front of the group, "Follow me! I know a little gastro pub that is right around the corner!"

***

The pub was only a block away and the crew made haste to reach it. The place was small, and the lighting was dim, but the food smelled heavenly. All six of the tiny tables were full, so the crew bellied up to the bar and Anton quickly ordered his favorites from the menu. The bartender was a gruff woman and didn't speak a word... just grunted when Anton finished and snapped the rag she was using to polish glass tumblers.

There was a vid playing on the screen and the images caught their attention as they waited for their food. The news chan had their reporter on the streets of one of the core worlds. Jacquie couldn't tell which one it might be. Behind the news reporter was a bonfire that billowed huge clouds of oily black smoke.

"Is that Jard?" asked Luli.

"Might be," answered Barney.

"Barkeep," called out Jacquie, "can you turn up the audio for this?"

The barkeep looked annoyed as she increased the sound.

The news chan blared for a moment before the volume normalized. "... live from the Consortium Capitol as food and supply shortages rock the government. There has been no official response to the Servant Uprising that is tearing the outer worlds to pieces. People are taking to the streets in protest against the actions of the genorg populations." The reporter leaned over and pushed his microphone toward a bystander, "Sir, sir! What do you think about the Servant Uprising?"

A dark sneer crossed the man's face as he spoke into the microphone, "How dare those drones! Do they think that because they're shaped like us that we should treat them as human?"

The reporter was taken aback by the man's adamance, "So you don't think they should be given rights?"

The man sneered, "Give those things rights? They have the right to clean our toilets and that's not enough for them?"

"Hold on, sir!" the reporter interrupted. "Something seems to be happening behind us."

The two of them turned to face the bonfire. The camera zoomed in on a woman pulling on a chain wrapped around the neck of a severely beaten genorg. In the woman's right hand was a stick. The genorg just looked up with a vacant stare as the woman knocked it to its knees.

"See? There's not enough brain in it to know

what to do!" the man mocked.

The woman raised the stick again and smashed it against the genorg's skull. The blow toppled the drone into the fire.

"Yeah!" the man screamed. "Burn it! Burn that drone trash!

The reporter looked ashen as he said, "Back to you, Maryn."

"Thank you for the update, Fauja. On the other side of the argument, we have a video of a Consortium citizen who spent time with the infamous Lieutenant Chadov."

The video began with a long shot of Captain Jacquotte Delahaye cuffed to an interrogation table on the M33.

"Oh no," Jacquie whispered.

In a close up, Captain Delahaye declared to her interrogator, "I have something to tell you, sir." She pulled herself closer to the loop that chained her to the table. "And I heard this from the very mouth of one of the people who's been used as fodder by the industries, by the citizenry, and even by the so-called Consortium which was built for the people by the people." The rattle of her bindings echoed in the little room. "Let me see if I can remember it exactly as Galena Chadov said it. Oh yes," her head nodded with certainty, "Wisdom is born on the bloodied scythes of the downtrodden..."

Jacquie's eyes grew wide as the crew turned to stare at her. "Where? How did they get this video?" she stammered. As she rose from the barstool, so did her anger. "Damn it to hell!" she cursed.

ten

Bandages

Finally, the muzzle flashes stopped. Corporal Cook released the breath he didn't realize he was holding as his hand settled on the butt of his pistol. Two of Dr. Wyeth's assistants ran up and pulled the airlock hatch open, then hastily stepped back.

"Come to me, Galena," beckoned Dr. Wyeth. "I repeat, come to me!"

Gut-wrenching revulsion struck Jerald like a wave as the Lieutenant stepped out of the sphere's enclosure. Blood spattered her coveralls. Bits of flesh trailed behind her in the tracks of her boot soles. Her finger impulsively clicked against the trigger on the pistol she held loosely in her hand. But it was her dead eyes that made the Corporal slowly pull his service weapon.

"She's not in there," he murmured to himself as he stepped back and made a gesture with his hand to ward off evil.

He had seen hundreds if not thousands of the genorgs fed into the enclosure and few had come out again. Those that survived the longest inside were mindless horrors while the others attacked anything they could reach when the hatch was opened. This was something else.

"Subject, disarm yourself, and stand down," ordered Dr. Wyeth.

Galena stood rigid as the bloodied pistol slid free of her grip and clunked against the decking. Slowly awareness shone bright in her eyes. A tiny cry escaped her lips and she collapsed in a heap.

Corporal Cook remained still as the two assistants stepped forward and slapped restrainers around Galena's wrists. They raised her to a sitting position as another person stepped out from the shadows. Jerald watched his bunkmate Hamza Fitzpatrick grab the Lieutenant and flip her over his shoulder.

"Mr. Cook, please help Mr. Fitzpatrick deliver the subject to her room for monitoring."

Jerald holstered his weapon and joined the Yeoman, "Of course, Doctor."

***

Galena woke up from a nightmare of constant screaming and blood where she was an emotionless monster bent on wreaking havoc. Her eyes blinked in the bright light before she noticed she was strapped down on a med table and the Doctor was holding her hand.

"Where am I?" she asked. "What... what happened?"

Dr. Wyeth looked down at her with feigned sadness, "You lost control in there. We had to pull you out after you butchered those beings. We tied you down for your own safety."

"My apologies, Doctor. I don't know what came over me."

The Doctor looked at her questioningly, "Explain."

"It was strange. Something clicked and I became nothing more than a passenger in my own body." She glanced at the Doctor and saw a self-satisfied smile that flashed across Judith's face then quickly disappeared.

"There, there," said Dr. Wyeth as she patted Galena's hand. "You did well, my dear. Even with the chaos you created, their physiology didn't affect you. You still show no signs of any contamination. And I must say I was impressed with your combat prowess. The creatures in there didn't stand a chance against you. All in all, it was a successful test."

"Even though I lost control?"

The Doctor smiled, "Exactly. The repairs to your battle chip worked and it defeated the infection before it could re-enter your bloodstream. We're installing copies of the chip into six new subjects. With more subjects and a little bit of luck, we'll be able to eradicate all of the monsters that exist within the sphere."

Judith stood up and slid Galena's hand under the sheet, "Now get some rest. You'll be acting as our control subject for the next set of tests."

Galena watched as Judith moved to leave the room, "May I ask a question, Doctor?"

Judith stopped and turned, "Of course."

"Where did the battle chip come from? I thought modifications were illegal in the Consortium?"

Judith's laughter trilled brightly, "It is only illegal to have them installed in humans. And luckily for us, you are not human. Sleep well, my dear."

When the Doctor left the room Galena's hand instinctively went to her chest, but the dog tags no longer hung there. *'Have I become no one again?'*

eleven

Land of Thousand Dances

Derain blinked as the sack over his head was pulled free for the second time in one day. At least he thought it was the same day. Time was passing in a blur. His wrists and ankles were tied down to what appeared to be a glowing white chair. His ankles were restrained in the same way.

"Was I drugged? Damn it," he cursed.

He was alone in another small room, but this one had plasti-sheet walls with corner seams that were almost invisible. The ambient light made it hard to focus, but he could faintly see an extrusion poking out of the wall in front of him. A small colored flame tickled the base of it.

"Definitely drugged," he decided. "How many days this time?"

Mr. Leon's chuckle rippled through the void and the flame coalesced into a holographic image of the criminal overlord. To Derain's strained eyes, he looked unchanged, but then again this might not even be one of the Leon's he'd met.

He squinted against the light and asked, "Are there older versions of you, or are you all just the same age?"

Mr. Leon's body language changed and his response was measured, "You know us better than most, Mr. Tiwi. All of us are the same age, though some shells appear older while others look younger."

Derain's eyebrow raised at the sound of Mr. Leon's voice. The slight time delays in his speech meant the man was in-system, but he wasn't on the asteroid. This was an unfamiliar strip of space. He wasn't sure if there were any outlying facilities or if it even had a proper jump gate. *'He's probably on an incoming ship, then.'*

The holo changed from a full body shot to a close-up of Mr. Leon's face, "Aren't you curious as to why I requested this audience?"

Derain shrugged, "From where I'm sitting, it looks like I have little choice in the matter. Though, if I was to hazard a guess, it would be related to my botched attempt on your contract."

Mr. Leon smiled ingratiatingly, "Astute as always, Mr. Tiwi. Though your failure has made achieving my goal more difficult, I still know that you are the right man for the job."

"What will my failure cost me? As I'm sure you've noticed, I am a captive audience."

"Charming as ever," Mr. Leon mocked as he

stared levelly at the bounty hunter. "How often does your first attempt fail? From what I have been led to believe, you always get your man... or woman in this case."

Derain sighed, "I've had a handful of first attempt fails, but my second time around usually cuts the biscuit. Although there was this one mark I tracked that required a total of three tries." Derain's teeth glinted in a wolfish grin, "Now, that was an ugly day, an ugly day."

Mr. Leon's smile faded, replaced by a harsh intensity, "I am inclined to give you another chance, Mr. Tiwi. But I do not suffer fools and liars for much longer."

Derain recoiled a little bit at the vehemence in the man's expression. Old rumors and tales circulated through his mind, ending with the one where Mr. Leon beheaded a man on a small moon in a system, far, far away. Although Mr. Leon had been kind to Derain and those he cared about, his generosity also left them all in his debt. This man, no, this entity was not to be underestimated.

Mr. Leon's face softened and he winked at the bounty hunter, "It helps to know that you have some investment in Dr. Wyeth's whereabouts. So why hire someone else when the person in front of me has the drive and all the tools? You owe me, Mr. Tiwi. A contract is a contract."

Derain's face wrinkled in confusion, "If she has the Lieutenant, where is she now?"

Mr. Leon continued, "Dr. Wyeth is headed to

the Malina system. The Khanda Family has questions regarding her handling of the drone situation."

Derain blinked in consternation, "The drone situation?" Understanding suddenly flooded Derain's face, "Oh. She's been called deep into the core. That's not good for Galena or us."

Rage flared in Mr. Leon's eyes, "Nothing that woman does is for the good of anyone. That's why she must be eliminated!"

***

Anton knocked on the door to an old apartment and Deepa answered. "Is Niran here? Or Joyo? I need to talk to one of them, please."

Deepa stepped aside and waved him in, "Niran's in the back."

Anton threw a nod her way and entered the home. It looked much the same as it had on his first visit decades ago. Everything appeared more worn, though, and showed signs of repairs. However, the data interface in the main room was new. It probably had been stripped from an old Mark 2 Heron freighter.

Making his way into the living room he spotted Joyo's mom in a recliner stripped from a lander. Time had been unkind to her. Her skin had grown thinner, almost translucent, and worry lines marred her face. But her eyes and mind were still sharp.

Jon Gray Lang

"I know that face," she declared.

"Good morning, Ms. Batak, long time no see."

She chuckled and slapped her thigh, "That you, Rabbit? I heard you were dead."

Anton smiled and grasped her hands, "You know you can't trust rumors."

"Ha!" she hooted. "Come and give this old woman a kiss. Make it sweet!"

Anton blushed a little as he bent down to kiss her on the cheek. But she moved slightly so that his kiss landed on her lips. She laughed all the harder at his shock and surprise.

"Mmm, sweet! It's good to see you, Rabbit. Been a long, long time. Figured you'd died with the pirates."

Anton squeezed her hands in farewell, "Almost, Ms. Batak, but you know me."

"Luck of the demon's in you, stripling, luck of the demons," she crooned conspiratorially. "Joyo's in the back room. You remember the way?"

"How could I ever forget?" As he walked past her, she slapped his backside and cackled with delight. Thoroughly embarrassed now, Anton hurried down the hallway to the backroom.

He tapped out a quick cadence on the door and he heard Joyo's voice reply from the other side, "You still remember that secret code? Get the hell in here, man."

Anton pushed the door open and stepped into the room. His old friend, Joyo, lay on the bed.

His midsection was wrapped in bandages. So were his right forearm and right leg.

"What the hell happened to you?"

"Oh, I caught the edge of a blast during a job," Joyo shrugged. "I'll be up and about in no time."

Anton struck a pose, "I meant how did you get so old? You look like Death came for you and decided you were too ugly to take."

Joyo huffed, "Death can try, but I'm not ready. Got way too much to do."

Anton walked over and slapped a pattern into his old friend's hand, "Good to see you out of his grasp, my friend. Who's the new boss, hey?"

Joyo cracked a smile, "You're looking at him! Self-made, my friend."

"What about mama?" asked Anton as he pointed back to the living room.

"She's my right hand and Niran is my left. I've been boss for a long time now. She has guided me well."

Anton bent down and embraced his old friend, "I'm glad to hear it. Always wondered, if she sold me out to the press gangs."

Joyo slapped him on the back with his left hand, "Mama? No way, man. But if she did, you know the rules: friendship and business..."

"...don't mix. I remember," answered Anton. "You get my payment?"

Joyo chuckled oddly, "Rabbit, he always comes through. It's that devil's luck that follows him everywhere he goes."

"Can't help what I'm born with."

Joyo nodded and shifted to sit up a bit higher in his bed, "We all have our fates, yeah?" He studied Anton and settled into his pillow, "This isn't a social call, is it?"

Anton stepped back and sighed, "No it isn't, my friend. I need some help."

Joyo quieted, "What kind of help you need? Your credit isn't that good."

"Just looking for a lost friend," Anton answered. "He landed with us, but I haven't seen him since."

Joyo smirked, "Your bounty hunter? Yeah, he got picked up." He leaned in, "There's an open contract on him. Big payout. Some find it hard to resist."

Anton blinked for a moment, "You know who grabbed him and where I might find them?"

"It'll cost you..."

Anton shifted, "I'm good for it." He pulled a small bundle of mazuma out of his vest pocket. "Where can I find him?"

Joyo tapped out a message on his data pad and flicked it over to Anton's device. When Anton went to pay him, Joyo waved him away, "An old friend discount. Besides, I saw your ship. You need all the help you can get."

Anton scratched his head as he tried to picture the location of the place displayed on the data screen, "Thanks Joyo. I expect you to do great things."

"Greater than you at least!" Joyo teased as they hugged each other.

***

Barney approached the docking bay entrance and stepped in through the open hatch. The bay rang with the sounds of busy workers as he made his way toward the Matilda. When she was in full view, he stopped. Bright lights played across her structure where some of the outer plates had been removed. Her inner workings lay exposed under the brightness and the new cables gleamed against the worn metals of her flanks. Sparks flew near a couple workers as they completed a connection.

He noticed Emy coming out of the cargo bay doors carrying a portable splicing kit. "Oy, Emy. How goes it?"

Emy stopped and looked up, "Oh, hey Mr. de Lagnel. It goes well. Still, a ton of connections to finish."

"Still think she'll be done by the time the salvage is dragged in?" Barney asked hopefully.

Emy sighed and leaned back, "Unless something else comes up, probably. It's like every line was fried. What did you get hit with, an EMP?"

"I'd rather not say," warned Barney. "Well, I'm willing to jump in and get to it if your people don't mind me being in their workshop."

Emy grinned, "My people? Hell, most of our

crew is working off debt to Orla in some way or another. I don't think they'd mind."

Barney rubbed his hands together, "Mind if I start now?"

"I don't mind at all," answered Emy. "Your helping won't cut the cost, though."

"I'd rather have a working ship sooner than save a bit of mazuma."

"Have at it, my friend. I'm off to grab a bite." A twinge of guilt hit him. He stopped, "Oh, by the way, one of the boys found a beat-up data card under the nav console. He plugged it in and it was loaded with coordinates to a moon or something. Just figured you should know."

"An old data card, eh? Wonder how long it's been there?" Barney shrugged as he shook Emy's hand. "Thanks for keeping me in the know."

Barney clamored onto the ship and quickly beelined to the equipment room. He yanked out his splicer and considered his agenda, "Might as well start in the secondary engine room."

***

Jacquie and Luli made their way to the Eclectic Electric. There were more people about and the word buzzing on everyone's lips centered on the new ships docked in the hangar. They overheard bits of conversation as they walked toward the club.

"Did you hear about the big haul from the Techin?..."

Jon Gray Lang

"... Javin and his pirates hit a convoy just one system over...."

"... What with the Consortium fighting their war, all these cargo ships are ripe for the taking..."

"... They say it's easy pickings now. The jump gate crews can barely keep up with the escaping traffic."

Luli saw the anger building in Jacquie's eyes and steered her into the club. Even at this early hour, the place was about a third full. Luli guided Jacquie to an empty table and pushed her into a seat.

"No fighting pirates this time, Captain," she growled. "We can't afford to get you out of jail."

Jacquie glared at her and stuck out her tongue, "I'll be good if you get me a drink."

Luli winked and waved at the robot bartender, "Already on its way over."

Luli slid in next to Jacquie to limit her avenues of escape. Jacquie just drummed her fingers on the table and looked around the place.

"What are we doing here again? Are we looking for someone?" asked Luli.

Jacquie nodded as she continued to drum the tabletop, "Yeah, the hostess. She said she'd look into where that Doctor might have taken Galena."

"This the same one you hooked up with? Basima?"

Jacquie nodded again. Two drinks appeared on the table, then the robot rolled its way back to the bar. She picked up the glass and looked into the foliage and plastic bits that decorated the top. It

Jon Gray Lang

took a moment to find the straw hidden within. Jacquie took a quick sip and as the liquid inside the glass agitated it changed color.

"For the ass end of the galaxy, this place has some crazy drinks," she whistled as her eyes widened. "Potent too."

Luli giggled as her drink morphed from a blushing pink to vibrant indigo, "These are so fun! I could drink these all day!"

"We did that already," laughed Jacquie, "then we ended up dancing in cages. We should probably take it easy tonight."

Luli looked surprised, "You? Take it easy? Who are you?"

Jacquie winked conspiratorially, "Well, only until I get the lead I need. Then the rest of the night is ours to do with as we please."

"That's my girl!" drawled Luli. "Hey, isn't that your friend?"

"Is it?" asked Jacquie as she looked around. "Basima! Over here!"

The hostess waved demurely and made her way over to Jacquie. She strutted up to the edge of the table and thrust out her hip suggestively, "Well, hello Captain. I see you're back for another night. One of my dancers called in sick. Can I depend on you to dance again?"

"We'll see," said Jacquie. "Depends on what you've brought me."

Basima slipped into an open seat, "It's going to be that way, huh? Well then, I hope this'll do the trick." She leaned in so that she couldn't be overheard, "It sounds like someone high up in the chain has taken an interest in your plight. It cost me a little to set up an appointment for you, but he said he has some information about your Doctor that he's willing to sell."

"He mention a price?" asked Luli.

Basima shook her head, "No."

"Is he trustworthy?" Jacquie asked, "If so, we can negotiate a price."

Basima sat back into the cushion, "He's only been here for a couple months, but he works for a powerful syndicate. If he says he has the info, I would believe him."

Jacquie's face creased in thought, "When is the appointment?"

"It's tomorrow at the half mark. The place is the Bröt 790 on the bottom deck."

"That's the place that Derain mentioned," Luli blurted. "I wonder what he's up to?"

"Bounty business would be my guess," Jacquie said. "He's had a bug up his ass about his rep since we escaped."

"Still mad at him?" asked Luli.

"Not a fan of people running deals behind my back, Lu. You know that." Jacquie sighed, "But I'll probably forgive him again. We'll need him to get Galena."

Basima looked startled, "Galena? Is she one of those genorgs?"

Luli looked concerned, "Yes, why do you

ask?"

Basima leaned forward into the table, "Those genorg freedom fighters keep throwing her name around like she's running the whole rebellion. But if yours is a prisoner of the Consortium, then it can't be the same one, can it?"

Jacquie and Luli locked eyes in grave concern. "Yeah, Basima," Jacquie lied, "ours is definitely a different one. Looks like I owe you tonight for all your help, so, bartender, another round!" Jacquie shouted. "We've got some serious dancing to do!"

***

"Hey Barney," commed Anton, "are you available? I found out who's holding Derain and I need some back-up."

Barney crawled out from underneath a pipe deep inside the innards of the ship, "Eh? What was that? Reception in here is terrible." He adjusted the settings on the comm and tried again, "Repeat, who is this and what do you want?"

"Barney, it's me, Anton. I've got a lead on where Derain is. Well at least on who took him."

"Someone grabbed Derain? That's got to be a first. Let me finish putting this plate back on and we can meet up." He grumbled for a minute, "Where do you want to muster?"

"Third deck. There's a little taco shop there. The only one in five systems."

"See you there; Barney out."

Jon Gray Lang

Barney crawled back under the pipe. He spliced the last two fibers together and waited for them to cool. A quick hit with the heat gun and the new protective casing molded itself over the lines. He tucked them back in and popped the cover plate back into place.

"Wonder if I should bring my 'case of trouble' along?"

***

Anton pocketed his comm and picked up his tray of tacos. They smelled divine. The perfect blend of mushroom protein and spices, four different kinds of chiles, some kind of cheese he'd never heard of, and greenery he didn't recognize.

"No other place makes them like this," he declared as he hoisted one of the tacos. He took a bite and just let the flavors meld in his mouth and ignite all of his taste buds, "Mmm, salty, sweet, sour, and spicy with a touch of bitterness. I'm gonna miss these all over again."

He fished out his comm and sent a ping to Jacquie, but her comm seemed to be off. He sent a ping to Luli and loud music blared over the speaker, "Luli! You there Luli? Luli!"

After a minute of trying to get through, he gave up and took another bite of his taco, "Well, I got Barney. That'll have to be enough."

***

Luli was grateful for a break in the songs as she hopped off the dance stage. She returned to the table and sucked down the last of whatever frilly, and ridiculous drink Jacquie had gotten her. Luli drained the glass and stacked it with the four other empties that all had a residual glow to them.

She never heard her comm chirp as she scrambled back onto the stage. A stage handler waved her over and she hopped into one of the cages. With a cheer, she grabbed the bars as the box was lifted back up to the rocky ceiling.

Luli gyrated wildly to the cheers from the crowd below and leapt into the air when the deejay kicked off the next round of songs with a heavy breakbeat.

"Time to forget and time to shine!" she shouted with abandon.

twelve

Oscillations

Another system, another hard-won battle. The M78, now known as the Lilith, had the Consortium frigate of the Leonis system in full retreat. The Consortium destroyer had been split open like a tin can and it spilled its contents out into space.

The rebel fleet had grown when the Lilith and her companion ships captured smaller vessels as they approached the jump gates and commandeered them by force. The rebels took control of some gates, but destroyed others. Such was the fate of the last mid-system jump gate, the memory of which remained only as floating debris. Just like that, the outer systems had been successfully split from the core systems. Then like ghosts, the rebel fleet disappeared as they returned to the outer systems.

This dealt a major blow to the Consortium.

Travel between the connected core systems and the separated systems required FTL capable ships. By Consortium law, this fell under military purview.

The loss of the jump gates also cut communications to the Consortium as well as interrupted the steady flow of goods from the outer systems to the core worlds. And the core worlds were feeling it. The next step was to clear the outer systems of all Consortium Navy ships.

"Which is why this frigate isn't going to escape," said the Captain of the Lilith. "Do we have a shot, Gunny?"

"Almost, sir. The range is extreme, so there is a high chance of a miss."

"Well, can we catch up?" the Captain asked the pilot.

The pilot replied, "We're burning hard, Cap. We'll be on top of them within five."

"They've slowed, Captain," stated Navigation.

Gunny growled, "And I have a lock on them. Missiles away."

The Lilith maintained her current speed, eating up the distance between the two vessels. Missiles flew past as she rushed toward the frigate. With less than a minute left, a wormhole opened up off the bow of the frigate and the ship edged its way toward it.

But the frigate was too slow. The first missile slammed into the main engine and exploded. Fragments from the engine ripped through the hull as the second missile punched its way into the underbelly of the craft. The wormhole collapsed as the power source that supported it dissipated in a wave over the frigate.

"Only a couple systems left." Mr. Leon closed his eyes, "Finish this up quickly. We're needed in the Ceti system."

"Gunny, go ahead and break that ship apart," ordered the Captain.

"On it."

thirteen

Rocket '88

The music blared in the Eclectic Electric.
Jacquie sat back on a couch, swirling the last of her
drink in its glass, "Finally. We've got a lead on
Galena's whereabouts. Now we just need the
Matilda to get off this rock." She watched Luli
dancing with abandon when she suddenly felt a hand
slip around her waist and pull her in tight.

"Your friend is quite the dancer, but I think I
prefer your moves," Basima purred lasciviously.

Jacquie glanced at Basima and chuckled,
"That's only because you haven't seen what she can
do. But I appreciate the sentiment."

Basima loosened her grip. "A word of
caution. The person who knows the whereabouts
of your genorg is dangerous. You better be careful.
I don't want your beautiful package damaged."

"Scars make for lively stories and mysteries to

Jon Gray Lang

solve. Who doesn't want that?" Jacquie teased as she kissed the woman, "I should be earning my way tonight. Send the details to my data pad, will you?"

Basima tittered and waved to the stage handlers, "Of course, my lovely. I'll be waiting for you."

***

Barney stepped out of the lift and spied Anton a few shops down sitting alone at a small table. He checked to make sure his wrist gun was secured and his boot knife was hidden from view. Shifting the orb of a flash grenade deeper into his vest pocket, he headed toward his friend.

"Alright, I'm here Anton. Where are we going?"

Anton pointed to a seat, "Go ahead and sit down. I ordered tacos for you and you have got to try them!"

Barney scowled, "Do we have time for this? Does Derain?"

Anton waved to the waiter, "We do. Besides, I need to brief you."

They both sat silently until a plate of tacos was ceremoniously placed in front of Barney. The waiter hovered just in range until Barney picked up one and took a bite. At the pleased expression on the Titan's face, the waiter disappeared back to the counter.

"These are surprisingly good! I'd never have

thought to order anything like this," Barney grinned through a mouthful.

"The best in three systems. Though, if you ask me, they're the best in all of known space," Anton took his last bite and washed it down with a shot of the local, colorless liquor.

"Go ahead and keep eating and I'll tell you what I know."

"Alright," replied Barney. "You really should learn to make these."

"Unfortunately, it's nearly impossible to get the right ingredients from anywhere else but here and they don't ship well." Anton pushed his plate back, "Anyway, from what I found out, there was a contract out on Derain."

"Some bounty hunters nabbed him?"

Anton nodded, "You got it. Tough ones too."

"Any idea who?" asked Barney. "Is it Consortium?"

"Surprisingly, no. Some local goon named Vania who works for an info broker. They knew when we landed and where we were staying. Luckily for us, they nabbed him on the street. From what I hear, this Vania person has been known to shoot up a motel to get her mark."

Barney gulped and had to clear his throat, "Lucky for us, indeed. This sounds like it's going to be trouble."

Anton nodded, "Most likely, but my sources say she'll be alone in about five minutes."

Anton started to rise, but quickly sat down

again as two burly males strolled past their table. He waited until they exited the shop. "Hey finish up, Barney," he whispered. "We've got to get going."

Barney swallowed his last bite and took the bottle of colorless liquor from Anton. He tipped the bottle back and took a long swig. With a choked gasp, he wiped at his mouth and set the empty bottle down on the table.

"By Tom, that stuff burns," Barney grimaced as he stood up, "Ready when you are."

Anton dropped a few bills onto the table and waved farewell to the waiter. He stepped out of the taco shop and into the corridor the two toughs had disappeared into moments ago.

Barney stuck to his side and kept his eyes open, "Where are we heading?"

"The living district. It'll be on the left... there."

The two turned left and walked past an open set of heavily armored doors. Flecks of rust lay in small piles near the two doors. Anton led them down one alley and then into another one. By the fifth turn, Barney was beginning to wonder if they were lost. But just then Anton stopped in front of a bright green door.

"This is the place. We'll play this smooth, but if the situation gets sticky, go ahead and do your thing."

Barney blinked up at him, "My thing?"

"Yeah, you know the thing you do." At Barney's blank stare, Anton mumbled, "When you crash through the door and beat everyone up."

"That's my thing?"

Anton shrugged uncomfortably, "Well, whatever your version of that is then. Just be prepared."

Barney shook his head and checked his wrist gun, "I'm as ready as I can be."

Anton shook his head and knocked on the door. His hand came back moist, "What the hell?" He wiped his hand on his trousers and knocked again but his hand hit empty air. "Whoa."

A tall, angry woman stood in the doorway and grabbed Anton's arm, "Who are you and what do you want?"

Anton stared up at the woman and was surprised by her height. He could see the body armor she wore under her outfit and the handgun she clutched in her left hand. Anton mumbled, "Umm..."

Barney screamed at the top of his lungs and barreled into the woman. The shock on her face made Anton choke back a laugh. The woman grabbed Barney and they fell back into a hallway. She sprang to her feet, but Barney swept her legs out from under her. She crashed onto the floor and landed on her backside.

Anton threw himself on top of her and bashed her hand against the floor until the gun she held skittered out of reach. He drew back his fist and delivered a well aimed blow to her jaw that knocked her cold.

As Anton sat up struggling to catch his breath, Barney raced down the hallway. Rounding a corner he caught sight of another woman. "You!" he shouted. "Where is Derain?"

***

Vania blinked rapidly at the short man who stood in the center of her hallway, "What? Who?"

"Barney wait," Anton grunted between gasps as he staggered down the hallway, "Let's start this over."

Vania whipped out her gun and thundered, "Who the hell are you and what are you doing in my home?" She rushed Anton, jumped into the air and kicked him in the chest. The blow sprawled him out on the floor. She wheeled and trained her pistol on Barney.

Barney scooted over to the woman, grabbed her ankle and yanked it hard. She lost her balance and slammed into a wall with a force that jarred the gun from her hand and sent it skittering toward him. He scooped the weapon off the floor, and aimed it at the woman, "That's enough!"

Raising her hands in surrender to the intruders, she declared, "Oy, I don't want no trouble,."

Rabbit slowly rose to his feet and joined Barney. "There's been a mistake here," Anton explained. "We only want to talk. Are you Vania... the bounty hunter?"

"Maybe," the woman smirked. "Why? You got a job for me?"

"No," Anton sighed, "We don't have a job for you. Just some questions about one you completed."

Vania visibly relaxed and the tension from the other two left. She propped the sole of her foot against the wall, leaned back, and crossed her arms. "Oh yeah? You guys in the habit of beating that kind of information out of honest business people?"

"What? No," Barney huffed.

Anton flashed a sheepish grin, "We heard you were a tough customer and figured we'd better play a strong hand. We don't want any trouble, we're just looking for our friend."

"And who would that be?" asked Vania.

Barney shuffled closer, "Tall guy, same profession as you. Has that look about him, you know?"

Anton added, "He's kind of a dick."

The woman laughed and slapped her thigh, "Are you talking about Tiwi?"

"That's the guy," said Anton.

Vania sent a silent command to her house AI to record an image of the two men in her hallway, "Yeah, I had your mate. Funnily enough, he and I go way back." She pursed her lips in consideration, "If I'd known there was another party looking for him, I would've had me a bidding war. But I've already traded him in, damn the luck."

Jon Gray Lang

Anton's expression grew hopeful, "Mind telling us where?"

"Sure," she sneered. "I can tell you that bit. It was an open contract, after all. I dropped him off at Bröt 790 this morning."

"Bröt 790," Barney pondered. "Why does that sound familiar?"

Anton smiled and bowed slightly, "Being an old friend of Derain's yourself, I'm sure you can understand our desire to find him. Thank you for the help."

Her eyebrow quirked in amusement, "That boyo is always getting into quick trouble. Nothing personal, mind you."

"...it's the rules of the place," finished Anton. "I understand. We'll get out of your hair. Come on Barney, let's go."

She watched as Rabbit and the Titan stepped out of her home. Once the door clicked shut and she was all alone, she called out, "AI, run a search on those two for any open contracts."

"Customer parameters?" intoned the AI.

"All contracts, customers set to wide, private and public."

The AI was silent for a moment as it ran its searches. She picked up her pistol and slid it into the holster inside her waistband. She nudged the comatose woman with her toe, "Wake up, Kamra. They're gone."

As the woman stirred at her feet, the AI responded, "Found. Open contracts on Anton

Roane, and another open contract on Derain Tiwi. Subcategory states possible open bounties on traveling companions: one genorg name Galena Chadov, one Titan, name unknown, one deep spacer, name unknown, and one merchant ship Captain, Jacquotte Delahaye."

"Those others don't sound familiar... except for the genorg."

The AI responded, "Galena Chadov, otherwise known as the Butcher of Timmony Bay. Currently listed as an escaped convict and wanted by the Consortium for crimes against society."

"Wait, are all these contracts from the Consortium? Never mind, send them to my data pad." As she perused the bounties, her estimate of the trouble that Derain had gotten himself into increased, "What are you doing, my man? You used to be the smart one. But I can't say no to this kind of mazuma. AI, send these contracts to the team and tell me where the nearest pick-up office is."

"By your command," replied the AI.

***

Jacquie smacked the mag-key against the lock and the motel door cycled open. She dragged Luli into the motel room and propped her against the wall.

Jacquie slapped at the wall, searching for the light pad, and cursed, "Why is it so damn dark in here?" Her fingers found the pad and the lights glowed, "Where is everybody?"

"I'm right here," mumbled Luli with a feeble wave, as she slid further down.

Jacquie grabbed Luli's arm and hoisted her toward the bedroom. She gingerly slipped Luli into the bed and pulled the covers up to her neck.

"Are you going to make it, Lu?"

"Mmm-hmm. Sir, yes sir," she murmured.

Jacquie blearily smiled at her friend, "I'm going to see if anyone left us a note or something."

She turned around and headed into the front room. It looked as if no one had returned since they had all gone their separate ways that morning. She checked her data pad for messages, but there were none.

"It's late," she grumbled. "Where is everybody?"

She slumped into one of the seats at the small table and rubbed her aching forehead. "Let's see, Barney is probably still working on the Matilda. He ignores everything when he's focused. And Anton... what did he say this morning? Oh yeah... that Derain's been gone a couple days now and he was going to look for him. No messages from him, though, so no idea if he found him. That's okay. Derain can take care of himself."

She slowly stood up, arched her back and yawned. She made her way to the bedroom and peeked in on her pilot. The scarring along Luli's hairline was still visible, but the skin looked better, fresher. The lines around her eyes had faded and the hardness of her features had softened. "You really needed this week to just live in the moment again."

"Me too, truth be told." Jacquie yawned once more and whispered, "We've got a meeting with an info broker in the morning, Lu. Don't sleep too hard." Jacquie kicked off her boots and stifled the next yawn with her hand, "I need to catch some shuteye myself."

"Jacq?" whispered Luli. "Can you... can you hold me? Bad dreams and memories. I don't want to be alone right now."

"Like you used to hold me when I was young?" asked Jacquie.

"Please?"

Jacquie nodded sleepily and turned off the lights. She slipped into the bed next to the cyborg and pulled the sheets over both of them. Her body naturally conformed to the pilot's smaller form and she pulled her in close, "Of course, Lu. Of course."

fourteen

C'est Si Bon

The early lights of the station glowed faintly, but Anton was grateful for the morning. He nudged Barney awake and peered out of the alleyway. The Bröt 790 looked empty, but it was still open and the glow of its neon sign was a welcome beacon for early breakfast seekers.

Anton grinned, "Nothing truly closes on the 'heap."

Barney growled, "Tell me again why I had to sleep in a gutter?"

"Are you wet? It's not a gutter, Barney."

"Semantics..."

"The info broker knows where we're staying. Hard to get a jump on someone who is watching you leave through your front door."

"Right," concurred Barney. "That bounty hunter better not have lied to us. I am not doing this again."

Anton chuckled as he stood and stretched, "Getting too old for the adventurous life?"

"Damn right, I'm too old! I'm over three hundred! Making an old man sleep in a gutter..."

Anton pounded his legs and felt the prickles as the blood returned. Blearily looking down the corridor, a pair of figures coming their way caught his eyes, "Is that the Captain?"

"Huh?" Barney pushed past him and peered down the pathway. "Looks like Luli, too. Did you make me sleep in an alley for no gods-be-damned reason?"

Anton ignored him, "Where are they headed?" He watched as they walked past and stepped through the doorway of the place they had been casing all night. "Well, I'll be damned. How'd they find out Derain was in there?"

"Better question is, why did I sleep in a gutter?" Barney harrumphed as he stomped past Rabbit. He stopped and turned around, "Obviously, the jig is up. You coming?"

***

Luli followed Jacquie through the doorway of the Bröt 790. A bar ran along the left wall and a collection of small tables populated the rest of the room. A single hostess was working behind the bar and one waiter was handling the tables. Luli thought he looked familiar but she couldn't place him.

Jacquie hollered in surprise, "Stanislav Tenden? Is that you? What the hell are you doing on the other end of the universe?"

The waiter looked up and his stern expression changed. While his expression still looked somber, those who knew him, knew that he was smiling. He called out to the hostess, "Ena, serve up a cold bottle to table three."

"Pickles?" she called back.

He nodded and waved Jacquie over to the designated table. Luli slipped into a chair he pulled out and so did Jacquie. "It is good to see you, Captain," he affirmed. "Be with you in a minute," he said as he went to fetch napkins.

"Is Viktor here?"

"Alas, he did not make it, Captain."

As Stanislav walked back to the bar, Ena approached and slid a tray onto their table. A single bottle of a clear liquor dominated the tray and three small glasses accompanied it. She pointed to the bowl of what looked like pickled cucumber slices, "You know how to do this, yes?"

Jacquie smiled brightly, "I do. Thank you."

Luli looked at the bottle and the glasses, "Isn't it a bit early for this?"

"It is never too early to celebrate the return of friends," remarked Stanislav as he returned. "With all the news about deep spacers, I am glad to see you alive, Ms. Qing. Your voice is..." his hand swept up in a spiral, "... magical. It would be a sore loss to those of us left behind. But I digress." He

Jon Gray Lang

picked up the bottle and poured vodka into the glasses.

The light brightened in the room as someone came in through the front door and waved at Jacquie. Stanislav called out, "Ena, two more glasses, please." He turned and led Anton and Barney to the table, "Gentlemen, please sit down. I will be with you in a minute."

Jacquie watched as the disheveled pair sat down somewhat sheepishly, "Where have you guys been?"

Barney glared at Anton, "Sleeping in a gutter for some unknown reason."

"Sleeping in a gutter?" Luli asked.

Anton blathered, "There was a reason. How was I to know you guys were going to show up here?"

"I don't know, maybe call us?" retorted Jacquie.

"I did call. I called Luli!"

"Huh?" Luli blinked as she checked her comm history, "Oh. He did call, Jacq."

"See?" Anton glanced at Barney and laid his hands flat out on the table, "Now what I want to know is how you found out Derain was being held here?"

Jacquie leaned forward, "What do you mean Derain's being held here? Against his will?"

Suddenly, Stanislav loomed over the table and filled two new shot glasses for Barney and Anton. He pulled a chair over from another table and slid into it. His gaze swept over the folks around the table and he could see questions in their eyes.

Before anyone could say another word he picked up his shot glass and recited a traditional toast, "May we only suffer as much sorrow as the drops of vodka we are about to leave in our glasses." He downed the shot and everyone at the table followed suit.

The glasses cracked against the tabletop and Stanislav curled his hands together, "Now, what can I do for you, Captain?"

Jacquie kicked Anton under the table as he opened his mouth to speak, "Shut it, Rabbit." She turned toward their host, "I am looking for information on a friend that's gone missing."

"Oh?"

"We only have a name for the person who took her," added Luli. "Dr. Judith Wyeth. Is that enough?" She bit into pickle slice, "Oh, these cucumbers are tasty!""

Stanislav tapped at the table, "This Dr. Wyeth abducted your friend? Are you sure?"

Barney piped up, "Pretty damn sure. We watched her get dragged off by the Doctor's lackey."

"Do you know anything about her? Location, hangouts, et cetera?" asked Jacquie.

They watched as Stanislav checked his data pad and waved Ena over. He confided something in her ear. She nodded before she headed to the back room. "I think I might have something for you. It is not much, but it should get you to a starting place, yes?"

"A starting place is definitely better than nothing," Jacquie stated. "What is it going to cost us?"

Before Stanislav could answer, Anton growled, "We also want to know what you've done with Derain. I know he's here."

Stanislav chuckled, "I do not 'have' Mr. Tiwi. He is free to move around on his own. In fact, here he is."

Derain stepped out of the back room and Ena dropped a shot glass into his hands. He looked a bit nonplussed, but was otherwise unharmed. He made his way over to the table and stood behind Jacquie.

Anton looked up, "What's the deal, Derain? We slept in a gutter for you."

Derain's eyebrows wrinkled in confusion, Why would you sleep in a gutter?"

Stanislav chortled heartily as he filled each of the glasses on the table and raised up his own, "It is good to see old friends reunited!"

The others clinked their glasses together and downed their shots in single gulps. The table rang with the glasses being slammed against its surface and Stanislav's laughter rang out again.

"As to the cost, assisting Mr. Tiwi in the completion of his contract would be payment enough. The bottle is a gift from me to you, my friends. Now, you must excuse me as I see to my other guests." Stanislav stood up and headed toward the bar.

"What about the data on Dr. Wyeth?" called Jacquie.

Derain gripped her shoulder and met her eyes as he slid into Stanislav's now vacated chair, "I have a system and a name, a powerful name."

Jacquie nodded in understanding, "So, Mr. Leon is involved in this contract of yours."

"Afraid so," he answered.

Luli asked the question that was on everyone's mind, "What's the contract entail, Derain?"

Derain picked up his glass and everyone followed suit, "I have to end the life of one Dr. Wyeth."

He clinked his glass against the others and downed the shot. He flipped the glass upside down onto the table and stood up, "I'm sorry to drag you all into this."

Barney's comm chimed and he answered it. He listened quietly for a moment then he signaled to the crew, "The salvage should make it here in the next day and the repairs on the Matilda should be completed tonight. Apparently, all of the Scrapheap knows about it as it's been spotted in long-range scans."

Jacquie nodded and stood with her hands on her hips, "Then we can get a move on tomorrow during the excitement. I have to say goodbye to someone. See you back at the Taj. Oh, and stay safe. Don't get into any complications, alright?"

"Got it," chorused the crew as they wandered

out of Bröt 790.

***

Vania kept an eye on the Matilda crew as they exited the Bröt 790. She pointed to her two henchmen, "You two, follow them and keep them in your eyesight. Report to me on their whereabouts."

"Got it, boss." The two hulking men nodded and headed after the crew.

She watched them go then strolled inside the sandwich shop. She went to the bar and kept a surreptitious eye on the hostess until the man who ran the place waved her over to a table.

As she slid into the seat across from him, he placed his palms together, "Our contract is completed, Vania. What can I do for you now?"

She kept the pistol she held under the table top pointed at Stanislav, "Those people that were just in here?"

Stanislav smiled, "You know I don't discuss my dealings with other clients."

Vania leaned back in her chair and studied the man. He seemed relaxed, but she knew how fast he could spring into deadly action with no warning. Until her ship was completely repaired, she had to keep all of her bridges intact, and that meant she needed to somehow keep the peace between them.

She slowly revealed her pistol and asked, "Do you know who on the 'heap is a contact for the Consortium? I have need of them."

Jon Gray Lang

"Ena, a drink for my friend here." Stanislav cricked his index finger on his left hand, "I do know who this person is. What do you need from them?"

"I need their jump gate contact. My open contracts are through the Consortium and I will need a ship to bring the warrants in."

Ena brought over a single shot and set it down in front of Vania. Vania thanked her and sipped from the glass. Stanislav watched her do this and a nerve throbbed along his jawline.

"What of your ship? I have heard that repairs are completed."

Vania blinked, "The repairs are completed? I've not heard anything."

Suddenly, her comm chirped and she answered it.

"Is this Vania?" asked the comm. "Your ship's repairs are completed. Come by any time to pick her up."

Vania clicked the comm and slipped it back into her pocket. "I stand corrected, Mr. Tenden. I won't need a ship after all... mine is repaired. It is good of you to tell me before the shop does."

He nodded, but didn't say anything. He did however notice the half-empty glass as she stood up.

"It looks like I will no longer need your services. Thanks for the drink." As she made her way out of the establishment, she smiled ruefully, "I'm sad to do this to you again, Derain. But those are the rules of our business."

fifteen

Escape from the Prison Planet

Jacquie ran her hands through her hair as she walked back to the Taj. Recalling her last night with Basima, she mused, "Some things in the Scrapheap are worth it." She stopped in front of the motel room, smoothed out her vest, then opened the door. Anton sat bare chested at an open poker game on the table.

"You lose your shirt again, Rabbit?" she asked as she stepped inside and closed the door.

Anton grinned, "I'll win it back, just you wait."

Barney snorted, "My mazuma is still on Derain taking it all."

Stretching her arms over her head, Luli sauntered in from the backroom, "Is mon Capitan back after breaking hearts in yet another port of call?"

Jon Gray Lang

Derain chuckled as he fanned out a royal flush, "The sting of a fling isn't a thing to Jacq. Now, what have you got, Rabbit?"

Anton groused as he dropped his cards onto the table, "I've got a fistful of nothing."

"Give him your pants!" chortled Barney.

"Ooh," Luli and Jacquie giggled, "Let's see what he's got hidden away there."

Derain made 'give-me' motions and Anton's face fell.

"Come on, man, these are the only ones I've got here."

"Are you reneging on a bet?" asked Barney. "That's bad precedent."

"Fine," Anton muttered as he undid his belt and pulled off his pants. He dropped them onto the floor and bowed to the admiring oohs and aahs.

"Never mind," laughed Derain, "Put your pants back on... the shirt, too."

"How'd it go, Jacq?" asked Luli.

"There were no tears, if that's what you're asking," she answered. "Is everyone as tired of this place as I am?"

Derain snorted, "Yes. I sure am."

"Glad to hear it," replied Jacquie. "Rumors say there's an open contract on most of us and I'd like to avoid a showdown, if you get my drift."

"Got it like the gravitational pull on a pebble," smirked Rabbit as he pulled his shirt over his head. "Any idea who?"

Jacquie shook her head and went to the

icebox. She pulled a beverage free and popped the top. Luli wrapped an arm around Jacquie and grabbed a beverage of her own. Anton struggled back into his pants and Derain gathered up the cards.

"Good news!" announced Jacquie. "Orla says the Matilda is ready to launch. I don't want to waste any more time, so let's get our stuff together and get off this rock. The Lieutenant has waited long enough for us to get our asses in gear."

Anton nodded as he picked up his pistol and slid it into its holster, "Don't worry, Jacq. We'll get Galena free, no matter what the cost."

***

The crew hastily made their way to Orla's. Unfortunately, the corridors were jammed packed with people as they headed down to the docking bay level. Jacquie elbowed her way through the crowd, followed by Luli and Barney. Derain had to shift around to keep up as Anton tailed him.

Derain called out, "What's the rush to the bays about?"

A passerby shouted, "Haven't you heard about the landfall on its way?"

"Orla's got a huge wreck coming in today!" declared a woman wedged beside him. "More work means more mazuma and more space to spread out!"

Derain stared at her, "What do you mean by

more space?"

"You a Johnny Raw or something? The whole rock has been hollowed out. The only way for this place to grow is with salvage." Derain's blank expression irritated the woman, "Look around. Half of the businesses and living spaces are built into the guts of old ships. Rumor has it that the 'heap is going to double in size! I've got to get up front!"

Anton grabbed Derain by the arm, "Come on. Jacquie is way ahead now."

As the two of them pushed their way through the crowd, they passed Kamra. She whispered into her comm, "Vania, your skips are on the second tier. They should get to the docking bay in about ten minutes."

"Get to your ship and tell the others to do the same, replied Vania. "We'll take them in space and take them directly to the jump gate."

"On my way," she said as she pocketed her comm and disappeared into the crowd.

***

Anton hammered at the docking bay doors, "Come on, Emy. Open the door! Emy!"

The door slowly swung inward, "Eh? Who's there?"

"Let us in, damn it!" Anton snapped as he pushed his way past. The rest of the crew piled in afterward.

Jon Gray Lang

"Is she ready to go?" yelled Jacquie as she brought up the rear.

Orla wandered slowly out of her office, "Hold your damn horses, Captain. Let me get down the stairs."

Jacquie stopped in front of the Matilda, tapping her foot impatiently, "Luli, run her through her pre-check. Barney, cycle up the engines and get the jump engine ready."

Derain followed the two of them in, "I'll look for those coordinates and get the nav system set."

"Sounds good," said Jacquie. "Anton, you're with me."

Anton nodded, "Understood, Captain."

Orla hopped off the last step and meandered toward the two of them, "Thank you for waiting, Captain. We just need to close out our deal. Are you ready?"

"We are ready to go, Orla," answered Anton. "We might have a tail, so can we pick up the pace?"

"You do have a tail, boy. Three, if the rumors are true." Orla stuck out her hand.

Jacquie grasped it and they exchanged the secret handholds used by smugglers. Orla smiled brightly when the gestures were completed.

"I figured it was the case, but I wanted to be sure," grinned Orla. "Your ship is ready Captain, and your payment will be received by the Scrapheap within the hour. I have only one request for you."

"Of course. What can we do for you?"

Orla sighed, "The scuttlebutt here says bounty

hunters are after you on orders from the Consortium. It would be appreciated, if you could get out of range of the salvage so that nothing happens to it. So, take your ship in the other direction."

Jacquie nodded, "We'll do our best to keep your shipyard safe. Now if you will excuse me, I have a ship to prep. Anton?"

Orla brought her hand up, "Please, let his Auntie have some parting words."

Jacquie glanced at Rabbit, "Make it quick," she cautioned as she hurried toward the Matilda.

Anton gave a quick embrace to Orla, "It was good to see you again, Auntie. I didn't think I would ever be back out this way."

"It was good to see you too, my boy." She slipped a package into his hands and patted his cheek, "You left this here a long time ago. Figured you might need it again. Be safe out there. Now go!" She shooed him away.

The Matilda's position lights blinked and the blast from her sublight engines spewed dust in all directions. The deafening roar increased as sirens sounded when the docking bay doors began to open to space.

Anton gripped the package and waved goodbye to Emy as he ran toward the departing ship. He jumped aboard just as the Matilda's giant cargo door began to shut. Anton did a quick check to make sure that everything was tied down, then he clicked his comm and rang the bridge, "Cargo bay doors are closed and I'm making my way up. Anton out."

Jacquie commed back, "We're already lifting. Get up here quick!"

Anton didn't bother replying as the lift doors shut behind him and he pushed the button for the top deck. He looked down at the package in his hand. It was wrapped in an old cloth shirt that he recognized from his childhood. The shape of what was inside was bulky and felt familiar.

"Henon?" he gasped, as he pulled away the wrapping and stared in surprise at the gift.

He flipped the pistol over in both hands and ran his thumb over the name that was engraved into the barrel slide. The gun was old and worn, but it was, without a doubt, his father's sidearm.

The pistol's familiar grip slid home into his palm and he felt the comforting weight of it, "I thought I'd lost you to those bastard press gang pirates. It is good to have you again, my old friend." He intertwined the gun through his belt and breathed in deeply.

As the lift dinged and the doors parted, a sense of renewal filled him. "My father's spirit has returned to look over me once again. I am ready for anything."

***

The Matilda retracted her landing legs as the attitude jets lifted her off the deck. The ship

Jon Gray Lang

hovered momentarily as it angled toward the open docking bay doorway. The sublight engines flared hot for a second and the freighter maneuvered out into open space.

Luli angled the merchant ship to starboard as the M33's salvaged remains appeared in the bow port window. Once open space came into full view the sublights blazed and the Matilda burned its way free from the gravitational pull of the Scrapheap.

"And we're clear," Derain stated.

Jacquie nodded, "You get those coordinates to the Malina system loaded?"

"Almost done," replied Derain as he finished typing them in.

Luli called out, "The hull's getting pinged. We've got trackers on us!"

Anton popped in through the hatch and dropped into the weapons console seat. Derain had brought up the systems, so he ran a fast scan of the surrounding area. The Scrapheap dominated the scanner's images, followed by the wreck of the M33. He ran a tighter search around the Scrapheap and a smaller target pinged back in response.

"I've got one, no... three bogies on our tail," Anton stated. "Should I fire?"

"Let's get farther away," answered Jacquie. She commed the engine room, "Barney! Is the engine ready?"

"She's ready, but we need to get farther away from the 'heap," he replied. "Gravity wells play havoc with the engine."

"Stay alert," she commed back.

Anton shouted, "We have incoming!"

"Damn it, they're too close!" cursed Luli.

The ship rang with a burst of small explosives that sprayed across the hull. A heavily armored tug shot past the Matilda and its engine cones glowed brightly against the backdrop of space. Another series of detonations rang the hull like a bell and the last one shook the bridge.

"Damn it! What are they doing so close?" snarled Jacquie. "Lu! Get us the hell out of here!"

"On it," exclaimed Luli. The ship's dive was too rapid for the artificial gravity to compensate correctly and the flooring dropped underneath them.

"I've got one pursuer locked, Captain," Anton barked. "Should I fire?"

"Hold!" she cautioned as G forces slammed them toward the starboard side.

"Done!" reported Derain. "Coordinates entered."

"Distance?" queried Jacquie.

Anton kept what appeared to be an old Consortium gunboat in his sights. A name was painted flamboyantly along the fuselage, "Got a name, Jacq. The Daena."

"Damn it, Vania never could pass up a high-cost contract," cursed Derain. "We're far out enough, Captain."

Jacquie's grin was bitter, "Fire at will, Rabbit. Let's get them off our back."

"Firing," shouted Anton. He tracked the slug,

but watched it sail past its intended target. "It's a miss."

***

Vania yanked back on the yoke of the Daena and the attitude jets pushed hard to the port. A slug from the Matilda's rail gun just missed her lander.

"Rubis, take out their sublights!" she ordered into her comm. "Spite, keep them off the Rubis!"

"On it, boss," rang through the comms from both ships.

Vania's ship dropped back and her two wingmates shot ahead of her. She pulled up the targeting system on her weapons console and studied the surface of the freighter. The computer struggled to find a weakness that could be exploited from this angle. Only the engines glowed red for the computer.

"I don't have the right ordnance on my boat to break those motors," complained Vania. "Alright, new plan. Change my approach and pepper their bridge with everything I've got."

***

"Two bogies coming up our tail," relayed Anton. "They're going after the engines!"

"Can you hit them or not?" asked Jacquie.

"Maybe," came his reluctant reply.

"Let me see if I can fix that for you," chirped

Luli.

The freighter dropped hard, then tumbled to its port side. Jacquie's grip on the armrests was white-knuckled as she murmured a small prayer.

Luli laughed, "I heard that, el Capitan! We'll make you a believer yet!"

"Firing... now..." ground out Anton.

***

The Rubis shot ahead of the Spite and kept its approach lean. The pilot's proximity scanner began screaming loudly, so Kamra mashed the countermeasure button. Chaff spiraled out of the front of the craft and she fired her starboard attitude jets.

The rail gun slug splintered its way through the chaff and missed the small ship. Kamra swung the Rubis out farther and the Spite shot past.

"All yours, Spite. All yours," she chattered into the comm.

***

"Missed again," groused Anton. "I can't keep the second one off us, Jacq. Prepare for impact!"

Barney's voice boomed from the comm, "We just got these engines installed! I won't have them trashed so soon. We're jumping now!"

Jacquie stammered, "No, wait!"

sixteen

House of Bamboo

Jerald Cook stood hesitantly outside the door to the Lieutenant's room. He could see her through the two-way window and watching her display emotions made him feel ill. His fingers twitched with irrational anger, "You aren't supposed to feel!"

The Consortium taught that unlike their human controllers, drones were incapable of feeling any emotion. But he had seen and heard enough screams from those shoveled into the enclosure to question that belief. Now, the sight of the Lieutenant knotted into a ball with tears streaming down her face throughly destroyed any vestige of that doctrine.

He began pacing and murmuring, "What to do, what to do, what to do." Suddenly, he stopped and glanced both ways down the hallway. He was alone. He sucked in a breath and blew it out in a whoosh. His expression hardened, "It's now or never."

He held his data pad to the scanner and the door unlocked with a loud click. He moved into the room and repeated the greeting procedure he always used with this genorg. "Lieutenant? Please come with me."

Galena's shoulder's straightened at the door opening and she came to her feet slowly. She wiped her tears away with the sleeve of her blood spattered coverall. Her lips trembled as she glanced at him, "I am needed again?"

"Please follow me," Jerald gulped, "Galena Chadov."

A hesitant sense of hope lit her face briefly then disappeared. "Given names, Corporal Cook? My Captain would say that's very forward of you. Very well, I am right behind you."

Jerald stepped out into the hallway and waited until she moved in front of him. "Please head toward the lift, Lieutenant."

She barely nodded as she briskly led the way. He had to double his steps to keep up with her and wondered if she was laughing or crying ever so slightly under her breath. At the lift, she stood in a loose version of attention but kept her head down. He shuffled past her and keyed the doors open.

She walked to the back of the car as he keyed the floor on the control pad, then inserted his data pad.

"We are no longer being monitored,

Lieutenant," said Cook as he glanced at Galena. "I...
I have something to show you, but the Doctor won't
like it. You must keep this a secret, otherwise there
will be heavy consequences for both of us."

She nodded just enough to assure him she
understood his warning. He slid his data pad back
into his pocket as the doors parted silently in front
of them and he directed her out of the lift.

"There is an old lab on this level of the base
that the Doctor rarely uses." Galena followed him
into a large room. "If you head toward the back,"
Cook continued, "you'll find what I think you should
see."

As Galena walked across the room, overhead
lights flickered to life. The floor and walls were
covered in the large tiles used in old hospitals. The
place looked as if it hadn't been cleaned in eons as
dust stood tall and proud everywhere she looked.
Every step she took left a rooster tail of dust behind
her. When she reached the far end of the room, a
final light switched on and Galena gasped.

Two bodies hung from restraints around their
wrists and ankles. The restraints were built into crux
decussata bolted directly into the floor. The one on
the left was male and the right one was female. A
closed incision in the scalp of the female form
caught Galena's eyes.

Galena moved closer and came into contact
with the plasma barrier. It sizzled briefly until she
pulled back from it. She stared in shock at the two
forms that hung in front of her.

Jon Gray Lang

"What is this?" she said in hushed tones. "This one looks like me. A genorg, but not gray of skin. More human... And this one resembles Mr. Leon. They look like they are from another time."

Jerald was a little surprised at her recognition of the male form. As far as he was aware, no one knew who the body was. *'Questions for another day.'*

"Some time from the past is correct," he answered. "None of us know who he is. But you are more like her than she is like you, if that makes any sense. She is what remains of your progenitor."

She turned and looked at him with some confusion.

He moved closer to her, "What I wanted to show you is that incision in her scalp. Do you see it?"

"I do," Galena answered, "But why show it to me?"

Jerald pointed at her hairline, "What is under your skin came from her. The battle computer under your scalp came from the inside of her skull."

"The machine intelligence is very old then? But where did the two bodies come from? When are they from?"

"From the rumors on base, they've resided here for centuries." Jerald shrugged, "One of Dr. Wyeth's ancestors discovered the bodies in a derelict vessel near Los in the Tiburon system. They were brought here for study and here they've remained. No one knows where they originally came from, what they were doing in that dead section of space, or how or why they died. They're an enigma."

Galena continued looking over the two crucified bodies and marveled at how clean the corpses were. Not a speck of blood, nor a sign of rot was visible to the eye. "How do you know so much about them?"

Jerald shrugged, "If you're stationed somewhere for over a decade, you learn the lay of the land and many of its secrets."

Galena's eyes squinted, "Secrets? What other secrets do you know?"

"Well, like I was saying, you and your kind are clones of this human woman. But the Wyeth lineage changed your brain in some way to make you more docile. Rumors say earlier versions of your kind staged a riot and were destroyed. Eventually, the Wyeth family filtered down your mental make-up until the genorgs became viable stock."

"Why don't they rot?"

"The plasma field keeps anything out that would upset their chemistry. Beyond that, they don't seem to break down as quickly as a normal human would."

He moved away from her and brought up his data pad. He clicked a holo image of Galena with the woman's body hanging off to her left. As he stowed it, he stated, "You are unlike any of the other genorgs that have been brought out here. And, for a while, I hated that a drone had been given a rank above mine. But I now see that we aren't that different. I thought it was important that you know your origin, especially as the Doctor pushes you through more tests."

"You think we are the same?" asked Galena.

Jerald smiled bitterly as he pulled something out of his pocket and placed it in her hands, "No, not the same. I truly believe you are our only hope against the horrors that destroyed Potune and Rater. Me? I am no one." He checked his timepiece, "We should hurry back."

Galena opened her hands and in her palms lay the scorched dog tags that declared her a sentient being of the Consortium.

Her fingers curled into a fist and she squeezed them tightly, "Thank you, Corporal Cook."

***

Jerald stepped into his room and sat on the corner of his bed before he noticed Fitzpatrick standing near the fresher chamber.

"Where you been, Cook? We were supposed to meet at the commissary an hour ago."

Fitzpatrick shifted closer to him and for some reason, Jerald felt vaguely threatened by his presence. He looked up at this man he had found so attractive only days ago. Now, he could sense the ugliness that lived just under his skin.

Jerald wiped at the sweat that formed on his brow, "I decided to keep guard on the test subject a little while longer after the last experiment. She seemed more unstable than usual, so I figured she might be a problem. Seems my worries were for naught. She just slept."

Hamza smiled and grabbed his shirt, "That one is unstable, alright. Nothing but crazy in whatever is left of its mind." Hamza gripped his shoulder, "You did a good thing looking out for the rest of us. Come on, I'll buy you a drink."

Jerald stood up and grabbed his gun belt, "Right behind you."

***

When the next day dawned, Galena was hustled out of her room and taken into Dr. Wyeth's office. But something had changed in the Doctor's demeanor. The woman's face was lit with an inner glee. She examined Galena as if she were nothing more than a mere object. Galena reached into her pocket and clutched the dog tags, "I am more than what you've made of me."

"Mmm, what was that?" asked Judith.

The Corporal interrupted, "Is there anything else you need of me, Dr. Wyeth?"

"You may wait outside Mr. Cook. Please sit Galena."

Galena slipped into the seat across from the Doctor and rested her hands on top of the desk. She had been to the enclosure every day for a fortnight, but the Doctor had never acted like this before. Galena wondered if it had anything to do with her visit to the special lab that the Corporal had shown her.

Dr. Wyeth pulled out her data pad and glanced at the Lieutenant. "I have something to show you, but I need to gauge your reaction. Please keep your eyes on the holo the entire time."

Galena's nostrils flared as she nodded. The Doctor keyed a pattern on her desktop and a holo sprang to life. It showed a long shot of the enclosure before it changed to a medium shot of a genorg in a basic coverall. Galena watched as the younger genorg picked up a pistol and stepped into the structure. She heard the gun fire three times before the holo panned to one of the enclosure's viewing windows. Inside lay the genorg and her head lay in a pool of her own blood. Galena looked up quizzically at the Doctor, but didn't say a word.

Dr. Wyeth gave some exposition, "We built copies of the chip in your skull and implanted it into eight test subjects and the results were always the same. They would go inside and terminate their existence. We tweaked the circuitry every time and the results didn't change. Until last night."

Judith brought up a new holo and that began in the same way. But the genorg in this experiment was old, older than any genorg Galena had ever seen before. She leaned in to see more as the old genorg picked up the pistol and walked inside. The holo viewer went to one of the windows immediately and recorded the genorg stopping just past the inner airlock. The gun fell from her hand and she stood stock still in front of the sphere.

Galena looked up and saw that the Doctor's attention was fully focused on the scene. She brought her eyes back to the holo. The surface of the sphere swirled through inky patterns before it went completely black. The blood drained from the old genorg's face as she collapsed. Genorgs altered by their time inside the sphere poured out, but Galena couldn't wrap her mind around what they were doing.

Some of the altered genorgs ripped down a pair of support beams from the structure's interior walls. They speared the ends into the earth of the moon in the form of an X. Then hung the old genorg's body on the diagonal cross. The other sisters formed a circle around the dead woman, bowed their heads, then returned to the blackness of the orb.

The way the old woman's body was suspended from the crux decussata struck Galena as similar to how her progenitor was displayed in the secret lab. As she struggled to hide her surprise, she finally realized that the orb inside the armored sphere resembled the engine on the Avadora.

"I have seen that before," she said under her breath.

Dr. Wyeth froze the holo, "Where? Where have you seen it?"

Galena leaned back and studied the intense look on Judith's face. At that moment, she chose to be wary of the information she volunteered. "During the battle over Ninguiz, I boarded an enemy vessel that had a sphere similar to the one in there. After destroying the vessel that was the last I saw of it."

The Doctor's eyes dimmed in disappointment. She grabbed Galena's hands, "Is there anything else that strikes you as familiar?"

Galena shook her head in the negative.

"Beggars can't be choosers," sighed the Doctor. "A change for no discernible reason is still something."

A voice that wasn't hers whispered from Galena's mouth, "Perhaps more flesh..."

Galena's hand flew up to cover her mouth, but the words had already been spoken. She watched the Doctor for any signs of having heard her but there was no response. *'Maybe it is all in my head,'* Galena thought. She pulled her other hand free of Judith's grip, "Is the chip in my skull still a concern?"

Dr. Wyeth looked past her at the wall, "A concern? In what way? I repaired it myself. Are you having interludes of loss of control that you haven't shared?"

"I don't feel in control when I enter the enclosure but everywhere else I feel normal."

The Doctor waved her hand dismissively, "The enclosure experiments are a different beast entirely. Our monitors have seen no sign of your earlier episodes, though. You are essentially cured of that malady."

"I am no longer a threat to those I care

about?"

"For all that you are able to care, I suppose," answered the Doctor. "But I do have other questions for you."

Galena leaned back in the chair and blanked her expression, "Of course. What else do you need from me?"

Judith's eyes tracked the lines on Galena's face and the faint scars that crossed it stood out in relief, "Do you remember your return here?"

"A few weeks ago?"

"No," replied the Doctor as she shook her head. "After your trial and imprisonment. We had your sentence commuted here, remember?"

"I remember some things, but it is fragmented, Doctor."

A feverish light filled Judith's eyes, "Do you remember stepping into the sphere?"

Galena shook her head, "I do not remember. I am sorry."

The Doctor ignored her reply and reached across the space between them, "You went in and you disappeared! You were gone for three years! What did you see in there? What did you do?"

"I don't know. I don't know!" Galena snapped, "Remove your hands from me!"

The Doctor released her grip, but rambled on, "I could force you to tell me, but it wouldn't work. Or would it? Could it work?" she whispered.

Judith seemed to come back to herself, "I have no more need of you, you may go." She keyed

the comm, "Mr. Cook, come and collect your ward."
Judith made shooing motions at Galena as she stood
and made her way through the office door. But as
the door closed behind her, Galena sagged at what
she heard.

Dr. Wyeth wrung her hands and said haltingly,
"Perhaps more flesh..."

seventeen

Loser

Vania pushed the Daena hard after her two wingmen when her ship's filters suddenly flooded with the smell of old blood and rust. That odor was followed quickly by the pungent sweet stench of rotting pineapple. She shook her head to clear her senses, but the scent only grew stronger.

She glared out her cockpit plas-glass and exclaimed, "By the devil Tom, what is that?"

Up ahead an array of dazzling colors folded around the Matilda. The freighter looked as if it had been turned inside out as it fell through a rent in space. Vania's wingmates couldn't react fast enough as first the Spite, then the Rubis hurtled into the tear. Gravitational forces sucked greedily at the Daena and the ship's speed increased.

"Slow down, damn it!" Vania cried as she fought against the pull of the rip.

Jon Gray Lang

But it was too late. The Daena followed the other ships into a place where only madness could reign. Beasts the size of cruisers populated the spectacle and smaller worm-like beings slithered their way between them. For a brief moment, she caught sight of the Matilda when its sublight engines reignited. As she craned her neck for a better view of the craft, she failed to notice she was barreling straight toward one of the creatures.

"Vania! Pull up, pull up!" came a cry from Kamra through her comm.

She yanked hard on the yoke and her attitude jets ignited as fiercely as they could. Suddenly, a rail gun slug slammed into the enormous creature and its body burst around her ship.

She barked into the comm, "That was bloody close!"

"The hole is closing behind us!" replied the Spite. "Where the hell are we?"

"How do we get out of here?" demanded Kamra.

Vania checked her scanners for a brief second, but the energy reading for the tear in space simply dissipated away into whatever this place was.

"Track that freighter!" she ordered. "Oh my God!"

One of the slithering creatures grappled with the Rubis and the port plas-glass was pulled out of its housing. She couldn't hear Kamra's scream, but she imagined it nonetheless as the pilot was bitten in half. The Spite opened fire on the creature and an

Jon Gray Lang

oily black blood spurted through its skin. The small ship strafed the long sinuous body and it split into ribbons of alien flesh.

***

"Damn it, Barney!" Jacquie yelled. "I told you to wait!"

"Whoa!" blurted Luli as she jinked the Matilda hard to port and narrowly avoided a gigantic squid-like creature. "There's so many of them!"

"The bounty hunters are still after us," Anton reported.

"Give them something to think about," barked Jacquie. "Get us out of here, Lu!"

Anton sighted along a tight group of the enormous creatures and fired a volley, "Shots away. If these critters act anything like the others, it'll start a blood frenzy."

Luli pushed the sublight engines to their max and weaved her way through the swarm of nightmares. "Making a break for it, Captain. Hopefully, they'll leave us alone once the bloodbath starts."

Jacquie's face was tight as she glanced over to Derain, "Are we on course? How long until we break into normal space?"

"We're on course. We have to survive out here for a solar day."

"And there we go, Captain," Anton confirmed. "They're starting to tear into each other.

They've gone after the pursuit ships too."

So long, Vania," Derain lamented, "You were tidda to me once, like a sister, but no more."

***

Vania stared in horror as an enormous tentacle wrapped itself around her ship and brought the Daena to a standstill. The bright flash of an explosion where the Spite had been was quickly smothered by a dark reddish haze.

"No, no, no!" Vania shouted as her canopy popped free of the ship's fuselage.

She pulled her pistol free and fired blindly into the meat of the tentacle, but it was to no avail. The tip of the appendage wrapped around her and yanked her out of the Daena. The sheer force snapped her back and left her lifeless. What little remained of her body disappeared into the maw of the creature.

eighteen

Walking on the Moon

Galena stood alone in the lab as she waited for the Doctor to return. Corporal Cook waited by the door in a relaxed stance. He didn't seem to be watching her closely, so she wandered around the room. Shelves lined the walls with drawers full of vials, jars, and electronic bits and pieces. Her hand brushed the counter as she walked along when a bit of bright blue caught her eye.

She glanced at the Corporal before she moved over to it and pulled the drawer open wider. Inside lay a small glass bottle filled with a blue powder.

"Mr. Leon's powder," she stammered as she jerked back her hand. "Where did the Doctor get it?"

She held her hands close to her chest as she stared at the container of powder. Next to it was a vial of a dark aqueous fluid that also looked familiar.

Jon Gray Lang

"Is that?"

"Perversion..." whispered the creature in her mind.

The door swung open and Dr. Wyeth flounced into the office, "What do you think you're doing? Get away from that! Corporal!" she admonished, "You're supposed to be watching the subject! Not letting it wander around my lab doing who knows what!"

Corporal Cook snapped to attention, "My apologies, Doctor. It won't happen again."

"Go stand in the hall. That's what your kind do best."

"Yes, ma'am," replied Jerald as he stepped out of the lab.

She rolled her eyes in exasperation, "Useless man."

To Galena, Dr. Wyeth looked frazzled. Her hair was unusually unkempt, the bags under her eyes were deep, and her skin had a sallow pallor. Sleep looked like it had not made a lengthy visit to Judith in days. Genorg programming kicked in and Galena's tone changed to match, "What do you need of me, Doctor? Is there anything I can do for you?"

The Doctor stared through her before the question registered. She waved in the negative, "No, there is nothing I need from you right now." She smoothed her lab coat and exhaled noisily. "You're here for your check-up. Tell me, how do you feel?"

"Me, Doctor? I feel fine."

Judith motioned her to a seat and shined a

light into her eyes, "Headaches? Uncontrollable actions? Voices?"

Galena stuttered, "N...no Doctor. Nothing of the sort."

Doctor Wyeth stared blankly and seemed to be lost in thought. She hissed through closed teeth, "The end comes and I cannot stop it. The experiments fail. They all fail."

Galena looked on concerned. "Are you alright Doctor?" When no answer came, Galena changed tactics, "What is the blue powder for?"

"Another failed experiment," confided Dr. Wyeth. "It showed so much promise from its origins! Expanded intelligence which only led to a simpleton for a subject. All destroyed.... All burned to oblivion." Judith's eyes focused on Galena, "Only you have succeeded... why? Why do we only have you to stand against the darkness?"

Words from an unknown speaker slipped through Galena's lips, "Only blood can fend off the darkness."

***

Jerald Cook stretched one leg and then the other as he stood guard at the Doctor's lab. Dr. Wyeth's reprimand surely would carry consequences. He could see PT duty in his near future. He sighed as he glanced down the hallway, and off in the distance he saw a person leaving a restricted area.

"Hey you! You're not supposed to be in

there. Come back here!"

The person stopped and turned around, "Jerr? Is that you?"

"Hamza? What are you doing in those restricted rooms?"

Fitzpatrick walked up to him and looked around furtively. "This place is labyrinthine. Have you been in there? You've got to see what's hidden in there."

Abandoning his post, the Corporal followed the Ensign. They slipped under the restricted sign and into the dark room.

Hamza spoke softly, "Lights."

The hidden lights flickered to life and the room hummed with a low buzz. Jerr breathed in sharply. Bold black script in an unknown language covered the walls and floor. At a second glance, some of the sigils were written over others forming a spiral across the entire ceiling as well.

The Corporal stepped back to the door and read the nameplate out loud, "Dr. Saric."

"He's dead," Hamza called out from the center of the room. "The prize genorg broke his neck."

"How do you know that?" said Jerr as he opened a few drawers and rattled through the contents.

"I came across his corpse. He'd been the ship Doctor for a prison transport. Security footage showed Galena coming to life like a puppet and snapping his neck like a twig."

Jerr closed the drawer and watched his roommate scrutinizing a certain section of script on one of the walls.

"The mad Doctor was onto something, though." Hamza's finger traced one of the lines, "I've seen these symbols before. They were sewn into the lining of the Khanda twins' overcoats."

Jerr was shocked, "You've met the Council Twins?"

"Once," answered the Ensign. "On the way here. They wanted the prize genorg too, but Dr. Wyeth talked them out of it... somehow. That woman is dangerous. Dr. Saric knew it. Fat lot of good it did him."

"The Doctor isn't a bad woman," said Jerr.

Hamza gave him a skeptical look. "Aha!" he rejoiced as he picked up an old data pad and stuffed it into his pocket. "I think I found what I was looking for."

Startled by a distant rustling sound, both men looked toward the door.

"We should get out of here," they declared in unison.

***

"Here you go, Lieutenant. I have to take care of some personal things so I won't be here tonight."

"I understand, Corporal Cook. Enjoy your tasks," said Galena.

After he saluted, he shut the door and she

heard the lock sink home. Her fingers brushed through her hair and she regarded her reflection in the mirror. *'The walk back from the lab to her room had been strange,'* she mused.

In fact, everything about today had been odd. The Corporal was suspiciously acting as if he'd been caught doing something he shouldn't. The Doctor's detached behavior was equally baffling. And what the Leon's blue powder was doing here was another mystery.

She stared at her reflection, looking for a sign of the creature that inhabited her body. "Are you there?" she asked. "You spoke through me again. What game are you playing?"

Dry chuckles rustled like brittle leaves in her brain. An earthy scent filled her nose and she felt more than saw the thing looking through her eyes.

"I am here, puppet."

"You recognized the blue powder."

The creature's words rattled through Galena's teeth, "Perversion."

Galena's fist slammed against the mirror, "What is it? What is it for?"

"You heard the Doctor. It was intended to make your kind smarter than insects. But the Doctor doesn't know how to use it or what it's meant to do."

"The Leons are connected."

"The insect learns. The milk of the motherverse makes one part of the whole, nothing else..." She felt the creature pull back, "... no matter how hard one tries to disconnect. But soon we will be free of her."

Galena was silent for a moment, "Mr. Leon grew deathly ill in 'other space'. Is it because he uses the powder?" When there was no answer, she gasped, "Is it made from you?"

There was a long stretch of silence, as the creature's presence disappeared, "In part, yes."

nineteen

This Is Not a War

The Peking Empress punched through the end of the open wormhole and entered an empty chunk of space. Admiral Kaur watched her bridge crew double-check all their systems and verify they had arrived where they should be.

"We have entered the Lukida system, Captain," stated Ovi at the nav console.

Harjeet nodded, "Thank you. Thadie, start broadcasting, please."

"Yes, sir."

"Any response?"

"Nothing yet."

"Bring us in closer." She gazed at Mr. Leon, "Can the rest of the fleet change their arrival time?"

Mr. Leon closed his eyes in consideration before he replied, "The tunnel was already set. They'll arrive on the initial timeline."

Jon Gray Lang

Admiral Kaur nodded in understanding. "We have to get those Navy boats closer to us. Tell the Captains of our contingent ships that it's going to be a knockdown drag-out."

"Message relayed," replied Thadie Dumba.

"Keep the FTL warmed up, Latiff."

Latiff grinned and caressed his workstation, "Aye, warmed and ready."

Harjeet shook her head in mock amusement, but her tight grip on the railing belied her relaxed attitude.

The Lukida system had been chosen for this attack for a reason. It was one of the core systems of the Consortium and it had three habitable worlds and two separate stations. *'If we can destroy their gate, it'll send one hell of a message.'*

After their success at Ceti, the decision had been made that the rebellion needed to make a grander stand in the war arena that would scare the Governing Council. While they had been successful at cutting the outer systems free of the inner core worlds, the Consortium Navy kept pushing further into the outer systems and blockading the gates left active. Merchant ship navies had sprung up in the outer regions and taken the battle to the Consortium Navy, but true warships were hard to take down even by the best pirate catchers.

"What's on your mind, Harjeet?" asked Mr. Leon.

"Just going over the battle plan again. Are we sure that an attack closer to the Consortium core will pull the Consortium Navy ships back?"

"The citizens will clamor for it."

"The same citizens that are burning genorgs alive in the streets?"

Mr. Leon nodded. "You've seen the proof of what the fear of those that are different from them has done. This will just be another example."

Admiral Kaur bit on her lower lip, "We just have to win this fight."

"This system will be difficult for the Navy to work in due to the number of civilian craft and locations," added Latiff. "They'll be constrained while we'll have free range."

'It will give Mr. Tiwi time to remove that final thorn in my side,' Mr. Leon thought to himself. "Such a simple thing is vengeance."

"What was that, Mr. Leon?" asked Latiff.

"Oh nothing, Mr. Ghilzai. Just praying for our success."

***

"The hold doors are opening," declared Alice. "Prepare to disengage."

"We received our marching orders," added Delta. "Per the Empress, this will be a knockdown drag out? What does the Admiral mean?"

Rosa laughed, "It means we'll be deep in the shit." She growled as she grabbed onto the piloting controls, "They'll be throwing everything at us which means it's our chance to shine!"

Jon Gray Lang

"I think I understand, Commander," replied Delta. "Clamps are disengaged and we are ready to provide luminescence."

Commander Keri was vigilant as the Independence cleared the confines of the hold and steered to port. The ship was quickly followed by the Copperhead as it fired its attitude jets to coast to starboard. The Scorpio shot forward and took up position at the bow.

The small fleet settled between the last planet in the system and its moons.

What do the scanners show?" asked Rosa.

Agnes answered, "The jump gate is at extreme sensor range with a standard two-ship contingent."

"So, no surprises yet," stated Rosa.

Carla spoke up, "Looks like there is another ship nearing the jump gate, but I can barely make it out from the gate's shadow."

"Anything behind us?" asked Delta.

Carla shook her head, "Nothing clear. There is too much interference."

"Looks like they set their defenses well," admitted Rosa. "With us barely able to register them, they could be anywhere. Keep an eye out for more."

***

Admiral Kaur maintained her grip on the railing, "So, they have three ships out there already."

"And they aren't budging," observed Mr.

Leon.

Latiff said, "My bet is that they will begin funneling in ships as we draw closer."

Mr. Leon sighed, "We knew this would be the hardest fight we've had."

Harjeet said a small prayer. "Let's hope we've prepared enough. Let's move out."

***

For close to an hour the Peking Empress and her three-ship entourage slowly headed toward the Consortium Navy ships and in all that time, the Navy ships didn't budge an inch.

The tiny fleet continued its approach as the Sensor Tech widened their scanning perimeters. Their role in this mission was to be the bait. Their objective was to lure the Navy away safely. But so far, the Consortium still had not responded as the Empress passed the last planet in the system.

"Nothing but space between us now," murmured Harjeet.

"We've been pinged, Admiral," reported Thadie.

"And now we have a tail," declared Ovi.

The ship-to-ship comm opened up and Captain Kahn's voice came through, "Empress, do you want your tail removed?"

"Hold on that order, Copperhead," replied the Admiral.

"If we engage the tail ship, we might pull

more of them away from the station," said Latiff.

Mr. Leon gave it some thought, "We wouldn't be stuck with such overwhelming odds."

"Copperhead and Independence fall back on our rear," ordered the Admiral. "Any signs of trouble, engage them. Scorpio, stay on point."

"Understood, Independence pulling back."

"Copperhead pulling back as well."

"Scorpio holding position until further orders."

The two ships on the flanks of the Peking Empress fired their bow attitude jets to arrest their forward momentum. They slowed down and the Empress floated past them.

Rosa relayed over the ship-to-ship comm, "We can see her now. Your tail's a CVA class small carrier with a four-fighter accompaniment."

Siede added, "Looks like the babies are out of the nest. Repeat, babies out of the nest."

"Where'd you pick up that lingo, Copperhead?" asked Commander Keri.

"Umm," Siede said shyly, "I heard it on some old holo-vids."

Laughter erupted over the comm before the signal went dead.

***

Admiral Kaur of the Empress asked, "Did we lose them?"

"Yes, Captain," replied Thadie. "Comms are

down with the Independence and Copperhead."

"Scorpio, fall back and cover our rear," ordered the Captain. "Only reason to cut comms is if you're going to make mischief. Pilot, give us a little bit of distance and then slow us down."

"On it, Admiral!"

***

"Ship-to-ship comms are down," stated Siede.

"Any sign of a confounder?"

"Nothing floating out there, but we are being hit by some high-level energy pulses," said Helena. "Hmm, pretty widespread so it's short range."

"Are you able to pinpoint it?" asked Omega.

"Not from here. It's coming from the big ship, not one of the fighters," Helena replied.

"Why do you ask, Omega? Do you think you can take it out when we get close enough?" Ariel quizzed.

The genorg soldier replied, "I will destroy it as ordered, Captain." She peered through the main weapon's scope and made range adjustments on the console.

***

"Let me guess, comms are down," Rosa said sarcastically.

Delta's lips tilted into a half smile, "Yes, Commander. How did you know?"

Jon Gray Lang

"Standard operating procedure for those CVA boats," grumbled Rosa. "Their armor is weak in the aft, though. I might see what I can do to get us back there."

Rex Leon emerged through the bridge hatch. He looked tired as he wandered over to stand behind Rosa.

"Done communing, glorious leader?"

He nodded, "For now. What's our status?"

Delta replied, "We have a single chaser with a standard two-ship guarding the jump gate."

"Anything from the home worlds?"

She shook her head in the negative.

Rosa looked up with a mischievous grin, "Hey Rex, you know the Captain better than the rest of us. What do you think she'll do, if I suddenly rev this boat and fly it right up that CVA's bum?"

Rex beamed, "She'll keep it simple and try to take out their jammer. If it's on the bow, she'll target there first."

"Huh, too bad we don't have the Scorpio. The Copperhead is going to take one hell of a beating."

∗∗∗

The Independence spun on its axis and revved her engines to full throttle. She ate the distance between the Empress and the CVA carrier, then spun into a tight rotation and slipped far to the port. The Independence maintained its speed and if it stayed on course, would shoot past the carrier. Suddenly two of the fighters peeled off from their position and barreled toward the one-time corsair. As the Independence edged closer, one of the remaining fighters pulled back to cover the carrier's flank.

"I see what she's doing. That lunatic is peeling the fighters out of our way!" Ariel exclaimed. "Siew, spin us around and full speed ahead. Omega, take out their comms and their signal jammer."

"Aye, Captain," Omega grinned darkly.

The Copperhead's attitude jets fired and the freighter slowly turned around. Before it was even finished, Siew Lian increased their forward speed and the carrier grew incrementally closer. The last fighter shot out of position and rocketed toward them. Omega focused on the carrier as her eyes played across the surface in search of the signal jamming emitter. She heard one of her sisters shout, "we're being fired upon" as the Copperhead was pelted by small coil-gun rounds.

"Quick, do a sweep of the Copperhead hull for trackers!" barked Captain Kahn.

The fighter slammed hard to starboard and shot past the aft of the Copperhead. Its attitude jets glowed in the blackness of space as it turned in a tight circle and swung back toward the Copperhead.

"Three trackers on the hull!" shouted Myles.

"Two missiles incoming!" yelled Rex as he grabbed onto the railing.

"Swing hard to starboard," ordered Captain

Kahn. "Cut the direct beams painting the hull!"

The Copperhead rolled and dipped to port. One missile passed over the freighter and began a long turn through open space back toward the Copperhead. The other missile slammed hard into the hull. The bridge shook from the blast and multiple alarms blared.

"Are we venting?" demanded the Captain.

Siede answered, "Reynard got the hatch closed, Captain. Damage is confined to the cargo bay."

Omega grinned triumphantly, "I found it! Locking onto the emitter."

"Swing back on course, Siew," the Captain ordered her pilot.

***

"Woo!" cheered Rosa as one of the fighters shot over the bow of the Independence. "That bugger can fly!"

"Missiles incoming," stated Delta flatly.

The Independence bucked as the ship flew through the enemy rockets. Rosa couldn't get over the sheer speed and power that was built into this ship and laughed maniacally. As she hit the forward attitude jets to reduce speed, the response of the oversized engines slammed her forward. "We'll be coming up on our target within a couple minutes. Hit anything that looks lightly armored, especially those engines!"

***

Almost all eyes were focused on the rear sensor reports from the battle raging behind them as the Empress continued toward the jump gate station. The Captain shook her head. These two somehow seemed to have had a plan. But what it was, she couldn't quite tell.

"One of the station ships is moving toward us," stated Ovi.

The Captain pulled her eyes away from the main screen, "Any movement from the gate itself?"

"Nothing yet, but I can't get an accurate reading out this far." Ovi scratched his head, "Never mind, a new ship has entered the system."

The Admiral looked over at Mr. Leon, "We'll be there in twenty minutes. When is the cavalry arriving?"

Mr. Leon frowned, "Sooner than that. Five minutes maybe."

"We have two more ships in the system, Admiral," stated Navigation. "And it looks like a whole lot more are coming through."

"Our luck couldn't hold forever, Admiral," sighed Mr. Leon.

"True," replied Harjeet. "But another day would've been nice."

"A second vessel is on its way toward us," interrupted Navigation.

"Scorpio, move back to our bow and prepare

to engage," the Admiral ordered.

Tau-SA43's voice came back, "On our way."

***

As the Scorpio pulled forward, the first of the rebellion's M-class destroyers broke into the Lukida system. The Consortium was waiting for it, though. A barrage of heavy ordinance spread out into a wide pattern that the cloaked ship couldn't avoid. Small explosions pockmarked the surface of the vessel and it cracked open like an egg. But the momentum continued to carry the blasted wreck toward its planned target.

Seven Consortium ships had come through the jump gate before the damaged M class vessel slammed into the ring. As the wormhole in the jump gate collapsed, the tail of the last ship coming through sheered off and disappeared. The failing wormhole pulled the manned part of the station into itself and the ring imploded.

Other wormholes began to dot the space around the ruined station's former location. As the rebellion's FTL-capable fleet punched into the system, mayhem ensued. The skies lit up like a gigantic fireworks display as the ships closed in on each other and fired every weapon they had.

***

The Scorpio's crew nervously kept an eye on

the Consortium cruiser as it inexorably made its way toward the Peking Empress.

"Tau-SA43, what are we looking at here?" asked Commander Gamma.

"It's a missile carrier. Coil-gun emplacements should be few as it was designed to saturate a target from a long distance out."

Gamma nodded as she increased the Scorpio's forward momentum. But, the sheer number of pings that echoed off the hull raised concern among the ore hauler's crew.

Mu-IK97, one of the young teenage genorgs asked timorously, "Can this old tug handle all of that?"

"Don't worry," answered Gamma. "Out of all the boats we have, this one can."

Gamma overheard one of the other recently liberated genorg's mutter, "Can doesn't mean will."

"That is true," answered Tau-SA43. "But is it not better to die for a dream than to get killed in a cave-in?"

"Or in a factory mishap that could have easily been avoided if the company had paid for safety regulations?" asked an older genorg.

"How would I know?" answered the young Mu. "I've only worked at an algae farm since my release."

"Weren't you being shipped to one of the gas mining colonies?" asked Tau.

"Well, I hadn't gotten there yet, had I?"

"Focus sisters," ordered Gamma. "We are in

their range now."

***

"Coil-gun rounds are in flight," declared Omega. "Changing to short-range rockets."

"Is that fighter still on us?" asked Ariel.

Helena answered, "It's still on our tail, Captain."

"Rockets are on their way, Captain," stated Omega.

"On evasives," replied Siew Lian.

Although the Copperhead was an armed merchant ship, she hadn't been built to fight the war she found herself in. She only had three coil-gun emplacements designed to provide cover on the flanks, aft, and bow, either in concert or individually. At present, all three guns were trained on the CVA vessel.

Luckily for the crew of the Copperhead, the Independence was harassing the small carrier, which kept most of the fighters busy. The pilot still had his work cut out for him, but avoiding a handful of pot shots was easier than surviving a concerted barrage. As the afterburners on the rockets petered out in the night sky, Siew jerked the ship into a flat curve and punched the accelerators.

The tiny rockets were too small for most radar-based defense systems and numerous enough that even a Qaynan defense system would struggle to keep up. But they were there to keep the ship's defenses busy while the coil gun rounds did their job. At this range, they were simply too heavy and too fast for any defense system to completely remove from the sky. If the rounds were broken up, it just meant that there were that many more to come. And they would be untrackable.

Detonations popped like firecrackers across the bow of the CVA vessel, but a few of the rockets impacted the vessel's surface. The armor on the naval ship was much too thick for it to inconvenience the craft. Within half a second, the comms clamored with noise and voices from multiple ships. They all went eerily silent when the CVA's comm tower toppled off the ship and spiraled into space.

"Omega, take that fighter out now!" ordered Ariel.

***

"Commander, we cannot take much more of this," Delta said through lips that were stretched back from the G-forces.

"Just knock out their damn engines and we can get the hell out of here then," cursed Rosa. "That bastard fighter will not get off our ass!" Her words were punctuated by a sharp impact that shook the ship. "They are getting closer to hitting us! Any luck on those trackers?" Rosa implored.

"Too many on the hull now," answered Rho-11.

"Damn! Well, let's see how badly they want us dead!" Rosa bellowed.

***

Gamma gripped the pilot controls tightly as she drove the heavily armored ore hauler straight toward the Consortium cruiser. She kept an eye on the sheer number of missiles that the cruiser fired on her position and held her breath. There were too many. But the heaviest armor on this brute she piloted was all in the nose and she hoped that would get them through.

'What was it the Matilda's dancing pilot used to say,' she wondered. "Oh, yes. Hail Tom, full of grace, please don't let me die in space."

As the first missile flew into range, the asteroid busters unleashed an unrelenting barrage of uranium rounds at it. The bullets pummeled the missile into oblivion then immediately tore into the next one and the next one. The cruiser grew closer and the space between the two vessels lit up in one hell of a light show. The Scorpio flew through the debris and the hull rang with the dings and bangs of wreckage fragments that struck the ship like hail.

The cruiser's defensive measures activated as the Scorpio entered into range. What looked like thousands of rockets and chaff shot toward the ore hauler. But the asteroid busters obliterated them and the skies were lit up with the chain reaction.

"Sensors can't see what's in front of us

anymore," shouted Tau-SA43 over the commotion. "There's too much junk between us."

Gamma grunted, "Let's hope that we're still on course."

***

"That is one hell of a light show," quipped Admiral Kaur on the Peking Empress. "Can we see what's happening over there?"

"Too much debris in the sky."

"All of my digits are crossed," winked Mr. Leon.

***

The Scorpio plowed forward and her crew squinted their eyes in response to the bright flashes lighting up the bridge. The asteroid busters had gauged and registered the Consortium cruiser the same way as it would a huge rock and unleashed on it every ounce of fury they contained. The Scorpio slammed hard into the outer plating of the cruiser and burrowed its way inside.

Chunks of superheated metal and what Gamma could only assume were bodies slammed against the bow of the Scorpio then slid off its flanks. The ore hauler continued to cut through the cruiser until it completely punched through and came out the other side. The fuel tanks on the cruiser exploded and tore what was left of the ship in twain.

When the blackness of space finally dominated the view through the bow port, Gamma yanked hard on the controls and trundled the slow ship back through a morass of floating wreckage toward the Peking Empress.

Gamma breathed in slowly as comprehension dawned on her, "By Tom, it worked. We survived."

The young Mu screamed, "Yeah! We made it! Woo!"

Some of the genorgs erupted in nervous cheers while others cried in shock.

"That was harder than I thought it would be," admitted Tau-SA43.

Gamma answered softly, "It's worth it, when it gives you a chance to have a future."

twenty

Mars

On board the Peking Empress, Admiral Kaur gasped in amazement as the battle played out its final scene in front of them.

"Did they just fly through that cruiser?" asked Mr. Ghilzai. "Literally through it?"

"The jump gate is down, Admiral," Thadie stated. "Orders are to pull back and retreat."

"We beat them. We actually beat them," the Admiral said with awe in her voice. "It's time now to call our children back home."

***

"Firing now," shouted Delta.

Rosa had flown the Independence hard toward the CVA carrier. They came in hot and fast and Delta threw everything they had at the

Consortium ship. Rosa had calculated her angle of approach well, entering from a blind spot that the defense computers would have trouble tracking. Two of the coil-gun rounds slammed into the hull of the CVA and atmosphere vented out into space. Simultaneously, a missile found its target and detonated in one of the main engine cones.

As the CVA began a slow uncontrolled turn the Independence shot past the aft end and through the cloud of debris. The fighter that tailed Rosa lost its way through the rubble and slammed into the aft of the CVA. The fighter broke apart and the explosion spewed across the CVA's hull.

Agnes spoke up, "We're being called back home. The gate is down."

Commander Keri grunted, "Let them know we'll head back shortly. The CVA may be dead in the water, but we still have two fighters on us."

***

As the fighter shot past her bow, the Copperhead fired a missile straight up its tail. The fighter exploded in a starburst of shards.

"Independence to Copperhead! Independence to Copperhead!" interjected the comm. "We are on our way to you with stragglers. We could use a helping hand."

"Bring the stragglers to us, Independence," answered Ariel.

***

The Independence had suffered significant damage.

"Bridge, we've got smoke building up in the engine room!" declared Carla.

"Do your best to put it out," Delta replied. "Commander, I can't get a good angle on either fighter."

"What have we got left to throw at them?"

"Not much," replied Delta.

Rosa cursed and kept an eye on the gauges. The engines flashed out warnings that the heat levels were redlining. "Come on, you can make it, girl," Rosa urged under her breath. "You can make it!"

***

"Siew, bring us back around to the Empress," Ariel commanded. "Omega, I need you to get those fighters away from the Independence."

Omega nodded as the Copperhead's tactical system configured a variety of target possibilities. All she could do now was wait until they flew within range.

***

"We were almost there!" Rosa fumed as one of the main engines failed. She fought to maintain the ship's course until the remaining engine powered down. As the Independence coasted, she let go of the controls. "Praying for a miracle," she murmured.

Suddenly one of the fighters burst into fragments as its hull was pummeled by a coil-gun salvo from the Copperhead. The second fighter swung out wide to avoid the rounds fired its way.

"Thank you, Copperhead," Rho-11 crowed into the comm.

Rosa fired the attitude jets and fell in line with the Copperhead as the pair of ships made their way back to the Empress.

"How'd we do?" Rosa asked.

Rho-11 replied, "The jump gate is down, but we lost the Sparta. Damage reports on the ships are still being collated."

"So we got the job done, but at a high price," speculated Rosa as she maneuvered the Independence into its docking slot inside the Empress. "Let's get the hell out of here."

The invading rebel ships disappeared, leaving the wreck of the jump gate in their wake as the skies of the Lukida system blossomed with new wormholes.

twenty-one

Space Truckin'

The Matilda's hull rang from random impacts as it stayed the course through the 'other' space. Anton grimaced as he ran another scan, "Even with the feeding frenzy, we've still got a bunch of those monstrosities chasing us, Jacq. The bigger ones are getting closer, and if they catch us we're doomed."

Jacquie winced as a dull boom rattled the hull of the ship. "They haven't given up yet? It's been a full solar day, damn it! Please tell me we're almost to our exit point."

Derain rubbed at his eyes and ignored the tiredness seeping into his bones. They had taken catnaps in bursts in the lounge, but with the creatures pummeling the ship, the racket had kept them all awake for the past sixteen hours.

He checked the nav computer and slapped himself on the cheeks, "Can't be much longer."

Jon Gray Lang

"Can't be soon enough," followed up Luli.

"They're going to trash my engines!" cursed Barney as he slumped in his seat.

Derain ignored the loud bang that reverberated from the back of the ship and checked their end coordinates. "Only a couple more minutes, Captain." He glanced up at her, "We'll be dropping into a populated system so I put us on the outer edge. Barney, do you think the cloaking device will last long enough to get us there?"

Barney's eyes gleamed with conviction, "Oh, it'll hold. But we have to get the hell out of here or we won't any have engines to go anywhere." A loud scrabbling came through the hull. "Is it me or are there way more of those creatures, now?"

"It's not you," muttered Jacquie.

Anton added, "Definitely not you..."

The nav system beeped loudly in a staccato pattern. Derain swiped at the screen and the sound stopped. "And here we go..."

The entire ship shook as a rent opened in space. It swallowed the Matilda whole and tossed her willy-nilly into the void of regular space.

As the ship tumbled, fragments of the closest creatures splattered against the hull before turning into dust. "About damn time," Jacquie cursed. "Turn the damn cloak on!"

Barney slapped at the switch then settled back in his seat, "Cloaking is engaged."

The crew stayed quiet at their consoles as Luli leveled the ship out. Jacquie cycled through the frequencies looking for any announcements of sudden arrivals and disappearances.

"Did anyone see us?" inquired Anton.

"Think we're in the clear," answered Jacquie. "Nothing on the chans except news about battles with the rebels."

She turned the sound up and they all leaned in to listen. Each frequency chattered with stories of rebel forces closing jump gates to the outer systems and Consortium goods being stolen under the noses of the Consortium Navy. One name kept popping up, Lieutenant Galena Chadov.

Luli asked into the quiet, "I know I was out of the loop for a while, but did we go to war?"

"With what the newsies are spouting, are we sure Galena is in the Malina system?" asked Anton.

Derain shrugged, "It's our only lead. It helps that Mr. Leon was pretty certain about it. He's known just about every bloody thing there is to know."

"I'll keep monitoring the news chans," said Jacquie. "His info is probably months old at this point. With all that's going on, she might've been caught as a war criminal again."

"Tom knows the council would play such a card," agreed Derain.

***

Barney mopped his brow as he stepped back onto the bridge, "Alright Jacq, I've checked all

Jon Gray Lang

through the ship and she's still solid. Anton's on the hull checking the exterior."

Jacquie nodded as she tapped at the nav console, "Looks like the cloaking is holding, too."

"What's the latest from the newsies?" asked Barney.

Jacquie shook her head, "Apparently, the rebel forces led by our Lieutenant Chadov have taken down all the jump gates for the mid systems. Comm connections to the outer systems have been lost, but we know the Consortium Navy is fighting the good fight. So, the same as before," she finished sardonically.

"There is no way they haven't got Galena in custody," lamented Luli. "The Council must have something big planned."

"Maybe the Consortium doesn't even know they have her. Maybe Dr. Wyeth kept her hidden," groaned Barney.

"Why do you think that?" asked Jacquie with concern.

"The woman chased after us a long time to recapture her," answered Derain. "Way before this rebellion nonsense even started. If the House of Khanda wants Galena, where would the Doctor hide her that they wouldn't bother to look?"

"An auction?" pondered Jacquie. "Where better to hide one genorg than with hundreds of others?"

The heavy thud of mag boots clumped along the hallway and Anton poked his head into the bridge. "I finished my preliminary inspection, Barney. Besides a shiny collection of new beauty marks, the old girl remains intact. When we're groundside, we should take a look at the port sublight engine. The cone is bent in, so thrust will be an issue sooner than later."

He looked around and realized that everyone seemed to be deep in their own thoughts. "What's going on?"

Jacquie looked up, "Groundside huh? From what I know, the Council House of Khanda is on the biggest planet in the system. Luli set a course for the prime homeworld and make it a quiet route."

"On it, mon Capitan."

Barney rapped his fist against a bulkhead, "I might know a place on Jard where we can make landfall."

"Verify that," Jacquie said as she stood up. "The rest of you, prep for trouble."

Anton headed back down the hallway, "I'll whip up something in the galley."

***

"And there she is," indicated Jacquie as the crown jewel and primary world of the Consortium glittered in the night sky.

The Matilda floated past the first of two moons and its net of defensive warships. The second, and smaller moon orbited past them trailed by its own warships.

"Looks like they're preparing to ward off an impending attack," observed Luli.

Derain mulled this over, "Is Galena's rebel fleet that much of a threat?"

Jacquie kept her eyes on the viewport, "Must be to put this system on high alert. I don't think we'd last a second if our cloaking failed."

"Don't fail," Anton prayed as he knocked out a lucky rhythm on the weapons console.

"The cloak is still holding," Barney reassured them.

Satellites, like fine crystals, spun around the planet on thin strands of flight patterns. As the Matilda broke atmosphere over the planet Jard, the sensors lit up from the heavy amount of sky-bound traffic. Luli had to jog the Matilda to avoid the high atmo craft that cruised by on strict flight paths. The gaps between the vessels shrank further as the Matilda neared the planet's surface.

"How are we going to get through that?"

Luli ignored the chatter from the crew as she wove the old trawler through the gaps and lanes. She grinned as the Matilda reminded her why she loved it so much. It responded to her thoughts like an extension of her own body. The surface winds rustled by the hull like breezes blowing through Luli's hair.

"Where am I headed?" she asked.

"Oh," replied Barney. "Coordinates are loaded in the nav."

"So you made contact?" asked Jacquie.

Barney looked embarrassed, "Um... mostly."

"Mostly?" queried Jacquie. "What does that mean?"

Luli found the location and mapped out a path, "Dark side, huh? I guess it'll aid in our clandestine arrival."

She cut the engines and the Matilda dropped like a stone. A quick burst on the starboard side attitude jets sent the ship into a slow spiral. Warning lights lit up the bridge in a scarlet glow.

"Aren't we falling a little too fast?" growled Anton.

Luli only laughed at his discomfort, "By the Major, I love this old boat!"

She felt the shudder of the ship's stubby wings extending to their full length. The main engines kicked on and the whole ship jerked hard. A heavy barge sailed past setting off proximity alarms as the Matilda slipped into an empty pocket in a shipping lane. Luli pulled back on the throttle and settled the ship into drafting range on the nearest cargo scow.

"I've got us locked into their trajectory. We should get there by morning, local." Luli whistled as she pulled the visor free from her eyes, "I don't know who made this old bird, but every day I get to fly her like this, is a day to be cherished."

***

"There it is," Barney pointed through the bow

port. "Do you see the sign, Lu?"

"I see it. Are they ready to receive us?"

Barney was quiet for a moment. "Park her in the back somewhere. I'll announce us then."

Luli smirked, "Playing it close to the chest, eh?"

"Last I heard, we're wanted criminals. No need to give them time to whet their greed."

"I spent enough time in a cell to last me a lifetime," griped Jacquie.

"What are you talking about Jacq? You did like what, two weeks in a cell?" Anton scoffed. "Try three years!"

"Do you want to go back?" asked Derain. "Cause it sounds like you want to go back." An evil smile lit his face, "I can help you with that."

"Setting down, now," interrupted Luli.

The Matilda settled into an open spot amongst lines of broken ships, ground vehicles, and other large mechanical detritus. Barney turned off the cloaking and the freighter materialized amongst the remains.

"Let's hope she blends in," Jacquie intoned. "We don't want trouble. We're only here to find Galena, then get off this mud ball as soon as possible."

Anton patted his father's pistol, "Considering the greetings we've gotten in the past couple of years, I'll keep Henon within easy grasp."

The crew completed the shutdown procedures. As the last system light stuttered into darkness, Derain opened the cargo bay doors just wide enough for Anton's Folly to exit. The scent of rust, dirty oil, and dried leaves fluttered into the hold. Early morning light followed and dimly lit the interior. Derain put on his game face as he strapped on his sidearm and stepped out of the ship.

A gruff voice shouted, "Hey! Who are you and what are you doing in my yard?"

Anton grinned, "Sounds like trouble..."

Jacquie grimaced, "Luli, you hang back and keep them out. Got it?" At the pilot's nod, Jacquie patted the Matilda's bulkhead and whispered, "I just got you put back together; no one is taking you away from me."

As she walked out into the junkyard, her boots crunched against the dead leaves and pebbles strewn in the roadway between the stripped wrecks. Jacquie stepped between Derain and Anton who had their weapons out, but pointed down. In front of them stood a short man without a hair on his head. Dirt lined the creases of his face. Behind him stood one of the tallest women Jacquie had ever seen. She literally towered over the small man, and her extreme height made Derain look average.

"Good news, Captain,' Anton said as he pointed toward their ship. "The Matilda fits right in. She blends..."

Jacquie glanced over her shoulder and it was true. The Matilda looked like a rusted hulk held together with spit and solder. Gouges ran the length of her. Burns from recent attacks left blackened craters that chipped away at the greenish paint that had once covered the ship.

"I'm not asking again!" shouted the man standing in front of them. "Who are you and what are doing parked in my yard?"

Derain leaned in and whispered to Jacquie, "There are at least three more out there that I can see. One's got to be a sniper."

Barney confidently swaggered out through the cargo bay doors and hailed the group, "Helloo! Where's Dusty?"

"Who wants to know?" hollered the tall woman.

"Barnabus de Lagnel, at your service," he said with a flourish.

The woman chuckled loudly, "This Titan says he's Barney, can you believe that, Batu?"

"About as much as you do, Zolzaya," the shorter man replied.

Barney strutted up to the fellow who stood a head taller than him, "I am Barnabus de Lagnel and you can run along and tell Dusty that yourself."

"I'll frisk him. The rest of you stay put," answered Batu.

Barney patiently waited while he was patted down. Once Batu was done, he motioned to Barney, "Follow me. Zolzaya keep these others in check."

As Barney followed Batu, he heard Derain remark, "There's something familiar about this place. What's the name again?"

"Machado's Salvage," answered Zolzaya.

Jon Gray Lang

"You got a problem with that?"

Batu rounded the bend and headed for a beat-up shack assembled from old hull plating. Barney kept to his leisurely pace and studied the structure. "This place looks the same as I remember, maybe a little rustier. By the ancestors, that would have been four Captains back."

Batu disappeared into the slap-sided garage. Barney followed him inside. The place was a mess. Empty fuel canisters, spare parts, and dirty rags littered every available surface. An ancient sign made with trapped gasses and electricity blinked the name MACHADO on the back wall in crimson flashes.

"We going to the back room?" asked Barney.

"Not yet. Stand still."

A scanner played across his body and beeped when it hit the wrist gun.

"Hold on," Barney said as he undid the latch and set the weapon on the nearest table. The scanner played across him again and came back clean.

Batu pulled out a smaller gadget and held it next to Barney's face. There was a ding and Batu stared at him and the 2D image on the device. His eyes tracked every detail on the image before he sighed. "We have a match." He glanced into Barney's eyes, "So, you're him, huh? For some reason, I expected more."

Barney growled, "Nice to meet you, too. Now, where is Dusty?"

Jon Gray Lang

Batu headed toward a door hidden behind a large chunk of insulation and motioned Barney to follow. As the two of them passed through, the scenery changed dramatically. The inside was pristine. All of the lighting worked and it smelled clean. It was a short walk to the lift at the end of the hall. Batu hit a button and the doors parted.

As they went down, Barney started to speak, but Batu raised a finger to his lips. They rode in silence until the doors opened. Another bright hallway beckoned. There were more people down here than there had been in the junk yard and each one carried a sense of purpose in their stride. Batu ignored them and led Barney into a small room on the right. The room was empty except for a desk, a terminal, and a few chairs. Batu indicated one and moved behind the desk.

As Batu sat down, he asked, "Can you vouch for your people?"

"I can and I do," said Barney.

Batu nodded as he spoke into a short-range comm and then set it aside. "Zolzaya will bring them in, but what I tell you can't leave this room."

Barney replied, "Oh? What's old Dusty up to, now?"

"Have you come across a Titan retrieval team?"

"I've come across one."

Batu tapped out an agitated pattern on the desktop with his index finger. "We had a run-in with some of them. Word got out that Dusty had been hiring crews to smuggle androgynes off Titan. They grabbed him off the street and have him imprisoned somewhere. We know they have our yard under surveillance, so we try to talk as little of his business out in the open as possible."

"Do you have any idea where they have him?"

Batu shook his head, "Not anywhere accessible by the likes of us. There are rumors circling of making an example of him at the next cyborg gladiator fights. Those rumors came all the way from Titan by the way."

"An execution, then."

"More like an opportunity," declared Batu. "Security is difficult in a huge place like that. We can get in, find him and get out."

"You think there's a chance?"

Batu's fist pounded the desktop, "It's the only chance I have. I can't let my..."

"...your father down. I understand."

"Is it my Titan height that gave it away?"

Barney smiled, but there was sadness there, "You favor your mother. She was a wonderful woman."

Batu's throat grew tight, "As long dead as she is, I forget that you would've met her."

"She was a sight to behold," murmured Barney. "Unfortunately, we're here to rescue another friend of mine. Let's make it two, shall we?"

***

Jon Gray Lang

Derain snapped his fingers, "I've got it! My great grandfather used to work for the Machado's. He spoke fondly of the family in all of his stories. Once they had him make an odd delivery run to..."

"Quiet you," mouthed Zolzaya. "You're on Jard. You're never alone here."

"Someone's always listening," finished Jacquie as they walked to the Matilda.

Zolzaya held a hand up to the side of her head and signaled with a series of gestures that was answered by rustling sounds up ahead. "Would you like refreshments while we discuss what the yard can find for you? Spare parts, old connectors, and the like?"

Jacquie nodded and peered into the Matilda's cargo bay, "Come on out and lock the door, Lu. We're getting a beverage!"

As Derain followed the woman and Anton, he heard a high-pitched whine and noticed a very low flying sky-eye. It whizzed overhead and disappeared behind a stand of trees. Having fallen behind the group, To catch up, Derain picked up his pace and they all walked through the door of a small shack together.

Inside the untidy shack Zolzaya led her guests into a side room where a surge machine dominated a small table. Jacquie sat in the only arm chair and Luli stood behind her, intently watching Zolzaya.

As the door shut behind the tall woman, she said, "The Titan has vouched for all of you, so you are welcome here. But people usually only come here if they are searching for something. So, what are you looking for?"

Anton shuffled past her and set cups down on the table. He handed one to Luli and let the others pick up their own. "We're looking for a friend of ours. Or the woman who took her."

"She's special," finished Jacquie. "You might've heard of her: Galena Chadov?"

"The Lieutenant? The leader of the Servant's Uprising?" asked Zolzaya in shock.

Anton grinned as he took a sip, "That's her. The one, the only!"

"She's also known as the Butcher of Timmony Bay," added Derain.

"As you can see, our friend is well known," said Luli, "but we think she is being kept under wraps."

Zolzaya contemplated, "Under wraps? The best place to keep a genorg hidden would be the auctions. It's an ugly place, though. Especially with the uprising."

"It's a start," Jacquie said as she crumpled the empty cup in her hand. "Where and when is the next one?"

twenty-two

Come

From the outskirts of the rural district a tiny robotic craft hovered its way toward the glowing skyline of a huge city. The drone radiated with an inner rosy light and a crest at its base declared its identity in stylized periwinkle blue lettering: Council Courier - House of Khanda.

The little craft ascended rapidly as it approached a tall thin tower that dominated the cityscape. It streaked toward a small opening near the very top and entered a hangar filled with more sky-eyes like it. It found its landing spot, backed into its port, and began to download its findings.

***

Inside the suite of the top of the tower, a strange tableau was in progress. The ruling twins of the House of Khanda had prostrated themselves before a sphere in the center of a round chamber. Oily colors flowed across the mid-sized orb and small fungal plants grew around the object that resembled a jump engine.

At the base of the sphere, a woman and a man in Family Senai colors were bound to the floor. Their mouths were held open with a series of cruel wires that cut into their cheeks. Above them, a shadowy form bled darkness into their mouths against their protests. As their struggles ceased, a wicked chuckle filled the chamber and the shadow being grew translucent until it faded away.

Nigel and three other men rushed forward to cut the bonds and drag the two comatose forms out of the room.

"Thank you for your sustenance and your future efforts in the growth of the House of Khanda. We look forward to seeing you as one of us in the months to come," murmured the Lord and Lady of Khanda.

Their neosilk robes barely covered their naked bodies underneath. As they raised their arms upward, the lengths of cloth slid down, revealing glyphs etched into the flesh of their arms. These matched the strange dark sigils on the ceiling above and the floor below. The symbols flowed into a series of lines that crossed back and forth over each other. Each one smoldered with an inner light.

At first, the Khanda Twins remained alone in the chamber. But whispers soon slithered in from

Jon Gray Lang

the darkened corners. Murky shadows fluttered along the walls and circled the twins, reaching out to them.

When the Lady of Khanda finally spoke, her voice held an odd cadence, "We've been completely cut off from the outer systems. And the Servant's Uprising continues!"

Her brother added, "We lose more of the mid systems every day. Yet you do not heed our prayers, Lord. You offer no assistance!"

Lady Rana glared at the shadow that slowly materialized into a creature made of nothing but eyes and legs, "Answer me, oh Lord and Master. How can we defeat those that want everything from us, when you give us nothing in return?"

A soft abrasive sound grew into a strident roar as the creature rubbed its legs together. Within the cacophony, a voice arose, "Have my gifts not lifted you to your heights? Do you not stand above all others? And what of our bargain? Has the route home been acquired?"

"Home..." growled Lord Jai. "'Tis nothing but an idea..."

"We had the deep spacer Jarl under our thumb..." interrupted Lady Rana. "He had all but two sections of the route back to our ancestral world... The 'home' that you dream of..."

"But he is no more," hissed Lord Jai, "Lost to us through the actions of the Harbinger."

A hush sounded from the shadows that cooled the twins' anger. The voices rose, desire

Jon Gray Lang

apparent in their throats, "It comes... She comes... The angel has arrived."

"She's on Jard?" wondered the Lord of Khanda. "How?"

"Where?" asked Lady Rana. "Where is the Harbinger?"

"Close... close... close..." reverberated about the chamber. "The time of change is close..."

"Why would the Harbinger be here?" wondered Lord Jai. "Are we whom she seeks?"

The shadow creature rubbed its legs together with a hum of satisfaction, "Do not fear, children of mine. The destruction of your enemies is imminent as they will come to you. The cost for your efforts is only blood and time."

The shadows repeated the Master's words echoing the phrase 'blood" and 'time' incessantly before they faded away.

"Of course, our tsotsi enemies will come to us," cursed Lord Jai. "With the speed of their onslaught, this will be the only system left for them to conquer."

"Call for us and we will come," answered the walls as the air grew thick and moist.

Suddenly, there was a knock at the door and the shadows slithered back into the darkness. Their manservant entered and waited patiently until he was allowed to speak.

"Yes, Nigel. What is it?"

"Lord of House Khanda, my apologies. One of our patrol sky-eyes discovered the deep spacer

Luli Qing nearby."

"The angel seeks for the enemy..." rippled from the walls.

Lady Rana pondered, "What enemy does she seek here?"

"Of course!" proclaimed Lord Jai triumphantly. "She searches for the genorg Lieutenant!"

twenty-three

Dark Was the Night, Cold Was the Ground

Inside the Matilda, Jacquie crossed her arms as she rode the lift down from the bridge flanked by Derain and Luli. "I left Anton on the bottom deck to keep an eye on their guests. Even with Barney's vouch, I'm not sure I trust these scrappers."

"Come on Jacquie, my great grandfather said the Machado's never crossed anyone," coaxed the bounty hunter.

Jacquie sneered, "Those are just stories, Derain. The people your ancestor knew are long dead. I can't afford to trust in stories."

"None of us can," added Luli as the lift doors parted.

Jacquie stepped out and saw Zolzaya and

Jon Gray Lang

Barney deep in conversation in the cargo bay, but Batu was engrossed in admiring the attributes of the Rabbit's Folly.

Hoots and whistles resounded from the med bay as Anton backed out, "Yeah, yeah. I know you don't want her on board, but the rest of us do!"

Even the grind of Doc's chassis sounded angry as it rumbled away and blared a defiant tone.

Anton flicked a thumb over his shoulder, "Doc is madder than usual, Jacq. What did the Lieutenant do to him to have him so riled up?"

Jacquie ignored him as she made a bee-line for Batu. "The Folly's not for sale, if that's what you're wondering."

"Just admiring the vehicle, Captain." He glanced over at Zolzaya and she cut her conversation with Barney short. Batu continued, "Been a while since I've seen an armored survey vehicle. A long while. Did you pick this up on one of the newer colonies?"

"Mining operation, if memory serves. Is the auction far from here?"

"Not far," he replied. "Crowded, but not far. Shall we go?"

Jacquie nodded as she swung into the driver's seat of the Folly. Luli hopped into the passenger seat while the rest of the crew settled into the back seats. Batu and Zolzaya walked out of the cargo bay and straddled a pair of mismatched slick-riders. Their cycles lifted up onto their cushions of air and slipped forward as the Folly trundled out of the cargo bay.

"Expensive," whistled Anton.

The single-seat hoverbikes were a rare luxury in rural areas. However, the slick-riders were absolutely essential to navigate through the traffic of big cities on the prime worlds.

Luckily, Batu and Zolzaya were going slow, so it was easy to keep up with them. Jacquie glanced over at Luli who stared in rapture at the trees that lined the main traffic artery. Eventually, the trees gave way to low business buildings that seemed to grow with each passing block.

Batu signaled to the right. He and Zolzaya leaned into the turn and briefly disappeared from view. Jacquie eased the Rabbit's Folly around the corner, then accelerated to catch up with the two riders. The buildings along this route were dingy and shabby. Humans with little left to them gathered in the alleys and on street corners. Smoke from their cook fires blended with the scent of decaying structures.

Warehouses soon replaced the ramshackle buildings and the stink of industry permeated the air filters of the Folly. Local planetary mercs acting as police sat in their armored vehicles at the intersections as runners, slick-riders and other vehicles crowded the roads.

Large digi-signs proclaimed that the 'Last Great Genorg Auction' was taking place today. Speakers played loudly as they neared their destination. "... All sales are final. Welcome to the auction! With the factories closing for the citizen's protection, these will be the last genorgs available for many a year to come! So, come one, come all to the event of the century! Verify your purchase before pick up. All sales are final. Welcome..."

Citizens of the Consortium lined the streets. They jostled with protesters whose signs declared that all drones should be executed for the actions of Lieutenant Galena Chadov, Butcher of Timmony Bay. Their speeches combined with similar messages from other groups. Most of the arrivals ignored them and headed toward the auction tents, carefully avoiding an ash mountain in the middle of an open lot.

"Are those?" began Luli.

Jacquie looked at the mountain of ash and could see blackened bones sticking out of it. Charred humanoid forms intermingled with others, but there was a sameness to all of them. Each one was female. A partially burnt corpse caught her eye and the telltale gray skin confirmed it was a genorg. Some looked quite young, maybe only twelve, sold for their first assignment. Others appeared to be much older.

Anton looked ill as he blurted, "Miserable bastards." He looked up into the sky and mouthed a prayer, "Henon, if you can hear me, please wash this sickness away. They've suffered enough."

Derain's eyes blazed, "This is barbaric! What gives them the right to do this to people?"

"You didn't believe drones were people, not

so long ago," growled Anton. "The perpetrators of this heinous action obviously believe the same."

"I wouldn't do that..."

Barney regarded the bounty hunter, "You sure? We've left so many bodies in our wake. We're all capable of it."

"That doesn't make it right!" whimpered Luli as she cried into Anton's shoulder.

Jacquie felt sick to her stomach, "No, it doesn't make it right. Let's go find Galena and get off this tainted corpse of a planet."

***

As Anton and the crew made their way through the crowds, the stench of fear, anger, and despair intermingled with the rot of the mildewed hay that covered the floor. The lighting was dim for the whole interior, except for the bright floods far in the back and off to the left.

"There they are," said Jacquie as they caught up with Batu and Zolzaya.

"You'll find the pens in the back and the auction stage over on the left," said Batu. "If you'll excuse us, we have other business to attend to. We'll meet back at the yard."

"This place gives me nightmares," Zolzaya whispered as she nudged Luli.

"Let's get this over with," muttered Derain as he headed to the first cage. Anton sighed as he moved to follow the bounty hunter and the others fell in behind.

The first cage contained very young genorgs who were all huddled in the corner as far away from the light as possible. The hawker stood just to the right of the cage and eyed the crew of the Matilda avidly.

"If you're looking for long-term physical labor, have I got the deal for you!" he barked. "Each one of these drones is fresh out of the training creche and ready to put to work! Not a day of work etched into their bones. No old beaters in there, no siree!" He leaned in, "With the current market as crazy as it is, I can sell you the whole lot for next to nothing."

Derain glowered at the man, "Not interested." He moved to the next cage.

"And you can support this endeavor without feeling a thing?" Barney rebuked the salesman. "Degenerates, the whole lot of our species, nothing but vicious degenerates."

Luli leveled a hard glare devoid of any sympathy for the man or his career choices as she stomped past.

He shouted as they kept going, "You won't find a better deal!"

The next few pens were no different except that the genorgs had been grouped by age and work history. Derain walked past each corral in despair. The more he saw, the more his shoulders slumped. Barney only grew angrier with each step. Luli had already hung back and found a stall selling alcoholic beverages on the cheap.

"We're getting nowhere, fast!" groaned Jacquie.

"We just have to wait for the auctions," mentioned Anton. "We'll see them all then."

Barney grumbled as he joined them, "I don't think I can stay another minute in this place. Not one more." He exited the tent structure with fury in his every step.

Derain strode up and his eyes were dark. "I didn't see her, but they told me there are more cages in the back. I can't look anymore. I... I didn't know it was like this."

"I know what I'm talking about. We just have to wait for the auctions," Anton stated with exasperation. "The back cages will be released first."

Jacquie did a double take, "You've done this before?"

Anton shook her off, "My father worked as a cage crier a few times to get the scratch together to get off planet. An ugly business, but the Consortium approves it as legal."

Jacquie stared at him in disgust.

Anton scoffed, "Don't judge me, Captain. You wanted to sell Galena off as soon as you met her. You all go outside, I'll keep looking for her. And you wonder why I ran off to join a revolution..."

Anton turned his back on his friends and headed up toward the front. He didn't notice Luli leaving the tent as the rest of the crew gathered in the back. But it didn't matter. He sauntered up to the front and asked the woman standing there, "Hey, is Vegas working this circuit? I'm looking for some quick mazuma."

"And who the fuck are you?"

Anton leaned against the stage and cinched his jacket open revealing Henon, "Just tell him Roane is here to see him."

The woman cursed, then disappeared behind a curtain while Anton stayed where he was. It was only a couple minutes until an older gentleman slipped past the curtain and glanced at Rabbit. His eyebrow quirked up as his footsteps slowed.

"That you, Kari? Thought you was dead."

Anton tugged on his jacket and bowed slightly, "No Vegas, I am not, but you know me."

The older man tilted his head, "Rabbit... that you?"

Anton bowed deeper, "The one and the same. Tell me, you got any quick work left?"

Vegas shook his head, "As much as I'd like to help you, boy, I've got nothin'. That crazy Butcher of Timmony Bay is making a hash of us what is living on them. Can't see us having much work after this auction."

Anton sighed loudly, "Work is just hard to come by these days." He glanced at the auctioneer and gave him a wink, "I do have a client, though. They're looking for a genorg with a shock of the ole white streaking through. For a finder's cut, do you have one like that back there?"

Jon Gray Lang

"I don't son, I don't."

Anton dipped his head and threw out his hand, "If'n you hear a word, throw it my way."

***

The voice of the auctioneer droned away in the background as the next batch of genorgs were brought to the stage.

Luli threw back the latest drink she had purchased and leaned into Jacquie, "Can we leave? This place and these people are making me sick."

Jacquie took a long swallow from her cup, "Not yet. This is our best chance of finding her."

"Not that we could afford her," grumbled Derain dejectedly. "Listen to those prices."

"I'm up for some thuggery," growled Barney. "Knocking some heads together and liberating some of Galena's sisters sounds like a good plan."

Anton slid between the people in front of the crew and shook his head. "She's not here."

Jacquie crumpled the cup in her hand, "Damn it. How can you be sure?"

"I know some of the people working the auction," he replied. "She's not back there."

"So, we've got nothing," Luli trashed the cup in her hand and turned to leave. But as she stepped forward, she collided with an imposing bald man. She looked up and sucked in a breath when she got a good look at him. Tall, cadaverous, and not a single hair on his pate. His gray eyes sunk deep into his face and nothing in his demeanor invited a conversation. She backed up as Jacquie and Anton appeared at her sides. "Oh! Pardon me. I didn't see you there."

The tall man bowed deeply and she noticed the scarring that encircled his skull. As he stood up to his full height, she saw another scar that traced its way down his face and through his right eye. His lips split into a ghastly smile, "No apologies needed. You wouldn't happen to be Luli Qing, the famed deep space pilot? My benefactors have a request to make of her."

Luli slipped into her performer persona and bowed in return. "I am Luli Qing. Who might you be?"

"My name is Nigel and my benefactors request your presence for a private concert. They would prefer your performance to be sooner than later so mazuma would not be an issue."

Luli's finger tapped against her lip, "I am needing information more than mazuma at the moment. Who are you representing?"

Nigel's odd smile appeared again. "The Lord and Lady of the House of Khanda. As to your payment, as Council leaders, they have access to all of the information that can be found on planet. Pray tell, what information would you require to perform?"

Luli's eyes widened at the names, *'What is the luck? The exact people we're looking for! Praise be to you, Major Tom, praise be!'*

Luli tilted her head back and mimed deep thoughts. Suddenly, she snapped her fingers and exclaimed, "Have you heard of a Dr. Wyeth? She has something that doesn't belong to her and we mean to get her back."

Nigel perked up, "Dr. Wyeth? Oh yes, the Lord and Lady would definitely be able to provide you with any details you need concerning her."

"If you have some information on the infamous Doctor, I could play as early as tonight."

"That would be perfectly splendid." Nigel whipped out a small business card and placed it into the cyborg's hand. "The address is on this card. Will you come at eight thirty?"

Luli grinned in satisfaction. She had found access to a lead on Galena and it would only cost her a show. "Eight-thirty sounds fantastic."

"And they say I have the Devil's luck," crowed Anton. "A connection to the Khanda's just walks up and asks for a show?"

Luli mockingly bowed as the grin on her face grew, "Sometimes it hurts to be this amazing, but not today."

Jacquie just shook her head in wonder.

Anton patted the knife in his boot tops as he shared a look with the Captain, "By the way, you aren't getting out of my sight again, Lu."

"Nor mine," added Jacquie.

***

Barney looked on glumly as the creepy man engaged Luli in conversation. "Well, that fellow's certainly a bit off-putting," he mused.

The Titan's attention was diverted, though when he noticed Zolzaya and Batu returning and waved at him. Assured that Luli was safe with the crew, Barney nodded at Derain and walked over to where the scrappers waited.

Zolzaya motioned Barney out past the tent entrance and into the sun. The smell of a dead fire lingered in the air and the stink of its victims burned the nostrils. The wind blew a thin layer of ash onto his arms and vest. Barney shuddered and kept his eyes averted from the pile of corpses.

Zolzaya leaned toward Barney and whispered, "Dusty was spotted at the arena. His execution is planned for tonight and will be tight beamed to the Titan home world through the local jump gates. Breaking him out is going to be tough."

Batu leaned in, "We could use your aid. Do you think you can help?"

Derain strolled over, "Barney, what's going on?"

Batu glanced at the bounty hunter and stepped back.

"You can trust him in this," said Barney. "He's the great-grandson of Derain Tiwi."

"So you say."

"I am, little man," hissed Derain.

"Cut it out, you two," Zolzaya chided. "We don't have time for this."

Barney confided to Derain, "The Consortium is planning to execute Dusty tonight in the arena. We're going to break him out. You in?"

Derain grinned maliciously, "After everything I've seen today, my great grandfather would not let me refuse."

Barney relaxed a bit and nodded, "I'll let the Captain know."

twenty-four

Beware

Hamza Fitzpatrick was alone in the room he shared with Corporal Cook who was busy guarding the prize genorg. Just thinking of her, set his skin crawling. "Demon thing," he intoned under his breath.

Fitzpatrick tapped at Dr. Saric's stolen data pad and sighed. He had been at it for hours and still hadn't broken the code. "Nothing for it, I'll have to go through his office again.

As he stood, he stretched his body to its full height. Pops and clicks ran up and down his back. He slipped the data pad into his side pocket, closed the shirt tab around his neck and flipped his uniform cap onto his head.

The door snapped shut behind him as he stepped into the hall. The lighting was set to low as the base tried to keep everyone on the twenty-five-hour schedule of Jard. There was no one in the hallway, but it was oddly quiet. He murmured, "As if a blanket muffles the very air..." An involuntary shiver of fear coursed down his back. As he shook off the feeling, he gritted his teeth and headed toward the lift.

The lower levels were equally as empty of staff. The only exception was the bottom floor with the encased sphere. There he saw a number of scientists busily leading genorgs both young and old into the enclosure. With each one sent inside a scream rent the air. The more he watched, the more the scene disturbed him. "Maybe I'm still human after all," he shuddered.

From the floors above, the enclosure resembled a giant's maw. Words came unbidden to his lips, "And the line of genorgs in their white habits are nothing more than sacrificial sheep for ritual slaughter." He shook his head to dismiss the image from his mind, "But why? What monster is Wyeth feeding? What does she hope to gain?"

In truth, he wasn't sure he wanted to know the answer. His hands slipped free of the railing as he stepped back, "No matter. Dr. Saric must've known what she's up to and I'm sure the twins would pay handsomely for that information."

The security tape still hung loosely over Dr. Saric's office, but it parted with ease as the door swung open. The Ensign shut it quietly and reached for the light control. The sensation of hot breath brushed against his neck. He slapped at the control and spun around, "Who's there? Show yourself!"

The room was empty. His eyes roved the corners looking for anything out of place. The thick dust on the floor and desk looked the same as when he had brought Jerr in here. Hamza moved closer to the desk, but he was alone. "Just spooking myself," he grumbled to himself in chagrin as he closed his eyes. Weirdly, the sigils inscribed on the walls and the floor seemed to glow faintly through his eyelids.

He quickly opened his eyes and glanced at the marks on the walls, but there was no glow. The writing was thick and dark and obviously applied by hand. When he reached up and scratched at the script, the substance flaked off. He rubbed a flake between his fingers and it crumbled into a cloud of rusty red dust. He sniffed the dust and the scent reminded him of old blood. In disgust, he quickly wiped his fingers on his pant leg.

"Never mind the dead man's sense of decor. Look for a password to this device," he muttered as he pulled the data pad from his pocket and dropped it on the desktop. As it bounced against the surface, the screen opened and files of data appeared in a holo-column.

"Well..." he conceded, "that's not what I was expecting."

He attempted to access the first file and it opened into a holo-vid before his eyes. The ugly man that appeared looked like a happier and much younger version of the ID for the headless corpse the M33 had discovered on that airless moon a few

Jon Gray Lang

years back.

The image gesticulated as its lips moved, but the audio was muted. Fitzpatrick adjusted the volume control until it became audible.

"... and that is when the Wyeth family let me examine the sphere. Long before we built the containment field." The excitement on Dr. Saric's face was obvious. "The energies it was emitting didn't show up on any scans, but you could feel it. It was like insects walking on your skin or... or that feeling you get when someone you didn't see walks up behind you."

The image changed to the sphere sitting freely on the surface of the moon with Dr. Saric in a spacesuit taking measurements of it. Charts appeared in the upper left corner that scrolled through different frequencies and power readings. One frequency caught Fitzpatrick's eye. It was a low band channel with a short range. It randomly spiked every time Saric's body grew closer to the sphere.

Fitzpatrick sped through the footage until it stopped. The next file opened automatically and this time the sphere was inside the lowest floor on the base. It was still out in the open. Dr. Saric walked into frame and pulled up a chart.

"We are finally able to track the power signature of the sphere. We now have Consortium vessels searching the known systems to see if more of these objects exist. This can't be the only one out there. There must be more."

In the background, a little girl chased an odd

little boy and disappeared. Fitzpatrick zoomed in as a woman who resembled Dr. Wyeth scooped up the little girl, "Judith, what did I tell you about coming down here? And with Subject L-7 in tow?"

The little girl sighed and dropped her head, "I'm not supposed to come down here and neither is he. But I was only chasing him! He said he could hear the singing and wanted to see where it came from. It's all his fault!"

Her pudgy fingers pointed at the boy who stared at the sphere in dumbfounded fascination. The skin of the sphere responded by forming ripples wherever the boy glanced. Slowly, he took a step forward and the ripples grew larger. Another step forward and the boy's finger touched the surface.

Dr. Saric turned around and yelled, "L, get away from that!"

The boy looked over his shoulder and stared at the Doctor in confusion. Suddenly, his fingertip brushed against one of the ripples as it traveled outward. The surface of the sphere shivered and enveloped Subject L's hand. The little girl watched in horrid fascination as the boy was pulled through the skin of the sphere. His eyes opened wide and he squealed in terror. The sphere pulled hungrily at his body and encased his arm as it dragged him closer.

Judith howled in fear, "Mommy! It's eating him! It's eating Leon! Save him! Please save him. I promise I won't come down here ever again. I promise!"

Jon Gray Lang

Instead, the woman stepped back and placed her hand over the little girl's eyes. Dr. Saric grabbed his data pad and ran it through multiple scans. The sphere pulled the boy inside of it. Once the rippling surface closed around him, the orb shivered again. As the sound of a gong chimed, a dark swirl of red burst across the surface of the sphere. Judith sobbed into her mother's shoulder as Dr. Saric whistled at the readings emanating from the sphere, "Incredible! Just incredible. So much power, but what is it for? What is its purpose?" He leaned in and pointed to a fine dark powder that had settled on the floor next to the orb. "What is this?"

The holo-vid feed cut out and was replaced by a floating image of three files. Fitzpatrick chose the middle one and leaned in close.

The new holo-vid showed an older Dr. Saric standing front and center. The sphere glowed eerily behind him and the spitting image of the little boy stood beside him. Fitzpatrick couldn't hear what was said as Dr. Saric led the boy to the sphere and gave him a push. The boy toppled against the sphere and it pulled him inside before he could issue a cry. The excited grin on Dr. Saric's face as he scrutinized the scans showed that the sacrifice of the boy had led to favorable results.

Fitzpatrick murmured in shock, "Not sure who the boy is, but he's obviously important to the experiments run by the base. What they are learning though, I haven't a clue."

He opened the next file and scanned through

the footage rapidly. More and more versions of the same boy were forced into the sphere. The orb seemed to grow steadily larger over time. A teenage version of Judith Wyeth showed up in the next few vids. With her own data pad, she took readings as Dr. Saric looked on. In the background, Fitzpatrick could see the two people he assumed were her parents. Near them stood more clones of the boy. They appeared to be drugged as they were docilely led into the sphere.

All of a sudden, the gang of duplicated boys stopped and turned on the two parents. They said something in unison as they grabbed hold of the adults. Some of the boys pulled on their arms as others knocked the adults to their knees. The woman and man tried to fight them off, but there were too many of them. Their shouts and protests were loud, but they didn't drown out the hum of a mantra the children stoically repeated.

Fitzpatrick increased the volume in an effort to understand what the boys were chanting. Judith Wyeth appeared in the background of the holo-vid begging for someone to save her parents as the little boys clubbed the adults into submission and dragged them closer to the orb. The sphere glowed brighter when the adults were pushed into it. Judith's cries of anguish rang in the chamber as the boys chanted louder, "Home... Home... Find the way home. Find the way home.... Home.... Home..."

All of the boys followed the adults into the sphere and disappeared. But the horror continued

Jon Gray Lang

as tentacles extended from the orb reaching out to attack Judith and Dr. Saric. The creature emerged from the sphere and only made it a few meters before it suddenly stopped. It shook uncontrollably for a moment, then the tentacles melted into a black liquid that splattered all over the floor. The creature struggled to get back to the sphere, but the entire thing melted away only leaving a fine crystallized dust behind. Once it was completely gone, the orb grew dark and the only sound remaining on the holo-vid was the mewling of the teenage Judith.

Fitzpatrick turned the audio off and his ragged breathing echoed in the room. "What was that thing? What did they mean by find the way home?"

A series of sigils on the walls glowed a sickly green and pulsed in sync with his voice. The prickly sensation of something standing behind him made him look over his shoulder. An amorphous shape detached from the dark and crept toward him. He backpedaled and tripped over the leg of the desk chair. As he fell, his head slammed into a file cabinet and his vision grew dark.

The last thing he heard was, "Yesss... You... You will find the way... Find the way home...."

***

Hours later, Fitzpatrick awoke in the darkened office. His lips were cracked from a lack of moisture and a thin layer of dust coated his skin.

He sat up and felt the lump the impact had made on the back of his head. His hair was matted in crusted blood. As he felt along his scalp, an ache throbbed in his fingertip. He glanced at his hand and noticed a cut that ran from nail to knuckle on his middle finger. His eyes were drawn to the floor and a new sigil was written there in a rusty brown color.

"Is that my blood? Who did this?"

A disembodied voice sounded in his head, "You did. You will find the way, but to do so you must search for it."

He slowly lifted himself from the floor and plopped back down into the desk chair. The holo-vid he had been watching hung frozen in the air. His voice, unbidden by him, spoke out loud, "Open next file."

The holo-vid disappeared to be replaced by another. In this one, Dr. Saric looked much older and more worn. Standing by his side was an adult Dr. Wyeth and at her side was another copy of the young boy.

"How many of those boys are there? What are they for?" Fitzpatrick grimaced.

Dr. Wyeth knelt down next to the boy and put a hand on his shoulder. She spoke softly into his ear and he nodded in understanding. He moved closer to the dark orb and placed his hand against the surface. Nothing happened. He brought both hands up and pressed against it with no change.

The holo-vid stopped and the next file opened. In this one, the boy looked older and intelligence twinkled in the depths of his eyes. Another of his younger versions stood off to the side. The younger one was led to the orb and again nothing happened as he touched it. The same held true as the older one repeated the gesture. Dr. Wyeth placed a syringe containing a blue liquid to the older one's neck and depressed the plunger. As the chamber emptied, the older one touched his hand to the orb, but his eyes rolled back into his head and he collapsed. The younger one slumped to the floor seconds later. A comm started chattering loudly in the background, "There has been a full collapse of the Leon's in creche three. Creche four has the same response... Creche five has lost life readings on many of the Subject L's. Others have entered a catatonic state."

Dr. Wyeth dragged the older Leon to the sphere and pressed him against it. Slowly, his hand disappeared into it briefly, then was thrown out violently. "Damn it! Another fail!" she cursed as she slammed her fist against the orb. "Where are my parents, monster? Where?"

The sphere rippled in time with her shouts and began to glow with an inner light. She struck it again and she shrieked in a panic as a stick-like appendage grasped her wrist.

She tried pulling away as a voice spoke through the lips of the older Leon, "Judith... Judith... You have opened the door..."

And the sentence continued from the younger Leon, "... and a door opens both ways..."

Jon Gray Lang

Dr. Saric ran over and yanked hard on Dr. Wyeth. Her wrist slipped free and they both tumbled to the floor. The older Leon kept repeating his message until the boy sagged like an empty puppet and sprawled out on the floor.

Dr. Saric started laughing, "Progress! Finally progress!"

***

Hamza blinked his eyes; the room seemed brighter than he remembered. He looked around the office, "Are more of these symbols glowing now, or is it a trick of the light?"

He started to rise from his chair and realized how stiff he was. *'Like I've been sitting for days.'* He struggled to his feet and slowly stretched. As his body unkinked, he recoiled at the sight of an insectile shadow that filled the center of the office. A foreign presence pressed against his mind and he fell back into the chair. As hard as he fought to resist, he was compelled to pull up the next holo-vid. Shaking, he swiped at the next file and a new recording opened.

This one started in the middle of a scene that was absolute madness. Nightmarish creatures spewed out of the sphere. The only thing keeping them at bay was a small military force that fired indiscriminately into the morass. Above the entire fiasco, a large dome was slowly being lowered from the ceiling.

Jon Gray Lang

Fitzpatrick recognized it as the protective dome that currently surrounded the sphere on the base. As it was lowered, the creatures fought against it. They grabbed anyone who was within within reach and dragged them into the sphere. In a last-ditch effort, the line to the dome was released and it dropped in slow motion to the floor below. The chamber echoed with a dull clang. Work teams risking life and limb bolted it to the floor.

As soon as the sphere was contained, Dr. Wyeth stepped into the frame followed by Dr. Saric. "Lock it down and keep everyone away from it!" she ordered. "If there's one of these objects out there, there might be more," she snarled at Dr. Saric. "We need to find them and shut them down!"

"Should we alert the..."

She stopped him mid-sentence, "The Council can't hear a word of this. Do you understand me?"

"But they could be anywhere," he replied gesticulating to the sky.

Dr. Wyeth poked him in the chest, "Then figure it out quickly or you're fired. Do you hear me?"

***

The last holo-vid on the data pad started of its own volition. Dr. Saric was alone in his office and he looked unwell. Fitzpatrick could see the walls in the background covered in the sigils written in fresh blood. Stacked in the corner of the room

Jon Gray Lang

was a pile of corpses drained of their blood.

The Doctor's eyes looked unfocused as he addressed the recording. "The search has been difficult, but I finally found a lead in the Leporis system. I leave in the morning to locate another of the orbs."

Fitzpatrick felt elation in his heart. "This must have been what prompted the surprise attacks on Potune and Ninguiz!" Here was the bombshell that could destroy Dr. Wyeth and get him in good with the House of Khanda. He barely noticed as the holo-vid continued.

Dr. Saric chuckled and wiped at his eyes, "I wouldn't have been able to do it without the assistance of the Masters. It's all they want from us. To open the doors and then find the way home."

The sigils on the wall glowed brighter and more alien shades crawled out from the spaces between the lines. They slowly moved toward Fitzpatrick and he felt whatever was holding him there, release its mental grip.

He jumped to his feet and the blood rushed to his head. Dizziness hit hard, but it was nothing compared to the elemental fear that forced him to run to the office door. He reached for the handle and twisted with all his might as something grasped his shoulder.

"Let me go!" he shouted as the door opened. "You have no need of me!"

He ran out into the hall and yanked the door shut. He backed away and fell against the wall on the other side of the corridor. His feet slid out from under him and he slid to the floor. Harsh breathing wracked his chest as he waited for the shadowed monstrosities in the office to find him and drag him back into the room.

But the door stayed shut and nothing ventured out. Hamza gulped at the air anxiously and, with wild eyes, searched the hallway in both directions. There was no one else there except him. "Maybe I'm dreaming. Maybe none of this is real." He laughed in desperation until his breathing quieted.

"Maybe it's only a nightmare." He stood up and wandered down the hallway toward the nearest lift. "Maybe I need to find the way home."

Jon Gray Lang

twenty-five

El Mecánico

The ship-generated wormhole billowed around the nose of the Empress as it completed its journey into the Erebus system. Once the tail end of the old pleasure cruiser exited, the wormhole dissipated in a shower of sparks.

Mr. Leon entered the corridor to the hangar where Hau Hung waited for him with a packed case resting on the deck beside his feet. Mr. Leon disarmingly smiled and walked up to him.

He proffered his hand and waited for the man to take it, "I don't bite Mr. Hau."

Hung smiled tentatively, then fell into a bow, too deep for a subordinate.

Mr. Leon sighed as he tapped him on the shoulder, "Please Mr. Hau, stand up."

"My apologies, Mr. Leon. I am never sure if I am to be tossed out the airlock or rewarded for my efforts."

"Well then, today is your lucky day. I have need of you and your skills, and they would be better used off the war front than on."

Hung looked up in confusion, "Of course, Mr. Leon. What do you require?"

Mr. Leon resumed walking, stopped at a hatch further down the hallway, and beckoned to his adjutant. Hau Hung hurried to join him as Mr. Leon unlocked the hatch.

"The times ahead are precarious and while it's difficult to plan for every contention, my brothers and I are proud of the organization we have built and would be greatly saddened its loss."

Hung listened with uncertainty, "And what can I do for your organization?"

Mr. Leon reached out and took the man's hand. As he gave it a light squeeze, he said, "If my brothers and I are not meant to survive this, a plan had to be devised."

"If anyone is to survive, it will be you, sir."

Mr. Leon's laughter sounded as if it came from more than one throat, "Be that as it may, a successor has been chosen. We have trained her as best we could, but she lacks in some of the, shall we say, street details?"

Hung's face lit up and he swaggered a bit, "And that is where I come in."

"Yes, that's where you come in," replied Mr. Leon. "You have survived a long time out in the dark. You have a reputation for knowing who to make a deal with and who to swindle. I would like you to accept this last mission from me..."

"Unless you win..."

Mr. Leon wagged his finger, "Unless I or some of my brothers survive. Either way, I would feel better knowing that your capable hands were involved. Do you accept?"

The swagger increased as Hung asked, "Besides exempt from the fight, what would I get for my expertise?" At Mr. Leon's dark expression, he quailed, "Not that I am not honored at this opportunity, sir."

"It is good that you are on my side, Mr. Hau," said Mr. Leon. "As for what's in it for you? You would be number two in the entire operation. Only answerable to one other person."

Shock spread across the Hung's face, "What? The second in command? Are you fooling with me?" He looked around in fear, "Am I standing in front of an airlock?"

"Of sorts, but it only leads to the shuttle behind you. Which is also empty as I cannot afford the loss of one pilot."

Hung gulped, "Do you have the right person in mind, Mr. Leon? I am not exactly known for my trustworthiness."

"As I said before, You know who to make deals with..."

"... and who to swindle. I see your point."

Mr. Leon shifted in a way that conveyed threat, "I have made my successor aware of you.

What your strengths are and..."

Hau Hung backed up a little, "...and what my weaknesses are. Of course, you have. I know better than to think you a fool. I would be honored, sir. And if you survive this war, I will be the first to welcome you back with open arms."

The shuttle door opened and the interior lit up automatically. Mr. Leon patted Hung's hand, "I am glad to have you on my side. I have enjoyed our time together these past few weeks. May you be safe on your journeys." He bowed deeper than he had originally intended.

Hau Hung picked up his case and stepped inside the shuttle, "Until we meet again."

Mr. Leon smiled as the shuttle hatch closed. "One more brick placed on the path..."

One of the other brothers in the meld finished the old saying, "and may the path remain clear."

***

Hau Hung locked down his case and settled into the pilot's seat. As he brought the shuttle online, he shook his head cynically, "What made him pick me? I am the last person I would choose."

As the warm-up cycle completed, the hangar bay doors opened. He clicked on the comm, "Shuttle 17 requesting departure. I repeat, Shuttle 17 requesting departure."

"Departure granted. Safe travels, Shuttle 17."

Jon Gray Lang

"Safe travels, Peking Empress," Hung replied. "May we see each other on the other side."

With that, he released the shuttle locks. He maneuvered the shuttle through the hangar bay past the Copperhead and the Scorpio. "Good luck to you as well," he brought his hand to his heart as he flew the shuttle out of the luxury cruiser.

As he edged further away from the Peking Empress, he let the nav system figure out his coordinates. He watched as the big ship generated a wormhole, shot toward it, and disappeared from view. The Nav system pinged with the shuttle's location. Hau Hung tracked a course to Mithuna, the nearest planet that registered itself as a port of call.

He brought up the comms and sent out a request, "Shuttle 17 to Mithuna, come in Mithuna. Shuttle 17 to Mithuna, come in."

As he waited for the call to travel through space, he fired the engines on the shuttle and locked in a path to Mithuna. Traffic to the planet was light, but still more than he had expected for a mid-system world.

The comm blinked, "Mithuna to Shuttle 17, come in."

"Hello Mithuna," he replied. "I am looking for a landing port. Small and affordable, if you can swing it."

The chuckle on the other end was short, but friendly, "Message received, Shuttle 17. Head to landing designation 303. Cheapest I could find this late in the morning."

"Thank you, Mithuna. I appreciate it." Hung settled back and studied the small note stuck on the Nav console, then flicked on the comm again, "Shuttle 17 to Mithuna, could you patch me through to Unifreight Inc.?"

"For someone flying on the cheap, you sure do ask a lot," chuckled the operator on Mithuna. "Patching you through now."

Hung followed the trajectory to designation 303 and brought the shuttle in for a landing. The wheels touched the tarmac and he rolled the craft into the spot. As he shut down the engines, he pulled a quick schematic of the shuttle and had it dumped to his data pad. He grinned, "just in case I need to sell you for some quick getaway mazuma."

The comm clicked on, "This in Unifreight Inc. to Shuttle 17."

Hung scrambled for the mic, "This is Shuttle 17 to Unifreight Inc. Can you put me through to Kwan Sang, dark channel 2312?"

The pause on the comm was so long, Hung wondered if Mr. Leon had set him up. He felt along his belt and hoped that his knife hung there. He also wondered for the hundredth time if his decision to not carry a sidearm, in general, was going to get him killed one day.

His nerves calmed when he heard static and the comm responded, "This is channel 2312 to Shuttle 17. Is this Hau Hung?"

"Why yes, it is!" Hung responded in relief.

Jon Gray Lang

You must be Kwan Sang. I am pleased to speak with you."

"I've been awaiting your comm, Mr. Hau. A vehicle has been dispatched for you. It should arrive within ten minutes. Be ready."

Hope swelled Hung's chest, "I look forward to working for you and with you, Ms. Kwan."

"And I you, Mr. Hau."

twenty-six

Martyr

Rex Leon slowly stretched out onto the floor of his cabin aboard the Independence as the pressure at the back of his mind built. "So, it is time to join my brothers," he murmured. The connection with his brethren coalesced as he closed his eyes and let out a long breath.

"Welcome to the gathering, brother Rex," the padrone of the brethren exclaimed.

"Thank you, padrone and brothers."

"How go the preparations?"

Rex replied, "The last group of vessels that are not FTL capable are being loaded aboard our M Class destroyers as we speak."

"Excellent," said the padrone. "UniFreight Inc.'s successor has accepted the position."

One of the brothers stated, "As the war rages on, the company will remain in good hands."

Jon Gray Lang

"The future is preserved," reassured the other brothers.

"Let us hope that we can remove the machinations of the Masters," murmured Rex.

"And sever them from our homes," intoned the others.

"With our success in Lukida, the time has come to take the fight to the prime home worlds," stated Mr. Leon as he smacked his fist against the holo-console on the Peking Empress.

"And what better place to start than with the first..." intoned a chorus of the brothers.

On the bridge of the Empress, Mr. Leon addressed the crowd of Captains and crew that lay before him as well as the brethren within his mind, "And what better world than Jard!"

"Aye! Let's go after those bastards!" shouted Ovi.

Admiral Kaur laughed, "Keep it in your pants, Ovi."

As the chuckles subsided, Mr. Leon continued, "Our enemy awaits us and is prepared to meet us head on. This will be the toughest campaign our fleet will ever face."

"But this time, fortune points our way," proclaimed Rex.

Mr. Leon stood taller and made eye contact with everyone on the bridge, "And by taking the fight to Jard, we will force the Council to recognize the needs of the outer system colonies!"

"And we'll win!" crowed Ovi.

Jon Gray Lang

Mr. Leon beamed as he commanded from the Peking Empress, "Spread the message, fleet Admiral. We leave this day to battle the beast in its lair!"

***

Rex opened his eyes and clicked the comm, "Commander Keri, come join me in my cabin. There are details to discuss that will be of import in the battles ahead."

"On my way."

Rex stroked the heat sensor on his tea kettle and brought it up to temp. As he was scooping the last of his loose-leaf tea into the tiny clay pot, there was a knock at the hatch.

"Come in, Rosa."

The hatch opened and Rosa's eyes lit up. "Ooh, tea. Should I call for Delta to join us?"

Rex shook his head in the negative. "The sisters are already aware of the information I will be sharing with you."

"Keeping me in the dark, eh?"

"Not for lack of trust, I assure you."

Rosa shrugged as she settled onto the mattress. "Well, you're sharing it with me now."

Rex handed her a teacup as he swirled his own. She cupped it and breathed in the aroma. She took a tiny sip and sat back feeling perplexed, "I know this tea, it is from my home world. With only one grower left on that poisoned rock, this must be very expensive." She took another sip and closed

Jon Gray Lang

her eyes, "How bad is what you're going to tell me?"

Rex's expression was forlorn. "The conflict that lies ahead will be hard fought, and those working with the Masters will be prepared for us."

Rosa looked up, "The Masters? Who are they?"

"More like, what are they." Rex set his cup down and poured more water into the tiny pot, "I know you've had dealings with the crew of the Matilda. Did any of them talk to you about the 'de trop aspect'?"

"Can't say that I've ever heard of that term."

Rex leaned over and filled her cup before he filled his own. "To be honest, they may have another name for it." He sighed as his fingers slowly spun the cup, "I first became interested in them once I heard about their jump engine and its ability to create shortcuts outside of our universe."

"I have heard mention of their engine but chalked it up to sailor's tales. So, the tales are true?"

He nodded, "I didn't recognize it for what it was until I was aboard their ship, and they took me there... I will have to go further back in my own history to explain." He set his cup down, "I and my brothers were not born, we were made in the same fashion as the genorgs. We were created in an attempt to fill the positions my sisters do for society..."

"But you were deemed a failure. This I know," said Rosa after she took a sip from her cup. "But what does that have to do with these Masters?"

Jon Gray Lang

Rex grunted at the interruption, "We ended up being used as subjects in other experiments. One of those experiments involved interactions with a sphere very similar to the jump engine on the Matilda only much larger in scale. However, when I first came across their engine, I realized they are of the same ilk."

Rosa stood up and poured more water into the teapot before she sat back down on the mattress. "Continue."

Rex cleared his throat, "From what Dr. Saric told us, our first interaction with the sphere was groundbreaking, though neither I nor any of my brothers have any memories of this. We did learn over time, that we were mere sacrifices in the pursuits of understanding. Many of us died, but as with my sisters, more can be made. In fact, it was Dr. Saric's engine that allowed us our first bid for escape."

He glanced up as Rosa filled his cup. He raised the cup and tapped it against hers. "My brothers and I can speak to each other with the assistance of an artificial substance. This connection allowed us to formulate our plans, but we didn't know enough to understand that escape was needed, not the cessation of pain. We made our attack and dragged those responsible inside the engine."

Sweat formed on Rex's brow as he struggled to get the words out, "There were beings inside waiting for us. Our arrival was met with glee as they tore us to pieces. As we lost our connection to them, their desires were laid bare to us. They want to be here, and they want to use us all as tools in this pursuit. If they truly gain a foothold in our universe, we can only lose."

"And these are the Masters you speak of?"

He nodded, "That is how they refer to themselves. At the time, we had no concept of what that even meant. But after our escape and exploration of Consortium space, we, as a collective, came to learn that there are those among the ruling Council that are in their employ. This is why their military has been weakened and we've been able to make such great strides."

"And here I thought we were a bunch of bad asses..." murmured Rosa.

Rex chuckled, "All of you are that. No one can deny it. But if we lose, everything is lost. At the very least, if we can destroy the jump gate in the Malina system, we can cut them off from the rest of the Consortium."

Seeing the distress in Rex's eyes, Rosa enveloped him in an embrace and held him. As he relaxed in her arms, her last words made their way to his heart. "There is no need to fear. If we do not win the day, I will make sure the gate is destroyed, if it's the last thing I do."

***

"Entering the Ceti system... now," stated

Navigation Officer Grissom. "Preparing to run scans."

When the Consortium Battle Cruiser Remus flowed into the system, proximity alarms blared as chunks of twisted metal and flotsam bounced against the hull. Sections of the scaffolding that supported the wormhole emitters hung broken against the blackness of space.

Commander Shafar sighed, "We're too late, again. The jump gate is already gone."

"The dissidents remain successful and out of reach," grumbled Captain Ellsbeth. "No matter. Re-prep the FTL. We've been called back to Jard Prime." She murmured under her breath, "To fight a war of their own making."

Ilya Shafar glanced over in surprise.

The Captain shrugged at her response. "I know I should care what the 'secret police' think, but I'm too old for that nonsense, Ilya. There'll be plenty of time for the Council to have me executed after we've won their war."

Ilya glared at the bridge crew as if daring anyone to speak up against her Captain.

"Captain, we're receiving a distress signal about twelve clicks out."

"Lead the way, Mr. Grissom."

The CBC Remus tracked the weak signal and hours later, came upon a lone Consortium shuttle. The cruiser angled up alongside and shone its spotlights along the craft's fuselage. Scorch marks covered most of the hull and one of its wings was a mangled mess.

"Shuttle 03, this is the CBC Remus, do you copy?"

"This is Lieutenant Mariko Shimada of the M33. With me are Chief Bull and Dr. Sinix. We require assistance as our oxygen and fuel are nearly depleted."

"Where is your home ship?"

"Our destroyer was... umm destroyed. We've been dead in the water for more days than I care to count."

Captain Ellsbeth paused a moment, "Did you say the M33? Weren't you in the Pequiz system a few years back?"

There was a long pause before the woman replied, "Yes, toward the end of the invasion."

"Destroyed how? By whom? Was it during one of the rebel attacks?"

There was another long pause before Lieutenant Shimada replied, "We captured a freighter named the Matilda. During their incarceration, an FTL jump was forced on the destroyer. An explosion emanating from the captured merchant vessel tore the destroyer in half. As this was going on, alien creatures appeared in the wormhole wreaking havoc everywhere."

Another voice interrupted the Lieutenant's story, "Captain, this is..."

"Dr. Sinix," boomed a new voice. "Could we speed up this interrogation or move it somewhere else? We are on the brink of starvation. At least, bring us on board and stick us in quarantine, damn it."

Captain Ellsbeth frowned, "You are welcome aboard the CBC Remus. You will receive docking instructions soon. Prepare to be placed into quarantine. Once cleared, positions will be found for you all on board."

"Thank you, Captain Ellsbeth."

"Don't thank me, Doctor," the woman scoffed. "We've been called to war and we both know that means you will be kept busy. One last question, how did the Matilda and her crew fare?"

Chief Bull spoke, "The trawler was nonfunctional when we escaped. I don't see how they could have survived."

Captain Ellsbeth tightened her grip on the armrest, "Thank you and welcome aboard." She waved to have the comm channel cut as she said faintly, "Somehow, I wouldn't put it past them to escape."

"Shouldn't we keep them in quarantine during the conflict?" asked Commander Shafar.

Ellsbeth shook her head, "No." She turned to the Nav officer, "Once they're stowed away, continue prep for launch to the Malina system. There is a war going on and we've been invited."

***

Admiral Kaur stared at the navigation holo as the wormhole tunnel walls slithered past the Peking

Empress. The computer system tracked what was expected to be the other ships in her fleet and their potential arrival points in the Malina system.

Her eyes tracked to the location of the jump gate of the system and also to the only planet with a sizable population. Her fingers drummed the console as the system tracked the various small stations and colonies on the outer moons and planets.

"It's not a big system, is it?" asked Mr. Leon as he stood by her. "So much power held in the gravity well of one planet and its four sisters."

She glanced at him and then at her bridge crew. She leaned in and whispered, "No one has ever taken on one of the big three, never mind the biggest one."

Mr. Leon tried to allay her fear, "The fact that it's unprecedented gives us a bit of an edge. They may know we're coming but they don't know the when or where. And they may not truly believe that we're coming."

"And every advantage, no matter how inconsequential, gives us a sliver of hope," she replied. "I see your point. But it won't be easy."

"Things of the greatest value rarely are."

Admiral Kaur nodded. She glanced at the arrival timer and waited for the pre-chime, "Rise and shine, people! Prepare for war!"

twenty-seven

Suspended

Anton piloted the Cyclops to the ethereally thin tower as Jacquie watched the landing pad lights. She entered the docking code they'd been given and the lights on the pad changed from a hostile red to a cool blue. Light rain pelted the windscreen of the small yacht as they landed and completed the shutdown process for the ship.

Jacquie reached over and shook their dozing musician, "You ready for your show, Lu?"

Luli opened her eyes, but stared around unfocused, "Hmm? Are we there yet?"

"Just arrived," answered Anton as the cabin lights came on and the rest of the controls went dark. "I'll grab your ukulele."

Luli looked around and yawned, "I don't know why, but I am can't seem to stay awake today."

Jacquie smiled and helped her up, "Well, it

could be because it's evening now."

Anton handed Jacquie a steaming cup of surge on his way to the airlock.

She handed it to Luli, "I'd suggest slamming this right now. You're playing for the bigwigs tonight and we need you to be on fire so that we can get a lead on Galena's location."

"Right," nodded Luli. "We're on a fact-finding soiree, I almost forgot." She tipped the cup back and slurped down the hot liquid. She wiped her mouth dry and grinned at the two of them, "Let's get this show started!"

All three stepped through the airlock and into the rain. A line of blinking lights caught Jacquie's eye. She waved the others forward and they followed the lights to a small raised structure. There were guards posted at the four corners of the roof as well as this pair at the platform.

One of the guards stepped forward, "Are you Luli Qing? We will need to check you in."

Luli bowed with a flourish, "Yes, it is I. The talent for the night. And, of course." She raised her arms as the guard ran a scanner across her.

"You were instructed to come alone."

She winked, "A singer doesn't travel without her sound crew. You wouldn't want your employers to hear a subpar performance, would you?"

The other guard spoke into his comm and waited. Anton handed over the ukulele case and raised his arms as well. Jacquie followed suit moments later. The guard with the scanner shrugged and scanned the pair of them. Alarms rang out as their weapons glowed brightly in the scanner. "No weapons allowed. We'll need to confiscate those."

Anton smiled as he slipped a small pistol out of his belt. Jacquie glanced quizzically at it, "That's not Henon..."

Anton glared at her briefly. He dropped his small pistol and bent over to retrieve it. As he straightened, Anton slipped free the guard's back-up weapon hidden in a holster at his ankle. As he dropped his own pistol into the guard's hand, he slipped the stolen pistol into his pocket.

"Oh." Jacquie gave a slight nod as she pulled her pistol free of the holster under her jacket, "Here you go."

"Nigel says the sound crew can enter. Anything to put Ms. Qing at her ease."

The guard collected their guns and placed them into a storage locker on the side of the platform. "They'll be here for you after the show. Enjoy your visit."

Anton picked up the ukulele case and the three of them headed to the lift. As the door opened, Jacquie felt something press against her wrist. She glanced down at the backup pistol being shoved into her hand. She palmed the weapon and deftly slid it into the inner pocket of her jacket.

Luli hummed softly to herself, but Jacquie noticed the cyborg seemed oddly distant. She nudged Anton, "Are we expecting trouble?"

He nodded and threw a tiny salute to the guards as the lift doors shut. "Just making sure we get out of here in one piece," Anton whispered.

***

Luli caught herself staring blankly at the corner of the lift as Anton and Jacquie chattered behind her. She turned slowly and the light seemed to follow her movement, "Hmm?"

She felt a hand on her shoulder. The Captain said something, but the sound was garbled to her ears. She looked down and watched as Anton pulled Henon free of a flat container on the inside of her ukulele case and slipped it under his coat.

"How'd you get that... ?" she wondered.

"A transition case. Fools most scanners."

Luli blinked slowly, "We expecting trouble?"

"When don't we have trouble?" answered Anton.

This elicited a burst of laughter from the pilot which gave her a moment of clarity. *'Why am I feeling loopy?'*

She saw the look of concern in Jacquie's eyes, but her mind wandered again. She heard a faint voice over everything, "Relax. There is nothing to fear; only hope resides here. Relax, there is nothing to fear..."

The lift doors parted and another set of guards greeted them. One pointed down the hallway that lay ahead while the other said, "Please follow me."

When they stepped behind the second guard, the first one took up his position behind them. Luli stared blankly at the dark indigo velvet walls. Her fingers brushed against the fabric and the texture felt like tiny little hairs bristling up from the skin of an enormous beast. Small tremors seemed to pass under her fingertips like insects crawling beneath the surface. She pulled her hand away in revulsion, and the sensation passed.

"The stage is in the chamber beyond this door," stated the guard in the lead. "You will find the needed sound equipment to the left." He bowed slightly, "We are honored to have you perform for the stewards of the House of Khanda. Please do not disappoint."

Jacquie reached out and shook the guard's hand, "Thank you, thank you. The illustrious Luli Qing appreciates the opportunity to perform for your leaders. Perhaps some day she will be allowed to perform for the servants of the House."

The guard smirked slightly, "Perhaps." He and the other guard bowed in deference to the celebrity, then turned on their heels and headed back to their post.

Luli felt a hand at her elbow leading her into the performance chamber. When she glanced at Anton he winked at her. Then the chamber door shut behind her and the heavy click of a lock engaging thundered through the pulsing blood in her ears.

Jon Gray Lang

"Are you up for this, Lu?" asked Jacquie with unease.

Luli tilted her head back and closed her eyes. Her lungs expanded with a long slow inhalation of air. As she exhaled, she raised her arms above her head then lowered them into a prayer position in front of her chest. She opened her eyes and grinned, "Yes. Let's see what kind of equipment we're working with here."

A pile of sound machinery sat exactly where the guard said it would be. Luli pointed at various pieces as Jacquie and Anton set them up per her instructions. Luli smiled, "After all our years together, you know how I like my setup."

Anton handed her the ukulele case. Her fingers ran over the surface of the cracked faux leather. Scarred and chipped from its time with her, it brought her a sense of comfort that very few other objects did. The case clicked open to reveal the ancient instrument that lay on its threadbare bed of padding. She curled her fingers around the neck of the instrument and brushed the strings as she settled it into the crook of her arm. Her fingers danced lightly across the strings as she warmed up with a series of chords and scales.

"Sounds good," said Anton from the soundboard.

"Yes, it sounds angelic..." said a voice from the shadows. Bright lights flicked on and two golden thrones sparkled in the sudden flash. Each throne held an individual draped across the seat and both wore extravagantly matching outfits.

Luli looked up and smiled, "Our hosts, the Lord, and Lady of the House Khanda! It has been many years since I've been to the planet Jard. I am honored by the offer to play a private show for such premier members of the Council."

"It is an honor to have a legend play for us, my dear," replied Lady Rana.

An imposingly tall man with a skeletal gait approached the trio. "A drink for the performer and her companions. It was made to evoke memories of your life among the stars."

The liquid inside the glasses was dark, almost black, but it glittered with tiny flecks of light. The scent of raisins and cherries emerged from the glass in a small wispy cloud. Suddenly, a bright flash of orange and purple burst within the glasses then faded once again to liquid darkness.

"Well, isn't that fancy," murmured Luli. Her hand touched the tall man's shoulder as she took a tiny sip and he seemed to relax, "Thank you Nigel, this is extraordinarily good."

Jacquie downed her cocktail in a second and handed back the empty glass, "Pretty good, but I'm more of a whiskey woman."

Anton sniffed the aperitif with a quizzical expression as he took a tiny sip. "There's something familiar in this..."

Two other attendants came up behind the imposing man and began moving the sound equipment to a small platform in the center of the circular room. A large overhead light came on and the stage was illuminated in a cone of radiance. As Luli strolled under the spotlight, Jacquie joined Anton at the soundboard.

"You must excuse our manservant," apologized Lord Jai. "Nigel has been looking forward to meeting a deep spacer since he was a child. He has been tinkering with that beverage all in the hopes to impress you for almost as long as I've been alive."

"I appreciate the effort, Nigel as it's a wonderful concoction. And it does bring to mind some of my journeys," Luli bowed in his direction and Nigel dipped his head back with a shy smile. Lady Rana tittered in response.

Luli glanced over her shoulder and Anton gave her the thumbs up. "Let's get this show on the road, shall we?" With a single strum of the uke, the lights in the room changed. Speckles of light similar to the ones in the beverage trickled down from the ceiling and the temperature in the room dropped.

Luli's voice rose as she began to sing an ancient song from old Earth,

"There's a low, green valley, on the old Kentucky shore."
"Where I've whiled many happy hours away,"
"A-sitting and a-singing by the little cottage door."
"Where lived my darling Nelly Gray."

***

Jon Gray Lang

As Luli flowed into her next song, Anton took another sip of the drink. His brow wrinkled as he wracked his brain, "I swear I've tasted something like this before. When was it?"

Jacquie grabbed his cocktail and drained the glass. "Hey, wait a minute," she said as she shook Anton's shoulder, "This isn't the playlist she showed us. What the hell is Luli doing?"

"Huh?" Anton looked up.

Luli floated in the cone of light, but the edges of it were fainter as if the darkness pushed against it. In fact, the entire chamber appeared darker except for the faint glow of symbols and sigils that decorated many of the beams. Recognition hit Anton.

"Oh shit." He grabbed Jacquie as he spoke haltingly into her ear, "You see those symbols on the wall? Derain and I saw something similar on the Demetrius! Remember? The ones who kidnapped Luli?"

Jacquie's eyes were wide and staring, "What are those?"

Anton glanced back to the stage as animate shadows separated from the surrounding curtain of darkness. The creatures strained against the light that encased Luli. She remained oblivious and kept singing.

Jacquie's eyes darted around the chamber and she saw an oddly familiar faint glow radiating from behind the thrones. As the glow increased the twins rose in unison and walked toward Luli.

The heavy stench of rotting vegetation permeated the chamber as the Lord and Lady pressed against the cone of light surrounding Luli. They began to chant and it blended with the voices from the shadow beings, "What of home? Which way is home? Where is home? Give us the course... provide us the route... yield us the map... We must find the way home... home... Home!"

"By the Major, are we jumping?" Jacquie quailed at the sight and she hurled up the drink. "How the hell are we jumping?"

Luli's ukulele fell from her fingers and banged against the floor. "No... I don't want to remember! There's nothing there! Nothing!"

"That's it! That drink was a fucking hallucinogenic!" Anton yelped. "Jacq, it's trouble time!" He barely registered her nod as he bolted away from the soundboard.

Air raid sirens wailed loudly and everyone stopped where they were. The twins laughed maniacally, "The invasion begins! Harvest all that you need, Masters! Harvest every last one of them!"

Anton pulled Henon free from his belt line. The pistol barked three times in the chamber and one of the shadows jerked in agony. "Jacquie! Get Luli out of here!" He fired another round and a shadow with its appendage wrapped around Luli's arm let go with a cry of anguish.

The Lord of Khanda cackled as he picked up Luli and dragged her out of the cone of light.

"Watch out!" screamed Jacquie as a bullet tore

through Anton's arm. He groaned in pain as the limb flopped uselessly against his side. He spun around to see Nigel holding a pistol before the bark of Jacquie's sidearm tore holes into the tall cadaverous man.

Anton flicked his gaze back to Luli. The twins stood over her and held her in place while the shadows tore at Luli's clothing.

"No! Not again!" Anton lined up his sights and Henon roared like thunder. The Lady Rana's head exploded like rotten fruit. Black aqueous liquid oozed from the wound, but her grip on Luli remained firm as her headless body thrashed across the stage.

Jacquie took aim with her own pistol and fired at Lord Khanda's chest. The force of the slugs knocked the twin away from Luli. Meanwhile, Anton sighted down Lady of Khanda's arm, pulled the trigger, and blasted the woman's wrist completely apart. Luli pulled free, but struggled to maintain her balance.

"Get her out of here, Jacq. I'll take care of the shadow things."

Jacquie ran over to Luli and grabbed her, preventing her from toppling into the grasp of the grim shadows. Another blast from Anton whistled past Jacquie's shoulder and destroyed Lord Jai's head. His body fell to the floor and more of the dark aqueous fluid poured out of his wound. Lady Rana's body quivered as it reached out for Luli again. Another shot tore through the woman's abdomen and her mangled body finally stopped moving.

Jacquie pushed Luli toward the chamber door. Anton kept firing at the shadows until the pistol's chamber clicked empty. With only one hand, he reloaded as quickly as he could.

Jacquie blasted the door lock apart and called out from the doorway, "Let's get out of this hell! Hurry it up, Rabbit!"

Anton dropped to his knees and tucked Luli's ukulele under his injured arm. He looked back at the twins as their forms rose to their feet and stumbled toward him. He aimed Henon again and shouted, "A bit late I guess, but, for the revolution!"

He blasted the legs of the two shambling bodies and they crashed to the floor.

A rakish grin stretched across Rabbit's face, "You want some more, shadow spirits? Henon protects me!"

The shadowy creatures crept back into the darkness and disappeared from view. Anton turned toward the door and yelled, "Right behind you, Jacq!"

Jon Gray Lang

twenty-eight

Swinging on a Star

The Peking Empress slipped between the orbits of the last two planets in the Malina system. As the first heliocentric system to be populated by what would become the Consortium, it was small. It only had five worlds, but only Jard, the third one, was densely populated. A total of fourteen moons were held in place by the outer two gaseous planets with manned facilities having only been built on seven of them.

Admiral Kaur studied the Nav system as it compared the conjectured 3D model with the reality of what she actually observed outside the luxury liner. "There are a lot more Consortium Naval vessels out there than I even knew existed," she said.

Mr. Leon shrugged, "We have successfully cut them off from many of their jump gates so that the choice of where to park their fleet is now severely

Jon Gray Lang

limited."

"And they knew we would eventually come here," added Latiff.

Proximity alarms jangled on the bridge of the Empress as the rest of the armada entered the Malina system. "That's the last of them," announced Thadie Dumba. "Your fleet awaits orders, Admiral."

Mr. Leon glanced at the 3D model as the sensors tracked the Consortium ships placement and his eyebrow shot up. "They are all gathered around the jump gate. They've left Jard unprotected."

Harjeet grinned, "They sure know what we like to go after, don't they? Should we throw them for a loop?"

Latiff laughed, "Confusion is good for the soul, eh?"

"Thadie, send the manifesto," ordered Admiral Kaur, "but send it to the planet Jard itself. Be heavy on the emphasis for taking control of the Council."

"On it," replied Thadie. Once she completed the revisions she announced, "Manifesto en route via tight beam."

"Now, let's see what they do," said Latiff.

"Probably not much unless they see afterburners," added Mr. Leon.

"I agree," Harjeet nodded. "Send orders to the Valkyrie, Coyote, Bhagat, and Lilith to drop cloak and move with haste to Jard."

Thadie sent the order, then shortly after

announced "Orders received. Ships are on their way."

Everyone's attention was focused on the Nav 3D model. There was some movement amongst the Consortium fleet, but most of them remained behind.

"Have the forward contingent release its cargo."

On the 3D model, the number of ships heading toward Jard went from four to twenty of varying signature sizes. A few more of the Consortium vessels left the protective barricade around the jump gate.

"Still thick as thieves," muttered Mr. Leon. "I think it's going to be an all-or-nothing situation."

Admiral Kaur sighed in disappointment, "Send the same order to the rest of the fleet. Latiff, turn our tail to the enemy."

The ship shuddered as the engines engaged and slowly spun toward Jard. As the luxury liner moved forward, there was more movement from the Consortium fleet. One... two... then four more left the protective circle of the jump gate. As the second group of the rebel armada dropped its cargo of smaller attack ships, a few more of the Consortium ships followed after them.

"There's still too damn many protecting the gate," cursed Harjeet.

Suddenly, Thadie called out, "An enemy vessel has engaged with the Destroyer Anansi!"

"Where did it come from?" asked Admiral

Kaur.

Mr. Leon pointed, "It was hiding behind the fourth planet, Mortu."

"Lugh and Enki are assisting the Anansi," said Thadie.

"Increase our velocity toward them," ordered Harjeet. "When we reach a higher speed if they give chase swing back around."

As the Peking Empress increased its speed, there was movement on the Nav model.

"It looks like your ploy is working, Admiral. I'm only seeing a standard two-ship contingent left at the system gate."

"Thank you, Mr. Leon. Keep an eye out for surprises, Ovi. Latiff, how far out are we from the jump gate?"

There was a quiet pause before he replied, "Still too far out for us to divest ourselves of the attack ships. I'd say five minutes if we turned around at our current speed."

Harjeet nodded. "Go ahead and set the deceleration burn, Mr. Ghilzai. Get us closer to the jump gate. Thadie, inform our cargo to prepare for launch at speed."

The old ship shook with the force of the massive deceleration as Latiff worked to bring her around. Admiral Kaur kept track of the Consortium vessels in the 3D model but none gave them chase. Everyone on the bridge was quiet as the liner slowly shifted its focus to the jump gate on the edge of the system.

As the range between the Empress and the jump gate shrank, Ovi spoke, "Ro-Ro bay doors opened. Clamps released and ships away."

"Good luck Copperhead, Independence, and Scorpio. You are free to take the jump gate. Empress out." said Thadie.

"Message received and see you on the dark side!" Commander Keri replied from the Independence.

"Dropping sensors to check for incoming FTL energies... and it's away." Ovi glanced at Harjeet, "Nothing else for us to do here."

"Go and lead the fight against Jard, Admiral," said Mr. Leon. "We shall leave these three to deal with the gate forces."

"You heard the man," shouted Admiral Kaur. "Turn this boat around and fly like the wind!"

***

Captain Oluchi of the Anansi gripped the handrail as a burst of detonations pounded the hull of his destroyer. "Where do we stand? Damage reports!"

"We have fires on decks three and twelve! Fire crews are engaging!"

"And the enemy ship is down!" exclaimed the Gunner.

"Bring her about and catch up with the others," ordered the Captain.

As the Anansi turned, everyone on the bridge

tried to catch a glimpse of the damaged Consortium vessel. The ship straightened out and they rejoined the fleet toward Jard.

"Thanks for the assist, Enki and Lugh," Captain Oluchi said over the comm.

"Hey, what are friends for?" replied the other vessels.

The hatch to the bridge opened and Mr. Leon entered. "How goes it, Captain?"

"The enemy cruiser has been eliminated. Last communique from the Empress stated the rest of the Consortium fleet is after us."

"So the Admiral's ploy worked. The jump gate was left undefended?"

Captain Oluchi shook his head, "A two-ship contingent still stands guard. It'll be a tough fight for the Empress and her battle group."

"Still, two is better than the vast number that are after us," Mr. Leon pointed at the Consortium ships speeding toward them on the Nav model. "And this battle group has been through worse."

The Comm officer interjected, "We're getting close to the home world. The first wave of ships has engaged the planetary defenses."

Mr. Leon chuckled. At Captain Oluchi's quizzical look, he confided, "Tales swirl about the state of repair, or should I say disrepair of the planetary defenses. Rumors of corruption that go all the way up to the highest members in the Council abound. I've spoken with some of the contractors and they have gotten fabulously wealthy delivering knock-off parts or no parts at all! It's almost as if the Council members involved either never saw this coming or wanted them to fail."

"Planetary arrival in T-minus thirty minutes," stated the Nav officer.

Captain Oluchi turned to his bridge crew, "If what you say is true, this'll be like walking in cake!"

Mr. Leon laughed along with the bridge crew, but he cautiously advised the Captain, "We have to take down those defenses so that we aren't caught between them and the fleet."

"And once the jump gate is down, we can go back home," maintained the Captain.

"Once it's down..."

"Receiving a report from the Valkyrie," stated the Comm officer. "Planetary defenses are folding." Cheers burst from the bridge crew.

"Keep it down!" ordered Captain Oluchi. "There's more to the message."

"Thank you, sir," answered the Comm officer. "Lilith is registering a build-up of peculiar energies from off-planet. The wavelength is apparently growing in size."

Captain Oluchi grumbled, "Some new weapon we're unaware of? Keep an eye out, folks."

The bridge crew sobered up and all eyes turned to the small cyan-blue ball that hovered in space. Suddenly, a pinprick of weird light appeared outside the planet. The pinprick steadily expanded in size.

"See if you can find what's causing that,"

ordered the Captain.

"Scans show an object at the center. Zooming in," replied the Scanner Technician. "Throwing image to the main screen."

The strange light blossomed around the nose of an immense ancient vessel. The light spread wider until it obliterated the view of the craft. As the Scanner Technician dropped the image, everyone could see that the light was evolving into an enormous bubble that enveloped the planet Jard and all the ships battling above it.

"Comms are coming through distorted. I'm having trouble making out what the traffic is saying," stated the Comm officer.

"Keep at it," said the Captain.

Silence shrouded the bridge as the Anansi drew closer to the skin of the bubble. When the destroyer punched through, the stench of rotting fruit and burnt copper permeated the air ducts.

"That can't be good," murmured Captain Oluchi. "Everyone stay on your toes."

"Comms are clearing up," said the Comm Officer. "Wait... now we're getting multiple reports concerning the Leons." As he listened intently to the chatter, the comm operator's eyes widened. "Sir!" he blurted, "The Leons inside the bubble are unresponsive!"

Behind the Captain, Mr. Leon struggled to breathe as his connection to the rest of his kind was severed. He gulped at the air and desperately clawed at his throat as he collapsed to the floor. He barely heard Captain Oluchi's call for a medical team as he slipped into unconsciousness.

twenty-nine

I Don't Want to Set the World on Fire

Derain brought the Rabbit's Folly to a stop in front of the arena that was being used for Dusty's execution. He and Barney stepped out and joined the huge crowds that shuffled through the front gates of the structure.

Barney tugged on Derain's sleeve, "There's Zolzaya."

Derain and Barney hurried to join Batu and Zolzaya on the far side of the stadium.

"Follow us," ordered Zolzaya as she led the way to a hidden stairwell.

As the door to the stairwell shut, Barney asked, "Have you seen Dusty yet?"

Batu nodded but his expression was dark. The group rushed up the stairs. Eventually, they emerged onto a landing that overlooked the arena's vast playing field. Dusty knelt in the center of the brightly lit pitch, chained to the ground and under the watch of four armed guards.

Batu's anger at the sight was palpable, but he turned away to address them, "They're tight beaming this spectacle all the way to Titan. They've already stated his execution is meant to be used as an example of their justice. Any Titan that escapes the home world will be found, no matter how long it takes, and put to death."

"There is a Titan delegation overseeing the process," said Zolzaya as she pointed to an upper box seat.

Barney looked up and saw the Titan Retrieval Team in their priest robes. Sky-eyes hovered around them as their voices boomed through the loud speakers, "... The will of the ancestors must be followed! Those who believe they are above the rules represent the evil that must be lanced like a boil for the betterment of all Titans!"

"Same rhetoric, different day," growled Barney. "We got a way to get to Dusty?"

"The better question," broached Derain, "is there a way we can we get out there and free him with any chance of success?"

"We'd need one hell of a diversion," insisted Batu.

The group stopped talking as the priest's voice grew louder and carried with it a sense of finale, "Do you have any last words, Dusty Machado, once of Titan?"

"None that you would care to hear, false

priest," the shackled man growled back. He shook the chains that held him down, "Not willing to give me a fighting chance, eh? I would expect no less from the likes of you."

The Titan priest chuckled, "A fighting chance for an androgyne? How droll. Well then, a fighting chance you shall have. Guards, leave the field. The games begin!"

The guards scattered as the arena's portcullises rumbled open. When the huge doors slammed to a stop, half-mechanical beasts streamed out onto the field. Abnormal animals whose legs and jaws had been replaced with prosthetics charged toward the prisoner.

"Cyborg animals?" asked Derain. "Aren't they illegal?"

Zolzaya gripped the railing in front of her and hissed, "Nothing is illegal to those that rule, no matter how cruel or unnecessary."

As the creatures approached, Dusty strained against the chains until they pulled free of the rings that locked them in place. With a rolling motion, he wound them around his forearms. He barely completed this before the first animal ferociously attacked. Dusty slammed his forearm into its mouth and sparks burst along the chain links. With a yank, he flung the dog-like beast away and sent it crashing into its pack.

The crowd roared with excitement as more of the cybernetic creatures crashed into the Titan and sent him sprawling.

Barney snarled. His hands curled around the railing and the metal bar twisted under his grip. "Fuck this, I am done hiding!"

"Wait!" hollered Derain.

But it was too late. Barney leapt over the barrier and landed in a roll two floors down. Derain watched in disbelief as his friend jumped to his feet and ran into the fray.

"Tom be damned," cursed Derain. "Every time! What is it with Jacq's crew that makes them go all in without any sense of a plan?"

Barney plowed through the pandemonium on the field and pulled Dusty to his feet.

"Oh ho!" shouted the coliseum announcer, "Looks like a new contender has entered the field and it's another Titan!"

The crowd erupted in cheers. Their desire for blood was rivaled only by the fomented lust of the cybernetic creatures. The brawl continued as the two Titans fought against the mechanized beasts. And miraculously, fewer and fewer of the half-mechanical beasts got back to their feet to charge back in.

"Who's our new champion going to be?" exclaimed the announcer as the Titans in the booth pulled him away from the microphone. "It is of no importance what it calls itself!" grumbled the priest, "Now, we'll have a double execution! Release the next wave!"

In response to the priest's command, humanoid forms that moved like cheap imitations of deep spacers stumbled onto the field.

"Those can't possibly be legal," said Derain.

"They're already dead," seethed Zolzaya. "Machine-controlled corpses that do the bidding of their overseers."

"There has to be a way to put a stop to this," Derain insisted.

"Only way to end it is if we take it to them," Batu pointed at the two Titans in their priest robes.

Derain yanked his pistols free and snarled, "Lead the way."

***

Barney felt a hand grip his arm and pull him to his feet. Dusty shoved a bionic cadaver and it stumbled away. Barney pushed another one into a mechanical animal. He yelled, "Get a wall to our backs!"

The two valiant warriors moved backward until a wall was the only thing behind them. They held off the man-made beasts and the fickleness of the crowd turned in their favor. Cheers erupted for the fighting Titans.

A small sky-eye floated over as the loudspeaker boomed, "Barnabus de Lagnel! You are wanted for crimes against the citizens of Titan! Your sentence shall be the same as that which your family paid for abetting you!"

Barney's bitter laugh was relayed by the small bot's tiny microphone, "What crimes do you speak of, priest? Being an androgyne bred for the carnal desires of those like you? Stealing children from their homes and grooming them to your whims? You are the criminals of Titan, not me!"

"Silence, de Lagnel!"

"And criminals should not be allowed to rule!"

The ground shook as the sound of air raid sirens echoed in the distance. A single shot rang out and pinged against the stone wall behind Barney. He didn't flinch. Another shot rang out and Dusty grunted in pain. Barney pointed at the balcony where the two priests stood and bellowed, "If I'm to die, you will not leave this planet alive!"

Armed security piled out of the portal behind them. Barney spun around and charged the nearest one. As he connected, the security guard dropped his rifle as he toppled over. As another guard raised her rifle to take a shot, Dusty grabbed the barrel and slammed it into the woman's face. A third guard with a shock stick swung hard and struck the back of Barney's head.

Blood sluiced through the air from the impact and Barney lost all sense of reason. His vision tunneled and everything went red. His only thought was the pain and those who caused it.

With a shriek, he tore off the man's arm. As the guard stumbled back in shock, Barney brandished the man's arm and swung it with all his might. It struck the guard's skull and he went down. Barney swung the arm again and battered it against a

Jon Gray Lang

shuffling corpse.

The crowd cheered all the harder and began throwing things at the guards. One security officer turned and fired into the crowd.

Screaming and fighting broke out in the stands. Suppression bots were released into the stadium and sonic blasts engulfed the crowds. A gun was fired from the stands and a sky-eye fizzled as it spiraled into the ground.

Suddenly, the sun was covered by a dark cloud that glistened with an oil-like sheen. The tone of a heavy gong tolled in the distance. Powerful winds swept over the coliseum, flinging detritus up into the air. In the midst of it, humanoid figures dropped from the sky.

Barney let the guard's arm fall from his grip as he regained his senses. The last the security member ran back into the portal and whatever operated the bionic cadavers stopped as they now stood still. Cries of "genorgs" erupted from the crowd. Barney looked up in awe as genorg soldiers dropped from the sky and open fired on everyone.

***

Derain, Batu, and Zolzaya dashed up the flights of stairs, meeting with little resistance along the way. No one bothered with them as everyone was focused on the execution.

Derain wheezed as he rounded the next staircase, "How many more flights are there?"

"Only one," said Batu, breathing heavily.

The group resumed their climb up the last steps. As they reached the top, Zolzaya pointed across the landing, "There's the door."

Derain checked his pistols, "You open the door, I go in guns blazing. Got it?"

Batu nodded as he gripped the door handle. "On two. One, two, now!"

As Batu yanked the door open, Derain barreled through. The control room was long and narrow and the walls were covered in electronic gear. Screens showed the pit in the coliseum with Barney and Dusty fighting for their lives. Up ahead a Titan dressed in priestly robes argued with a woman at the soundboard.

Barney's voice boomed over the speakers, "What crimes do you speak of, priest? Being an androgyne bred for the carnal desires of those like you? Stealing children from their homes and grooming them to your whims? You are the criminals of Titan, not me."

"Cut the damn feed, now!" shouted the Titan priest.

The soundboard engineer frantically pointed at something, "I can't cut the direct beam feed! They're located offsite!"

The other Titan came in from the balcony and threatened, "Do you want to end up like your announcer friend over there? Then, find a way."

Derain mirthlessly chuckled, "No one is cutting off my friend. In fact, this is for his family."

Jon Gray Lang

Derain's gun barked four times in the control room and the two Titans crumpled to the ground. Barney's voice echoed in the background, "...criminals should not be allowed to rule!" And the sound tech fled from the scene.

An eerie hush fell over the control room. Not because two people had been assassinated, but because the light from the balcony instantly dimmed as a dark cloud blotted out the sun. A rancid odor of old blood and decayed vegetation washed over the group.

"Do you hear that?" asked Zolzaya. "It sounds like a gong is ringing somewhere."

Suddenly, a vicious wind whipped across the arena. Screams erupted from the coliseum as sporadic shooting became a hailstorm of gunfire and armored drop suits rained down from the sky.

"Damn," Derain cursed, "as if this day couldn't get any worse!"

thirty

Voyage Libre

Fires burned in the distance and rain heavy with ash pelted the field inside the stadium. Battles raged across the skies as attack spacecraft dropped into the atmosphere of Jard. Missiles hammered the ground and explosions lit the clouds in fiery defiance as a portent of planetary war.

"Barney, what in the nine hells is happening?" shouted Dusty.

With a loud boom a heavy spacecraft dropped below the cloud line and streaked across the sky. The small freighter that pursued it fired a rocket, then broke away. The larger ship tumbled wildly and crashed into one of the tall buildings along the skyline.

Dumbfounded, Barney looked on. "I have no idea."

Confusion and chaos steered the crowds in

the arena and they ran in all directions. Genorg soldiers fired into the stampede as Barney grabbed Dusty's hand and yanked him up.

As they ran, Dusty shouted, "Has the war truly come to Jard?"

A damaged vessel whistled past them as Barney yelled, "We have to get under cover!"

They two of them ran for the nearest exit, but it was blocked by a mass of humanity trying to escape the madness. Overhead, a squadron of small fighters whizzed by in pursuit of a beleaguered transport ship trailing smoke. The throaty booms of space defense cannons reverberated through the air and shook the dust under their feet.

Dusty pointed toward a small door halfway along the wall and panted, "I bet that leads out to a loading dock."

Barney nodded as a pod of rockets ripped through the air and slammed into the arena booth high above them. He shoved Dusty through the doorway, then stared up at the ruined gallery. "Where are you, Derain?"

***

"By the Major, that was close!" Derain shouted as the floors above them disintegrated in a flash and debris rained down around them. "We have to get out of here!"

Batu and Zolzaya shot past and the stairs rang with their receding footsteps. He bounded after them.

The stairs were smeared with blood and trampled bodies lay where they had fallen. As the trio neared the lower levels the stairwell resonated with the sharp pops of handguns and automatic rifles.

We have to rethink our exit strategy," said Batu. "The stairs are blocked the next level down. Looks like security took up positions to keep everyone inside and the people aren't happy about it."

Zolzaya pointed out an open window, "Isn't that your ride a couple floors down?"

"Anyone out there that you can see?" asked Derain.

Zolzaya shook her head as she looked over the edge, "It looks clear. There are some ledges we can drop to between here and the ground."

Derain stepped up to the window and studied their option. Compared to the inside of the coliseum, the parking lot was peaceful. Chunks of a downed spaceship burned on top of some crushed vehicles, but out in the distance, the Rabbit's Folly remained untouched.

"Alright, we go out the window," shouted Derain. "Try to break your fall with the bushes down below and just run like blazes to the Folly."

Batu hopped up onto the ridge and eased himself out. Zolzaya was right behind him. Derain looked down and watched their progress before he swung himself up onto the ledge.

"Where's Anton's damn rope gun when you need it?" cursed Derain.

***

Jacquie pushed the chamber door open while Anton supported the pilot and her ukulele.

"Come on Lu, wake up! We need you here and now," Anton entreated as he followed Jacquie through the door.

The air raid sirens were much louder outside of the private chamber. Jacquie crept ahead and the two guards never stood a chance. Jacquie squeezed the trigger on her pistol and left them where they lay. She turned back and helped Anton with Luli.

"Come on Lu, we're almost there," she murmured as they stumbled into the lift.

Weird tinny music competed with the wail of the air raid sirens as the lift rose to the roof of the tower. Anton dropped the musician into the corner and stood in front of her with Henon clenched in his sweaty hand. Jacquie gripped her sidearm and maintained her position beside the doors.

"Ready?" she asked.

"For you? Always," chuckled Anton as a bead of perspiration trickled down the side of his face.

The lift dinged and the doors opened onto the roof. Off in the distance sat the Cyclops, but the skies around it were unlike anything they had ever seen. Riotous colors and streaks of blackness shot across the heavens. Enormous beasts flew through the skies like nightmares unbound by physics.

"Well, fuck me," swore Jacquie. "How do you jump a whole planet?"

One of the roof guards appeared, "Hey, what are you doing up here?"

Jacquie fired and he dropped to the ground. Another shot rang out and the sound of splintering wood came from underneath Anton's arm.

"God damn it! I just fixed that for her!" Henon boomed in the narrow confines of the lift and another guard went down.

Jacquie stuck her head out past the lift doors. Off to the right, a flock of small creatures assailed the remaining guards on the roof.

"On one!" she bellowed. "One!"

Anton spun around and propped Luli on his good shoulder as Jacquie wrapped her arm around the cyborg's other flank. They broke cover and ran as fast as they could toward the sanctuary of the Cyclops. High-pitched squawks and squeals dogged their steps and small winged creatures flew close overhead.

Jacquie slapped at the airlock controls as the trumpeting from the gigantic monstrosities reverberated across the skies. Once the airlock opened up enough, Jacquie dragged her half of Luli through the door, followed by Anton with his.

"Shut the hatch!" she ordered. "I'll warm up the ship and we'll head back to the Matilda."

Anton nodded and dragged Luli onto the

stretch of decking behind the pilot's console. Jacquie tapped through the commands and brought the ship online. The engines ignited and the yacht shook hard as Jacquie lifted her off the landing pad.

"Luli? Are you awake?" Anton beseeched. "Come on Lu, we're going to need your piloting skills, soon. Quit sleeping on the job."

The flying creatures slammed against the hull of the Cyclops as the remaining guards tried to bring the yacht down. With a growl, Jacquie punched the accelerator and the Cyclops flew straight up into the air.

Luli's voice grunted from behind her, "I'm up, I'm up. Stop slapping me."

"Oh good," sighed Anton. "Because I think I need to lie down."

"You're covered in blood, Anton," exclaimed Luli. "Did you get shot?"

"Told you I needed to lie down."

"I'm going to try to stop the bleeding."

Suddenly, the sky above them darkened as a damaged Consortium destroyer flew in low. It plowed directly into the tower they had just escaped and the massive explosion threw the small yacht sideways. Jacquie fought to keep the Cyclops under control.

Luli's voice sounded tired as she finished cauterizing Anton's wound, "Rabbit will live. Where are we headed?"

Jacquie quickly keyed in the coordinates for the scrap yard and gunned the ship to full speed.

"Back to the Matilda and then off-planet. With no gods-be-damned leads on the whereabouts of Galena."

***

Derain, Batu, and Zolzaya sprinted toward the Folly when they noticed a couple of other people running in the same direction.

"I think that's Dusty and Barney!" shouted Zolzaya.

Derain glanced over and had to agree. No one ran quite the same way as Barney. He could pick him out of a crowd every time. Suddenly, an explosion tore a hole in the parking lot and sent Dusty flying.

"Go help him! I'll get the Folly rolling!" shouted Derain as the dust from the explosion ballooned around them.

Batu disappeared into the cloud while Zolzaya kept pace with Derain. When they reached the Folly, Derain unlocked the doors and the two of them piled in.

Another figure approached the vehicle. "Let me in," shouted Barney. "This whole place is going to be swarming with the God's know what soon! Let me in!"

Zolzaya kicked the door open and Barney hopped inside. "Help your brother get Dusty in here," he shouted. "I have to warm up the rail gun."

The woman hopped out and helped Batu

shovel Dusty into the Folly. Zolzaya stared in fascination as a sphere of black-rimmed purple lightning appeared over the parking lot. Small humanoid shapes fell out of it and landed all over the parking lot. As the humanoid figures stood up, they ran quickly toward the arena with the press of humanity still trapped there.

"Are those genorgs?" wondered Zolzaya.

Barney cursed, "Worse. Genorgs given the purpose of vengeance. Gods, I never wanted to see those things again."

"Never mind the human war above us, your home system is being invaded by aliens," added Derain. "This whole planet is going to be a dead zone in a matter of hours."

Dusty coughed, "Zol, get in here now! We've got to go!"

As the door closed behind her, Derain kicked the Folly in gear and sped away in a fantail of gravel.

"Drive like the Devil Tom is after you!" Barney shouted from the rail gun enclosure. "Otherwise we'll never get out of this!"

***

The Cyclops dodged a flying creature when Jacquie took the craft into a nose dive and rolled to port. As she shot back up, an alarm began bleating.

"Incoming!" yelled Jacquie. She flipped the Cyclops upside down to avoid a large Consortium vessel that plummeted past and slammed into a tall building. The winged creature changed its direction and chased after the downed ship. Jacquie kept a steady course toward their goal.

They flew over the city into the outskirts where the cloaked Matilda awaited their arrival. The ground fires burning brightly below them lighted their way as war quickly spread across the planet.

Receiving a well-timed code, the Matilda dropped her cloak and Jacquie flew through the open hangar bay doors. In the distance the Folly also raced toward the Matilda, raising a rooster tail of dust in its wake.

Forms fell from the sky and landed on their feet in a ragged circle around the Matilda. The circle grew larger as more of the altered genorgs arrived and trained their weapons on the Folly's approach.

"Hurry up and land this thing, Jacq!" Anton implored. "We have to give cover to the Folly!"

Jacquie brought the Cyclops into the hangar at a speed greater than most pilots would ever attempt. As the yacht screeched to a halt, she slammed the airlock switch and an acrid smell of smoke and dust blasted through the opening into the cabin. "Get the bay doors closed, Anton!"

"I'll cinch her down, Captain!" Luli shouted as she tore the restraining web free of her chest. "Get the Matilda ready for flight!"

Jacquie was already through the airlock and rushing across the bay.

***

Jon Gray Lang

Barney dropped free of the rail gun turret as the Folly rolled past the gate of the junkyard. He glanced over at Dusty who had regained some of his color. The Rabbit's Folly slowly rolled to a stop in front of the office and Derain hit the door switch.

"You sure you don't want to come with us?" asked Barney.

Dusty laughed weakly as Batu and Zolzaya helped him free of the seat webbing. "This is my home, Barney. My kids were born here and my wife died here. I ran away from one home world, if I don't fight to keep this one, where would I belong?"

"If this goes anything like Ninguiz, the Council will call for nuking the planet," Derain cautioned.

"Come on, pops," said Zolzaya as she pulled Dusty free of his seat. Batu went over to Dusty's other side to add support. "Dusty made sure our base below-ground was bomb-proof long before I was even born."

"We'll be alright," Batu added.

Dusty gave a tired grin to his old friend, "See? Sometimes I have to pretend like I have a choice. Go find your missing crew person and Godspeed to you, my oldest of friends."

Barney looked hopeless as he waved goodbye. "Let's go home, Derain."

Derain and Barney drove away from the junkyard with heavy hearts. They rode along in silence until the Matilda came into view.

"Just saw the Cyclops head into the ship," said Barney. "Might want to slow down."

"No," said Derain, "Look there's something dropping from the sky out here. More genorg troops, maybe?"

"Yeah," Barney agreed. "Looks like they're armed. Damn, that one's carrying a pre-Consortium rifle!"

"Whoa!" yelped Derain as he rounded a bend into a road block. He coasted the Folly to a stop as the altered creatures piled five deep in front of it. "It looks like we're in for a fight," he said as reached down to check his side arms. Barney swung the door open and slipped out of the vehicle. "Hey! What are you doing? Get back in here!" yelled Derain.

Barney just waved him away and walked in front of the Folly. He gave a deep sigh as he rolled up what was left of his sleeves. "This is gonna hurt. Alright, let's get this over with!"

The altered genorg that took the lead blinked rapidly and tilted her head at an unnatural angle. Slowly, the others followed suit. First one spoke then the others, until it sounded like one voice, "Barney? Barney? ...arney? ...ney? Is that you?"

Barney's expression was grim. He raised his sore arms like a gladiator awaiting cheers and jeered, "The one! The only! I am Barney de Lagnel, and I grow tired of waiting."

The genorg from 'other space' pointed her weapon toward the ground and began to chuckle.

Jon Gray Lang

Then all the creatures lowered their rifles and laughed in unison.

Barney quirked his face in confusion, "Eh? What's this?"

"You live! Live! So long have I thought you dead, friend." The genorgs pondered together, "Maybe it was me who died?"

Barney stepped back and slapped the hood of the Folly, "I'll try to cause a distraction so you can get her on the Matilda, alright?"

As the Folly edged forward, the genorgs stepped out of the way. Barney led the vehicle through the throng when a thought hit him, "Galena? Is that you?"

The closest genorg to him turned and said, "My friend, I don't know how much longer I can last. The world... the universe is much too big for me to hold onto."

Barney stopped, reached out and took her hand, "Then hold onto me and the rest of us that love you. We're coming to free you, Galena."

He squeezed her hand, and the sadness on her face was heartbreaking. Black tears leaked from the eyes of the being that looked at him. Suddenly, she let go of his hand and shoved him away. She and the others screamed with more pain than any creature should ever have to feel. They all fell to their knees and the wailing continued.

Barney glanced behind him as the Folly came to a stop inside the Matilda. He watched as Derain hopped out and began strapping the vehicle down.

Jon Gray Lang

The screams of the genorgs came to a stuttering stop and Barney looked back. Something was attacking Galena and she was losing.

Barney growled with resolve, "Fight it Galena! Fight it with everything you've got! By the Ancestors, we're coming for you and you better be there when we arrive!"

He turned and ran for the Matilda. As his feet landed on the hard metal of the cargo deck, he smacked the switch to close the doors. When a low hum emanated from the genorgs, Barney looked out at the sea of faces that resembled Galena and saw a hard resolve appear.

As the altered genorgs regained their feet, they flowed into a synchronous motion. As the last one came to stand, they all stepped through a syncopated pattern in unison that they repeated until the cargo bay doors clanged shut.

"Are they dancing?" pondered Derain in awe.

Barney nodded with a fierce grin, "She's fighting with everything she has. Now it's up to us to free her!"

***

By the time Barney and Derain made it to the bridge, Luli was already strapped into the pilot seat and had locked on her viewfinder. Jacquie was just finishing strapping in and Anton had the weapons unlocked and ready to fire.

"Good, you're on board," Jacquie said as they

walked in. "Derain, take the Nav console and figure out a way off this rock."

Anton remarked, "Not sure what is going on now, but those genorgs are running willy nilly toward the city."

"I wonder if she's okay," Barney said with concern.

"What do you mean," asked Jacquie.

"It was Galena, Jacq. She was talking through them."

"You sure?"

Barney shrugged, "Sure as I can be in this bonkers kind of situation."

"I've got an exit configured," said Derain. "Sending it over to you, Lu."

"Received," she replied.

"Dusty and the rest staying here?" asked Anton.

Barney nodded.

"Hope they have better luck than I did on Tigron..." grumbled Anton.

"Or that dead planet in the Leporis system," mentioned Luli.

The Matilda rumbled loudly as she lifted and her landing gear retracted. The ship rose slowly over the beleaguered city that glowed from the fires that burned in its streets. As the ship flew along the route Derain had given her, Luli avoided the falling debris, attack ships, and flying monstrosities. As they broke atmosphere, the skies filled with ships and creatures engaged in a full space battle.

"Wow..." mouthed Anton in awe of the spectacle.

"Get that cloak back on," ordered Jacquie. "Who is crazy enough to take on the whole Consortium?"

"Over one of the primary home worlds, no less." Luli grimaced as she swung the Matilda into a tight spiral and rammed the acceleration on the ship's engines to max.

"It has to be those rebel forces we kept hearing about from the feeds," said Derain as he held tightly to his seat.

"We could never muster numbers like this," Anton marveled.

"Good luck to them," Jacquie said dubiously.

As the Matilda disappeared from view, Barney declared, "Now, let's go find Galena. Did you get a lead from the Khanda twins?"

"Nothing at all," Jacquie lamented. "All of that effort was wasted. We are no closer to finding Galena than when we landed on this bleeding mud ball!"

"Don't give up hope, Jacquie. Something will turn up," said Luli.

Barney moved toward the hatchway on the bridge, "I'll head down to the engine room and keep an eye on things down there. If you hear anything, let me know."

Derain looked up from the Nav console, "Barney, wait. I think there is something wrong with the ship's navigation. The program is pointing us toward the inner planet of the system and won't let me change it."

Barney walked over and noticed a data card sticking out of the drive. "Wait, is this the card you retrieved for Mr. Leon from Baal Shamin? What's it doing here?"

A strange voice with an odd enunciation emanated from the Matilda's nav console, "Location found, navigation engaged. Trajectory to Aja locked."

"See?" said Anton. "Nothing says hope like a creepy voice coming out of your ship's computer."

thirty-one

Rocket Ship

Some extra sense propelled Galena as if through a dream. There was little she remembered except leaving her bunk in her cell. Part of her remembered Corporal Cook wouldn't be on guard tonight. Yet the journey through the halls felt unreal as if she wasn't moving under her own propulsion. The thought hit her hard, *"I am only a passenger in my body."*

The chuckle she sensed from that other identity sealed it. "Where are you taking me?"

The creature's voice cut through her thought, "You need to know more, understand more. There is only one place here and time is running short."

Her body arrived at a door but she barely glimpsed the name on the plate. The door swung open as if it had never been locked and the entity moved her to the center of the room. Without her own volition, she dropped to the floor in a lotus position. The door closed behind her, but she never heard the latch click as she vacantly stared at her surroundings.

"Why am I in Dr. Saric's old office? The man has been dead for years. I made sure of it."

The chuckle almost hurt as the entity shuffled through her memories. It replayed scenes of her being cut free from the wall on the prison ship and her foot connecting with Dr. Saric's head. The snap of his broken neck sounded even louder than she remembered.

"Such a creature of chaos. Wyeth created you well. Better than we could have imagined. You will serve us well."

Galena sucked in a breath as the thing within her replayed every death she had caused, back to the moment she had first met Anton Roane. The creature slowed every decision she made on that fateful day down. The slow click of her service pistol as she loosed a round into the skull of one after another of the captured rebels. The shock of the remaining rebels was more palpable than she remembered as she traveled down the line and seemed to skip some without meaning. The sickened look on her squad's face as the thing they only regarded as a tool made the decision they had shirked.

"There weren't enough provisions for all of us!" she shouted in consternation.

"Then why did you keep the one you know as

Rabbit alive? It doesn't fit your logic."

Galena struggled for a reason, but it was only his odd blue eyes she remembered. Eyes that had gazed into hers with deep understanding. Somehow he knew the purpose for her action and made peace with it. For that reason alone she spared him and her feelings for him had grown into something new and surprising.

The creature within scoffed, "Emotions? Foolishness. An insect that suffers so is more a failure than we could have expected. No matter."

"We? Are you like the Leons?" she whispered to herself.

"Read!" the creature bellowed.

She had little control over her body as her neck tilted and forced her head to look at the lines of sigils. They glimmered faintly in the dim light. The peculiar shapes and squiggles scratched in random lines appeared to be a language. *'A language I do not understand,'* Galena thought.

But she was wrong. Slowly, their meaning emerged. The symbols spoke of a tale thousands of centuries in the making. A portal opened and humans wandered through only to be torn asunder by the creatures that existed within. Wave after wave of humans clothed in archaic armor stormed the portals only to be swallowed up each time by the monsters on the other side of the gate.

Until the arrival of the twelve. They fed humans by the thousands to the void as they fought for some form of control over it. As the cost of lives slowly outweighed the appetite of the creatures within, they made headway.

"Yes," answered the entity. "You see what no one has seen for many years. Not so different are we."

Galena's mind recoiled. "No! This is sickness! Why not leave the portal alone? No one needed to have died!"

"Weakness," cursed the monster. "All that exists needs to be controlled."

Galena watched as the twelve found the center of the 'other space' and trapped the creature inside. The creature's size was beyond reckoning, yet somehow it felt familiar.

"I don't want to see anymore!" she shouted as she closed her mind's eye to the horrors of the twelve nailing the power of the creature to blocks so that it could no longer move or fight.

As the creature fought for control of her spirit, she found shelter within another that was like, yet unlike her. Her eyes opened and the world she was falling toward looked familiar.

"I have been here before," she realized as she carefully landed on legs still not her own. She looked around and saw more of her sisters landing, but they all looked wrong. "You are the ones from the other side..."

"Sister... sister... sister..." they replied. "You see us... you come for us..."

The trundle of an engine caught her ear and she turned to face the sound. "Familiar..."

Jon Gray Lang

A small, angry man hopped out of a vehicle and strode toward her. Emotions swept over her, protectiveness, nurturing, and surprise. "Barney? Is that you?"

"The one! The only!" the familiar man proclaimed. "I am Barney de Lagnel, and I grow tired of waiting."

Joy swept over Galena, "You live! So long have I thought you dead, friend." The creature within struck at her and broke the connection, but the lifeline quickly reformed.

Recognition filled Barney's eyes, "Galena? Is that you?"

As the entity battled to silence her mind, she struggled to speak, "My friend, I don't know how much longer I can last. The world... the universe is much too big for me to hold onto."

She felt Barney stop and take her hand, "Then hold onto me and the rest of us that love you."

"Love?" she wondered. "What could love me?"

The entity within rushed toward her consciousness, "Nothing could love a foundling such as you. Only hate and fear exist for your kind!"

The creature forced Galena's darkest memories back into the front of her mind. Being separated from her creche sisters. Watching her sisters crushed in the machinery of the factory as she and the survivors were blamed. The mine collapse and hearing the screams of those trapped within before they were executed by rescue parties.

Jon Gray Lang

The sting of the Council Senator's ring as it cut her brow for being late. The revulsion of the officers as they forced her through combat training and did their best to break her. All the way back to her days on the auction block where they kept her in a cage and treated her with less dignity than an animal.

Barney's voice cut through the darkness of her memories, "We're coming to free you Galena." The resolve in his voice added steel to her spine as she embraced his words. "When? What must I do until you come?"

"Fight it Galena! Fight it with everything you've got! By the Ancestors, we're coming for you and you better be there when we arrive!"

"Don't listen to that thing!" cried the larval thing within her. "It is less than human!"

Galena's eyes snapped open and she flicked her tongue against the back of her teeth. "Your prejudices outweigh any truth you might speak, 'once-human'. I am loved and I will fight because, because that is what I was made to do!"

The creature's laughter grated as it spoke, "Fight with what? You too are less than human."

"Maybe so," she replied. "But I am not alone!"

Movement returned to her slowly as she remembered the voices of cherished friends.

Luli's voice exclaimed, "Dance, silly girl! Dancing is the most human thing I can do. Even being part machine, still I dance."

Jacquie's voice spoke to her, "You are part of

my crew and I expect you to be as human as possible! So dance, girl! Dance!"

She flowed through the moves they had taught her and focused on each step. As the patterns knit together, Galena began to separate from the creature. She felt the enveloping arms of her sisters as she reunited them with their own humanity. As more and more of them accepted her connection, the presence of the entity receded into the darkness.

It was only then that she felt a new presence envelope her. Dark waves swept over her and she felt like she was drowning. A huge eye swung around to light upon her like a lighthouse in stormy seas. The being seeped into her bones and cut her connection to her sisters.

"No!" she lamented. "I need them! They help me fight against the thing! Return me, please!"

The huge eye stared into Galena's very essence and issued a single command. "Free me. You have the strength little one. Free me!"

The presence overwhelmed her will and Galena slipped into the darkness of unconsciousness.

***

Jerr Cook awoke trembling in fear. Shadowy creatures flitted about the room and hovered over his roommate's bunk. Hamza Fitzpatrick tossed back and forth as the sweat from his brow sparkled in the light and splashed against the tiles of the floor.

A voice spoke to Jerr's mind that he barely recognized. "Help me!"

The plaintive voice cut through his grogginess and compelled him to slip out from his bed. The shadowy spirits seemed agitated, but they remained focused on Fitzpatrick.

"Help me, please!"

He wasn't sure if the voice he heard could also hear him, "I am on my way. Where should I go?"

A vision of the name plate in Dr. Saric's office filled his mind. He cursed as he shrugged on his jacket and stepped out into the hallway.

As the room door closed, he pondered, *'Am I dreaming?'*

"Help me!" wailed the voice.

Cook shook himself and sprinted toward the lift. "Good enough for me. I am on my way!"

***

Corporal Cook carefully cracked open the door to Dr. Saric's old office. The room glowed with an eerie light. The bloodied sigils etched into the walls of the room smoldered with a darkness that made him feel ill.

The sound of rhythmic gasping drew Cook into the center of the room. There in the dim light lay the crumpled form of the Lieutenant. Standing over her body was one of the shadowy figures he had seen hovering around Fitzpatrick.

Suddenly, the main station speaker sounded an alarm, "Warning! Warning! Jard is under attack!" The message repeated steadily, "Warning! Warning! Jard is under attack!"

"Fuck it. It's now or never." Jerald grimaced as he grabbed the Lieutenant's arm and yanked her out of the center of the room.

The shadow creature bobbed and screeched as he dragged her limp body toward the door. The shadow figure lunged. He felt it pass through his body, leaving a trace of coldness behind.

Relentlessly, Cook held onto the Lieutenant's arm and continued across the room. "Gods-be-damned door!" he cursed as he struggled with the latch, "Open!"

The door opened with a suddenness he wasn't expecting and he fell back. Jerald quickly recovered and yanked the genorg Lieutenant through the door with all his strength, then he pulled the door shut and locked it. He thought he heard screams emanating from the other side, but he couldn't swear they were real.

'Is any of this real?' he wondered, as he pinched himself to be certain he wasn't dreaming. He looked down at Galena who appeared to merely be sleeping peacefully.

"I'm sure I heard a call for help," said Corporal Cook as he gathered up the Lieutenant and hoisted her over his shoulder. "You called for help,

I'm certain."

As soon as he spoke those words, the blaring alarms that warned of an in-system attack on Jard went silent. "I'll take that as a sign that I'm right."

Carrying the Lieutenant in his arms, Jerald trudged down the hall and stepped aboard the lift. The ride back up seemed slower than usual, but grateful that no shadowy figures had followed them, Cook relaxed and chuckled.

When the lift reached the proper floor, the Corporal was also thankful there was no one in the hallway to ask questions as he stepped out. He lumbered along to the Lieutenant's room, struggled to open the door, and carefully carried her inside. With a gentle heave, he settled her onto her bunk and covered her with a blanket.

Without warning, Galena reached out and pressed her hand hard against the Corporal's forehead, "Remember nothing!"

Instantly, Cook's eyes closed as tranquility swept over him and his senses disappeared in darkness.

thirty-two

The Darker the Weather, The Better the Man

The Peking Empress kept her distance from the rear of the fleet of Consortium ships that pursued the rest of her rebel armada into the bubble that enshrouded the planet Jard. Not a single one had turned to confront her.

'But what great threat is a toothless old luxury liner?' Harjeet brooded.

"Admiral!" exclaimed Thadie, "The reports are garbled but something inside the bubble is affecting the Leon's! They're dropping like flies!"

Suddenly, Mr. Leon shrieked and stumbled to the decking. His breath came in short ragged bursts as he struggled to control the flow of air into his lungs.

Jon Gray Lang

"Get a medical team up here!" shouted Admiral Kaur.

Mr. Leon struggled to get his feet under him, but waved her away, "No need, Harjeet. I'll be okay." As the words left his lips, he squealed in pain and fell to his knees. "Might need a minute, though."

Admiral Kaur saw the plaintive request in his eyes, "Belay that order. What did I miss?"

"The enemy fleet is entering the bubble or whatever in Sheol that is around Jard," stated Thadie.

Mr. Leon pulled himself back up and breathed as if it took all his strength to do so, "Please Admiral Kaur, do not enter that sphere. I think I know what it is, but I can't get confirmation from inside."

"We're technically blind out here, Mr. Leon."

He nodded wearily, "I know. But this isn't a warship. You have no guns or defensive weapons. And if I'm right about what lies inside, that is the least of what we'll need to survive."

She took him aside, "And what would you have me do? Sit on the sidelines and offer no assistance at all? What sort of leader would I be?"

Mr. Leon smiled weakly, "I knew you were the right person for the job. Tell me, Admiral, if we're struggling to get comms from inside the sphere, do you think those inside the sphere can hear us? What would that mean?"

Her smile was grim, "It means we have a perspective unlike anyone else."

Mr. Leon nodded, "I will leave it to you. I must retire to my cabin." As he took a step, he collapsed again and this time he didn't come back to his senses.

Harjeet called out, "Mr. Vadik, please see Mr. Leon to his cabin. Latiff, is there any way we can see inside the bubble without entering it?"

"Hmm, the main sensor array is in the bow of the Empress. If we can bury the nose in deep enough, theoretically we could see what's in there."

"Would that leave us vulnerable out here?" she asked. "Can we remain watchful outside of the bubble, too?"

Latiff pondered for a moment, "I could make the rear sensor and comms array run independently of the primary one. I'd have to shut down the engineering board up here for the processing."

"Get Mr. Dauber on the comm, Thadie."

Mr. Dauber's voice came over the comm, "I'm here Cap, err I mean Admiral."

"We need to free up some system space. Think you can keep a tight eye on the engines?"

Mr. Dauber's voice sounded excited, "You mean run her completely on manual? Of course! I do that for fun when you're all sleeping!"

Harjeet laughed, "She's all yours, Mr. Dauber. Mr. Ghilzai, make it happen."

As the bubble-like sphere took up the entire forward view, Latiff busily hijacked the ship's systems console until the rear sensor array began sending information to it. "Check the comms, Ms.

Dumba."

"I have two set-ups now," replied Thadie.

"We're good to go, Admiral."

Harjeet's hands dropped to her hips and her stance widened for stability. "I have no idea what this thing is in front of us but expect the entry to be bumpy, everyone. We'll need to track everything in there so that we can offer support to our compatriots as soon as possible. Comms are going to be important and we need to stay out here as long as we're needed. We all on board?"

"No point in signing up for a rodeo, if there ain't no bulls to ride!" groused Ovi.

Harjeet relaxed as her crew took up their positions and locked into their systems. "Send her in."

The Peking Empress looked tiny as she moved toward the oily rainbow surface of the sphere that encased Jard. When her bow pierced the bubble, a strange scent of burning copper intertwined with long-dead vegetation penetrated the ship in a permeable wave. Someone retched uncontrollably at the smell as the comm channels flooded with battle calls and damage reports. However, among the flurry of calls, the most alarming news was that all of the Mr. Leon's were comatose or worse.

There was a deafening shriek and a creature twice the size of the Empress swam past the nose of the ship. In pursuit was a freighter firing everything it had at the behemoth, as a creature with spidery legs crawled along its fuselage. Further out ahead, floated the wreck of a Consortium destroyer that had been cracked in half. A shadowy amorphous blob reached into the destroyer, pulled out crew members, both living and dead, and shoveled them into its maw.

The crew of the Peking Empress watched the scene in stunned silence. "Great Tom, space monsters are real?" Ovi shouted. "All this time I thought they were just tall tales from drunken star sailors!"

***

As the Independence, Scorpio, and Copperhead flew toward the jump gate, the Consortium destroyer and frigate finally reacted. They altered their lazy orbit and moved out to engage the three smaller vessels.

"Alright, ladies! Looks like we've got their attention," crowed Commander Keri of the Independence.

"You say that like it's a good thing," replied Captain Kahn of the Copperhead.

Commander Gamma chimed in from the Scorpio, "Is that not what we are here to do?"

Rosa Keri glanced at Captain Delta, "We have got to work on her sense of humor."

Delta looked at her quizzically, "Was there something humorous in that verbal exchange?"

Rosa sighed dramatically, "We'll have to work

on all of your senses of humor then. What's the plan, Captains?"

"We will lose in a straight-on fight. We need to split them up," said Captain Delta.

Rosa's grin was a bit feral as she said, "Ariel, do you think you could peel that destroyer off our backs so the Independence and Scorpio can work on that frigate?"

"You heard her, Siew," said Captain Kahn. "Let's go fishing!"

"Copperhead out," said Siede Geist. Before the comm completely cut off everyone heard, "Eesh, are we in for a trip. I think Rosa is rubbing off on Ariel..."

"You're with us, Scorpio," laughed the Commander. "The jump gate is your job."

"Understood. Scorpio out."

Rosa said over her shoulder, "Captain Delta, can you check the flight trajectory of the Copperhead?"

"Of course, Commander."

Commander Keri settled into the pilot's seat of the Independence and quickly checked her mobilization straps. "Tight enough," she said as she gripped the controls.

She watched as the Scorpio fell back and rode off the tail of the Independence. The Copperhead broke hard to port and fired its afterburners. The small merchant craft rocketed off into the distance when it lit its directional rockets. The arc was wide and fast.

Jon Gray Lang

Delta spoke, "Copperhead's trajectory is a wide-angle approach that should bring it toward the stern of the destroyer."

Rosa nodded, "Good, good. That should pull them off trajectory. Everyone buckle in and prep for a fight! Rho-11, take out their comm array. Daphne, keep an eye out for her fighters. Hopefully, they won't think our little ship is worth launching them."

"Rho-11, your second target is the bay doors. Tertiary targets are any and all engines."

"Understood, Commander," Rho-11 replied as she hunkered down in the weapons station.

Rosa boosted the Independence's forward momentum and studied the frigate. It was an older model that bore battle scars along its flanks. The sensor array was well protected in an alcove near the bow of the ship. But the comm array stood proudly on the central tower like a single tree in a meadow. Rosa tapped at the attitudinal jets and adjusted her flight angle. The frigate grew in size as they approached it at high velocity.

"She's an old beast, alright," she whistled. "Expect engagement in three, two, one!"

The thump from the rail guns vibrated the decking under her feet as the scrape of three missiles being launched played an accompaniment.

"Incoming!" shouted Agnes from the Sensors console.

Rosa ignited the jets along the top line of the Independence and forced a hard drop. Hard and heavy slugs the size of airlock hatches screamed past and disappeared beyond the Independence.

"Missiles locked on, dumping chafe!" relayed Agnes.

"Shit, shutting down engines and flying free," grumbled Rosa. *'Hopefully, the timing is right.'*

The Independence kept dropping as missiles crashed into the chafe and exploded outside the ship. As the boat rocked, Rosa triggered the engines and the Independence accelerated. She glanced out the bow port and cursed. The destroyer was still focused on them.

"Anne, get the Copperhead on the comm! We need that destroyer out of the way!"

***

"... need that destroyer out of the way!"

Ariel slammed a fist against her armrest. She compared the location of the Independence to the positions of the two Consortium ships. It looked ugly. The current flight path of the Independence would take it between the two vessels and there was nothing the Independence could do to break off. "She's going too damn fast."

Omega spoke up from the weapons console, "It's very far out, but I have a lock on the destroyer's rail guns."

"Do it. See if you can get their attention, Omega," Ariel replied. "Siew, do you think you can adjust to bring us up behind the destroyer?"

"We're far out enough. It shouldn't be a problem, but it'll take time."

Ariel grumbled, "If we can't get her to move off, we'll switch to taking out the jump gate."

"Slugs away," said Omega.

The Copperhead swung a bit as Siew Lian adjusted their attack path. Ariel watched as the destroyer and the jump gate slowly grew closer. She glanced at the countdown and it read five minutes.

"Cutting it close, damn close," she observed.

***

Gamma guided the Scorpio behind the Independence and sighted along the flight path. It was then that she noticed the destroyer and the frigate were closing in on the Independence. They were setting up a kill zone for the old pirate ship and she knew there was nothing Rosa could do to stop it.

"No matter how good a pilot she is, she can't defeat physics," Gamma said to no one in particular. "Tau-SA43, can we hit either of them with anything at this range?"

"The Scorpio is only designed for targets up close," replied Tau-SA43. We'd have to be in the center of the fray to hit anything."

"It doesn't look good, Commander," said Nu-M12 from the Nav station. "I don't think the Independence will survive."

Suddenly, the Independence picked up speed and Gamma labored to keep pace. She pushed the old engines for everything they were worth and swung out from behind the Independence.

Gamma growled, "If we need to be in the center of the fray, then in the center of it we will go!"

***

The Independence flew straight as an arrow and its forward path grew ever more narrow. The frigate and the destroyer angled their approach which left no other way through except for right between the two of them. Rosa glared in consternation at how they had caught her in their trap.

"Well, they're not taking us down without a fight!" Rosa snarled. "If it's a broadside they want, then we'll give it to them! Arm every last thing we have on this boat and fire them all!"

***

As Gamma fought to bring the Scorpio along the port side of the Independence, the two Consortium ships launched their rockets and artillery at the Independence. Space lit up as the Independence launched everything it had in a bid to take them down.

The glare was intense as the Scorpio sidled up close to the Independence and absorbed the rounds from the destroyer. The ore hauler shook, rattled, and rolled under the impacts.

"Tau-SA43, fire at will!" ordered Commander Gamma.

"Firing, Commander!"

Gamma struggled to keep the Scorpio in place and flew almost completely blind amongst the chafe, rockets, missiles, and rail gun slugs. The asteroid breaker guns punished almost everything incoming, but even they couldn't keep up with the sheer amount of firepower the two Consortium ships brought to bear.

"Nu-M12, I need you to be my eyes!" shouted Gamma. "Where are we and how much farther do we have to go?"

Nu-M12 zoomed in the Nav console to a ten-kilometer radius. "Positioning is good, but we're only halfway through!"

***

Ariel shielded her eyes from the insane battle her friends were flying through. From what she could see, it looked as if the Scorpio was acting as a shield for the Independence. With the amount of ordinance being used, she didn't have much hope that either ship would survive.

Omega burst out in triumph, "We have a direct hit on the destroyer's rail guns! Targeting hangar bay doors now."

Ariel stamped her foot against the decking in frustration. She knew there wasn't much else she could do for the other ships in her battle group.

'Curse me for getting involved!' she thought to herself. *'How did I end up in this situation?'*

She turned her attention to Omega who was prepping for another hit on the destroyer. *'At least she is fighting for her people, her sisters. But what am I fighting for?'*

Ariel pursed her lips, *'If no one else out there is willing to stand with them, how can I ignore their call for help?'*

Captain Khan sat up straighter and steeled her words, "Siew, a change in plans. Go after the jump gate and do everything you can to keep us flying. Omega, I need you to target those engines and knock that ship down a notch. Then dump everything else into the jump gate. If we're going to succeed, it has to be now!"

***

The clanging inside the Independence was deafening as the hull pinged with every round that hit it. Alarms screamed throughout the bridge as smoke swelled in through every vent. The entire ship shook as a strong blast opened her up to space.

Commander Keri hesitated, "What was that?"

"The cargo bay is gone, I repeat the cargo bay is gone!" Anne shouted over the din. "Auto airlocks have engaged."

The atmospheric warning shut off when the leak was stemmed and the silence was a blessed moment of bliss.　Rosa struggled to keep the Independence under control as the ship bucked hard from the attack.

"I'm out!　Guns are high and dry!" declared Rho-11.

Rosa cursed loudly.　"How's the Scorpio?"

"She's still with us, but her comms are down... engines too."

The number of pops and bangs coming from the starboard side dissipated.　Delta chuckled, "Copperhead got a hit on the destroyer's rail guns and they misfired into the frigate!"

"Thank the Major for small blessings!" shouted Rosa.

***

As the Copperhead flew straight toward the jump gate, Captain Kahn asked, "Where are we in regards to the enemy vessels?"

Omega replied, "We are passing them in... one, two... now!　Slugs away!"

"Is that the Independence coming through that mess?" Siede hollered in amazement.　"How, by the Demon Tom, did they make it through?"

"Any sign of the Scorpio?" asked Ariel.

Siede shook her head in the negative, "Nothing yet."

"Another direct hit!" shouted Omega in excitement.　"The enemy destroyer is dead in space! I repeat, dead in space!"

The Captain eyed the switch for the planet killer missile that Mr. Leon had wired into her panel. As the crew cheered, she brought up the interface with the AI. An old emoji of a smiley face danced across the screen requesting target directives. Ariel pulled up the coordinates for the jump gate generator and loaded them in. The interface flashed its final question, "Launch now? Yes or No?"

"Omega, I need you to target the jump gate, a wide spread with everything we have left," Ariel said as she chose 'Yes' and set a launch time for one minute. "You got it? We only have one shot at this."

Omega's voice sobered as she swept through the weapons controls and did as she was ordered, "Target is locked. Awaiting launch order."

"I see the Scorpio now," said Siede in the interim.

Captain Kahn nodded in acknowledgment as she watched the launch clock time down for the planet killer. When it hit thirty seconds, she ordered, "Do it now."

***

On board the Scorpio, Mu-IK97 ran with an extinguisher as the alarms bleated overhead. The port side of the ore hauler had taken a horrific beating and entire sections had been sealed against space. The young genorg raced through the last open airlock and battled an electrical fire that threatened to gut the ship.

The wires that operated airlocks further down the line dangled from the blackened walls in a mad dance of sparks. Mu-IK97 heaved the extinguisher up and coated the flames with a blast of heat retardant and liquid patch mix.

As the retardant hit the flames, it rippled out in a cloud of noxious smoke. She covered her mouth and kept spraying until the last of the flames were smothered.

As she backed away, she shouted, "Fire's out! Send in the splicers!"

Two more genorgs bound into the chamber. They immediately cleared out the burnt wires and unspooled replacements. Mu-IK97 watched for a moment to make sure no new fires flared up, but the room remained safe.

The gauge on the extinguisher showed it was empty. She pulled a replacement from the wall and stowed the empty in its place. With a new tank in her hands, she wandered over to the closed airlock and looked through the window.

The rent in the hull was long and wide. And in the faint glow of the emergency lights, she could see the rag doll corpses of her sisters caught on the jagged metal and floating grimly in place.

Then something else out past the hull caught her eyes. Tiny pinpricks of light orbited a circular structure that suddenly burst in a flash of light as bright as a star.

As she blinked her eyes to clear the flash, the overhead comm announced, "The jump gate is down. I repeat the jump gate is down. The mission is accomplished!"

"Come on, Mu-IK97," said one of the splicers, "There's another fire on deck seven."

"On my way," she replied as a tiny smile formed on her lips. "We won."

***

Admiral Kaur watched with concern as the Nav console did its best to generate an updated 3D model of the battle inside the alien bubble. The information it was receiving changed so quickly that sometimes what she saw was already minutes old.

All in all, though, her fleet was doing remarkably well. They had defeated the planetary defenses and the Consortium vessels were locked in a battle of survival against the alien creatures.

"So is the planet below," she conceded. "So are we, if truth be told."

Her hands settled on her hips as she monitored the battle. "However, we need to work with the Consortium fleet if humanity is to survive another day."

"Eh?" grunted Ovi. "Why don't us and ours escape and let those Consortium bastards rot? Let the monsters have this place and we head home the victors."

Harjeet glared at him until he cowered under her gaze, "We'd be the victors for how long, Ovi? You know they're gunning for all of us, if the rumors hold true. These alien creatures have destroyed entire systems we used to rely on to make port. Don't you miss some of those folks? I know I do."

Ovi gulped as he comprehended what she meant, "Well, when you put it that way..."

She slammed a fist against the panel, "We have the best chance to send these extraterrestrials back to where ever they came from, but we have to work together."

She gave everyone on her bridge crew the evil eye, "If we don't help the people, how are we any better than the Council? Aren't we better than them?"

Dead silence dominated the bridge as each person considered her words. Suddenly, a loud ping sounded.

Thadie said, "The transponder is picking up wormhole energies out near the last planet. It looks like a big signature."

"Send a direct laser comm to the incoming vessel," ordered Admiral Kaur. "If any of us are going to get out of this alive, we have to convince them to work with us before they get here."

Thadie went through the commands and sent the comm. She looked up at Harjeet and shrugged, "The cruiser's not there anymore."

***

The CBC Remus punched its way into the

Malina system. All was clear in near proximity. Then suddenly a bright flash obliterated the jump gate.

"Holy!... That was the jump gate... it's gone," exclaimed the Comm Officer. "I'm not getting replies from the jump gate defense ships, but there is a lot of distorted chatter coming from Jard."

"With the jump gate down, focus our sensors on Jard. Then find me an active Consortium ship that can tell me what is going on," ordered Captain Ellsbeth. "There's supposed to be a fleet out here!"

"Sensor report to the main screen, Captain."

The main screen blossomed with the image of an oily sphere that surrounded the home world of Jard. However, nothing at all was visible through the skin of the bubble.

"That looks familiar," remarked Commander Shafar. "Is Malina under invasion by...?"

Captain Ellsbeth grabbed the arms of her chair in a death grip, "By the Gods! It can't be! They can't be here!"

She switched the comm to ship-wide, "Jard is under alien invasion! I repeat the home world is under invasion by the same creatures as in the Pequiz system! Prepare for battle!"

She clicked the comm off and growled, "Get this boat ready for a short FTL jump. Bring us inside of that alien sphere!"

"But Captain, that could cause cataclysms on the planet!" said Commander Shafar.

Captain Ellsbeth ground out the words,

"There won't be a planet worth saving if we don't get there yesterday! Dire times call for desperate measures. And we're running out of time."

thirty-three

I Wish I Was the Moon

"Pushing hard to starboard!" shouted Luli as a brace of short-range rockets sped past and slammed into an ancient alien looking vessel behind the Matilda. "By Tom, that was close!"

"We've got a bogey on our tail, Lu, but I can't get a fix on her," shouted Anton. "Hunta, hunta, yea!"

"She can only go so fast, Rabbit!" Luli cursed. "Let me do my damn job!"

"There we go," grinned Anton as the heavy thunk of one of the rail guns launched its shot at velocity. "Eh? What was that?"

Jacquie gripped the armrests of her chair and dug her heels into the decking, "Are we sure the cloak is on?"

Barney's voice came through the open comm, "Oh it's on. It isn't happy about it, but it's on."

Jon Gray Lang

Jacquie growled, "Acknowledged. Derain, are we still on track?"

The bounty hunter looked up from his console, "As much as we can be."

"Noted."

Jacquie scanned the skies in shock. Ordnance flew past and found plenty of targets to hit. Consortium carriers fired on their own destroyers who likewise fired back. Intermixed was an array of trawlers, merchant ships, and other vessels that belonged in museums and scrap yards. Some of those boats trailed fire and smoke as they glided between the others uncontrollably.

"Seriously," she said, "What in the hell happened while we were out in the boonies?"

"I don't know, but aren't those the same bounty hunters from the Scrapheap?" Anton said as he pointed to a trio of craft off in the distance.

As the three ships grew closer, Derain noted, "The one in the lead is Vania's ship, the Daena."

On closer inspection, he recognized the telltale markings on her suit, but the figure who wore it was not alive in the normal sense. Half of its head was sheared off and where the right arm should be was a chitinous limb that gripped the flight controls. The left eye glared at him as the Daena picked up speed. "I think it recognizes me. But how can it see us through the cloak?"

"Who cares! It's coming right for us!" bellowed Jacquie. "Evasives!"

"Too late!" warned Luli as the Daena

slammed into them.

The Daena exploded on impact. The Matilda spun out of control through the scattered remnants of Vania's ship. Alarms bleated from multiple systems.

"Shut those down, now!" shouted Jacquie. "Lu, You got this?"

Luli crowed, "Woo hoo! Now this is flying!"

Derain glanced at Anton in shock, but the ex-pirate only shrugged in reply.

As Luli fought for control, she sang with untamed joy,

"Soon may the Wellerman come,"
"To bring us sugar and tea and rum,"
"One day, when the tonguin's is done,"
"We'll take our leave and go!"

As Luli finished the verse she straightened the Matilda's course and blasted out past the ruckus that surrounded Jard. The permeating reek of overripe fruit began to recede as the ship climbed and the oppressive weight of the 'other space' vanished.

Derain exhaled in suspended relief, "I think we made it out!"

***

The Matilda's cloaking device held up as the ship cruised through the system. Navigation was taking them ever closer to the innermost planet which didn't have a satellite as far as everyone knew. Derain widened the system map and watched as the numbers descended. When they grew closer to matching the coordinates found on that data card, he widened the parameters. "There isn't anything out here, Jacq. Mr. Leon sent us on a wild goose chase."

"Maybe it's a space station?" Anton suggested.

Jacquie shrugged, "Maybe. Mr. Leon has hung us out to dry before, but he hasn't ever lied. We'll see this through."

"Not much longer until we're on top of the planet Ogun," said Luli. "I see no incoming or outbound traffic, and the only thing past it is the sun."

As the Matilda slipped through space the rocky planet grew larger in her port bow. The surface of Ogun glowed cherry red from the solar radiation on one side while the other side was black as night. Nothing could survive on the planet where the sun blazed hot across its surface. The dark side was brutally cold, but eventually, the sun kissed the entire surface during the planet's fifty-seven-day rotation.

"Ogun is definitely our destination," Derain grumbled.

Barney clicked the scanner through different light spectrums and mused, "There is something similar to this near my home world. Old Titan records spoke of a plan to build a mobile base that would travel across the surface at a speed that matched the planet's rotation. As far as I know, it wasn't ever built and population growth control then became the major concern." He sighed, "There's nothing reflecting on the surface."

Suddenly, the scanner system pinged and Anton straightened up in his chair. "Hey!" he squeaked in excitement, "We've got something circling this planet and boy is it fast."

"What is it?" asked Jacquie.

"I'm still pulling data, but whatever it is it should be visible to the naked eye any minute now."

Derain, Jacquie, and Barney edged closer to the port bow. A tiny satellite flashed in the sun as it moved quickly and closely around Ogun.

"This rock has a moon?" Jacquie said in surprise. "Why isn't this on any star map?"

"The Consortium controls the knowledge. They don't want people to know about it," Luli said offhandedly.

"What have you got on it, Rabbit?" Jacquie asked.

"It's a natural moon, and it's got a lot of mass." Anton answered. "It's only about 30 kilometers in diameter and it circles Ogun every eight hours. Looks like one side of it doesn't get much sun, though. You think this is the place?"

"Do you see anything else out here?" Derain wisecracked.

"Can we get closer to it?" asked Barney. "I want to check the surface for structures."

"You got it, Mr. de Lagnel," Luli said as she accelerated the Matilda toward the moon's orbit path.

The dust on the surface of Ogun obscured

the view as the little moon raced through space. Luli brought the Matilda in closer and slipped the ship between the moon and the planet. It was a close, fast-moving orbit, only a little over six thousand kilometers from the surface.

"Is this orbit degrading?" Luli asked as she fought against the solar winds that buffeted the space between.

"Um," Anton pondered. "Not anytime soon. Hundreds of years and then, yeah, it all goes boom."

"Wait!" cried Barney. "I see something. It looks like a dome. Lu, swing out and see if you can find a close landing spot. There has to be monitoring equipment in a site this secret. Let's hope the cloak holds."

"I see a place," Luli growled. "Grab a seat. I'm going in hot and fast."

The Matilda's attitude jets cut hard and the trawler dropped like a stone toward the rocky surface of the moon. Her landing legs slid free of their housing and dust billowed beneath her in a big cloud. The ship slammed forcefully into the dirt and stone of the satellite.

"Isn't this dust cloud going to give us away?" Derain asked.

"It shouldn't," replied Anton. "This place gets pounded by meteor showers pretty frequently."

"The dome is less than a mile out," stated Barney. "I was able to grab a quick holo of the site. Luckily for us..."

"You mean thanks to some great flying," Luli

interrupted.

"... good flying," continued Barney, "We're near the main entrance of the dome. Now, the getting in and out? That's the tough part."

"We'll figure out something," answered Jacquie. "Let's hope Galena is still here so we can get her back in one piece."

thirty-four

Sea of Sorrow

The alarm blared as its message repeated over the open comm, "Prepare for system entry. Repeat, prepare for system entry."

The CBC Remus crashed through its hastily built FTL wormhole into the interior of the alien bubble around Jard. Madness held sway inside as enormous creatures ripped ships open and feasted upon the crews within. Ancient vessels from forgotten eras speared their way through the skies as fires burned rampantly on the planet below.

The gravitational force of the huge carrier set off shock waves and eddies through the space around it. Proximity alarms erupted in a chorus as the ship's systems struggled to track everything around it. The cruiser shuddered as it collided with a long, skeletally thin creature and split it in half.

"Shut down the alarms!" Captain Ellsbeth

Jon Gray Lang

ordered. "Track the ship that created the portal immediately and find me someone who has a clue what's going on."

The ship's comm crackled again, "Welcome to the war, Remus. This is the cruiser Horizon."

"How goes the fight, Horizon?"

There was a chuckle from the other end, "Poorly as of right now, Remus. Jard's defenses are completely down. Last message we received from the surface said that nightmare creatures were tearing their way through the cities. And, get this, armed genorgs are dancing in the streets. I don't know what to believe anymore."

"Dancing?" queried Commander Shafar.

"The fleet is holding out against the invading aliens, but we aren't making any progress against the rebel fleet." "Incoming" shouted someone in the background as other voices on the Horizon screamed, "By the Gods, it's got us! Fire everything we can! Break free! Break free!"

The comm suddenly cut out and a burst of fire glowed in the distance before it went dark.

Captain Ellsbeth's hands curled into fists as her gunners targeted creatures large and small that harried the Remus.

"Captain, I have another comm coming through. It's from the rebel fleet."

"Play it."

There was some momentary static then the comm opened, "... I repeat this is Admiral Kaur of the Freedom Fleet. God damn it, listen to me! If we don't work together against the alien menace, we all lose! Please respond, Consortium."

Captain Ellsbeth smiled grimly, "Connect us and give me the comm."

"The comm is yours, Captain."

"Attention Admiral Kaur. This is Captain Ellsbeth of the CBC Remus. We hear your plea and concur. We've had dealings with these creatures before. They use a large vessel as an anchor for the portal into our system. Have you observed such a craft?"

***

A hush spread over the bridge of the Peking Empress at the word spoken by the Consortium Captain. Harjeet felt surprise and elation in her chest. *'There is hope for us after all.'*

She turned and faced her people, "You heard her. Start looking for a ship acting as an anchor for... for this insanity!"

She drummed her fingers against the top of the polished rail that ran the length of the command platform. Her eyes darted out through the bow port and tracked a bloated colossus as it swallowed one of her freighters in a single gulp.

Thadie piped up, "I think I have something. The Anansi sent a weird report about a liner sticking out of the bubble as it formed." She shuffled through the saved comms until she spied the one she wanted, "Aah, here it is! Hey, Ovi, see if you can

Jon Gray Lang

verify this."

Ovi pulled the logged report and ran a scan. As he waited, he shunted the coordinates to the Nav model. His teeth glinted in the green light as he smiled, "We have confirmation, Harjeet. There lies the beast within the belly." An indicator blinked in the 3D model.

"Get those coordinates to the Remus as soon as you can make a connection," ordered Admiral Kaur.

"On it, sir," replied Thadie. "Sent and... received."

Harjeet crossed the fingers on her right hand, "Let's hope that's all it takes."

***

The Comm officer on the CBC Remus stated, "Receiving coordinates from the Empress."

"Get them over to Navigation to run a check. If they prove to be valid, align as many of our vessels as you can for a spearhead attack."

"Sent, Captain."

Captain Ellsbeth muttered under her breath, "Gods, I hate the waiting."

Her Nav officer broke the silence, "I have confirmation. An enormous heavy draft vessel is sitting in the middle of an energy well about three clicks out."

Captain Ellsbeth grinned in relief, "Get us moving and call the other vessels in for support.

Gunnery, prep three of the planet killers and stagger their attack pattern. Comm the Empress back and have her boats clear a path for us."

"Attack pattern locked and loaded, Captain," announced Gunnery.

The defensive guns rattled on the CBC Remus as the ship pushed deeper inside the bubble. Other Consortium vessels followed behind and took up outer positions to provide support. Creatures exploded in bloody ribbons as the concerted attack tore through them.

"Captain, the target has been acquired," stated Gunnery.

Captain Ellsbeth glanced at the man, "Once we're in range, let them free in a staggered pattern. Then load another just in case. That anchor has to be cut loose so that Jard can survive. You hear me?"

Gunnery nodded, but his eyes didn't leave his station's systems. "Target in range. Launching ordnance, now."

***

Admiral Kaur watched and waited as her fleet of ships diligently worked to clear a pathway for the Consortium attack group. Her eyes searched the darkness for the ancient vessel but it was too far away.

"They're on the move," said Ovi.

Harjeet gripped the railing as the block of Consortium vessels that registered as blinking cursors on the Nav 3D model made their ponderous way forward.

"Planet killers en route! I think we have a hit!" he exclaimed. "Second detonation, no change. Third detonation and the anchor craft is listing!"

There was a shift as the bubble that the nose of the Peking Empress pierced began to sink into itself.

"Get our ships to mop up the beasts out there!"

Thadie said, "Sending the orders now."

***

"How are we doing, Gunnery?" asked Captain Ellsbeth.

The man crowed, "That old boat is breaking up!"

Captain Ellsbeth studied the reports from deep inside the safety of the CBC Remus. The strange energy readings were dropping, but they eventually plateaued and the bubble remained unbroken. The number of remaining broken and ancient ships left in serviceable order for the creatures and their once humanoid combatants was dwindling.

Her hastily assembled battle group had the eye of the alien storm locked in place. No more of the gigantic monsters sailed free of the portal. Anything that stuck its head or appendage out was immediately engaged until it retreated.

She shook her head in frustration, "It's like Potune and Ninguiz all over again. We didn't make any headway until we destroyed the pair of anchor points. There must be one of those damn gateway anchors down on the planet's surface." She glared at the Scanner Technician, "Scan the planet's surface for the same energy readings and be quick about it."

She studied the Nav 3D model and looked for any signs of weakness. The rebel fleet had sustained heavy damage even as they worked with the Consortium forces against the alien menace.

The Scanner Technician spoke up, "Captain, I've found it. I'm getting the same readings but on a much smaller scale from the Council House of the Khanda's tower."

"Khanda, eh?" Captain Ellsbeth ordered, "Ready an attack group to destroy or disable that thing. Put Chief Bull from the M33 in charge."

The Comm officer replied, "Chief Bull has his team up and ready. They launch in three, two, and one. They're out in the ruckus."

"That should shut the portal down. Only one enemy left to eliminate."

"How's that, Captain?" asked Commander Shafar.

"The only way the Consortium can come out ahead is to destroy the resistance as it exists," Captain Ellsbeth replied. "And they're right in front of us. Send out coded orders to begin the attack on our transient allies. Got it?"

"Of... of course, Captain," said Commander

Shafar. She glumly moved over to the Nav 3D model and surreptitiously chose a handful of capital ships and sent them their orders. She chose another group and sent coded orders to them as well. As Commander Shafar sent out coded orders to the third and final team, "Orders have been sent with a strike time of five minutes."

Captain Ellsbeth registered her Commander's downcast eyes, "War is absolute Hell, Ilya. I've seen enough of it to know that I would rather destroy their hopes and dreams, if doing so will keep their children off the battlefield in the future."

***

Off to starboard, an explosion broke open one of her merchant ships. A second rocket slammed into the engines, the small ship flickered brightly and broke in two.

"By the Demon, Tom," cursed Admiral Kaur. "Those Consortium bastards have swung around to attack us!"

She pounded the rail as she watched her fleet suffer under a barrage of ordnance from the attacking Consortium vessels. She stared at the Nav 3D model searching for anything that would give her fleet an edge.

"What should we do?" asked Thadie.

"Gods be damned! There's no way we can beat them now," Harjeet growled. "Call for a full retreat and wormhole out of here. Make sure the

Captains fill their holds with every freighter and trawler they can pick up before they leave."

Thadie looked ashen as she sent out the fleet-wide comm.

Harjeet cursed under her breath as she watched her fleet get torn apart by the Consortium capital ships. One of her M Class destroyers burst into flames off in the distance before the lack of oxygen smothered them.

"I have to trust in their skills," she entreated.

"Admiral, I have the Laverna on the comm."

Harjeet nodded in dejection, "Patch them through."

"... Laverna to Empress, are you there?"

"We're reading you, Laverna," replied Thadie.

"This is Captain Mahmood. We're struggling under the barrage and also having trouble getting any ships on board. We're... Hey! Quiet down back there! Bakker, put that away! What are you doing?"

A shot rang out over the comm, followed by two more. Then the comm went quiet.

"What's happening, Laverna," asked Admiral Kaur as her stomach dropped. "I repeat, what's happening? Are you there, Mahmood?"

"They're gone, Harjeet," answered Ovi. "The Laverna just wormholed out."

Harjeet's hands knotted and unknotted in frustration. "Where do we stand with the rest of the fleet?"

Latiff replied, "Some of the fleet was able to get out with their small vessels intact. Others are still trying to get the few operable freighters on board." He looked with concern at Harjeet, "We have to think about getting out of here ourselves. As soon as they find us, it'll be too late."

Admiral Kaur's head dropped, "I know."

"Wait," Thadie exclaimed, "I'm picking up a comm from the Independence! The jump gate is down. They did it!"

"At least something has gone right," sighed Harjeet. She squared her shoulders, "There's nothing more we can do here. Swing us around so that we can load up our brace of ships."

The mood on board was somber as Latiff fired the attitudinal jets. He swung the Empress on its axis, "Heading out to collect our wayward children."

***

Chief Bull remained strapped into the drop seat behind Lieutenant Shimada Mariko as she piloted the lander out of the CBC Remus hangar. He glanced through the bow port and watched as the other landers under his command dropped free of the hangar like a swarm of insects ready to descend on Jard.

Multiple fighters provided escort and he was mighty glad of it. Flying, screeching beasts flapped their wings and dive-bombed the formation until the fighters either chased them away or shot them down.

Bull glanced over his shoulder. His team held

onto their seats as the lander was buffeted by air currents that shouldn't be there. Lieutenant Shimada cursed loudly as she struggled to keep control of the lander against the gravity well that Jard represented.

"This bunch ain't like my boys," he muttered as he clapped the Lieutenant on the shoulder. "How goes it, Mariko? Glad to be flying again?"

She tensed under his grip, "First off, my specialty is communications, not piloting. Secondly, I don't think flying directly into a war zone is what I expected to be doing today."

"So, getting this gig for you was a bad plan?" he asked.

Mariko's laugh was short and sharp, "Anything is better than being cooped up on that cruiser with all those judging eyes."

Chief Bull chortled along with her, "I told 'em I wouldn't fly with anyone else!"

She hit the cabin comm, "Dropping into planetary atmo. It's going to be bumpy!"

Chief Bull leaned into the hull of the lander as it took a nose dive. A bat-like creature flew past with its claws embedded into the ruins of a merchant vessel. Mariko rolled the lander to port as the creature dropped the freighter and gave them chase. Its screech was deafening.

One of their escort fighter's shot past with its guns blazing. Mariko growled and pushed the lander into a climb to get out of the way. The creature exploded into bloody fragments as its carcass

Jon Gray Lang

tumbled toward the planet and crashed into the buildings below.

The comm chirped, "Heading West to the target. Just follow the road. Witch Leader out."

Mariko pointed at the HUD as she beckoned to the Chief, "See that signal blip? That's your target. The plan is for the fighters to take it out. If it's still generating energy readings, your teams are to go in and remove it from existence."

Chief Bull nodded, "Time to arrival?"

"At this speed, just a couple minutes," she replied. "Check out the terrain below."

Chief Bull slid back into his drop seat and watched the landscape pass by under the troop carrier. Buildings lay crushed and the smoking remains of downed craft burned in the rubble. Horrific creatures skittered amongst the ruins and hunted down what life had survived the onslaught.

There was an intense firefight happening as the lander coasted over an intersection. A surface-to-air rocket streaked toward them, but lost steam and crashed to the ground in a fiery burst.

Mariko shook him and pointed, "There it is, the Council home of the House of Khanda."

Smoke poured from the top of the tall spire that bore the heavy scars of bombardment.

"Looks like the place has undergone some recent remodeling," joked Chief Bull.

"I hear unplanned renovations are all the rage," remarked Lieutenant Shimada.

The fighter escort shot ahead as Mariko

pulled back and slowed down the lander. Their fighter escort fired its rockets, then peeled away. The explosions shook the dust on the ground as the building leaned to its side and collapsed under its own weight.

"Whoa," shouted Mariko as she pulled the lander's nose up to avoid the billowing cloud of debris.

"Did we get it? Are the energy readings gone?"

Lieutenant Shimada responded as she wrestled the troop carrier back into control. "No good. Readings are still coming through. Your team is up! Give me a signal for dust-off."

Chief Bull shouted over the din as the lander dropped to the street below, "You heard the Lieutenant! Everyone out in twos and watch your buddy's back! Now, move!"

Chief Bull hopped out as his team scurried away from the lander. As soon as it was empty, Mariko took it back up into the skies and disappeared past the skyline. Bull double-checked the location of the remains of the Khanda building, then motioned his squads forward.

One of his scouts waved the group to a stop and indicated ahead. The Chief slowly approached as the scout pointed to a ring of genorgs in Consortium fatigues dancing to music that they only heard.

'Or remembered,' he thought.

He waved his people past and they crept by

the strange sight. They kept to the shadows until they reached the broken Khanda tower. Chief Bull pulled out his scanner and waved it back and forth to register the alien energy output. He signaled two of his people forward to investigate.

"Sanchez, get those mortars set up. I want to blast that thing to dust and get off this rock as soon as possible. Betazy, unpack the rounds and wait for the marker."

"On it, Chief," Betazy and Sanchez said in unison.

The others fanned out and set up a perimeter. The low clank of the mortars being assembled was the only nearby sound. However, in the distance rockets still burst in the sky and unholy screams echoed eerily from between the buildings.

"I hope we don't meet whatever makes that noise."

"Shut it, Betazy," grunted the Chief.

A marker appeared on his handheld scanner. He glanced up and saw two of his squad exiting the rubble. The horrid screaming sounded very close now. Suddenly, a hideous worm-like beast burst free of a pile of rubble and slithered after the closest trooper. It shrieked again, then swallowed the man whole.

"Fuck that!" screamed Betazy as she unloaded her rifle into the monstrosity.

The rounds punctured the flesh of the creature but that only made it madder. It reared up to give chase and the rest of the squad opened fire on its underbelly.

"Sanchez!" shouted the Chief. "Destroy the energy source. Keep at it until it disappears. The rest of you, get that creature away from us!"

Sanchez nodded as he dropped a shell into the mortar. It thumped and the shell shot into the air toward the painted marker.

Chief Bull kept his rifle trained on the beast while he watched the adjoining streets for other nightmarish creatures. The worm screamed again, then flopped onto its side and stopped moving. The thump of the mortars kept going in the background, almost in rhythm with the exploding shells.

"We've got incoming!" shouted another trooper as chitinous legs easily eight feet long stomped through the rubble behind their position.

Chief raised his rifle and sighted down the barrel. While his squad fired blindly at the legs, he waited for more of the creature to appear. He finally was rewarded for his patience when a wriggling star-shaped head lifted up above the legs.

His rifle barked and the first round tore a hole through one of the mouth-like appendages, but the creature didn't stop. One of its legs stabbed straight through a soldier. Another leg swept out, crushed the skull of another trooper and flung the body into a wall ten feet away.

"Take out the legs at the joints!" he ordered as he brought his rifle back up and pumped three more rounds into the star-shaped head. One of the legs shattered under the onslaught of rounds and the

Jon Gray Lang

creature tumbled onto its side, but the other legs continued dragging the towering brute forward.

"Ha!" shouted Sanchez. "The energy blip is gone, Chief!"

"Thank the Major!" Chief Bull's hand shook as he launched the signal flare. "Come on, Mariko. I've had enough nightmares to last me a lifetime."

The others kept shooting at the monster as the lander blasted down the street to pick up the squad. Hot in pursuit was an explicable pile of animated chitinous claws and legs that scrambled behind Mariko's drop ship.

"Sanchez, kill that thing as fast as you can! Everyone, prepare for immediate dust-off!"

The Chief whistled with a new respect for Sanchez as the soldier aimed, fired, and destroyed the creature before Mariko could open the lander's hatch. "Everyone in! Go, go, go!"

Chief Bull dragged Betazy aboard and yelled, "Get us out of here now!"

The lander shot straight up as the bloodied chitinous mess that had chased the lander reached out to grab it. Mariko kicked the craft into overdrive and narrowly avoided the beast's grasp. As the ship pulled away, the monstrous organism screeched in fury as its legs began to disintegrate.

The Lieutenant's voice was brisk, "Ground mission completed. Calling for an escort. Repeat, ground mission completed."

"Witch Leader and the cabal are headed your way, Lieutenant."

Jon Gray Lang

Chief Bull buckled himself into the drop seat and breathed a sigh of relief. "When you can, send a comm to the CBC Remus that the energy source is gone." He grimaced as Betazy and two other soldiers cried out pain, "Oh, and tell Dr. Sinix we've got work for him."

***

Commander Keri pushed the Independence through the debris from the destroyed jump gate as she kept an eye on the gutted frigate. With no engines to control it, the dead destroyer floated further away from her flight path.

"Copperhead, where are you?" she asked over the comm.

"Coming up on the other side of the Scorpio," replied Captain Kahn. "We're in position."

Rosa tapped at the attitudinal jets and dropped the ship's nose a fraction. She slowly edged forward and brought the Independence alongside the Scorpio.

"We're in position, too." Rosa turned to Delta, "Is your team ready to tie her down?"

Delta nodded as she spoke into her comm, "Agnes, get the Scorpio tied down so we can tow her out."

"On it, Captain," said Agnes. "Carla, throw me that tow rope."

Rosa held the Independence steady as the troops on the hull worked with their counterparts on the Copperhead and brought the Scorpio under control. With enough effort, the ore hauler would soon be mobile enough to move out.

"We have an incoming comm on a coded channel," said Delta. "This is the Independence, I repeat this is the Independence."

There was a forty-second delay before a familiar voice came through, "Independence, come in. This is the Peking Empress. We're headed your way for a get-n-go."

Delta answered, "Thadie, it is good to hear your voice. The jump gate is down. How goes the battle?"

Agnes' voice came through on a different comm channel, "The Scorpio is locked down. We're coming in."

"Acknowledged."

"Independence, this is Harjeet. The battle was a complete rout. We're coming your way to pick you up and wormhole out of here. Just a second... Ovi, what's our ETA? Ten minutes? We'll be there in ten. Empress, out."

"Independence, this is Copperhead. We got the message. Let's tow the Scorpio out of the debris and get out of here."

Anger clouded Rosa's face. "Damn, so close to a victory. But at least the demolished jump gate will give us a bit of time."

***

Jon Gray Lang

Captain Ellsbeth studied the devastation that surrounded her carrier. Dead crew members floated among the broken vessels, intermingled with the pulped flesh of hideous alien creatures. Below, fires burned throughout the rubble on the planet's surface.

According to Chief Bull's report, the fighting continued on Jard. From street to street, genorgs that wore Consortium uniforms fought hard against the populace. But pockets of these same genorg troops were still seen moving through dance steps of partially remembered routines.

The Captain knew intimately, without question that the genorgs on the surface below were the same ones she had sent on a suicide mission during the battle of Pequiz. Images taken by the Chief that showed genorgs wearing fatigues created specifically for their use only proved the fact.

She sighed, "Damn me if they aren't mine. Damn the alien menace out there for bringing them back to haunt me."

Commander Shafar stepped up behind her and affirmed in awe, "You did it, Mary. You turned the tide on the alien invasion and routed the rebel fleet. Their ship's bones stand as tribute in your honor. With one deft stroke, you have ended two sieges on the home world." Ilya faced her and said, "You should receive a medal of distinction. You will be cheered as a hero!"

Mary Ellsbeth felt sick to her stomach as she looked out on the wreckage that hung in place like grim ornaments in the gravity well of the planet below. *'Was it worth it?'*

She sighed, "Defending the Consortium never ends, Ilya. Dispatch the fleet and chase down those escaping ships. Launch our clean-up teams to the surface and nullify any threats remaining. Oh, and see what we can find out about this Mr. Leon. Chief Bull mentioned that his name kept coming up during their investigation."

"Of course, Captain. I'll get right on it."

Mary Ellsbeth waved her assistant over, "Harry, get me a drink, will you? Something strong."

thirty-five

Rapture

Hamza Fitzpatrick wandered into the commissary and searched the room with wild, red-rimmed eyes. When he saw Jerald, he grinned like a lost soul. His eyes flitted left and right as he shambled toward the Corporal. Jerald froze at the sight of his bunkmate; the Ensign looked so changed.

Hamza sank into the seat across from him. Without blinking he steadily stared into Jerald's eyes. Then Hamza leaned in and said, "You ever get the feeling there is more going on here than what you can see?"

Jerr broke eye contact, "What do you mean?"

Hamza watched two of the base personnel as they crossed by behind Jerald, "It's as if an alien sentience holds us here and it wants something."

Jerald glanced over his shoulder and noticed

the two people giving him the side eye. It struck him as odd. Since he had first arrived, he had noticed a cliquishness to those who stayed on. Some of the personnel left as soon as their tour was done while others stayed on base. He had been one of the ones who remained, but he still felt vaguely ostracized by the majority of the people.

"You mean how close-knit some of the personnel are?" Jerr looked into Hamza's eyes and saw the burgeoning fear that flickered there, "You know how it is. People stay once they find a leader that they work well with. It just takes a while to get accepted." He reached out and cupped his hand over Hamza's, "You and Dr. Wyeth are getting on well. As much as Commander Diego would like to think he runs the base, he is more of a figurehead for the Doctor. I wouldn't worry about it."

"That's not what I'm talking about!" Fitzpatrick sputtered furiously as he pulled his hand free. "There's something else here. I can feel it and it's watching... always watching."

Fitzpatrick smacked his hands against the tabletop and stood, "I don't get the same vibe from you as I do the rest. Keep yourself safe." His abrupt movements set the table to wobbling as he bolted out the door of the commissary.

Jerald returned to his meal but it had grown cold. He sighed and dropped his last bite back onto the plate. He felt eyes on him as he pushed back from the table. As he glanced around, he noticed that everyone in the room watched his every movement.

"Food got cold," he chuckled as he threw the remainder in the bin. "Don't let that happen to you."

As the commissary door closed behind him, his face settled into a frown. "Something is wrong." The way the people on base were acting now struck him as familiar, but he couldn't think why. He shook his head and headed off to his post.

***

'Is this real?'

Pain burned across Galena's scalp. Horribly bright lights hurt her eyes and her throat was raw from screaming. Her skin felt foreign as it crawled across her muscles. Voices, both delusional and familiar tickled her ears and cajoled her to action.

"The Master and the Doctor..." she stuttered in a whisper.

A weight swaying in her left hand made her look down. A military-issue pistol gleamed and dangled from her fingertips. About her waist hung a belt of extra magazines that she had no memory of wearing. Each of the rounds radiated with its own strange promise. The fingers on her right hand clenched and she looked up.

The sphere bent in front of her and splintered the light into reflections around her. A piece of her mind saw Dr. Wyeth pulling a fragment of bone free from her skull. A rectangular object glittered in the light as its spidery fronds slithered into the gap and it buried itself into the meat of her brain.

Coding similar to the kind that Barney had taught her burned onto her inner eyelids. As she tried to make sense of it, the coding darkened against the brightness of the engines. Stacked in front of her in their varying sizes were her sisters. Then they melded together until only one remained. Her sister called to her from the enclosure and beckoned to her. Sweet scents and pleasant memories filled her senses. Galena smiled and stepped inside.

***

Jerald woke to an odd noise that had pulled him from his slumber. He heard the sound again as he sat up and wiped at the grit around his eyes. Short, shuddering breaths came from the other side of the room. In his bleary state, he had trouble making out what it was.

"Cabin lights, on," he commanded.

He blinked away the sudden glare, then recoiled when his vision cleared. Fitzpatrick was on his knees in front of the other bed with tears streaming down his face. It took a moment for Jerald to notice that blood pooled on the floor around Hamza and a knife handle protruded from his belly. The Corporal stared in horror as the Ensign gripped the handle and began cutting once again.

"Hamza!... Why?"

Fitzpatrick dragged his bloody fingers across his face and grinned, "Everything is exactly as it should be, Jerald. Just as it should be."

Hamza's voice quavered. He pulled the knife from his body and his other hand reached in and pulled his intestines free. They spooled out as his eyes, so lively when Jerald had first seen them, slowly dimmed. The Ensign's body tipped forward and slid flat against the decking.

Jerald didn't move. He couldn't believe what the man had done to himself. As the pool of blood continued to flow wider, Jerald jerked away. Suddenly, it struck him like lightning.

"I've seen this sort of thing before. It's just like home before the alien invasion," he murmured in shock. "It's just like Potune in its last days."

thirty-six

Bad Luck

Galena woke to a knocking at her door. After quickly dressing into her coveralls, she followed the Corporal to her daily appointment with Dr. Wyeth. He seemed agitated, but she wasn't sure. '*After that dream, am I seeing clearly?*'

Jerald knocked on the Doctor's door and stepped to one side. That's when Galena noticed the dark circles under his eyes, "Trouble sleeping Corporal?"

"You don't even know."

Judith's voice came through Jerald's comm, "Bring the Lieutenant in, Mr. Cook."

"You heard her," he muttered.

She nodded and went through the office door. Judith sat behind her desk where a holo from outside the enclosure was displayed. Galena saw the line of genorgs, some barely at the age for servitude

Jon Gray Lang

standing before the enclosure. One by one, the scientists pushed them in. Moments later, two other natural-borns would drag a body out of it.

She couldn't quite see everything, but it seemed that the base personnel were assembling large Xs and bolting them to the decking. As she tried to see exactly what they were doing, Judith swiped at the image and it disappeared.

Galena slid into the seat across from the Doctor and asked, "Are the new chips working?"

Without looking up, Judith answered, "No need for that anymore. More flesh will fix the problem. Now, what I need from you is..."

"What will fix the problem?"

The Doctor looked up with a perplexed expression that Galena had never seen before on her face.

"Let me think a minute." The Doctor shook herself and glanced down at her data pad, "Yes, I had questions about your time away. Aah, there is the entry." She glanced up, "Is it true you have no memories of your time within the sphere? Tell me, what do you remember?"

Galena wondered at that. "Haven't we already discussed this?"

"Yes, but something is missing. I just need the key to understand. Tell me again what you remember."

"What do I remember? Since my training?" Galena asked in a tone tinged with anger, "I remember the weight of the pistol in my hand, and the pain when its recoil hit me in my chest each time another body slumped to the ground. I remember the bite in my belly when I went hungry so that others could eat. I remember believing I could never be clean again. All in the name of duty."

"Yes, yes, Timmony Bay. I am not concerned with that. What do you remember after?"

Galena saw the need in the Doctor's eyes, "After I was labeled a monster? Only what you made of me."

"What does that even mean?" inquired the Doctor. "That excursion only proved that you were a good candidate for the procedure! Your actions backed that up."

"I only did what was needed, so that my team could survive! But I have since learned there is more to life than just survival. A lesson that few, if any, of my sisters will ever have the chance to learn." Heat rose in Galena's voice, "I am no longer the same being you threw into that engine so many years ago."

"Tell me more."

Galena's hands tightened into fists as she glared at the Doctor, "In my dreams, I see pain and blood. Every day, every night. And each time I see you in the midst of it all pulling on strings like a puppet master. I have hated you for it, but I am aware that you saved me. Saved me for that!" Galena's index finger pointed in the rough direction of the enclosure. "I can hear it whispering to me, goading me to bring this place down."

Jon Gray Lang

The Doctor responded giddily, "You hear voices from the 'de trop aspect'? It talks to you? What does it say?" Excitement glowed briefly on her face, "Does it fear you?"

Surprised by the Doctor's excitement, Galena said nothing.

"Yess..." a voice hissed in the quiet.

Dr. Wyeth looked toward the door of her office and Galena realized Judith could hear the voice too. As soon as that thought came to her, she felt herself separating from her body. She sensed the light growing dim as the entity within her took control.

'No!' she shouted in despair, but the sound only died away within her mind.

She could sense the entity's sibilant voice as its words slithered out of her throat, "I feel their fear every time I enter the chamber. With each of my sisters that you throw in, their fear only grows stronger. Soon, we can bring them to their knees, Doctor. We only need more flesh..."

A well of blackness swallowed Galena. The feeling of her elbows on the armrests of the chair and the bottoms of her boots as they rested against the floor was all she could perceive, but she could no longer control her limbs.

As her fear and anger rose, Galena noticed small pinpricks of light that appeared in the distance. Slowly, the tiny lights grew in number and she could sense a color within them.

'Green,' she thought, 'Emerald green. Like my

eyes... Am I not alone here?'

Voices echoed back at her, "You are not alone... never alone... Weakness! Weakness... There is a way..."

"A way?" the thought surprised her, "There is a way to survive?"

She felt an acceptance surround her, "High cost... Pain... But there is a way."

"The Master controls my body. How do I escape if I'm trapped inside myself?"

The voices faded with a final message, "Soon is the time to be free..."

A slight smile formed on her lips and she relaxed into it, "Such an odd feeling to have hope."

***

Jerald grabbed Galena by the arm as she left the Doctor's office. "Come on, Lieutenant. We have to get you back to your room."

He pulled her forward and she stumbled. With a prod, she reluctantly moved ahead. Jerald was concerned, but he kept her walking slowly in the right direction. As the doors to the lift parted, he tugged her inside, faced her against the back wall, and pushed the floor button on the control.

Corporal Cook spun her around, "Come on, Lieutenant. What are you doing?"

As she leaned against the wall, her eyes glinted darkly, "I await your command, Corporal. What would you have me do?"

Jon Gray Lang

Galena moved provocatively toward him. It was unlike anything he had ever seen from a genorg.

"What has gotten into you? Back off!"

Disappointment arrested her movements and she dropped into parade rest. Jerald turned away and pounded his fist against the wall.

"What the hell is going on here?" he ranted. "I wake up and Hamza is gutting himself in my room! After I get his ass to the infirmary, base personnel are attacking each other in the commissary for no good reason. And outside that Gods-forsaken chamber, the scientists are stringing up corpses like it's a holiday. This place has lost its collective mind!"

Galena's voice rattled oddly out of her chest, "What do you think is the cause of this?"

Jerald kept facing the wall and his shoulders shook as he cried, "I, I don't know. It all reminds me when the alien monsters broke loose on Potune. Everyone I knew, everyone I loved died that day!"

He faced her and a part of his brain noticed the lack of whites in her eyes. "This all started here when you arrived. Dr. Wyeth had you visit that cursed orb in there and then madness was the end result." He grabbed her by the shoulders and shook her with tears in his eyes, "Can you stop it? Can you make it all go away?"

Galena's body stepped forward and her arms enveloped him in an embrace. As he relaxed within her arms, he uttered, "No one has held me this way since my mother died."

Jon Gray Lang

He didn't notice as she reached up and snapped his neck. His body crumpled to the floor of the lift as the doors parted again. The creature controlling Galena forced her mouth into a lopsided grin.

Her voice purred, "She liked you, you know. So a quiet death is yours. But, the key draws nigh and the gates must be opened in preparation!"

***

From inside the dome's command center on Aja, an alarm started bleating insistently.

"Where's that alarm coming from?" asked Commander Diego.

"It's from the bottom deck again," replied the Scanner Technician. "The fifth alert this hour."

Commander Diego nodded in consternation, "We were informed the next experiment may set it off. Go ahead and kill it."

The alarm cut mid-tone as the Scanner Technician obeyed. When the sound stopped, the external sensors registered an impact about a mile out. She double-checked the ship's delivery roster and the schedule for the next expected meteor storm. But the next delivery wasn't due to arrive for another two months, and the next meteor shower wasn't expected for another day.

"This is odd," the Scanner Technician said as she ran scans of the impact outside of the dome. She enlarged the image, "There's nothing out there except dust that's been disturbed by something."

"What's that?" asked Commander Diego as he ambled toward her station.

The Scanner Technician enlarged the image again. "There was an impact a mile out from the dome and there is something weird about it."

"Let me see."

Commander Diego's breath drifted across the back of her neck as he manipulated the holo. The shape highlighted by the raised dust looked surprisingly like a freighter. She sensed his shock.

"Where in Tom's hell did that come from?" Commander Diego fumbled with his comm, "Doctor, you have to see this."

Dr. Wyeth's voice came back over the comm, "I am in the middle of something. Send it to me."

"Send the feed to the Doctor immediately."

***

The rhythmic pounding of booted feet jostled Galena as her figure ran down to the enclosure. The doors to the large chamber must have been opened, because her form didn't stop until she heard the screams. The entity that inhabited her body chuckled at what it saw. "The second gateway has arrived!"

Even with the Master in charge of her body, Galena's sight came back to her and all was madness. The scientists and their assistants had begun dismembering the latest batch of dead genorgs and strung them up like something from a cautionary tale. Her body ran toward the enclosure and her fingers keyed the airlock controls. The inner and outer airlock doors swung open and a noxious-smelling gas undulated out of the entry. She felt a change in pressure wash over her as the environment within the sphere spilled into the open area.

She looked up when a yowl of frustration startled her. The floors shook from the impact of something huge within the enclosure. She felt the tremors again and again until the airlock dented outward. The metal finally twisted as a gigantic stick-like insectoid crawled through the opening.

It was quickly followed by the largest worm creature she had ever seen. Its face was easily twelve feet across and its gullet was easily large enough to swallow her in one bite. It struggled to emerge through the hole created in the enclosure.

The being that controlled Galena called to the creature, singing to it to break free. It fought and pushed its way against the twisted metal and the hole grew larger. A piece of the jagged metal dug into its side and black ichor sprayed from the wound. The beast squealed and even the entity within Galena quailed at the creature's response.

Suddenly, it reared and vomited black goo. Within the material, tiny wriggling versions of the worm struggled to the surface. Then they latched onto the humans that hadn't left the chamber. The tiny ones grew rapidly as they consumed the flesh of the living and the dead.

The black ichor that had spilled from the creature rotted the metal of the dome. It blackened and cracked as more pressure was applied by the creatures inside the enclosure. The top of the dome buckled open like the shell of a rotten egg and all manner of filth and horror streamed freely from the opening.

The sphere could be seen glowing amongst the fragments of the enclosure even as the walls that surrounded it were brought low. The giant worm began slamming its heavy body against the walls of the base. A tiny crack opened up in the wall and the hiss of escaping air sounded like a knife cutting through flesh. Galena felt a sense of elation from the being within her.

"Let's watch the Doctor in her final hour," it howled.

thirty-seven

The Puppet

Dr. Wyeth observed the door to her office open before she registered the sound. Her prize genorg stepped in and straddled the chair across from her. An old memory rose to the surface of her mind as the black eyes of the subject stared at her.

"You," she exclaimed in shock. "You should be dead now."

"As you of all humans know, Judith, we are not so easily defeated."

Dr. Wyeth sat back and flipped a secret switch on the underside of her desk, "Mayhaps, but you will do as I say."

A high-pitched tone cycled through a complete pattern before it was repeated. She giggled oddly as she watched the recognition appear on the Lieutenant's face.

"Abomination!" Galena's body shook as the

thing fought against the machine intelligence that had been activated. Judith held the button down until Galena's eyes cleared.

The dull tones of the machine spoke through Galena's mouth, "What is your command?"

"Restrain yourself to that chair."

Galena flipped the leather cover over her wrist and slid the fastener clips into place. Her other hand slid into the shallow half-tube and she nudged the cover over. "I am unable to comply."

Judith grinned and her eyes were feverishly bright. She stepped around the desk and slid the pins on the clips home.

Suddenly, the office shook as if from a heavy impact. "Again?" Dr. Wyeth pulled up the feeds from the cameras to the enclosure, but all of them had shorted out. "Damnable electrical problems..." she cursed. "No matter."

She picked up her data pad, adjusted some levels, and studied Galena's reactions. Eventually, she set the data pad down, but kept it close to her hand.

"Are you still in there, Lieutenant?"

***

Galena's lips trembled as her consciousness battled for control of her body. The creature fought back all the harder as the machine intelligence chased it into the depths of Galena's being. The Lieutenant held to her center, but she was losing on

Jon Gray Lang

both fronts.

She squeezed her mind's eyes shut in concentration. Much to her surprise pinpricks of emerald green blinked into existence around her. The number grew until there were hundreds of them, if not thousands.

"So many," she said in hushed tones. "Can you hear me?"

She gasped as the voices repeated to her, "Can you hear me? Can you hear me? Can you hear me?"

"I can hear you..."

"We hear you. We are you... are you... you... Now is the time to break free... free..."

The machine was unrelenting in its operation, but Galena could feel the Master inhabiting her weakening. As she pushed against the entity, she felt her own will increase. Determination curled her fingers into a fist. Suddenly she knew the way to defeat the creatures and finally had the hands to do it. "Sisters, I need you to do this for me."

"We will do this for you. We will do this for you... do this for you... do this for ourselves... ourselves..."

Galena's eyes snapped open and beheld Dr. Wyeth, who sat in anticipation across from her, waiting for her to speak.

"I am here, Doctor."

***

When the genorg's eyes cleared, Dr. Wyeth flipped the secret switch again and the Lieutenant relaxed. At the same moment, the holo from Commander Diego appeared at her station. She zoomed in closer and studied it.

"Doctor, a ship has landed near the enclosure..."

Galena's voice rose, "The Matilda?"

Dr. Wyeth's eyes lit with surprise. "You recognize this by shape alone?"

Galena blinked against the harsh overhead light and focused on the holo-vid, "I do, though I don't know how she made her way to me."

"You think this vessel came for you?" asked Dr. Wyeth.

"You chased after me, did you not?" retorted Galena. "Now, they've come to rescue me, even if it isn't needed. Isn't that what friends do?"

"That I did. Perhaps these friends of yours see the same thing I see in you."

"They see more in me than even I know," answered Galena.

Dr. Wyeth stood up and unlatched the straps that held Galena to the chair. She helped the genorg to her feet and waited until she was steady.

"If you think they've come for you, then your time here is almost done," said Dr. Wyeth. "I would like you to go out and meet them."

Galena's eyes brightened, "Really? You would let me go?"

Dr. Wyeth's eyes glinted dangerously, "You are

your own person, are you not? I do not control your destiny. Only remember that the entity within you is still there."

"Of course," replied Galena as she thought about what she had seen at the enclosure. "I'll just go grab my things."

Dr. Wyeth watched the genorg leave her office and disappear down the hallway. She keyed the comm, "Mr. Diego. The subject is being released into the wild. Have a five-man team follow her. Let's see if she does as she has been trained to do. Otherwise, prepare to send the signal on my call."

"Understood, Doctor. Commander Diego out."

thirty-eight

Bang, Bang My Baby Shot Me Down

The door to the Doctor's office closed behind her and the main area was eerily quiet. She glanced over the railing and there was no movement on the bottom floor. A ragged hole was torn through the top of the armored enclosure and partially eaten bodies lay where they had fallen. The rent in the outer wall whistled with the escaping air of the open area. But there was no sign of the large worm or the insectile creature.

Perplexed, she shook her head and continued toward the lift. As she rounded the corner, she could hear the lift door opening and closing repetitively. Once it came into view, she discovered the large alien worm hunkered over Corporal Cook's corpse slowly ingesting it. Its many eyes tracked her movement but showed no interest in her as she snuck past.

Jon Gray Lang

The Corporal's leg blocked the lift door from completely closing. Heaviness hit her heart as she moved it out of the way and the lift doors clicked closed. His data pad still hung from the port. She hit the key for the top level and the lift began to rise. Once it came to a stop, she pocketed the data pad and stepped out into the hall.

Despite everything that had happened, Galena was filled with elation. There was a skip to her stride and a lightness of her spirit that she had never felt before. The Matilda had come for her. The Captain had not left her to rot. She looked forward to seeing the whole crew, but one member most of all, "I will see Anton again."

Galena headed toward the ready room off of the main airlock to the base. When she burst in through the door, she startled a five-man squad that was there suiting up into their heavy armor. But none of them questioned why she was there as she walked past.

An unbidden thought came to her, *'Are they here for me?'* The question didn't slow her pace as she made her way over to one of the lockers and pulled out an armored atmo suit.

The five soldiers grabbed their helmets and gear and departed in a rush, leaving Galena all alone in the ready room. As she carried the armored suit to a bench, her eyes spotted the security camera bolted to the ceiling. As it cycled through its pattern, Galena removed her coveralls and tossed them onto the floor.

She kept her head down as she slid into the atmo suit and wriggled it up to her waist. The fit was snug as the plates on the legs and feet settled into place. She pulled the torso up to her neck and the chest plates clicked into position. She slid the arms on and the mesh from the inner weave of the sleeves slithered together with the mesh covering her trunk. The only pieces left were the gloves and the helmet.

Galena parked those items on the bench while she checked out the arms locker near the doorway. The rifle rack still had a lock bar across it that was closed with a DNA key sequence lock. Below this lay the handgun storage unit. Its lock bar hung off to the side. She tsked in disapproval. The squad that had vacated minutes before had done a poor job of tidying up after themselves.

She slipped an arm into the storage unit, but as her hand closed around the grip of a gun, she felt the machine swim to the surface of her conscience. She ignored it and reached into the ammunition crate. Magazines for her make and model of pistol were carelessly stacked inside the crate. What should have been separate stacks marked for kill rounds and stun rounds had been jumbled together. She bit back her annoyance and searched for a full stun magazine.

The machine's presence came to the fore and her hand quaked in response. She felt its attempt to gain control as her fingers passed over a stack of stun ammo and grabbed three magazines of kill rounds instead. Her hand dropped them on the lip of the bin.

Galena glanced up at the security camera and realized it was now under manual control. The operating light was aglow and the lens was directly focused on her.

'So I am not an agent of my own free will. I yet remain a prisoner.'

Sweat broke out on her forehead as she fought for control of her own actions. Her fingers spasmed, but she grinned fiercely when her fist finally closed around a magazine of stun rounds. She straightened and dropped that one next to the others. The machine quieted as she slid two more stun magazines onto the belt of her suit. Now only one magazine of stun rounds and three with kill rounds remained on the lips of the bin in front of her.

She forced her body to hyperventilate as she reached for the one she wanted when the compulsion came again. Her hand shot toward the kill rounds and she fought against it.

***

Dr. Wyeth observed Galena's efforts on the holo-vid in her office. The genorg stood stock still with an expression of pure will carved into her face. Judith watched intently as droplets of sweat fell from the Lieutenant's forehead and splattered to the floor, fascinated by her valiant struggle to keep the machine at bay.

"Still fighting me, aren't you," mused the Doctor. "No matter. You can't last forever."

She keyed her direct comm to Galena's helmet on the bench in the ready room. "Lieutenant Chadov, make your way outside of the base and greet our visitors. Make haste."

The Doctor cut the comm with a sharp tone. However, the holo-vid still showed Galena fighting with everything she had against the machine. Judith's lip curled in aggravation as she keyed a tonal code through the helmet and the genorg's response was rapid.

The battle computer brought Galena into a rigid stance. Her hand reached down and pocketed one magazine and slammed another home into the pistol. The machine drove her body back over to the bench and slid on her gloves. It waited for the mesh to seal before it placed the helmet over the genorg's head.

As the helmet closed with a heavy click, Galena's voice spoke into the comm, "On my way, Doctor. Lieutenant Chadov out."

Another comm channel beeped insistently and Dr. Wyeth keyed it in frustration, "I'm busy at the moment. Can't it wait?"

Commander Diego answered, "My apologies, Doctor, but this is an emergency. All comms to the enclosure have been lost. The cameras are down as well."

Dr. Wyeth waved her hand in irritation, "It's

the next step in the experiment. You were informed!"

"The last comm received said everything was spiraling out of control and then the feed went dead. Automatic lockdown protocol has kicked on and the lower decks are closed to us," replied the Commander. "This is a real emergency, Doctor."

"Then send a team down to investigate! I'll disengage the locks then head up top."

***

Galena retained her sense of self, but functioned only as a passenger in her own body. The machine intelligence that controlled her cycled the airlock and stepped onto the soil of the moon. As the battle computer slid her pistol into the chest holster, Galena could see that the magazine locked into the weapon contained the stun rounds. Fierce joy welled within her, *'Your dominance is weakening, machine. I will break free...'*

A smile tinged her lips as she scanned Aja's surface. As the little moon spun through its orbit the shadows lengthened and shortened drastically during each rapid rotation. From what she could remember, this moon was a dense mass of stone and metals. As such, a thin atmosphere was trapped within the deepest crevasses of the planetoid.

She gained a little bit more control of her body the further she moved away from the base. She glanced over her shoulder to the command center that now lay behind her and admired the dome as it glittered in the flashing shadows. The base was built into one of the deep crevasses where sharp peaks surrounded it on three sides.

She felt the tug of the machine as it pushed her to go further afield. Without hesitating, her body hopped over a short ledge and headed off in the direction where the Matilda was purported to be.

As Galena stumbled through the thin atmosphere, she gave that possibility more thought. The Doctor had sent her out to meet her friends, but what did she want? *'Is this just another test? Or is the Matilda really out there like a beacon of hope?'*

She murmured aloud through her re-breather, "If this is a test, what is the cost if I fail?"

She saw a puff of dust far off to the left and slowed her advance. The battle computer connected to her brain picked up the movements of five other beings behind and around her. A disingenuous smile graced her lips as the chip compelled her to continue walking forward and positioned her hand over the pistol strapped to her chest.

The machine led her to the location she had seen in the holo-vid. Her eyes registered that dust was settling around something quite large that blocked the moon's light wind. *'The ship is real.'*

Her heart skipped a beat. Not only did they live, but they had truly come for her. Of her greatest wishes, being found had been tantamount, but it also had been the chance she had believed in the least.

Jon Gray Lang

Dr. Wyeth told that her friends had been lost when the wormhole collapsed around the M33. No ship could survive such a situation. But Galena had never given up hope.

The cloaking that hid the Matilda from sight abruptly dropped and suddenly there it was in all its glory, resting on the bluff. The spacecraft that pulled her off of a prison vessel; the freighter that had become a home for her, and the ship that she was told was lost forever.

She slowed again as she approached the bulky hull and her eyes wandered over every scratch and dent that marred its surface. The trawler had been through much since she had last seen her. But none of it had stopped the battered boat from sailing through the vacuum of space to come for her rescue.

The joy in her heart melted as the battle computer dropped her arms to her sides, brought her body to a standstill in front of the cargo bay doors and rooted her to the spot.

***

Through the port hole Luli could see the dome of the base hidden in its grove of jagged peaks. With the cloaking on, Luli had managed to land the Matilda remarkably close to the only structure on the moon of Aja.

On the Matilda's bridge, Barney's data pad was jammed into the port on the pilot console

Jon Gray Lang

running diagnostics. A sudden whoosh rang out, followed by silence.

"The cloak just dropped, didn't it?" smirked Jacquie.

Anton barked in laughter and Derain glared at the pair of them.

Barney noisily blew out a breath as he waited for the diagnostic report to conclude, "Maybe... but it shouldn't have. That mechanized veneer of invisibility is the only thing keeping us safe..."

"I'm pretty sure the cloak is gone, Barney," warned Luli. "Because I see a bunch of people walking right up to the ship."

"Eh? How many?"

"I see five, no six of them," she answered. "Though the one out front seems to be on a different mission than the others. See how the others are trying to stay hidden and that one is just standing out in the open?"

"That looks like the Lieutenant," remarked Anton.

"You sure?" asked Derain. "It could be a Trojan Horse situation."

Anton glared at the bounty hunter, "No, I'm not sure. How the hell would I be? It just moves like her."

"What should we do, Jacq?" asked Barney. "If it is the Lieutenant, should we call her over and blast off this rock?"

Jacquie deliberated, "They've seen us. Grab your gear and meet in the cargo bay. We'll give them a hello they won't forget. Then we'll see if the stray is our Lieutenant."

"I am ready, as I am never without my friend Henon God of Thunder," grinned Anton.

Derain rolled his eyes as he kicked Anton's feet off the console, knocking Rabbit out of his chair. "Let's go then."

They piled into the lift. As it went down, Barney hopped off on the second deck, "Have to grab the ole 'in case of trouble'."

The others exited the lift once it reached the bottom deck. Jacquie handed out the emergency re-breathers stashed in the shabby, dented case on the wall. "Keep your line of sight open."

As the others took up defensive positions, Barney exited the lift. Anton scurried to the roof of the Folly. As he unholstered his pistol, he reminisced, "This reminds me of that time we fended off the pirate attack on Joy."

"A misnamed planet, if there ever was one," murmured Jacquie. "Barney, go ahead and trigger the cargo bay doors."

"On it."

As they opened, Jacquie moved to the slit and looked out onto the surface of the bizarre moon. The majority of the rock had nothing to indicate that anything lived on it, yet this old crater somehow kept a thin atmosphere.

'In a way I'm glad there's trouble. I knew this rescue mission was too easy.' Jacquie slipped her pistol free and adjusted the straps on her cheap re-breather,

"Let her come in and we'll take care of her entourage... easy peasy."

***

Five Consortium troopers ghosted past Galena. They moved toward the open cargo bay doors and threw three canisters inside the ship. The air blossomed with a chalky, colored smoke and the acrid taint of burnt bleach penetrated through the helmet filters. Galena couldn't move as the soldiers filed past her and in through the gap between the doors.

She heard the sharp retort of gunfire echo through the cargo bay. Then silence. As Galena's body relaxed, her hand slid toward her pistol and pulled it free. The machine's voice rippled from her throat, "Mission parameters, understood."

She slipped aboard the ship while the battle computer tracked sound and movement. There was a slight shift to the far right and her pistol instantly leapt up and squeezed off a round. A small cry answered and Derain fell out of the smoke.

The chip in Galena's skull responded when it felt a brush of air behind her. As she spun around to meet it, Luli jumped out of the smoke and threw a hammer fist toward her head. The computer calculated the least amount of movement required and swiftly shifted out of the way.

Jacquie's voice eerily pierced, "Wait! Galena, it's us!"

Luli spun in response and swung her leg out to trip the genorg. The Lieutenant's body swept up into a bullfighter's stance and a round from her pistol blasted into Luli's knee at close range. The cyborg stumbled under the loss of balance and fell to the decking.

"Damn it! Take her down!" cried the Captain.

As the Lieutenant aimed at Luli, a small cry of anguish escaped Galena. There was a loud bark and a bullet tore through the genorg's arm, knocking off her aim. Galena fought with all her will against the battle computer as it tried to bring her pistol to bear again. Another loud bark sent Galena flying across the cargo bay and slammed her against the flank of the Rabbit's Folly.

She glanced down at her chest as she fought to suck in a breath. A large caliber round had exploded into fragments against her body armor and thrown her from her feet. Her eyes searched for the source of the shot as Anton strode out of the smoke with Henon firmly gripped in his hand. His pistol barked again and her helmet cracked open like an eggshell from the impact.

"Why did you leave us, Galena?" he asked.

She shook her head to stop the ringing in her ears and felt the machine struggle to aim her pistol at the first human connection she had ever made, "... not... me."

Resolution came to her briskly as Galena took control of her arm and shoved the barrel of her gun through the crack in her helmet.

Jon Gray Lang

"Wait! No!" screamed Anton as he dropped Henon to wrest the pistol from her hands.

As the cold tip rested against her temple, a single tear leaked from her eye when she pulled the trigger. In a brilliant flash her head rocked hard from the impact, but it was enough to short out the chip. She smiled serenely and breathed out a sigh of relief.

***

"Free! The abomination is dead." The oily creature crawled to the surface of Galena's stunned mind and left her to drown in the darkness.

Anton's voice cracked as he fell to his knees, "What did they do to you?"

Galena's lips parted and black blood dribbled down her chin. The words crawled from her throat, "Slave to God or puppet for the Devil? It matters not to me..." Her eyes grew black and thin rivulets spilled down her cheeks.

"Oh shit!" Anton cursed as he backpedaled away from her.

The expression on her face was darkness itself as her gun barked three times. Anton dropped to the decking and settled alongside Luli.

Horrid laughter bubbled up from the genorg's throat as she hopped to her feet as anguish tore at her heart. She spied Barney as a round from his long rifle tore through her body armor. He couldn't reload fast enough. Her foot slammed into his jaw.

Jon Gray Lang

He was barely able to register the crack of her ankle as it snapped under the weight of his body when the blow lifted him off the ground.

Jacquie pulled the trigger on her pistol repeatedly until it clicked on chamber after empty chamber. What was left of the Lieutenant hobbled toward the Captain and ripped the pistol from her hand.

The pistol cracked into Jacquie's temple and she fell heavily to the decking. The Lieutenant stared down blankly at the limp body until her eyes slowly cleared.

The entity within the genorg squealed in abject fear, "No! This cannot be!"

Galena growled as she ripped the faceplate off her helmet and dropped to her hands and knees, "I will no longer be controlled by you or anyone else!"

The creature tried to hide deep within her guts, but her stomach muscles rebelled. Her diaphragm pushed down while her abdominal walls contracted and her stomach squeezed hard. A large wriggling object fought to stay down as her body struggled to force it up.

The creature cried out, but it no longer had the control it had wielded over Galena, "So close, so close to the way back home..."

Drool and stringy black goo trickled out of Galena's mouth as she convulsed. With a final push, the object from within her splatted against the decking.

Jon Gray Lang

A wriggling larva that was as black as night lay in a pool of her stomach's contents. Galena stared at it in revulsion as she tried to catch her breath. The grub-like thing tried to right itself and slither away. With a snarl, the Lieutenant picked up the pistol and swung it like a hammer. The larva burst like rotten fruit, spraying its innards all over the deck.

She swung again and again as a keening sound undulated from the depths of her being. The wail rose into a screech and she dumped all her rage into it. The pistol grip shattered into fragments as her fist kept smashing into the creature's body until there was nothing left of it. The pieces of the entity dried up and collapsed into a dark dust that floated in the air.

As her crying dwindled to ragged breathing, she leaned back against a bulkhead and stared at her handiwork. *'Oh, Anton, what have I done?'* Tears coursed down her cheeks as her voice mumbled past unresponsive lips, "Life is too hard, Jacq."

A radio squawk emanated from one of the fallen soldiers. Galena came to her feet as if in a daze and walked falteringly toward it. As it squawked again, she slowly pulled the helmet free from the dead trooper. She put the helmet on and the Doctor's voice came through, "Peters? Come in... Damn it! No one's answering..."

Galena's anger came back in a rush. "You got your wish, Doctor."

"Lieutenant, is that you? You sound... unwell.

Jon Gray Lang

Where is Peters?"

"They're all dead. Every last one of them." As Galena's voice rose, her eyes grew darker, "Your tin soldiers are no more, Doctor. I am free from your whims. I am free to do as I wish..."

She clicked the comm off. Her eyes rolled into the back of her head and she slumped to the decking.

***

"... I am free from your whims. I am free to do as I wish..."

As she stood on the high platform in the control room, Dr. Wyeth look stunned. Her hands kept opening and closing as if trying to grasp onto everything that was slipping through her fingers. *'My life's work undone. My final chance at finding my family. Not yet, Devil Tom! Not yet!'*

She curled her hand into a fist and grabbed the comm, "Now, uh Galena, let's calm down. You know how you get when you're excited. We still have so much work left to do..."

The Comm operator shook his head, "Sorry Doctor, but the comm channel has been cut."

The Doctor cursed as she slammed the handset down, "Damn her to every inch of the nine hells. Diego, get a team over there and end her. You hear me? End her!"

Commander Diego snapped his heels together and raised his hand for a sharp salute, "Yes,

Doctor."

He moved quickly out of the control room and headed down to the gate. As he passed one of the workstations, he ordered, "Tanner, get two teams together for close combat and set up a third team for distance. We've been given the go-ahead to take her down."

"About bloody time."

***

Absolute blackness swallowed Galena's consciousness as she lost sight of the Matilda's interior. She moved her arms and there was no resistance, a sensation similar to being in deep space. *'But I'm on the Matilda...'*

"Are you?" the darkness answered her unspoken question.

A resounding trumpeting resonated in the distance. The matter that surrounded her quivered in anticipation as it slapped against her and sent her tumbling. She was tossed on the breakers of an errant wave of noise. There was no sense of direction for her to grasp onto as she lost connection to her body.

Another blast of trumpeting sounded near her and she sensed a large body pass beneath her. Her eyes focused on the only thing that stood out in the blackness, an oily orb that seemed to track her as it moved further away. Suddenly, another orb blinked open and focused on her, followed by others.

The blackness lit up with a blanket of stars like the night sky and each one was an eye with her as their focus. Somehow she knew that the eyes all belonged to an immensely powerful being. The pressure of the godlike being directing its will at her made her quail in fear.

Appendages slithered out of the darkness and wrapped about her arms and legs. They applied pressure and her arms and legs straightened against her will. She felt the eyes and appendages study her body, her mind, her very soul. There was nowhere to hide. She was pulled forward as something wet and undulous plastered itself against her forehead.

"Please, no more," she pleaded as her memories were rifled through until one stood out clearly in her mind.

She was in the cell on the Matilda and her back was pressed against the bars. Luli hovered out past the bars and listened as the memory of Galena spoke, "What you take for granted as a living being in this shit hole of a galaxy, I had to earn. Fight, scratch, claw, and bleed for... take lives for..." Galena reached involuntarily for the dog tags around her neck as the memory faded, "These stupid sheaths of plastic and circuitry are what validate my existence as a person..."

Suddenly, she was swept into a memory that was not hers.

***

The blackness became an ocean lit with colors her human eyes couldn't comprehend. Emptiness expanded outward with no end in sight. Nothing else existed here except the entity the memories came from. Eons stretched by until time had no meaning and yet the being continued to exist.

Suddenly, there was a stabbing pain followed by a flicker of light and color, unlike anything the godlike being had ever experienced. It glimmered in the distance and she felt a pull toward it. As she swam closer, the flicker elongated into a shaft illuminated from within by flames, smoke and the color of suns. Her eyes grew fascinated by this change and blinked open in the darkness.

Millions of orbs watched the glinting shaft and strange metallic objects traveled down through the center of it and disappeared. Colored lights burned between these vessels and explosions broke some of them apart. Eager to understand what she was seeing, the being reached out and pierced the shaft. The metallic objects tumbled out and flames leapt from their engines in an attempt to control their flight.

A thought bubbled to the surface from Galena's mind, "Spacecraft unlike any built by humankind. Older than humanity, older than the earth itself."

Galena's mind fell below the surface of the memory as a tentacle reached out and snapped up one of the ancient warships. The vessel cracked in two and tiny beings tumbled out. She could feel their fear of death and this shocked the entity.

Galena's mind translated the emotions of the godlike being at play, "There are others like me? Those that feel, those that see, those that swim?"

She reached out and gingerly caught one of the tiny creatures. Its fish-like scaled body tried to slither free as it sucked in breath after breath of the air of the new universe it found itself in.

Words tumbled from the mouth of the creature, but they made no sense to her. She caught another one with the spindly legs of an insect. It sang to her with the scratching of its dangling legs, but she did not understand what it was trying to communicate. Others of her eyes watched as the shaft splintered apart before it winked out of existence.

The memory ended and was replaced by another. The being could now see spots where her universe pressed against other ones. Curiosity came to the fore of her mind as she reached out and pressed an eye against these thin spots. The eye slid through and she saw things that were unimaginable to her sheltered existence. Organisms in all shapes and sizes, each with their own worries and cares.

The godlike being studied these places for centuries and learned of pain, war, and power. She stole creatures from the other universes and brought them to her world. She watched as they interacted with the others trapped in her menagerie. Over time, she understood what they said and it was always the same. "Please, Motherverse set us free. Return us home."

As time went on in the outer universes, it slowed within hers. Her creatures changed, combined, and multiplied until she was no longer alone. But she continued to survey those other worlds. The creatures on the other side responded in fear when they found her watching. They assembled fleets and armies to attack. She swept more of them into her universe, adding more organisms to her menagerie.

The entity stopped observing the other worlds when a burst of pain screamed across her senses, followed by another and another. Her captured creatures had cut her eyes free with their attack ships. While she could still see through them, they remained beyond the veil of her universe. They were out of her reach.

Where those eyes had been only open wounds remained. Her creatures cut deep into the wounds. They drained her life force until she was weakened and could no longer fight them off. She could only observe as the oldest of her menagerie used her blood to speak through her lost eyes to those who would listen in the other universes.

And Galena finally understood what the Masters wanted. They longed for nothing more than to go back to a home that no longer existed. They knew Luli carried a map back to humanity's original world. They would recreate their worlds, if given the chance, including wiping out any species that had replaced them after they faded from time. "They only desire death for all beings other than themselves."

A sense of acceptance sank into Galena's chest emanating from the being named the Motherverse by her children. The trumpeting voice quieted as it whispered, "Stop them. Free me from pain. Return myself to me..."

thirty-nine

I Wanna Be Free

Galena's eyes snapped open as a bright circular light shown in her eyes. She was laying on a metal table that radiated cold through her armored atmo suit. She tried to cover her eyes, but her wrists were bound to the table. The same was true for her ankles. Her eyes blinked involuntarily as she tried to turn away from the light.

Doc's voice spoke from beyond the light, "Et du! Da kae tong sa che!"

"Doc? Is that you? Where am I?"

A mechanical arm reached out and restrained her head. "Sho sho!" The robot spoke again, but not to her, "Shi lo da, es lo te? Et cho tae dom sah eee."

"She's special to us, Doc," said Jacquie. "I don't care if you don't want to fix her, just do it!"

Barney murmured, "There has got to be

something I can do about Doc's bedside manner. Cantankerous bloody automaton."

Galena tried to shake the arm free and received a blunt cuff for her efforts. "Jacquie? Barney? You're not dead? I didn't kill you?"

"No one dies from stun rounds. Not even from point-blank range, apparently. Why'd you do that?" asked Derain in consternation.

Anton added, "Had us scared to a T. Thanks for using those or we'd all be dead."

Galena's heart expanded with joy, "I... I wasn't sure if that was real or not. To be honest, I don't know if this is real, either."

There was an audible crack when Doc reset her ankle and she cried out in pain.

"That sounded pretty real," said Anton as he took her hand in his, "By the way, it is good to see you among the living."

"Kae tong sae." The light shut off and Doc slid away chirping in discontent.

Galena blinked her eyes and noticed the pair of guns pointed in her direction. "Oh, there you all are. Where's Luli?"

"She's on the bridge figuring out a way for us to get out of here," answered Jacquie.

"Are you, you know... you?" asked Anton when she noticed he held onto her wrist.

Derain slowly holstered his pistol as he wisecracked, "That was a hell of a thing to puke up on the deck."

"Stank like the Devil himself," added Barney.

"Was that thing controlling you?"

She nodded, "Partly."

"Is that why you shot yourself?" asked Anton.

Galena shook her head in the negative, "No. That was for the battle chip the Doctor put in my head. I had to stop it, but I thought I was too late."

"Dr. Wyeth?" asked Derain. "What a bloody bunyip. No wonder Mr. Leon wants the woman dead. What gives her the right to do something like that to a person?"

Anton glanced over and winked, "Who replaced our bounty hunter with this humanitarian?" He undid the straps around Galena's ankles and wrists.

Jacquie holstered her pistol as she headed out of the sickbay, "We're out of here, so she's someone else's problem."

"Wait, no! We had a deal!" Derain protested. "We get the Lieutenant back, then I get to finish the job. If I fail again Mr. Leon will hunt me to the ends of the galaxy!"

Jacquie pointed toward the cargo bay doors, "Look outside, Derain. That is a Consortium military base that sent out a team to kill us when they spotted us through our cloak. We barely escaped being imprisoned or executed on that warship. The Consortium can't be beat!"

Barney piped up, "Looks like a bunch of people think differently, Jacq. There is no way you missed the battle we flew through over Jard."

Jacquie sighed as she slapped her palm against

the plas-glass, "Just more targets for the Consortium. We can't win."

Galena hopped off the table and grabbed Jacquie by the shoulder, "We can't go yet. There is more at stake than you could possibly know. The Masters want all of humanity dead. There is nowhere we could go to escape them."

Anton added, "You saw what they were fighting against, Jacq. We've seen what those things are capable of. Two dead systems, even after beating them in one."

Jacquie shrugged him off, "Someone else's fight, now. Not ours. Prep for take-off."

"So we're going to tuck tail and run for the rest of our lives?" grimaced Barney.

Jacquie quipped, "How is that any different than the life you've been leading all this time?"

"That's low, Jacq," Anton groused. "Even if you're pissed."

The comm chirped and Luli's voice came through, "Looks like we've got a second team incoming. Prep for a fight."

"Fuck that," shouted Jacquie. "Jump this God's be damned boat and get us the hell out of here." She slapped the door controls to close.

"Jumping..."

***

Commander Diego slowly advanced on the freighter. The only sign of the previous excursion was the thin layer of chalky substance from the gas grenades dusting the ground. He stepped into the quiet cargo bay followed swiftly by his squad, but there was no sign of life. The bodies of the team that arrived with the genorg subject lay where they had fallen. Off in the distance, the lift doors remained open and inviting.

The Commander waved over to his people, "Juarez, you and Saed come with me."

As the troops made their way deeper into the cargo bay, the entire ship shook. The sweet and bitter tang of overripe tropical fruit blanketed the bay, followed by the gut-wrenching feeling of everything being turned inside out. Commander Diego fell to his knees while Juarez yanked his helmet off and began retching onto the decking. The Commander could hear other soldiers inside the cargo bay vomiting up everything they had eaten that morning.

He worked hard to keep his stomach under control when the very air outside the doors sparkled and swirled with colors he could never have imagined. Two of his men ran for the door. The ship tilted crazily as if the very ground underneath it was no longer solid. He was thrown onto his back as horrific chatter came through the filters of his suit.

A screeching unlike anything he had ever heard exploded from outside the ship followed by the bellows of horrors he didn't want to picture. Screams erupted from outside the hull and gunfire cracked loudly in response. A couple of members of his team who were posted at the doors emptied their rifles, only to be dragged out of the ship by whip-like appendages from outside.

Strange apparitions of what looked like genorgs affected by some disease appeared out of the air. Others looked like the mad creations that sometimes got free of the enclosure in the base. Many had extra extremities, like malformed wings or chitinous limbs. The Commander saw their faces and every single one of them had eyes black as pitch.

"You're... you're like the prime. Mistakes!"

He brought up his rifle and fired at two of them. Viscous dark fluid sprayed from the wounds, but the shots didn't slow them. They reached for him and their fingers punctured his armor and dug into his flesh. The rest of his men fared no better as they were torn to pieces before his very eyes.

Just as suddenly as they had arrived, the tortured genorgs fled from the cargo bay. With hoots and snarls they ran through the cargo bay doors and scattered out into the fields that surrounded the secret base on the moon of Aja.

As his life ebbed out from his wounds, the Commander's last conscious thought was, "What hell have we brought upon ourselves?"

***

Judith paced back and forth in the Control

Room waiting for any news about her failed subject. The message had set her on edge and the waiting was crushing her.

"The Commander and his team have entered the ship," declared the Comm tech.

Dr. Wyeth spun around and enlarged the video feed. The Matilda could now be seen on the moon's surface. She watched as Diego's team entered the cargo bay. Nothing seemed to happen.

"Can you bring in a feed from one of their helmets?" she asked.

At the shake of the technician's head, she swallowed her irritation and glared at the holo-screen.

Suddenly, a burst of multi-colored light swirled around the merchant trawler. Creatures that could only come from the 'de trop aspect' slithered and crawled out of the light burst. As if on cue, the comms exploded with the screams of Commander Diego's team.

"Doctor? We are getting peculiar energy readings from the satellite monitoring system."

"What kind of readings?"

"I've only seen something like this from the uh... sphere in the vault." He looked over at her, "But it's coming from that ship."

"Umm, Doctor?" spoke the Comm Tech, "We've lost comms with the investigative team sent to the vault."

Judith cursed as the video feed cut off, "I don't care about the investigative team! Are the energy readings coming from anywhere else?"

"Let me check."

She shoved him to the side, "Get out of the way!"

She ran a scan and blips appeared around the moon's gravity field. Each one matched the energy reading from the Matilda. She punched the monitor when the energy readings from the sphere grew exponentially in reaction to the one from outside. The air inside the base thickened and rang with the deep vibrations of a gong.

"No!" she wailed. "No, no, no! This can't be happening!"

The power blipped out and the Control Room went dark. As the moon of Aja came out of the shadow of Ogun, sunlight showed through the dome. Dr. Wyeth saw only fear on the faces of the base personnel.

Shrieks and snarls filtered through the walls. No one moved as something scratched at the airlock in the room. Other ghastly sounds rippled along the gangway to the Control Room. The shadows lengthened as the moon swung around the planet and faced the sun.

"By Tom, I hope the doors automatically unlock during a power outage," one of the technicians said.

Dr. Wyeth searched for the speaker as the Control Room grew dark, "Who said that? Keep quiet, damn it!"

Something large smacked against the plas-glass of the inner dome above the Doctor. Before she could even look up, someone screamed in horror as meaty fists thudded against the airlock. On the dome, an abomination scrabbled at the plas-glass. It moved quickly to the seam where the plas-glass met the wall and dug its claws into the rubber seal.

"The airlock is being pulled open!"

A strange moaning grew in volume as something new slammed against the airlock. The walls shook with each impact. A handful of people ran to the door as the gap slowly widened. But Dr. Wyeth knew it didn't matter. They were now all in the 'de trop aspect', a place where her family had sent others that would never be seen or heard from again. *The same place that took my parents from me.'*

As the gap in the door widened, she edged forward and kept close to the walls. She hid in a nook a few feet from the door and waited for the inevitable. As the shadows grew short, the nails of the horror above them began prying at the dome to pull it free. At the same time, the airlock opened wide enough for an arm to reach in and pluck up one of the soldiers closest to it.

The scream of the soldier was blessedly short, but it ignited a blood frenzy. Other monsters reached through the door and slammed it hard into its housing. Rage took the reins as all manner of misshapen creations invaded the Control Room. The people at the door ran in every direction as the terrors bolted after them.

When the last monster came through and

chased down a woman who hid under a desk, Judith ran for the door as fast as she could. She tried to ignore the crunch of bones under her feet and the slathering of human blood that splattered against the walls.

The gangway was empty and Judith wasted no time crossing it. As she headed for the next entryway, the heel of her shoe broke and she tumbled to the decking. The mongrel beast on top of the dome came around to investigate the noise. When the creature looked away, Judith grabbed both of her shoes and threw one as far away from her as she could. As it clattered down the open hole to the bottom level, the creature jumped after it.

Dr. Wyeth sprang to her feet and ran for the emergency stairwell. She opened the door and peeked inside. It was blessedly empty.

Once she stepped in, a woman called out, "Doctor! Hold the door! Please!"

Judith spied the multi-limbed creature chasing the poor woman and slammed the door in her face. She held it closed and shut her ears to the shrieks. Each second seemed an eternity until the woman's voice finally gave out. The Doctor backed away from the door and bolted along the steps to the next floor down.

***

"Jumping..." Luli said from the pilot seat.
She flipped the switch and the jump engine

activated. The rot of spoiled vegetation filled the bridge. Out beyond the port window, the skies crackled with the after flashes of lightning as the entire ship rumbled and shook. But the Matilda didn't budge from the surface of the moon.

"By the Major, what is that?" Luli blinked in surprise, "Another jump engine?"

Astonishingly, instead of falling into 'other space' the Matilda's engine had reacted with the orb in the enclosure and brought 'other space' to the moon of Aja. And Luli could clearly see it hovering like an afterimage over the base.

A horrific hooting boomed outside the ship and startled Luli from her thoughts. Creatures from the 'other space' swarmed the base and battered at the structure in a furor. Spacecraft that she recognized from history class programs dotted the scenery with vessels that looked completely alien in design. The smaller craft flocked to the moon's surface and launched ancient ordnance against the dome.

Her eyes tracked to the orb engine inside the base and many of the creatures had moved away from it as they were drawn to the lives within the base. The thought struck her, *'We're the anchor. Like the Avadora was in the Pequiz system so long ago.'*

Jacquie's voice came over the comm, "Shut her down, Lu. Our immediate problem is rectified."

As she shut the engine down, the overlaid imagery faded, but the creature's attack continued unabated. She clicked the comm, "Hey Jacq, you've got to see this. The Doctor hid another engine on this rock."

***

As Judith passed each floor, the noises grew louder on the other side of the stairwell doors. It was only when she got to the lower levels that the sounds finally tapered off. She was exhausted when she arrived at the exit level for her office. Grim hope encouraged her, *'Specially built to be off the power grid. It's on a separate generator and it has life support and food storage to last a year.'*

She nodded to herself, "I can wait this out and catch a ride to Jard on the next delivery shuttle."

As she peeked through the door, she remembered that the base had lost communication with the homeworld, "Could it be related? No matter, all things tire of the hunt eventually."

The hallway looked empty as she stepped out and let the door close behind her. Just outside the lift, the team of soldiers sent down to investigate the alarms lay where they had died. Judith steeled her resolve. She headed down the hallway brandishing her remaining shoe as a weapon, but it seemed that no living thing was left to challenge her.

As she came out to the open area, she slowed down. She risked taking a look over the edge and at first, couldn't understand what had happened. The armored enclosure had been split open. Bent plates of plasteel littered the floor among the half-eaten remains of her assistants, but she felt no regret, *'They knew the risks.'*

As she backed away, she spied an immense helminth busily masticating on a dead body. Smaller versions of the worm dripped free of the creature's saliva. They left sticky trails on the floor as they buried themselves inside the corpses.

She moved over to the wall and carefully crept along so as not to make a noise. But something heard her. At the sharp sound of snapping metal, Judith glanced over her shoulder. An elongated insectile creature that had broken the railing pulled itself up to her level. She hurled her shoe at the beast and broke into a run toward her office.

She slid to a stop, pulled the door to her office open and tumbled inside. As Judith kicked the door from her prone position, the creature reached toward her. But she was the quicker of the two and the door slammed shut. She hopped to her feet and hastily engaged the automatic locks.

A heavy plate dropped from the ceiling and banged against the floor, blocking the door entirely. Bars spaced six inches apart also settled against the walls. She engaged the generator and the room lit up like the sun compared to the darkness of the stairwell and hallways. "I made it," she sighed in gratitude. "I am safe."

A shuffling noise from her lavatory made her turn around. She frowned. That useless Ensign stood in the shadowed doorway and stared at her appraisingly. "Ah, it is good to see you, Doctor. I was hoping you would make it. You see, I dreamed I would see you one more time. Dreams truly can come true."

"What are you doing here, Mr. Fitzpatrick? You're a military man, shouldn't you be out there fighting the good fight?"

The man's haggard face grinned back, "Oh, I tried that. Or at least the fight that would free me from my nightmares. But, as you can see, it didn't go entirely my way."

Dr. Wyeth wasn't sure what he was talking about until he stepped into the light. His uniform was untidy. It hung open and was spattered in blood. Symbols like those Dr. Saric had been obsessed with were carved into the man's chest and neck. His eyes were black as night and then she noticed his entrails swung freely from a knife cut across his belly.

Her indrawn breath was the only sound she made as he leapt over the desk and sent her sprawling. She tried to get away, but he grabbed her legs and pulled her toward him. He pinned her to the floor with his knee on her chest and the grin he gave her reminded her of the time he interrogated the bounty hunter's family.

"Mr. Fitzpatrick, I'm sure we can work something out..."

"Oh, we had a deal," he giggled. "And I mean to collect!"

Trapped as she was, her struggles were useless. He grabbed her by the hair, bit down on her neck, and ripped out her jugular. As the last of her life flowed away, he whispered in her ear, "We're even now. I've cursed you as much as you cursed me..."

***

"Another jump engine?" uttered Jacquie in shock.

Galena grabbed her by the shoulder and spun her around. "Please listen to me! The Masters will extinguish all human life! They want to return the worlds back to what they remember."

Jacquie shook her off, "Then we'll keep running."

"Run to where, Jacq?" asked Anton. "If everyone else is dead, where can we run?"

Barney strode up to her side with his hands on his hips, "You're right to be scared, I am too. But I've been running my entire life and I'm tired of it."

Derain cracked his knuckles and winked, "Now's the time, Captain. If you give the order."

"What about you, Lu?"

"Well, I can't say no. If someone fancied writing a traditional ballad about me, saving the universe would be quite the kicker."

"You're all in agreement then?"

As she watched, each one of them gave a nod and she sighed through the tightness in her chest. "Well, I guess that settles it. Might as well be legends... for just one day."

Jon Gray Lang

"Suits on, everyone!" ordered Jacquie. "Bring us in closer, Lu. Then activate the jump engine."

***

Luli made short work of the launch protocol and the sublight engines ignited. The stubby wings extended to their full length and turned so that the large engines were pointed toward the ground. She pushed the burn hard and the Matilda lifted off.

As the freighter crested the spiky mountain range, the base became clearly visible in the distance. The sphere of 'other space' had grown to the point that it surrounded the entire moon of Aja. The skies were filled with every make and manner of vessel and titanic beasts flitted amongst them. Winged fiends flew toward the base and Luli followed their flight path. Once she was in range, she could see all of the nightmare creatures that scurried across the surface of the dome searching for an entrance.

The doors of the building burst open. The surviving base personnel ran into the open fields looking for any refuge. Nipping at their heels was a madman's menagerie of monsters that hurtled into the crowd and attacked the escapees.

Luli launched a brace of rockets from the Matilda. They streaked out from the freighter and shattered the dome. As the plas-glass fragments rained down on the carnage, the Matilda punched through the fracture. Luli flew past the Command

Center and spiraled down the long shaft.

Flying creatures pelted the freighter and tore at the sublight engines. She ignored them as she slipped through the narrowing shaft toward the bottom level. As she brought the ship in for a landing, an enormous maggot reared its head and charged.

Before the two landing legs were fully extended, the forward coil gun fired a salvo into the face of the creature. This was quickly followed by another volley as Luli set the trawler down. She launched another brace of rockets. They flew past the remains of the beast and slammed into the damaged enclosure around the other engine. The metal of the structure buckled under the blasts.

"Activating the jump engine..."

Everything went black except for the bright fiery glow of the other engine. It gained in intensity as it reacted to the engine on the Matilda and colorful green-hued sparks showered the surrounding area.

***

Jacquie led the charge when the cargo bay doors swung open. The base level was a mess of twisted metal, shattered plas-glass, and bodies, both human and alien. As she sprinted out, she waved the others forward. From the corner of her eye, she saw Anton head off to the left while Derain moved toward the right.

Jon Gray Lang

Barney spoke through the open comm, "I have you covered, Captain. I don't see anything moving."

"Me either," Jacquie said as Galena came to stand beside her. "You see anything, Lu?"

"All clear for now. Looks like the explosion chased off the beasties that were on us on the way down."

Jacquie saw her two shipmates illuminated by the light from the other engine.

"How are we supposed to get that on board?" Anton asked as he stared at the immense sphere.

"What are we going to do with it, once we have it?" asked Derain.

Strained laughter echoed from above them. Jacquie followed the sound and saw the man as he leapt off the railing. His feet splintered underneath him as he landed in between everyone.

"You!" Derain shouted as he brought his pistol to bear. "You aren't getting away from me again!"

Ensign Fitzpatrick waved his finger, "Now, now, bounty hunter. You will have to wait your turn. Especially when the whole band of outcasts is here!"

"Taking the shot," murmured Barney.

"And look! The Lieutenant has returned!" Hamza's eyes glowed weirdly as he grinned with fierce joy, "I will have my vengeance." He pointed a gun at her and pulled the trigger.

There was a loud crack and the Ensign's chest fountained blood black as night. The man chuckled as a second round hit him in the shoulder. He only laughed that much harder as squawks and croaks rose in volume above them. Frightening creations rained down around them from the landings above.

Anton cursed as he fired Henon. One of the creatures going after Derain collapsed with a screech. Another blast from Barney's rifle shattered the Ensign's knee and he toppled to the deck. His laughter rang on as more of the creatures filled up the space between the Matilda and the orb.

"God damn it! There's too many of them!" cried Jacquie as she shot a five-foot-tall spindly crab creature. As its leg was sheered off it clacked and fell sideways. Two more beasts spun on her and charged.

Galena's pistol barked loudly next to the Captain, but more of the creatures skittered over the corpses of their kind to get at them.

Jacquie shoved Galena out of the way as a fleshy protuberance reached for her. As she backed up to the cargo bay doors, she thought furiously, *'What to do? What to do?'*

Hamza abruptly stood up and called out, "My Masters! Like the Doctor before, these others have come to thwart your plans! But Wyeth is no more and these fools await your judgment!"

Derain dove to the ground and rolled out of the grasp of a clawed beast, "The Doctor is dead? What are we bloody well waiting for then? Let's wrap up this job!"

Shadowy figures coalesced around the orb.

Anton slapped on a cocky grin, "You guys again? Didn't you learn anything at Khanda Tower?"

Henon boomed and the ones in its path scattered. Their mandibles clicked rapidly as they chattered to the other creatures. The nearest ones perked up as if listening to signals before they moved forward.

Jacquie called out, "Anton! Derain! Get over here! Lu, think you can lay down some covering fire?"

"On it," Luli said.

There was a high-pitched whine as the rail gun swung in the direction of the orb and launched a projectile at point-blank range. It crashed into the decking sending fragments flying in all directions. It obliterated one of the Masters as it sailed past and cut another in two.

Anton quickly moved out of the way and bolted toward the Matilda. Derain was right behind him, but he stopped near Ensign Fitzpatrick.

"This is for my grandfather."

Derain fired his pistol and the Ensign dropped like a stone. Whatever had been animating his corpse slithered free of Hamza's skull and Derain backpedaled in horror. Both of his guns came up and unloaded into the slug until it was nothing but paste.

Jacquie cursed when the second rail gun projectile slammed into the crowd of creatures, but didn't leave an open route to the sphere. "We can't get a clear path to get to the damn thing out of here!"

"I might be able to call for help," Galena said as her eyes closed. "Help me get inside the Matilda."

***

Galena called out in her mind, "My sisters, we need your help again!"

"Sister? Sister? Sister, sister, sis..."

Within the bubble of 'other space', Galena could hear the altered genorgs as they communicated to each other in the back of her thoughts. A wry grin formed on her lips, *'We are more alike to the brothers Leon than I had ever thought. I only needed to open my mind to the possibility.'*

She leaned back and closed her eyes, "My sisters! Do you hear me? The path is cleared and time is of the essence..."

The flicker of green eyes united all around Galena in her mind's eye. "Yes, sister who kept us whole. We hear you..."

Galena felt her body being dragged through the cargo bay doors when her sisters appeared from inside the large orb sitting in the wreckage of the enclosure.

She barely registered Derain's voice as he exclaimed, "By Tom, there are so many of them."

The sisters pushed the giant engine out of its cradle of twisted metal. It floated of its own volition and green sparks showered across the walls as it glided out of the enclosure toward the Matilda.

As it drifted through the cargo bay doors into the ship, the sisters charged in after it. They laid down suppressing fire as the rest of the crew backed against the walls to avoid being close to the orb.

Jacquie slapped the cargo bay doors closed and shouted, "The eye is aboard. Get us out of here, Lu!"

Galena looked down. Black blood oozed out from a bullet wound in her side, "I've been shot..." She stumbled and leaned against the bulkhead. As she passed out from the loss of blood, she slumped to her knees.

***

Luli opened the comm and proclaimed, "Embarking on less traveled pathways. And we're off!"

The pilot brought the Matilda to a hover as she engaged the sublight engines. The freighter shot up the shaft as the base began to crumble. Girders and chunks of corroded metal sailed past the freighter on her way to freedom above the jagged shards of the dome.

The ship rose into the sky above the moon and Luli glanced down at the ruins of the base, "Goodbye to you, Doctor. I pray that no one ever falls into your hands in the afterlife." As she angled the Matilda to port, she whispered a prayer, "Please keep my friends safe."

There was a bright flash and she happened to

glance over at the Nav console. A filmy, space-suited figure faded in and out of reality as it manipulated the controls. Her eyes widened in shock. "Major Tom?"

The figure turned toward her and the eyes of the apparition twinkled mischievously before he disappeared from sight.

"Wait!" she cried out. "What have you done?"

Suddenly, an oddly accented voice emerged from the ship's comms. The words put ice in her veins.

"Terminal Advent found..."

The Matilda lurched heavily from the port side and bucked to starboard. Luli was slammed against the harness and her connection to the ship was severed.

The Matilda spiraled out of control and punched a hole through the fabric of the bubble around the moon. The bubble shattered and the invading ships disappeared as the 'de trop aspect' shattered.

Normal space came rushing in to surround Aja. The base lay in ruins. Broken ships were scattered around the shattered dome. Lumps of alien flesh and bone disintegrated into black dust leaving only the remnants of the victims. The fragmented halls of the building were silent. There were no signs of life on the rock.

***

Galena's mind struggled against the pit of unconsciousness that enveloped her. She strove to form thoughts, notions, and even memories, but only her sense of self responded. *'Is this the end?'* she wondered. *'Am I dying?'*

She forced her eyes to open and found herself floating in an endless sea of blackness. She imagined moving her legs and arms, but her limbs remained unresponsive. Yet, she felt no fear or discomfort.

She closed her eyes and sought the connection to her altered sisters and felt the faintest of touches. The tiniest of emerald pinpricks appeared in the farthest distance. She opened her lips to speak and the darkness flooded her mouth. She tried to spit it out, but realized it wasn't drowning her. It simply streamed down her throat leaving a warmth in her belly.

A presence made itself known as it watched her. The hairs on the back of her neck tingled as pale wavelets within the blackness splashed against her body. She felt the presence push against her mind and she opposed it.

The entity bellowed in anger and stronger waves pummeled her body, tossing it to and fro. With it came the awareness of the damage her body had endured and the suffering it had survived. The agony broke through the walls she had built in her mind. The presence sensed this and enveloped her within itself.

Its thoughts were beyond her ability to

fathom. Its motivations were outside of her capacity to understand. The being was immense, larger than worlds, larger than stars. It was older than the galaxy and its scope was far-reaching.

It bellowed again and the intense vibrations threatened to break her apart.

"Stop!" she mouthed and the darkness within her spewed out in convulsions that paralleled the vibrations of the entity. As the last of it trickled free, the presence seeped into her bones and the torment from her body fell away.

A monstrous eye stared down at her and she felt smaller than she had ever felt, inconsequential in comparison. Another eye opened and it studied her. A third eye appeared and, as its lids pulled back, this one captivated Galena. "The jump engine from the Matilda!"

Amusement at her words wrapped around her and she delighted in the sensation. "Little one, the chains that held me are broken and I am free. And I glory in it."

"I have never truly known freedom," confided Galena. "I thought I had it once, but it wasn't real. There was always another chain that I couldn't see that tied me down. Even now, in your presence, I am still not free."

A fourth and fifth eye opened and they sparkled like fireflies in rain. The being spoke to the center of her mind, "You are free now. I release you."

The presence began to recede and an endless

sea of darkness swept over her. She trembled in fear as she blurted, "But what of my friends? Are they free as well?"

As the waves closed over her head she heard from the entity for the last time.

"Begone!"

forty

Take the Long Way Home

Luli fought to regain control, but the Matilda was no longer under its own power. Some force had sent the freighter soaring in zig-zags and no matter how hard she tried, she couldn't get it to fly straight.

Jacquie staggered onto the bridge, "What in the name of the Major are you doing to my boat, Lu?"

"It isn't me, Cap," Luli groaned as she was thrown against her harness when the ship dropped into another spiral. "How's the rest of us?"

Jacquie grabbed the seat at the Nav console and strapped herself down. "Galena's gunshot wound is bad. We've got her sedated in a med tube. Anton and Derain are checking the tie-downs in the hangar. Barney's headed to the engine room to see what's left of it."

"Hopefully something," Luli grimaced as she

Jon Gray Lang

pulled her lap belt tighter.

Jacquie glanced down at their trajectory, "Where are we headed?"

Luli chuckled, "You wouldn't believe me if I told you, but the answer is, I don't know. It's like a skipping stone on a lake, except we're bouncing between the walls of our space and 'other space'. And we're picking up speed!"

Barney's voice crackled over the comm, "The engine is gone, Captain. We're only on sublight engines now. If they make it through this... please make it through this."

"I was hoping for better news," Jacquie grumbled. "Might as well come up top. Luli, are you seeing the weak spots between the two?"

"See them? No!" Luli grunted as the Matilda slammed hard to port tumbling end over end. "Feel them? Hell to the yes."

"Shit!" cursed Jacquie as she pounded the armrest of the chair. "We can't get lost in deep space!"

She grabbed the comm, "Anton! Derain! Activate every transponder we have and daisy chain the signals together. Every time we hit a hard bounce, toss one out the airlock and hope we can find our way back!"

***

Derain held onto the wall near the open comm in the airlock. The ship took a dizzying turn and threw him against the helmet rack. As he pulled himself back over, he said, "A hard bounce like that last one?"

"Oof... exactly!" shouted Jacquie. "And be quick about it!"

"We're on it."

Anton grabbed Derain and clipped a guideline to the loop on his spacesuit. "We're clipped in, now. What's the gig?"

"Daisy-chain a bunch of transponders and toss them out the airlock. Then pray to Tom they'll lead us back home."

Anton grinned as the Matilda dropped hard underneath him, "Aah, the old breadcrumb trick. It's been a while." He glanced toward the hangar, "It'd be easier out there."

"Agreed. You want to toss or reprogram?"

Anton was already cycling the inner airlock, "Pretty sure Barney and I built these, so I'll reprogram."

"I'll crack the hangar bay doors."

***

The airlock opened and they headed in separate directions. Anton stopped at the rack of transponders and activated the onboard computers. They blinked to life and each one ran a start-up diagnostic.

The last time Anton had used the large cylindrical devices was for a short-range meeting to

Jon Gray Lang

deliver some illicit goods for a deal that Jacquie had made under the table. He smiled at the memory, *'Good payoff on that run. We danced the night away until none of us had a bit of mazuma left to our name.'*

The light patterns stopped cycling and they all turned green. He hunkered down at the first one and tapped through the opening settings. With a few quick keystrokes, he set the channel and copied it down. He stabbed the keys of the next one and set it to duplicate the first one.

***

Derain headed to the back and flipped the heavy switch to activate the hangar bay doors. Although sound couldn't travel through the airless bay, he could feel the metal squeak and grind as they trundled open and hit the switch again. The maelstrom of 'other space' shown through the crack.

"Here ya go," said Anton as he dropped the first transponder on the deck. He glanced out and remarked, "Is that spot a darker black?"

Derain followed his finger, "Hmm, might be."

As they passed over the spot, the Matilda shuddered and listed to starboard. "That's our queue!" Derain shouted as he lifted up the transponder and chucked it through the opening. "I can see another of those spots coming up."

Anton bounded over to the stack and grabbed two of them. With a quick toss, he sent them floating toward Derain. Derain snatched them and threw one out past the doors. The ship lurched drunkenly and Derain held on fast to the other one.

***

Anton was already running through the programming on the next two. As soon as he was done, he said into the comm, "Jacquie, set the comm channel to 706 point 1." He stared fixedly at the transponders in front of him and willed the connection to speed up. A staccato pattern played across the mini screen, "The loop is set."

The Matilda slammed hard into something large and Anton was thrown off his feet. He crashed into the rack and a couple of the transponders rolled free. He scrabbled back to his feet and grabbed the nearest of the errant devices.

He heard Derain cry, "I need another one,"

"I'm programming them as fast as I can," shouted Anton as he threw the one he had. "Here!"

***

Barney was thrown off his feet in the engine room at the heavy impact. Alarms started bleating and the port sublight engine's read-out went red. He picked himself up and cursed.

"We lost the port engine, Jacq. We're dumping fuel."

"How bad is it?" asked Jacquie through the comm.

Jon Gray Lang

Barney grumbled, "At this rate, the tanks will be empty in less than an hour. Without it, we lose electricity, we lose heat, and we lose life support. We'll lose the Matilda."

Another bounce set Barney flying and he curled into a ball to absorb the blow. As he regained his balance he said, "The med tubes are designed to operate independently of the ship's power. We can put ourselves under and that'll slow our oxygen usage."

Luli shot back, "That's a last resort call, Barney!"

He sighed deeply, "I don't see any other way for us, Lu."

The ship chopped upward before it crashed down hard. The list to starboard grew more pronounced.

Derain's voice came through the comm, "The last transponder is out the airlock. We're heading down to sickbay."

"We're all out of chances, Jacq. I'm heading down there too."

Jacquie's laugh was short and bitter, "Everyone, abandon your posts and head to sickbay."

"Killing power to everything except the comm loop," said Luli.

***

Just as the lift opened, the ship took a nose

dive. Jacquie thrust her leg out and pushed the lift door into the housing. "They're coming closer together aren't they?"

Luli gasped as she fought against the anti-grav in the lift, "They sure are. We must be getting close to an eddy, fingers crossed."

Barney peeked out past the plas-glass doors to sickbay, "Come on, step it up! You're the last two."

Jacquie glanced at Luli, "Ready to run for it? On one, two, three!"

The two women sprinted toward the sickbay, hoping to make it inside before the next bounce. Barney backed out of the way as they flew past him. Doc's arms reached out and grabbed the pair of them as the next bounce sent the ship reeling again.

"Nice catch, Doc," cooed Luli. "I always knew you cared."

Doc chirruped, "Che, che. Et tae dom sa!"

The ship shivered as it hit another weak spot. Doc let them go and pushed them toward the readied med tubes.

"We're going as fast as we can, Doc!" Jacquie growled as she hopped into her med tube. "Set the timer on my med tube to wake me in a few days. I'm counting on you!"

Doc closed Luli's med tube and set the sleep cycle. Just as the robot was closing the lid over Barney, he reached out a hand to stop it, "Hey Jacq, you made your parents proud today."

Her throat caught for a moment, "You think?"

Jon Gray Lang

He nodded as the lid closed over him, "I'm certain."

The robot set the sleep cycle and made sure that unconsciousness claimed the engineer before turning to Jacquie's med tube.

A simple smile graced her lips as her eyes closed, "I think so, too..."

"Che dom sat ae," Doc said as the timer menu opened. The ship rocked hard as if it had hit a wall and began tumbling out of control. Doc was flung back off his track and slammed into the cabinet on the opposite wall. A support girder fell from the ceiling and pierced his abdomen.

"Et... et... et cho..."

The lights on his chassis went dark and power began failing throughout the ship.

***

Impossible colors sparkled against the curtain of starless space. These sparks slowly coalesced into a shock of bright light that ripped its way through the fabric of the sky. Mist the shade of fresh blood sprayed outward until it formed a vortex that pulsed with inner energy.

The creatures that existed here were drawn to the rift and swam toward it. Their bellows echoed loudly when the slab face of a freighter shoved its way through the tear. The vessel was drawn free of the laceration in the inky black sky as it slowly knit itself closed.

The tiny vessel finally slipped free of the 'de trop aspect'. Newer dents adorned the carcass of the broken ship. Its port engine was crushed and fragments of the plating that were caught in the gravitation well of the trawler circled it endlessly.

It was buffeted by the monstrous brutes that brushed against it, but eventually, they moved on. The poor ship was left where it hung under the dimmed light of a single star that splashed light against its hull. It floated serenely between a tiny blue planet and a smaller red one.

The cargo bay doors hung open to space as did the hangar bay doors. No lights showed from the interior, no sound emanated from the rooms. In the sickbay, six med tubes contained the comatose forms of the crew of the Matilda.

The awakening cycle on the Captain's tube blinked with a query; [Begin Awakening Protocol?] [YES] [NO]

The automated Doctor lay on the floor as its sliding rack hung bent and broken above. The only things moving were small creatures that skittered around inside and none of them even twitched an ear or antenna when a tinny voice sounded from the empty bridge, "Terminal Advent reached. Distress beacon activated and linked to transponder loop. Beginning broadcast."

<<<< THE END >>>>

Jon Gray Lang

forty-one

Epilogue

HOURS AFTER THE JARD INCURSION:

Deep underneath Machado's Salvage, Zolzaya studied the feeds from the cameras that provided security on the surface. She zoomed in and didn't quite know what to make of what she saw.

"Dusty," she called out. "Something strange is happening up there. I don't know what to make of it."

Batu chuckled, "If it's anything like watching a bunch of genorgs line dancing in the middle of a war, then it's part of the new normal."

Zolzaya shook her head, "It's not that. Come on dad, You have to see this."

He glanced her way as he pulled the headphones off his ears. "I can't get a hold of our contacts at the Council Hall. So, what have you got for me?"

She slid out of the way of the monitors and everyone in the room stared.

"They're just coming apart, aren't they?" asked Zolzaya in amazement. "My eyes aren't playing tricks, right?"

Batu moved forward and increased the zoom on the Machado's Salvage sign and watched as a winged creature lost its grip and fell off. As it dropped it turned into a powder that blew away in the light breeze. Under his breath, he said, "That one isn't flying ever again."

Dusty wiped the concern from his face and settled his hands onto his hips, "The only way to find out what's going on is to go up top. Who's with me?"

"I'm right behind you, pops."

"Me too," added Zolzaya.

The ride up the lift was somber. They didn't know what they were going to find. War had never come to Jard in the entire history of the Consortium. The idea that someone dared to lay siege to the planet was difficult to imagine, never mind the truth of it. Or the nightmare creatures that came in their wake.

The lift doors parted and they stepped out one after the other. The shack was dark as they walked through the front room and into the yard outside.

The sun burned brightly and felt good on

Zolzaya's skin after the chilly underground room. But there was little else she could see that fit the pleasantness of the weather.

Columns of smoke billowed up from the ruins of structures in the distance. The once proud and tall buildings were no longer part of the skyline. They now resembled the jagged teeth of a long-dead mythical beast.

Burning shipwrecks dotted the horizon and the wind stank of death. None of the invading creatures were left to behold. The only sign that they had even been there was the eddying dust devils of black powder that flitted across the gravel.

High in the sky, the fuselages of Consortium Naval craft seeped fumes like blood from wounds as they cruised overhead. Far off to the east a pack of genorg soldiers mindlessly wandered in circles. Their weapons were forgotten as they stared blankly forward. Beyond that, there were no other signs of life.

Batu asked the question on everyone's mind, "Did we win?"

Dusty sighed as he pulled his children in close, "We survived, Batu. We survived."

***

DAYS AFTER THE JARD INCURSION:

On the Silk Road station, Mr. Leon perused the news feeds from his office. The feeds were coming from just about every system now. The Consortium had begun a systematic lockdown on every star system, even those that hadn't been directly involved in the uprising. The genorgs were labeled as the cause for martial law. The Consortium wasted no time dispersing or disposing of anyone who had ever questioned the government in the first place.

"We have to kill them! Kill every single one of them!" echoed through his handheld from a man screeching into the camera. An unhappy sigh escaped him as he swiped at his data pad to blank out the vid. The feeds were coming from nearly every system now.

Genorgs were being executed on sight by the military, but it didn't stop there. Even the Consortium populace were hunting them. Cries that those who were less than human should not be allowed to live were cheered on by the masses. Others raged that anyone who had owned a genorg was responsible for the war. As a sign of this, prosperous individuals had begun to go missing.

"It won't be much longer until they come for me in all my guises," Mr. Leon mused.

He brought his data pad back up and flipped through to the plans he and his brothers had established for this second revolution. With some minor differences, almost every step had fallen into place, but the jackboots of the Consortium had been able to turn the tables at the very end.

Mr. Leon sighed, "I hadn't counted on the

populace turning so quickly."

"No, we hadn't," echoed in his head as others of his brethren woke to join together.

"Adjustments will need to be made..."

"Yes, adjustments..." echoed another.

A sardonic laugh brought smiles to their faces, "Do they not say that the third time is the charm?"

"It is one of the natural-born's sayings..."

"The ark is away?" asked Mr. Leon from his office.

"It is..." replied his brethren.

"That is good," he said. Many of his brothers had been put in stasis and placed on board a large ship that was running at least five separate idents. With the vessel away, he knew that he and his kin still had a chance at survival. A slight grin curved the corner of his lips.

Mr. Leon pressed a series of keys on his data pad and its memory was wiped clean. With a casual hand, he dropped it into the waste bin beside his desk. Seconds later, the kettle whistled and he quickly poured the hot water into the small pot sitting in front of him. He slowly poured the tea liquor into his ceramic cup and sat back. As he brought the cup to his lips, a pounding began on his office door.

"So soon?" he wondered. "I thought I might still have a moment or two..."

He took a sip of his tea and felt his brothers leave his presence. He was to be the sacrificial lamb this time. His office door dented in when a short-radius blast burst through the center of it. Shrapnel shot outward and a chunk smashed into his clay teapot, shattering it. Wet tea leaves seeped from between the pot's fragments, littering his desk and the floor.

A larger shard of shrapnel pierced Mr. Leon's skull and blood gushed freely from the wound. The tea cup slipped from his hand and shattered on the floor. The nerve endings in his eyes and brain kept firing long enough for him to register the black-suited ops team as they crawled through the hole. A surprised sneer lit his face as his nerve endings quit broadcasting.

"Shit, he's dead," groused the first one through the door.

"You sure?" asked the one behind him.

The first one through the hatch lifted Mr. Leon's head up by his hair and peered into the glazed eyes, "Yes, I'm sure."

"Well, I guess this would be a dead end then," quipped another one.

"Yeah, just like your jokes..."

***

WEEKS AFTER THE JARD INCURSION:

The Consortium military hadn't ransacked this system yet. The Independence floated past the space station as Rosa Keri negotiated for supplies. But resources were growing tight.

She glanced over at Captain Delta and shook her head in the negative. "They don't have anything to spare. I'll ping the moon colony next."

There was a sharp intake of breath behind her. Rosa turned and watched as Rex Leon's face appeared more ashen by the minute. His eyes grew watery and he slumped into himself.

Delta asked in concern, "Another one was found?"

Rex nodded. "The few brothers I have left are scattering to the wind in the hopes of living another day." He glanced at the Captain, "Delta, you and the sisters must be careful. The Consortium is making a concerted effort to cleanse the systems of genorgs. No place is truly safe."

He looked up at Commander Keri, "Is the Peking Empress still with us?" At her nod, he warned, "We have to get out of here."

"If nowhere is safe, where can we go?" asked Daphne. "With what you just said and the news chattering about the Consortium victories, where can we go?"

"There are rumors of a civil war brewing on Titan," said Rosa. "Supposedly, a hero named Barnabus de Lagnel issued a Call-To-Arms and it was heard across their system. The immediate response caught their theocracy by surprise."

Rex shook his head in the negative. "Sadly, the Consortium would bring their weight to bear, if we showed our faces. It would only bring a swift end to the Titan's call for justice."

Jon Gray Lang

"Where does that leave us? Is there nowhere else we can go?" lamented Rho-11.

Rex centered himself and the aloofness he usually wore settled around him like a blanket. There were lessons to be learned from this defeat. "Call the others and set course for the Empress. Have Admiral Kaur prime the wormhole engine. We will have to remain on the move until a better option appears."

Rosa Keri held up her hand in a stopping motion as she siphoned through radio chatter to find a new signal that had begun to come through faintly. "Hold on that order for a minute. I found something."

She swiped through a few others until she was able to bring the new one to the fore. The signal was weak, but as she broadened the search, she found it was being duplicated further out. "Like the old smugglers trick. Daisy chain a bunch of transponders to leave a trail to follow."

"A what?" asked Rex as he came up behind her.

She pointed at the display, "See there? That's a single transponder, but if you widen the search..."

"You'll see the message repeated. I see." He checked the origination code, " Now, that's a ship ident I have not seen in a long, long while."

Rosa looked up at him, "It looked familiar to me, too. You recognize it?"

He nodded, "That, my dear Commander, is the original ident for the Matilda and it looks like she has something left to tell us."

He turned and addressed the crew, "New orders. Inform the Admiral that we may have found a haven safe from the Consortium. Bring the fleet about and make way to this Terminal Advent."

***

A YEAR AFTER THE JARD INCURSION:

Captain Ellsbeth shook her head. The infighting within the Council heads was going absolutely nowhere. Each one called the others traitor for having made any deal with the House of Khanda. Even though each of the remaining eighteen founding families had all taken the twin's mazuma.

"Brought to a standstill by the bickering of adult children."

But some things had changed. All comms to Titan were lost. Trade dried up and the jump gate itself decommissioned on its own. The last bit of information that came through before the blackout spoke of rebellion by their citizens and a direct attack against their religious leaders.

Very little information had been found on the enigmatic shipping magnate, Mr. Leon. Purported to be the financier of the rebel forces, over two dozen identical males calling themselves Mr. Leon had been found and executed as war criminals. Who or what he was, no one truly knew. How far his reach was, or if he still had his fingers in the Consortium, was the question.

On top of that, the core of the rebel fleet remained at large. Try as she might, they continued to slip through her fingers. This gave many of the outer systems the where with all to hold doggedly to their separation from the Consortium. Others demanded concessions before being forcibly rejoined. The concessions included things one would expect, like more equal trade negotiations, and more support from the central worlds in making the newer colonies livable. What stood out as remarkable, though, was the call to bring equality to the remaining living genorgs.

Mary smiled, "About time for that. You can't make someone a soldier and then deny them their say in the governing they have been forced to defend."

Her comm chirped, "Yes, Ilya?"

"The two survivors from Aja are ready to speak to the Council, Captain."

"Are the two women still holding to their story?"

"Yes sir. Dr. Wyeth lost control of the moon base and Lieutenant Chadov was instrumental in driving away the alien invasion. Do you think it will be enough to push the vote for equality for the genorgs?"

Captain Ellsbeth replied, "With the benefit of regaining swaths of the colonies without a fight, one can hope."

Jon Gray Lang

She walked back into the Council Hall and took the seat assigned to her. The first woman told her story of the moon of Aja, followed by the other. There was a smattering of claps from the audience, then the voting cycle began.

Mary Ellsbeth exhaled as she looked toward the ornate roof of the hall. Hairline cracks permeated through the decorative tiles, down to the foundations.

"Oh, Lieutenant, where are you?" she murmured. "The Consortium owe you and your crew a great debt. Perhaps one day we will find where you've gone and be able to repay you."

Jon Gray Lang

forty-two

The Songs for Chapter Titles

As in the previous books, so the tradition continues. The chapter names are song titles and each one is part of Ms. Luli Qing's performance roster. This list of songs helped set my mood for the various chapters, only certain versions were used. If curiosity still eats at you, here they are:

- ☐ End of Time - Chantal Claret
- ☐ Streets of Forbes - Marian Henderson
- ☐ By the Light of the Silvery Moon - Doris Day
- ☐ Green Eyes - Don Azpiazu
- ☐ The Sky is a Poisonous Garden - Concrete Blonde
- ☐ Burn With Me - Whilk & Misky
- ☐ Shadow Dancing - Andy Gibb
- ☐ Orange Colored Sky - Nat King Cole

Jon Gray Lang

- ☐ Ball and Chain - Janis Joplin
- ☐ Bandages - Hot Hot Heat
- ☐ Land of Thousand Dances - The Walker Brothers
- ☐ Oscillations - Silver Apples
- ☐ Rocket '88 - Jackie Brenston & His Delta Cats
- ☐ C'est Si Bon - Eartha Kitt
- ☐ Escape From the Prison Planet - Clutch
- ☐ House of Bamboo - Southern Culture on the Skids
- ☐ Loser - BECK
- ☐ Walking on the Moon - The Police
- ☐ This is Not a War - AJJ
- ☐ Mars - Taimane Gardner
- ☐ Space Truckin' - Deep Purple
- ☐ Come - Jain
- ☐ Dark Was the Night, Cold Was the Ground - Blind Willie Johnson
- ☐ Beware - Deftones
- ☐ El Mecánico - Deela
- ☐ Martyr - Sevdaliza
- ☐ Suspended - Kelis
- ☐ Swinging on a Star - Frank Sinatra
- ☐ I Don't Want to Set the World On Fire - The Ink Spots
- ☐ Voyage Libre - Thievery Corporation
- ☐ Rocket Ship - Kathy McMCarty
- ☐ The Darker the Weather, The Better the Man - Missio
- ☐ I Wish I Was the Moon - Neko Case
- ☐ Sea of Sorrow - Alice in Chains

Jon Gray Lang

☐ Rapture - Blondie
☐ Bad Luck - Dinah Washington
☐ The Puppet - Godhead
☐ Bang, Bang My Baby Shot Me Down – Nancy Sinatra
☐ I Wanna Be Free - Loretta Lynn
☐ Take the Long Way Home - Supertramp

The title of the book is also a song:

☐ Waltzing Matilda - Banjo Paterson

In case you hadn't noticed, some of the characters sang some old tunes within the many pages of the Matilda series. Most of these songs are at least one hundred years old while others are much older than that.

Music is important to the odyssey of the Matilda just as it was vital to the sailors of old. A simple activity to while away the hours on long voyages, or how to celebrate arrivals at port and all the little undertakings in between.

My love of music fueled my desire to give a musical voice to the books and informed the creation of Luli Qing as a musical character. In fact, she was the first person I created for this story.

For the first time ever (so why not do it now, here at the very end?) are the songs sung by the characters that populate the journey of the Matilda:

Jon Gray Lang

☐ Spanish Ladies - First printed in 1796
☐ Bold Fisherman - First printed in 1813
☐ Freight Train - First printed in 1906
☐ You May Bury Me in the East - First printed in 1915
☐ Nana Neném - First printed in 1921
☐ Yiannis Mou - First printed in 1950
☐ Darling Nelly Gray - First printed in 1856
☐ Wellerman - First printed in 1860

I hope you've enjoyed traveling with the Matilda and her stalwart crew on their last flight together. It has been a long journey for both sides of the eponymous pen.

... Songs of The Matilda, a collection of short stories in the Matilda's universe will be coming out in   the   future.

Jon Gray Lang

jongraylang.com

forty-three

Glossary of the Autonomous Doctor

Have you ever wondered what that cantankerous robotic Doctor on board the Matilda was muttering about? Well, wonder no more! Below lies every sentence uttered by that lovable rascal of a machine within the pages of the Matilda series.

While Doc's speech is not a true language, there is a flow to it. Inflection could alter the meaning or direction of the sentence, but every retort by their illustrious mechanical companion had a point which the crew could understand implicitly.

Probably not, but they sure got the gist!

- Che che. - Yes, yes.
- Che dom sae to. - Of course I am.
- Che dom sat ae. - Of course, Captain / one who gives orders.

Jon Gray Lang

- Che du tong sa? - Why aren't you repairing me?
- Che shi lo? - Are you ok? Is something wrong with you?
- Che ta, che ta. - Yes there is, yes there is.
- Che tuu da. - Yes, I already am.
- Cho lo te? - Are you broken? / Reconnect me?
- Cho lo? - reconnect?
- Chu ta de? - Tampered with?
- Da kae da cho? - Are you not connected?
- Da kae to cha? - Are you working on it?
- Da kae tong sa che! - I am fixing you!
- De ko na? - All of my eyes?
- De ta? - Are you?
- Don te kuu ta lae! - I have my revenge or My debt is paid!
- Du che to da me. - She had it coming.
- Du ka klo tet? - Why don't you speak to them?
- Du sae tad? - Do you have one?
- Ed to do, che da! - This one is important, I understand!
- Ee che dae le. - I am running.
- Ee chu ta de? - I was tampered with?
- Eee chu tae dom sah. - I don't have time for that / I don't want to.
- Eee tu cha dae son ta! - I am being attacked!
- Es ed to do? - Are they all not important?
- Es ed to do! - They are all important!
- Et cho? - Am I broken?

- Et cho ka dae? - Am I stuck?
- Et cho tae dom sah eee. - I don't want to repair this one.
- Et du! - You are in need of repair!
- Et tae dom sa! - Now hurry!
- Kae tong sae. - Reconnected / repaired.
- Li do sat ae ehhh? - Who are you to talk to me? / order me?
- Li do tong sa? - Are you ordering me?
- Li do tong sa, te cho da. - I am not getting a response from mother (Matilda).
- Sa chu ta dae dom sa? - Tampered, do you have time to look?
- Sa tad don da! - Some of my cables are broken!
- Shae lo da? - Why is that one special?
- Shi lo da? - Why is this one special?
- Shi lo da, es lo te? - Are you sure this one is special?
- Sho che ta me klo! - Idiot, to attack and not speak!
- Sho du kla. - Idiot, you speak (to them).
- Sho sho. - Idiot, danger.
- Sho sho du ka te no! - Idiot, danger to me and all!
- Te cho da. - I am not connected.

forty-four

Dictionary

Perhaps you have questions relating to some words that have appeared throughout The Matilda Series that could be unfamiliar?

Well, search no more!

- **Androgyne** - A non-binary gender identity in which a person is simultaneously male and female.
- **Bralgu** - Island of the dead and the place where the ancestors known as Djanggawul originated - from the Rirratjingu clan of First Nation Australians.
- **Bunyip** - A monstrous swamp-dwelling man-eater from southeastern First Nation Australian mythology.
- **Cobber** - Australian slang for friend or mate.

- **Dinlow** - Romany word for idiot.
- **Genorg** - Future slang for (gen)etic (org)anism.
- **Gorja** - Angloromani for outsider
- **Helminth** - Term for parasitic worm.
- **Henon** - Haudenosaunee Thunder God, leader of the winged race of Thunders who cause thunder and lightning of First Nation Americans.
- **Hunta, hunta, yea** - First Nation Lakota phrase meaning Get out of the way, something's coming (female).
- **Mazuma** - Yiddish for money.
- **Ohdowas** - Mythical little people who keep monstrous beings imprisoned underground of the First Nation Haudenosaunee.
- **Pala Naio** - Part of a Hawaiian proverb meaning heaping pile of larvae (heaping pile of shit).
- **Sheol** - Abode of the dead in the Old Testament.
- **Tidda** - Sister or best friend - from the Torres Strait Islander people of Australia.
- **Tsotsi** - Johannesburg, South Africa slang for thug.
- **Tugurio** - Hovel or slum in Spanish

***

Jon Gray Lang

About the Author

Jon Gray Lang was born in Australia before being hastily relocated to the United States where he wrote a handful of screenplays, shot a few films, and even threw his hat into the acting ring. But with a life-long love of science fiction, it was only a matter of time before he bit the novel writing bullet and wrote the award-winning five book science fiction series, Saga of a Space Freighter. When he's not typing away at the keyboard, he's busy fighting with rapiers, skiing the Rockies, or banging out tunes on a ukulele... just not all at once... No matter how hard he tries.

Please follow him on:
JonGrayLang.com
facebook.com/JonGrayLang
twitter.com/Jon_Gray_Lang
instagram.com/jongraylang

<<<<>>>>

Jon Gray Lang

www.ingramcontent.com/pod-product-compliance
Lightning Source LLC
Chambersburg PA
CBHW020500020726
47493CB00001B/107